Also by Joan Byrd
From Indigo Sea Press

The All My Tomorrows Series:

A New Beginning

Love Finds a Way

Today, Tomorrow and Always

The Seed Has Been Sown

The Shadow of the Moon Rider

Lost Stories of Jesus

The Box in the Attic

The Good Seed—the Bad Seed

Sunset Over Dixie

indigoseapress.com

The Devil's Revenge, God's Victory

Book Two of the
Good Seed-Bad Seed Series

By

Joan Byrd

Deep Indigo Books
Published by Indigo Sea Press
Winston-Salem

Deep Indigo Books
Indigo Sea Press
PO Box 26701
Winston-Salem, NC 27114
This book is a work of fiction. Names, characters, locations and events are either a product of the author's imagination, fictitious or used fictitiously. Any resemblance to any event, locale or person, living or dead, is purely coincidental.

First Deep Indigo Books edition published
March, 2021

For information regarding bulk purchases of this book, digital purchase and special discounts, please contact the publisher at indigoseapress@gmail.com

Cover design by Pan Morelli
Manufactured in the United States of America
ISBN 978-1-63066-515-9

I dedicate this book to all my loyal readers who are always looking forward to my next book being published.

When the last page is read—keep reading!

No two books are alike!

I appreciate each and every one of you!

—Joan Byrd

Chapter One

Ted stood smiling as the wind blew a gentle breeze through his shag hair and it whispered, "You are very happy my son."

"Yes, my Father! My heart is overflowing with love." Ted laughed softly. "Even now my sweet Jenny waits for my return and she has no clue she is with child. Two beautiful gifts, growing inside her at this very moment."

"You are correct, my son, beautiful and angelic." Came the soft voice through the wind. "The twins are a month inside her womb."

"I smile whenever I gaze into her beautiful eyes." Ted's attention fell below the top of Goldsburg Mountain. "I think the time to tell her has come, for I believe I cannot contain this news within me any longer."

"Yes, my son. You may tell Jenny now that she will have two beautiful girls." The soft voice seemed to laugh softly. "The girls will take their looks after you my son, fair, blonde, with angelic faces. They will be gifted with your powers. My heart tells me you have chosen their names."

"Yes, my father. The twin girls who I gave these names have returned to their parents after many tears, and resumed their birth names, leaving Mary and Martha open, so I felt these names appropriate." Ted closed his eyes and smiled when he felt a new familiar breeze kiss his face.

"Mary, my chosen mother's name, my loving brother. Also, the names of my very dear friends, Mary and Martha."

Ted smiled. "Yes, my Lord, my most holy friend and brother."

"Ted, you and Jenny have our blessings!" The Lord, spoke with tender love. "As the Father hath said, the girls will have your looks and right spirit."

"Tell me, what will they share with my Jenny? They must have some part of my beloved!" Ted's eyes filled with tears, not wishing his Jenny would feel left out.

The wind blew around Ted's robe as the soothing voice fell on his ear. "Young Ted, do not be filled with sadness. The girls will have Jenny's energy, the need for knowledge, and the one thing only she can supply them, her feminine charms. Do not worry, my son, you will see a lot of Jenny in Mary and Martha."

"Thank you, Holy Ones, for giving us this most special gift that will always be a part of me and my Jenny." Ted suddenly grew silent as he listened to the dark brooding wind that swept across the mountain, and he shook, involuntary, dreading its return.

"Yes, my son, you can sense its return." The voice grew serious.

"There is a new evil coming to Black Mountain!" Ted touched his chest. "My love one, my sweet angel will be in danger!" Ted fell to his knees, his sudden fear for the ones he loved. "Father, it is Jeff, he will be put through a hard test!" Ted closed his eyes.

"Ted, my son, your feelings are real. Lucifer has returned to claim his son. Jeff must choose between good and evil, but this time, he has to do it on his own. His sweet loving wife, Naomi cannot help much in this matter."

"No, she cannot, not this time. Their love for each other won him over to our side, but Jeff has only touched the service of learning everything. Jeff's love for Naomi will not be enough in his fight with his father. He must turn himself completely around and believe in you totally."

"Be at peace, my son and remember, love is stronger and it will ALWAYS WIN!" The voice faded away with the breeze and Ted let out a deep breath as his eyes fell on the path leading down the mountain.

"I will be there for Jeff and lift him up at the end of his trials, but for now, my Jenny awaits."

Chapter Two

Jenny sat quietly looking up the steep path that led up to the top of Goldsburg Mountain, where she had watched her handsome husband disappear up the path to speak to God. Jenny knew she could not go any farther. Only Ted was allowed on the summit, much like Moses on Mount Sini. Jenny shook her head, never quite getting use to being in love with someone like Ted.

"My strange, sweet husband, I suppose I shall never really understand everything there is to know about you." Jenny twisted the wooden wedding band on her slim finger and smiled. "But God in heaven knows how very much I love you, my darling adorable husband."

Jenny looked back up at the bright mountain top, high over her head. "I did get to go up once, on our wedding day, when the Father, Himself, joined us as one as we stood…on a rainbow!" She lifted up her finger and smiled at the bright, shiny wooden ring gracing her hand. "I knew in my heart it was not a dream, even though it seemed like one, hearing angels singing around us, me wearing a white robe, like Ted and holding a white Bible covered with beautiful white roses." Jenny gave a soft laugh. "The same beautiful white Bible I keep lying on my dresser, Ted's gift to me so I could always remember our special wedding day."

Hearing soft footsteps coming down the mountain path, Jenny's attention fell on her handsome husband making his way down to her. A beautiful loving smile graced his angelic face, causing Jenny to feel butterflies fluttering around in her stomach, like it did every time she saw Ted.

"Jenny, dear loving wife, I see you have not grown tired of waiting for me and seek a softer seat at home." Ted held out his hand for her and she stood to take it happily.

"When my heart is on the mountain, my waiting does not grow weary, my sexy husband. I would wait for you all day as long as I have the nights alone with you, Ted darling."

"Jenny" Ted blushed. "What am I going to do with you?"

Jenny laughed out, and looped her arms around his neck. "I can think of one very pleasant thing you may do with me." Jenny noticed the twinkle in Ted's eyes and stood back, trying to read his thoughts. "Ted Neenam, what is going on?"

Ted laughed. "Jenny, have you been feeling sick as of late? Perhaps, in the mornings?"

"No, I have not!" she glanced down when she noticed the frown cover Ted's face. "Well, maybe just a wee bit sick, now and then. It, sort of comes and goes." Jenny noticed his frown was replaced with a sly grin, so she reached over and slapped his arm, causing him to laugh. "Ted Neenam, what are you 'not' telling me?" Jenny placed her hands on her hips and narrowed her eyes. "I am waiting!"

"Maybe, you had better sit down, Jenny." Ted kept laughing.

"No, I will not!" Jenny gritted her teeth. "Now, tell me!"

"Very well, my darling wife." Ted took both of her hands in his and looked her in the eyes. "Jenny, you are with child, two to be exact."

"WHAT!" Jenny nervously felt for the rock and sat down, feeling dizzy over the shocking revelation. "Ted, this is not funny. Don't you mean, we are going to be parents in the near future?"

Ted could not control his laughter as he joined Jenny on the rock. "No, my beautiful Jenny. As of now, you have two twins growing inside you."

"Well, I just know you can tell me the answer to my next question." Jenny took a deep breath, prepared to ask when Ted spoke up.

"One month, my love, you have carried our girls for one month." Ted's eyes were filled with love as he touched her gently on the stomach.

"One Month?" Jenny almost shouted. "And you knew and I did not?" she composed herself as she added "I guess you know the exact moment they were conceived?" Jenny noticed Ted's eyes light up with love.

"Oh Jenny, it was such a special feeling when we created our beautiful daughters. I will always remember." Ted kissed Jenny tenderly. "I think you might remember such a special moment too, Jenny."

Jenny let her thoughts go back. Each time she made love to Ted was special but there was one special night that stood out.

"Yes darling, I do remember one Saturday night, about a month ago." Jenny closed her eyes as the night flooded back to her. "I thought it could not get any better when suddenly the wonderful feeling returned, twice as good."

Ted laughed and pulled Jenny up in his arms. "Enough baby talk, now little mother, we have guest coming for a visit."

"Not so fast, handsome daddy, you said girls so that means that you already know them, right?" Jenny took his hand and studied his eyes. "Well?"

Ted laughed out loud, and simply said "Jenny, I will have to wait for eight more months, just like you."

"Ted, I am certain you know how they will look, by some heavenly blessing you have been gifted with, so start talking."

Ted smiled and touched her face with tenderness, his voice coming soft. Blonde hair, blue eyes with angelic faces."

Jenny's laugh was beautiful. "So, my darling, they both will take after their dear sweet daddy, what a relief."

"But our Father informs me that they will have your energy, the love for knowledge and your feminine charms, which certainly worked on me." Ted smiled at her knowing laugh until he added "It is obvious they will be a handful, but we will manage."

Jenny narrowed her eyes as she turned him toward the farmhouse. "Ted, we have house guest waiting and I will not ask you how you know we have a visitor."

"Visitors, sweetheart. Naomi and little Teddy have just arrived." Ted took Jenny's hand and led her down the path that led to the white farmhouse.

Chapter Three

Moments earlier, Naomi stepped from the forest path that led from Wineworth Castle, little Teddy following close with his favorite wolf, Eden. Naomi smiled out at the white farmhouse where she had learned love and trust from a young man not much older than herself. The beautiful, short hair, brunette, snooped down next to her little boy, who was the spitting imaged of his father and the man Naomi had given her heart to.

"There it is Teddy, the children's home, your mama's home until I married your papa."

"I wuv coming here, Mama." Teddy rubbed his wolfs head as he smiled up at his mother. "Can my puppy come with us, Mama?"

"Eden is hardly a puppy any more Teddy. It's best if he waits here in the forest." Naomi patted the friendly wolf's head. "Sit Eden and stay here until we return." The large grey wolf wagged its tail and sat down to wait as Naomi took her son's hand and walked up to the front door.

Knowing she was still family, Naomi rapped lightly on the open door as she walked inside and called out.

"Is anyone at home?"

"Naomi, here, in the kitchen!" Kathy's voice came happily from the large open room, where pots boiled lively on the stove and the smell of fresh baked rolls drifted from the old oven. "Come on in! I hope you brought my favorite little fellow."

Teddy dropped his mother's hand and made a dash for the kitchen, calling out "Kathy! My Kathy!" The dark hair, dark eyed boy threw himself in her outstretched arms, where she picked him up and twirled him around.

"My, how you have grown, kiddo and you look more like your papa every day!"

"I'm getting tall like my papa too!" Teddy laughed happily. "Right mama?"

"A little taller every day! At the rate you're growing, you will be as tall as me when you reach ten." Naomi looked around, noticing how quiet the full house was. "Where is everyone?"

"Ted and Jenny left early this morning." Kathy pulled the bread from the oven and placed in several apple pies, with Naomi's help. "Ted was going up on his mountain and he wanted Jenny to walk with him then wait for him to come down." Kathy looked from the window at the tall mountain, then smiled. "They are so much in love."

"Yes, that is easy to see." Naomi joined Kathy at the window she had so often gazed from and looped her arm around Kathy. "And how are things going with you and Matthew?"

"Things could not be any better, Naomi. Matthew has proved to be a remarkable husband. He is funny, cute, and good…no, he is great in bed!"

Naomi blushed and prayed Teddy would not ask why Matthew was great in bed, so she quickly changed the subject.

"Where is Ruth? I thought she might like to play with Teddy."

Kathy laughed. "Ruth is, at this very moment, hiding from Teddy. She wants to see if he can find her."

"Ruth is under the table!" Teddy pointed from his spot beside his mother at one end of the long table with a white tablecloth hanging to the floor.

Naomi and Kathy gave one another a puzzled look before Naomi reached over to pat her son's black locks.

"Well, little Jeff, go and see if Ruth is hiding under the table."

"She is!" he giggled and ran over to lift up the long skirt on the tablecloth to reveal four-year-old Ruth, smiling broadly. "See, I told you!" Young Teddy squatted down and took her outreached hand.

"Hi Teddy! Wanta play with my new red ball?"

Teddy looked up at Naomi for an answer after asking "Mama, can I play ball?"

"Teddy, you can play with Ruth just as soon as you speak to Ted and Jenny. I see them walking up the front walk."

As soon as Ted and Jenny walked inside the airy farmhouse, Ted called out "Where is my little friend?"

Within seconds, little Teddy came running from the kitchen, right into Ted's arms. "My Ted! My Ted! I wuv my Ted!"

Ted laughed and picked up the handsome boy. "My, you are getting heavier every day, Teddy. You know I love you too, very much!"

"I know Ted, I can see it on your face!" the sweet child kissed

Ted's cheek before looking over at the beautiful woman with the chestnut hair. "My Jenny!" Teddy wiggled out of Ted's arms and ran to Jenny as Naomi laughed softly from the kitchen door. "When I get big like my Ted, I'm going to marry you Jenny! You will be 'my' girl!"

Jenny and Ted laughed as Ted's beautiful wife knelt down to hug the small innocent boy.

"Teddy, sweetheart, I'm already married to your Ted, remember? Besides, I am much too old for you." Jenny frowned up at Ted when he laughed. He patted her on the head and knelt down next to her.

"Teddy, what my 'young' wife means is, Ruth is more your age." Ted looked into Jenny's eyes and squeezed her hand lovingly. "Or maybe, you will fall in love with Mary or Martha?"

"Mary or Martha? Ted, the twins moved out almost a year ago! Besides, they would probably think Teddy was too young!" Naomi looked puzzled when Ted and Jenny started laughing. "Am I missing something? Besides Mary and Martha in the Holy scriptures, our two sisters are the only ones we know by those names, right?"

"My darling Ted is referring to our twin's girls, Naomi." Jenny smiled up into her husband's blue eyes.

"Twins? You...you are going to have baby girls?" Naomi jumped into Ted's arms as Kathy embraced Jenny. Naomi chuckled. "When did you find out the good news? Did you see a doctor?"

"I did not have to visit a doctor, ladies. Ted informed me a few minutes ago and said I was a month along!" Jenny's eyes lit up with joy. "Isn't it wonderful?"

"Oh Jenny! It is totally wonderful, pal!" Kathy reached for a tissue to wipe her eyes. "I was wondering which of us would get pregnant? Dang, two little Jenny's running around!"

"More like, two angelic, blue eyed, blonde hair girls with a lot of me hiding inside their adorable bodies." Jenny laughed.

"Speaking of Mary and Martha who took back their birth names after their parents returned for them, cleaned from their drug habits and alcohol abuse, I wonder if they ever got over leaving here and you Ted?" Naomi had tears in her eyes remembering the sad day they had to pack their things and move out. "They were such bright-eyed, sweet girls, always willing to clean the dishes and help out where needed."

"It was hard to let them go. They were a part of our family, Cindy and Mindy." Ted gazed sadly from the big window, remembering the sad day the girls he had named Mary and Martha left the mountain.

"I believe it was harder on them." Naomi touched Ted's arm. I can still see them clinging to you, crying uncontrollable until their parents, Paul and Olivia Johnson had to pulled them away from your arms and drive away."

Young Teddy had been listening and forced his small frame up in the middle of the small group and said loudly "I Want to Marry Mary and Martha! They will look just like 'my' Jenny!

"For starters young man, you may only have one wife when you are a man!" Naomi looked down at her son serious and Ted laughed, patting her head.

"Teddy is only a child, my angel, he is not aware how things work right now, but he will grow quickly into that knowledge on his own." Ted squatted down next to the young boy and looped his arm around the boy. "Teddy, I am afraid the girls will look nothing like my beautiful Jenny."

"Why not!" The young boy looked from Ted to Jenny. "She is the mama!"

"That is right sweetheart." Jenny sat down and gathered Teddy in her lap. "But sometimes, little girls take after their daddy. Trust me, they will be beautiful! They will have blonde hair, blue eyes and the same bright loving smile that their daddy has."

"No! No! No! Ted is NOT BEAUTIFUL! Ted is handsome, just like my papa and me! Boys are handsome, not beautiful!" Teddy jumped down and stomped his foot.

"Teddy Jeffery Wineworth!" Naomi grabbed his hand and pulled him around to face her. "Mary and Martha will be so pretty, you will have a hard time choosing the one you want!" She frowned down into his dark eyes. "But you can only choose one! Now, you owe your Jenny and Ted an apology! Got it, young man?"

"Got it mama!" He smiled up at Ted and Jenny. "I'm sorry." Not waiting for their reply, he reached for Ruth's hand and giggled. "In the meantime, Ruth is my girlfriend."

"Then you and Ruth can go sit next to the window and roll Ruth's big ball. Just don't start throwing it in the house." Jenny reached out and patted their heads as Ted took their hands and walked then over by the window then went over to get him and Jenny a glass of water. His attention went to Kathy as she pulled her pies from the oven.

"Kathy, how's Matthew's driving lessons coming along?" Ted laughed softly when Jenny made a face when she took a sip of the water. "No more wine for you darling, till the babies are born." He reached over and kissed her as Kathy walked over and flopped down.

"Ted Neenam, Matthew and I were going to surprise you with his driving lessons and how well he is doing. How did you…" Kathy stopped short, and Jenny and Naomi laughed. "What were we thinking, trying to fool you?"

"Matthew's reasons for wanting to drive are almost right." Ted laughed. "He wants to help take the children to school and…" Ted looked down at Jenny as he continued. "when you or Jenny are with child and get to fat to sit behind the wheel…"

"What? Get too fat to drive?" Jenny sat her glass down angrily. "Of all the nerve! Why, that Matthew Christian, I'll 'fat' his lip!"

"Jenny?" Kathy laughed along with Ted and Naomi.

"What, pray tell, is so funny?" Jenny raised her eyebrow as the three continued to laugh. "I will 'never' get too fat to drive that stupid station wagon!"

"Jenny, when Matthew said those words to me…" Kathy stared down at Ted. "in the privacy of our bedroom, I lost my temper too. I said some really cruel things to poor Matthew. Then I saw the genuine hurt in his eyes and I realized Matthew didn't know any better. He thought he was doing the right thing to help either of us out if we needed him. He wasn't seeing a big fat woman trying to drive, Matthew was seeing an expectant mother afraid of hurting the baby growing inside her and mashing it on the steering wheel."

"You see sweetheart, it's not as hurtful as it felt." Ted took around Jenny when she started laughing with the others. "Poor, innocent Matthew. You was about to smash him in the mouth and he was only being thoughtful."

Naomi reached out to hug Jenny. "Well, I must be off. Teddy and I left Jeff weeding his garden. He is probably looking for us. I am so happy for you both."

"Thank you, Naomi and please come back soon. We love having you and little Teddy. This will always be your home." Jenny gave her a loving hug as Ted walked over smiling and took around Naomi on her other side.

"Angel, be aware of this Mrs. Protor who is coming to watch young Teddy."

Naomi felt a sudden panic as she looked up into his serious eyes. "Ted, is it a bad idea? I never told you anything about this woman coming up today to apply for the nanny position."

"You have not told Jeff either, Naomi." Ted took her hands. "Tell him now! Jeff needs to know."

"I will Ted, I promise to tell Jeff when I get home." Naomi reached up and kissed his cheek. "Pray for us."

"Always." He smiled and cast his eyes on the small boy playing and giggling with Ruth. "Teddy, come along, your mama is leaving now. Tell Ruth goodbye."

"O.K, my Ted!" Teddy jumped up and grabbed his mama's hand as his eyes went around the room. "Bye, my Jenny! Bye, my Kathy! Bye my friend, Ruth!"

"Bye, bye Teddy! Come back soon!" Ruth ran over to Ted who scooped her up in his arms and kissed her fat little cheek. The Christian family waved at the back door as Naomi and her son disappeared in the forest to a waiting wolf call.

Chapter Four

Jeff looked across the neat rows of his garden, alive with all kinds of vegetable plants. He smiled as he reached down to rub the two wolves who sat staring up at their master, unsure of his change and alert for an angry remark from him.

"Thorn, Fang, this is my best garden yet! I believe every plant will survive my feeble attempt at gardening." Jeff laughed when his faithful companions gave a small whimper. "Not impressed, are you? I cannot blame you, even though it is only my second attempt. Maybe my precious one will at least be able to gather a few vegetables this summer."

Naomi slipped up behind her tall handsome husband and smiled at his words. Jeff had sensed her behind him and a smile fell on his lips as he spoke softly.

"My sweet one is sneaking up on me!" Jeff turned around and scooped her up into his strong arms and swung her around, laughing at her bright smile.

"Jeff Wineworth!" Naomi giggled like a schoolgirl as she managed to say "Put me down this instant!"

"You liked it when I carried you over the threshold on our wedding night, my dearest darling." Jeff's eyes lit up in mischief.

Naomi lend in close to his ear and whispered. "There were a great many things I 'liked' about our wedding night, my darling, but we must watch what we say around little Teddy." She slid from her husband's strong arms when he looked down to see the little boy watching with big eyes.

"My son, will you let your papa twirl you around?" Jeff held out his arms and Teddy ran over laughing.

"Yes Papa! Twirl!" Naomi stood back laughing as she watched her two favorite fellows at play.

"Jeff, don't make him dizzy, sweetheart. That is enough twirling for now." Naomi took Jeff's hand when he lowered Teddy and held him steady until he retained his balance. "Sweetheart, your garden looks wonderful! There is not one weed and I believe this year will be a bumper crop."

"Thank you, my one. I am pretty happy with it." Jeff looked lovingly down into Naomi's eyes as his fingers brushed back her hair. "It's still not as good as Ted's"

"No bodies garden is as good as Ted's, my beloved. He could always grow circles around all of us at the home." Naomi reassured him as she added softly "His gardens are…heavenly."

Jeff laughed and hugged her. "That is the word I too would apply to Ted's gardens."

"How would my boys like some nice cold lemonade?" Naomi chuckled when both father and son nodded their heads in unison.

"That sounds perfect, cold lemonade in the shade garden with my favorite girl and my handsome son!" Jeff checked his dirty hands and tried to brushed them off on his pants before declaring "I am off to wash the garden dirt off and you Teddy, boy, could use a little scrub as well. We men need to look sharp for your mama." Jeff reached down to kiss Naomi tenderly. "We will be waiting in the garden, beautiful."

"Then I am off to make the lemonade!" Before she made one step, she remembered the news Ted and Jenny had shared with her. "Oh, Jeff, I have good news!"

"Ted and Jenny are going to have twins in eight months!" Jeff laughed when he took Naomi by surprise. That is indeed good news! Two little blue eyed, blonde hair angels, named Mary and Martha!"

"Oh Jeff! You and Ted!" Naomi blew him a kiss and turned back to her lemonade mission.

As Naomi carried the pitcher of lemonade out on a tray with three glasses, she happily watched Jeff and their son on the ground rolling a big ball back and forth. She could not get over the big change in her husband when love found its way inside his evil heart and turned him completely around.

"Are my two fellows ready for lemonade?"

Jeff hopped up and brushed off his pants before lifting his son to his feet and leading him to a small, wooden bench to sit him down on. Naomi kissed the little boy before handing him a child's glass, half full of lemonade.

"Now, try not to spill any on you Teddy."

"O.K. mama, I will be careful. "Can I give…"

"No son, you may not share your lemonade with Eden!" Jeff snapped his fingers, causing the wolf to arise and wait for the master's command. "Eden, go and wait by the big tree." Quickly, with a wag of its tail, the big grey wolf walked over to the oak tree and laid down.

Like a true gentleman, Jeff stood, holding the glasses of lemonade until Naomi sat down on the garden love bench, then joined her, handing her a glass. Lovingly he draped his arm around her shoulder as his eyes met hers seriously then fell on their son, happily drinking the wonderful drink his mother had made.

"I hope our son grows up to be just like you." Jeff spoke softly, his attention tenderly on the small child. Naomi sat her glass down and gently turned his face around to face her.

"Jeff, what's wrong? Has the nightmares returned?"

"Many nights they do, dearest one." Jeff's dark eyes turned back on Teddy. "My blood runs through our little boy, Naomi."

"Yes Jeff, it does." Naomi touched her husband's arm lovingly. "Jeff, he is a good boy."

"Do you remember the night Teddy was conceived?" Jeff gazed down at his wife who stared down at her hands.

"I try not to think about that night, Jeff." Naomi whispered. "When I found out I was carrying your child, I must admit, I was deeply afraid. Afraid of your reaction if you found out, afraid what sort of baby I would have."

"And well you should have been afraid, Naomi." Jeff stared down at her. "The evil ran through me as though I was Lucifer himself, the very image of my father! I took you, knowing you were a virgin. I raped you, my darling Naomi." Jeff's eyes fell when Naomi looked up, tears lacing her beautiful eyes. "Naomi, I…I needed you so badly. At the time I took you, I did not onetime care about what you wanted. I only had lust for you and I could not have been stopped."

Naomi closed her eyes, trying to block out that frightening night. She finally found the strength to looked up into his dark eyes, that held hers steady.

"Jeff, it's true, you did all those horrible things to me and I just wanted to die and escape your madness." She lovingly reached for his strong hand. "But toward the end, my fear turned to desire for you and not by some power you placed inside me but the love I felt for you. I realized I wanted you as much as you wanted me. I felt so ashamed later, because I remembered just how much I did want you, needed you and I was overcome when at last I felt like fireworks were exploding deep inside me." Naomi smiled shyly and added "That's when Teddy was conceived."

Jeff took Naomi up into his arms as his voice came softly to her ear. "Forgive me, my sweet one. I loved you so much it was ripping me apart and I never knew what I was feeling." He kissed her tenderly then sat back, closing his eyes. "I think of everything I did, I think of the madness of this castle, the memories. All bad memories."

"Jeff, darling, you must put those memories out of your mind." Naomi took his hand and kissed it. "We both must bury them, Jeff. For both our sake and for little Teddy's. He must never find out. We can make new memories, darling, lots of good happy memories."

"I know you are right, Naomi. I love Teddy so very much." Jeff's eyes sparkled with tears as his hand caressed her cheek. "I would give my life for our son, But you, my darling Naomi, I love you more than anything or anyone."

"My darling, it's good for you to love me and Teddy very much, but..." Naomi took his face in her small soft hands. "you, my darling, the love of my life, to find complete peace and happiness, you 'must' love God first, above all."

"Dearest one, how can I when you are already in that spot in my heart?" Jeff looked at her with innocents, seriousness written on his handsome face. "I can love God second, then Teddy."

"Jeff, my sweet love, someday you will learn with God's love, there is more than enough to go around."

Jeff reached over and kissed her cheek, then took her hands. "Then someday, with your and Ted's help, I shall learn of this powerful love, but for now, my dear wife, tell me about Mrs. Proctor."

"Jeff, I know I should have talk it over with you first before putting that ad in the paper." Naomi looked down at her hands. "I thought it was something I could handle. I should have known you would know somehow. You are so much like Ted, in a good way."

"Just to let you know, the woman is on her way now!" Jeff stood up, helping Naomi to her feet. "Her car just turned onto Mountain Road. I do not feel good about this woman."

"Why Jeff, you haven't even met Mrs. Proctor yet." Naomi started gathering the glasses and pitcher. "She sounded very pleasant and she comes highly recommended."

"Recommended by whom, sweetheart?" Jeff's attention turned toward their private road as Naomi pulled a folded letter from her pant pocket and handed it to her husband.

"It is from Doctor and Mrs. Luther Raven living in Salem, Mass."

"Raven?" Jeff's eyes grew dark as his voice came out suspicious. "That name, Raven, it sounds very familiar. I have heard it many times, but my mind is cloudy of past disciples of Lucifer."

"Jeff, you're scaring me." Naomi hands trembled, causing the tray to tilt. Jeff's quick reflects grabbed it before it crashed to the ground. "Darling, Mrs. Proctor has come a long way to see us. Can we at least talk to her? She sounded so perfect for Teddy's nanny and it would really help me have more time for tending to this big castle and fixing our meals."

"What did Ted say about this woman?" Jeff looked her in the eyes.

"Ted was concerned about Mrs. Proctor, just like you Jeff. He knew she was arriving today." Naomi shook her head, never quite getting use to these two remarkable men in her life. "Ted said, you would know what to do and he told me to watch her."

"Darling, why couldn't you get help with the housecleaning and cooking, not to mention all the other things you do." Jeff opened the door with his free hand, still holding the tray up in his right. "That would free you to look after our little boy. He needs his mama, not some stranger."

"Jeff, darling, you know I love to do my own cooking and cleaning our home." She smiled. "And not to worry about me spending lots of time with our son, same as you, darling. Teddy needs his papa and his mama."

"Alright Naomi, I will approve of your judgement about this Mrs. Proctor but I will be watching her closely." Jeff's eyes shot fire when he heard the motor a short distance away. "We shall know what she is like soon. She is only a mile away and speeding this way quickly."

"Jeff, I know you. You are too protective of me and Teddy." Naomi looped her arms around him in a hug. "We will be safe, as long as you are here."

Chapter Five

"Mrs. Proctor is pulling her black Ford up the driveway. I will get the door sweetheart and Teddy, stay behind your mama, son." Jeff walked over to the big door and pulled it open as Mrs. Proctor was about to pull the rope. He stared down coldly at the middle-aged woman dressed in black. "Mrs. Proctor, won't you please come inside."

For a moment, the stout woman stood frozen, as she looked into Jeff's piercing black eyes, but soon gave him a shaky smile before stepping inside.

"Thank you, sir. You are Mr. Wineworth?"

Jeff nodded and stepped over next to Naomi. "This is my wife, Mrs. Wineworth."

"Naomi, I recall. A beautiful biblical name, is it not?" the stranger's attention went back to Jeff as Naomi smiled and stated.

"Naomi is in our Holy Bible, Mrs. Proctor. Are you a devoted Bible reader?"

"But of course. Some of the story books I read my little ones are from the Bible, like Jonah and the big fish." Even though Mrs. Proctor was speaking to Naomi, her eyes remained on the tall, serious man, who watched her closely. "I recall your name is Jeffery. Do you read the Bible also, master Jeffery?"

"You may call me Mr. Wineworth, madam, call my wife, Mrs. Wineworth." Jeff took her arm and led her to the sofa. "Please, have a seat, Mrs. Proctor."

"But of course, Mr. Wineworth. Whatever you think is best." The woman took a seat and looked around at the tidy room with the white walls and blue curtains.

"Jeff, we want Mrs. Proctor to feel at home here." Naomi reached over and shook the woman's cold hand. "You may call me Naomi. Tell me, was the air colder as you drove up the mountains, Mrs. Proctor? Your hands are freezing and its summer, even on the mountain."

"No, the air was fine, my dear. It must be the excitement of taking on another little child." She smiled "I am sure you must have a lot of questions for me."

"As a matter of fact, madam, we do." Jeff stared coldly at the stranger, his voice rich and low. "How long did you work for the Ravens?"

"Eighteen short years." Tears came to her faded eyes. "When I started being their nanny, their children were small like your Teddy. I do so love looking after little children."

Jeff cleared his throat, unmoved by what he considered a performance. "What made you decide to become a nanny, Mrs. Proctor?"

"The reason for my becoming a nanny, master…I mean, Mr. Wineworth came when I lost my wonderful, hard-working husband. He was a devoted husband as well as a fine Christian man and we had only thirty years together when he had a heart attack and left me a widow and alone. We never had children, although we tried, so the ideal came to become a nanny. I put my advertisement in the local newspaper and a week later, the Raven family called me." Mrs. Proctor flashed a smile at Naomi. "Well, mercy me, it was a blessing. I stayed with that good Christian family until the last child graduated and went off to college. They flew out of the nest, as the old saying goes."

"So now, you want another child to look after." Naomi smiled warmly, moved by the dear woman's story."

"How old are you, Mrs. Proctor?" Jeff stare was as cold as ice, giving the woman, the shivers and Naomi could not understand why her devoted husband was being so cold to this woman. Did he see something she couldn't?"

"Jeff, I really don't think Mrs. Proctor's age will hinder her from being a nanny."

Ignoring Naomi's statement, Jeff repeated his question a little louder. "How old, madam?"

"I do not mind telling my age sir. I am fifty-eight and my health is very good, despite my being a little overweight." The nanny turned to Naomi. "You mustn't blame your husband for his personal questions, Mrs. Wineworth. It only proves he is a protective father. I can assure you both, I have had plenty of experience taking care of children."

"What sort of things would you be doing with Teddy?" Naomi tried to act relaxed standing beside her cold husband.

"I love to take the small ones, especially boys like your Teddy, for short hikes in the woods and tell them all about the different birds, trees and small animals, like rabbits and chipmunks. I play fun games with them, according to their age, many I learned from teaching Bible school. I teach them their ABC's when they are small to give them a head start for first grade. I also help them with numbers, making games out of that as well." The woman smiled at Naomi but avoided looking toward Jeff as she continued. "I prefer tucking the tikes in bed at night, after of course, mama and daddy's goodnight hugs and kisses. I have them say their prayers then I read them a sweet little story to help them fall asleep."

"That sounds wonderful, Mrs. Proctor, a full, fun-packed, day." Naomi smiled brightly, knowing Teddy would enjoy all those things she spoke about. She looked up at Jeff when he took hold of her hand and gazed down at the woman.

"Mrs. Proctor, if you will excuse us for a few minutes. We must discuss this matter in private."

Before they could walk away, Teddy peeked around at the woman who had just described a full day of fun. He gave her a shy smile when she noticed him.

"Hello, you must be Teddy." Mrs. Proctor lovingly held out her hands toward the boy. "May Teddy come over to meet me?"

Naomi noticed Jeff had taken their son by his hand, so she ask him softly "Jeff, can they meet?"

"Teddy, you may go over to meet Mrs. Proctor." Jeff released his son's hand and stared down coldly at the woman who gathered Teddy up in her large lap. "We will be just over there, by the window."

"I certainly understand your concern, sir." Her voice trembled from his unwavering stare. "You can't be too careful whenever your precious little ones meet a stranger. I can assure you, sir, your son is in good hands with me. I can see I already love the little angel. We will get along fine, Teddy and Nana."

Jeff pulled Naomi over by the window, his attention never leaving the two on the sofa. "I can tell you now Naomi, I do not like that woman. I do not trust her!"

"Jeff, darling…" Naomi smiled up at him with reassurance. "She will be perfect for little Teddy. He already likes her and its obvious she is crazy about him." Naomi laughed softly as she watched them together, laughing and chatting away. She lovingly touched Jeff on his face. “Jeff, she is a good Christian woman. Can we at least try her and see how she works out?”

“Do as you see fit. I did tell you I would trust your judgement.” Jeff looked deep into Naomi’s eyes, his uncertainly still visible as he added sternly “But I will be watching that woman! That, you can count on!”

Chapter Six

Naomi began clearing the dishes from the table. She lovingly patted Jeff on the arm, causing him to look up and smile at her beautiful face. He stood up and gathered his son in his arms, gave him a fatherly kiss and sat him on the floor next to his collection of toy cars and trucks.

"Alright my boy, play with your cars while mama and papa do the supper dishes and put them away."

"May I be of some service, Mrs. Wineworth?" Mrs. Proctor carried her empty plate to the sink and Naomi took it with a bright smile."

"That is very kind of you to offer, Mrs. Proctor, but Jeff and I can manage. Why don't you take this time to get more acquainted with Teddy?"

Jeff turned to watch the woman as she went down on the floor with their son. "Mrs. Proctor, did you enjoy your dinner?"

"Oh, my yes, Mr. Wineworth, every bite. Your pretty little wife is an excellent cook." She kept her attention on the young boy as she pushed a red car over to him and watched him laugh with glee.

"I'm glad that you enjoyed my cooking. I have had plenty of experience, being the cook at the home on Goldsburg Mountain, our neighbor." Naomi dried off her hands as she watched them playing together. "I hope you will like everything I prepare, Mrs. Proctor. I have the habit of preparing my menus in advanced. It makes shopping a lot easier."

"If there is one thing I know, my dear, I can eat anything that is set in front of me, no questions asked."

Jeff's eyebrow flew up, having heard those same familiar words spoken before, when Jeff was young Teddy's age. His parents were interviewing a woman for their new maid, a Marna Mullican. Jeff's thought drifted back and he could hear his mother speaking to the stranger seated in their living room being interviewed.

"I trust your dinner was suitable this evening, Mrs. Mullican?"

"Oh, my yes, Mrs. Wineworth! Your cook is excellent." Marna had laughed before adding "If there is one thing I know, I can eat anything that is set in front of me, no questions asked."

Jeff was so caught up in his discovery, he had not heard Naomi's sweet voice call his name until she tugged at his sleeve. Jeff looked down and saw her holding a big clean tray.

"Jeff, can you put this platter up on the top shelf for me so we can get Teddy to bed. He is yawning and it is his bedtime."

Without hesitation, Jeff took the platter with one hand and placed it easily on the high shelf before he walked over to scoop his son up in his strong arms.

"Alright son, it is time to get you in bed. It sounds like you have a busy day ahead tomorrow, so you need your rest." Jeff carried the young boy down the hall to his bedroom while Naomi and Mrs. Proctor followed close behind.

The nanny reached over and took Naomi's hand as she looked around at the cheerful hallway. "My dear, you have done a great job in brightening up the big castle."

Jeff's mood grew darker as he focused ahead. "Did you expect to find something different, madam?" Jeff asked, never turning around as he continued his wide steps to his son's bedroom.

The nanny laughed nervously. "My goodness, no sir. This is the first castle I have ever been inside of. I was comparing it to those eyrie dark castles you see in the movies."

"This is a happy home, Mrs. Proctor." Naomi reassured the newcomer as she hurried to keep up with her husband who had pulled ahead. "Jeff has given me and our son a good cheer full loving home in which to live."

Overhearing his wife's comment, Jeff smiled to himself as he helped their son into his pajamas, then turning the covers back, sat his son down.

"Teddy, my boy, it is time you say your prayers and then your new nana can read you a bedtime story, just like mama does." He looked down into his son's concerned face, so he added "Your mama and Papa will stay in here with you tonight, until you drop off to sleep." Little Teddy smiled up at his father, hugged his neck then gave him a kiss on the lips.

"I love you, Papa."

Jeff laughed and gave the boy a tender hug before reaching back for Naomi's hand and gently pulling her beside him. "it's time to tell your mama goodnight and give her an extra big hug and kiss."

"Goodnight mama, I love you!" Teddy looped his small arms around her neck and kissed her on the lips.

"I love you too, my precious little boy." Naomi gave him a big hug and returned his sweet innocent kiss. "Now, kneel and say your prayers to Jesus. He loves you so much, darling."

"I love Jesus too, mama, bunches!" Teddy turned toward his bed and dropped to his knees as he folded his little hands together, closed his eyes and bowed his head. "Thank you, Lord Jesus, for loving me and watching over me."

As Teddy prayed, Jeff was observing the nanny who was standing rigid and unsmiling. The more the child prayed, the more uncomfortable she appeared.

"Thank you for my mama and papa, my Ted, My pretty Jenny, Kathy, Matthew, my good friend, Ruth, all my big family on my Ted's mountain, and my puppy, Eden." Teddy started to stand back up when he snapped his fingers and went back to his knees, "And oh yes, thank you for my new nana. Amen!" he smiled up at his parents as he climbed into his small bed and Jeff pulled up his covers when he laid back.

"That was a good prayer son." His dark eyes moved over to the stranger as his voice came out sternly. "You may read him a bedtime story now, Mrs. Proctor."

"Very well." The nanny forced a smile his way and she pulled a chair up next to his bed. "Teddy, this book is called, Little Red Riding Hood, one of my other children's favorite. Once upon a time…" before she could get halfway through the book, Teddy was sleeping soundly, so Jeff motioned toward the open door and without a word, the small group stepped out into the hallway and closed the door.

"Mrs. Proctor, you will be taking Teddy hiking in the morning, am I correct?" Jeff's cold stare gave her the shivers.

"Yes sir, that is what I had planned for us, if that is alright by you sir?" The nanny swallowed when Jeff remained cold, simply saying

"Good evening, Mrs. Proctor. "Rest well." With that, Jeff took Naomi by the hand and led her inside their bedroom.

Naomi watched her husband stripped off his clothes and climb into bed, placed his arms under his head and stare up at the ceiling. She walked over and touched his arm, his eyes taking her in.

"Jeff, darling, couldn't you try and be a little more pleasant with

Mrs. Proctor. I think you make her feel uneasy."

"Good!" He reached around her and pulled her in closer, then began removing her clothes. His lips slowly melted into a warm smile as he pulled her down over him and kissed her with passion.

Naomi began growing warm when his long hair brushed down her neck as his lips kissed each breast causing her hands to move over his tan body.

"Jeff, darling, I need you! I am so in love with you!"

"My sweet one, my Naomi, I love you with all my heart, even that part that never knew love, not until you, dearest one." In the dark of the night, the lovers made passionate love, blocking out the stranger in their mist. It was times like this that placed them in a world of their own, two people madly in love and a special love that kept repeating, over and over, the beautiful, exchange of ecstasy that sent both reeling to their own paradise.

The following morning, Jeff found Naomi standing at the sink doing dishes, a warm smile of the previous night's love making still on her mind. Moving quietly up behind her, Jeff slid his strong arms around her tiny waist and nuzzled her neck with warm kisses.

"Good morning, my beautiful bride. You smile because you are remembering last night in my arms."

"You would know." She closed her eyes, feeling his hands move over her. "Are you rested up, my darling?"

"I did sleep a bit late. Why did you not wake me up when you arose, sweetheart. I must have been completely out. I never heard you leave."

Turning, Naomi reached up and touched his handsome face. "You were sleeping so peacefully. You tossed and turned after around midnight until the wee hours of the morning."

"It is those bad dreams, they have come back." Jeff ran his hand through his thick long hair and walked over for a cup of coffee. He held up another cup. "Join me, my love." Jeff filled the second cup and carried them to the kitchen table. His eyes took in her body as she walked over and sat down in the chair he held out. "I did sleep very well, my dove, for the first four hours, after our night of love making."

Naomi blushed as she reached for her coffee and took a sip before looking up into his alluring black eyes. "It was very…rewarding."

Jeff laughed out as he caressed her cheek, then he picked up his coffee and looked around at the quiet, empty room. "Where is Teddy and that woman?"

"Gone for a hike in the woods, after I gave them a good hot breakfast of bacon, eggs and grits." Naomi reached over and patted his hand. "You should have seen Teddy. He was so excited, he declared he was finished with his breakfast after two bites." She chuckled. "He decided to eat every spoonful when Mrs. Proctor told him he would need to start out with a hardy breakfast to keep his energy up." Naomi noticed Jeff's concerned. "It will be fine, darling, you'll see."

Jeff lifted his tall frame and walked to the window to stare out into the forest. "We shall see." His eyes grew dark. "We shall hope."

After walking deep into the woods, Mrs. Proctor dropped Teddy's hand and glanced behind them to make sure they were not being followed. The small boy stood rigid, listening to all the different sounds around them. Only moments before, his nanny had showed him a lot of different flowers and small, cute animals among the ground cover. He jumped when the nanny spoke up in the stillness as she pointed to a frisky little squirrel playing happily under a tree.

"Oh, that's not good, Teddy. That is not good at all."

"What is it, Nana?" the young boy watched the innocent squirrel picked up a hickory nut and start eating. "It's just a little hungry squirrel playing, Nana."

"Now Teddy, it is a good thing Nana is here to help you spot danger." Her voice came out mysterious and soft. "That squirrel is not what it appears to be. That, young man, is a mad squirrel and it will scratch your eyes out and bite you! Then, you will become mad too and foam at the mouth!"

"No! No!" Teddy started to tremble. "I want to go home to mama and papa."

"We cannot outrun a mad squirrel, kid. Eden will help us." Mrs. Proctor snapped her finger and the wolf ran over to her. "This squirrel is mad, Evil! He wants to hurt Teddy.

"My wolf's name is Eden, it's not Evil!" the frightened child cried out. "I want my papa!"

"Well, young man, it was your papa that named your wolf Evil when it belonged to him. Your papa taught him how to be bad, to kill, to destroy things, even people."

"No, no Nana! My papa is good! Eden is good!" Teddy started to run but Mrs. Proctor grabbed his arms tightly.

"Stay put, Teddy! You listen to me. Your papa will get mad at you if you tell him!" the nanny squeezed his small arm, causing him to whimper in pain. "Your papa will hate you! He will hurt you, Teddy. Your father is an evil, wicked, man!"

Little Teddy shook all over as Mrs. Proctor ordered Evil to attack the helpless, little squirrel. Instantly the big wolf's lips rolled back over its sharp deadly teeth and he made a dive for the unsuspecting squirrel, tearing it to pieces. The frighten boy started screaming and the nana clamped her hand tightly over his mouth and stormed down at him, his eyes wide in horror.

"Just shut up, brat and not a sound or Evil will tear you to pieces just like that mad rodent! Do you understand?"

Teddy whimpered softly and nodded his head. The woman faked a smile at the frightened child and lightly slapped his cheek.

"Now, that's more like it. This is our little secret Teddy, so we must not tell mama or papa. We do not want your papa to hate you, do we?"

"No…no Nana." Teddy dropped his eyes sadly. "I won't tell, I promise."

Chapter Seven

Naomi and Jeff had noticed a change in Teddy. He had become a lot quieter and withdrawn. The boy would cling to his mother whenever Jeff was close by and he struggled to kiss him goodnight or tell him he loved him. At Mrs. Proctor's demand, Teddy said his Nana would help him with his prayers and putting him to bed. Jeff's son had become terrified of him and it was obvious to Jeff and Naomi.

Jeff stared out into the darkness, trying to piece together what had happened to his little boy, causing him to avoid any contact with the man he had loved so dearly.

"It is that woman, Naomi! There is something about her! I do not like any part of her!" Jeff angrily slammed his fist on the hall table. "That bitch is turning my son against me!"

"Jeff, maybe Teddy is doing too much, playing too many hours." Naomi lovingly took his hand. "Darling, we can ask Mrs. Proctor to cut back on the hours she spends with our son."

"I will not rest until I find out what that woman is up to! I grant you, it's not playing!" Jeff grew dark.

"Jeff?" Naomi squeezed his hand, worry mounting for her little boy. "I pray you are wrong, but whatever it is you are feeling, I know it is something very strong, very real to you. The fact is, you and Ted have a gift in knowing what is going to happen before it does. I pray you know something soon, for Teddy's sake."

Each night Mrs. Proctor would read a bedtime story to Teddy, only the endings were always the same tragic ending. The bad wolf would tear apart his victims and eat them. Little Red Riding Hood, The Three Little Pigs and her favorite story, The Little Lamb and Grey Wolf. The small girl, the three pigs and the innocent lamb, all torn up and eaten.

The evil nanny refused to let the frightened little boy say his prayers. She had warned him that Evil was always watching him and he would tear him up and eat him if he said one word to Jesus. The Nana had told the frightened child to stay inside his room and never leave at night or Evil would be waiting for him outside his door.

After being his Nana for one week, Mrs. Proctor took Teddy deeper into the forest, Eden always by her side. She stopped at a swampy looking spot where a tall tree grew, hanging covered with a creepy vine. Looking up high in the tree, the nanny smiled and pointed to a big limb where a giant red snake lay, looking down at the them.

Teddy trembled as the biddy eyes froze on him and he started backing up, feeling the need to run away. Eden growled at him, causing him to stop in fear of getting torn up and eaten.

"Now, Teddy Jeffery Wineworth, you have nothing to be afraid of. That snake belongs to your grandfather. It is a pet."

"I…I don't have…a…grandfather, Nana." A tear ran down his small cheek.

"Oh, yes you do boy!" she sneered. "Your papa's father. His name is Lucifer and he lives deep down in the ground where he is the ruler of his underground kingdom."

"NO! YOU ARE LYING!" Teddy pulled at her hand as she held him tightly. "LET ME GO!"

"Do you want Evil to tear you up and eat you!" The Nana stared coldly in the boy's scared eyes. "Now, shut up, brat, and relax. Phantom, come down boy and meet the master's grandchild."

Teddy stared wide-eyed as he watched the huge snake make his way slowly down the tree and crawl over in front of the startled young boy. When Phantom touched his leg, the little fellow's knees started shaking and continued to shake as the heavy snake slithered up his leg, then up his small chest until the hissing head stopped at the frightened child's face. Sweat was tripping from the child as fear gripped his swaying little body. So, overcome by fear, Teddy felt everything spinning around until he fainted silently on the moss-covered earth.

Naomi watched as Mrs. Proctor carried her limp child into the house, looking pale. Feeling sudden panic, she dashed from the house crying.

"Oh, my God! What happened to Teddy?" without hesitation, Naomi grabbed her limp son from the Nana's arms and ran inside the castle screaming for Jeff.

Jeff came running down the steps, three at a time. His attention fell on his limp son then straight over to Mrs. Proctor, who pretended to be upset. He laid his hand over on Teddy forehead, it felt hot and sweaty. He turned his dark eyes on the nanny and spoke loudly.

"What the hell happened to my son, woman? What did you do to frighten him so much he would pass out?'

The woman stepped back shaking.

"Speak Up, Bitch! NOW!" he yelled.

"Oh, Mr. Wineworth, my lady…I…it was that wolf of his, Eden!" Mrs. Proctor grew dramatic. "The wolf suddenly got angry and started growling at the boy, showing those dreadful sharp deadly teeth. He was scaring me too sir, I did not know how to defend myself or young Teddy."

"GO ON!" Jeff knew she was lying as he grabbed her arm and pulled her up closer.

"The wolf attacked a helpless little squirrel and tore it to pieces and…ate it, right in front of your little boy." The nanny covered her eyes and started crying. "I knew those wolves would come to no good! I do not see why any good parent would have something that dangerous around a small child."

"Mrs. Proctor, that will be enough! These wolves are pets and unless someone with evil intentions order them to do something bad, they will be as harmless as any breed of dog!" Jeff released her arm and turned his attention back on Naomi and Teddy. "He hasn't come to yet?" he whispered close to her ear.

"I felt him move." Naomi's voice trembled. "I will take him upstairs and give him a nice warm bath when he comes to."

"If you would permit me madam, to take young Teddy up." Mrs. Proctor stretched out her arms for the unconscious little boy, avoiding any contact with Jeff, who watched her closely, eyes blazing.

"You are not needed. His mother will take our son, Mrs. Proctor. You are dismissed! Go to your room until you are called." Jeff turned and stormed down the hallway and into the library and shut the door behind him.

Jeff had been sitting inside the library trying to put things together when the door opened and little Teddy stood staring at his father. His young voice came out soft.

“Papa…you…you hate Teddy?”

Jeff quickly put down his pen and stood up, sadness written over his handsome face. “My son, where did you hear this? Your papa loves you.”

“Papa, are you evil? Are you…bad?” Teddy’s voice shook, feeling so small beside his tall daddy. “Do you make Evil do bad things?”

“Sweet boy, your papa loves you dearly. Who told you I was evil, Teddy? Was it your Nana?”

“No…one told me, Papa.” Teddy nervously looked over his shoulder to see if he was followed. “Are you evil? Does your papa live in a kingdom down in the ground and make people do bad things?” Teddy blinked his eyes nervously. “Papa, do you kill things and…people?”

Tears filled Jeff’s black eyes, feeling his heart breaking from his son’s obvious distrust in him. “Son, my father, the man that raise me, is dead. I…I was once different, that’s true. I was a bad person, mean and evil, all true. I did some things I am not proud of.” He knelt down, making sure to keep some distanced between them, so as not to frighten his little boy any more than he obviously was. Jeff looked into Teddy’s eyes, with true love shining through. “Your mama saved me and brought me love. Your Ted saved me by taking away all the bad things and replacing them with good. Teddy, do you believe me, my boy?”

“I…I believe you, Papa.” Tears filled his eyes and danced down his red cheeks.

“Teddy, my sweet son, please listen, go to your room and shut your door. Wait for your mama and papa to come to you tonight.”

“Promise papa? Please papa, promise?” his young voice trembled.

“I promise Teddy.” Jeff gently took his son by the hand. “You have nothing to be afraid of, anymore. Your mama and papa will take care of you from now on.”

Teddy’s other hand reached over and patted his daddy’s big hand as the little fellow gave him a weak smile. He turned and made his way slowly to his room and closed the door, while Jeff watched.

Naomi stepped out from behind the door where she had been listening. She walked over and looped her arms around her husband’s waist.

“Jeff, darling, are you alright? I heard everything.”

Jeff pulled her up close and held her in his strong arms, his voice coming soft.

"I will be alright, my love. I know what I must do now. Everything is clear to me and I know just who this, Mrs. Proctor really is and who sent her."

Chapter Eight

Jeff stared at the picture on the wall directly in front of him. He could sense Mrs. Proctor coming up silently behind him. Her voice came out softly, his attention remained on the picture while she spoke.

"Master Wineworth?" he said nothing, only grunted with discuss. "I will put master Teddy down for the night, sir. The little tike has had a shock and needs to have his rest."

"Mrs. Proctor," Jeff turned around slowly and stared down into her eyes. Her body shook from the fire in his eyes. "where did you take my son today? What did you do, Mrs. Proctor, to make him so terrorize that he would break out in a sweat before blacking out?"

"I did nothing to harm your little boy, I swear. I took master Teddy for a walk in the woods, just like we have done every day. Up until today, Teddy loved the adventures of discovery we had while on our hike." She eyes dropped to avoid his glaring stared. "Fane and Evil went with us, sir."

"Mrs. Proctor, why do insist on calling Eden, Evil?" his black eyes flashed from knowing the reason but held it back for the present. "My son and I named him Eden. Who told you the wolf's name was Evil?"

"The…a…" for a brief moment the woman was caught up in a trance, like something showing her an answer. She smiled to herself as her eyes moved down the hallway, scanning the walls for a certain picture and found it near the end. Her transfixed eyes focused in on it and she made it out clearly. "the picture at the end of the hallway, that is what told me. Your long line of pet wolves, framed and labeled with each of their names beneath them."

"I see! It is quiet amazing you can tell which one was Evil among my loyal group of wolves. They appear to look exactly alike to everyone but me…and perhaps Ted, who knows pretty much everything, Mrs. Proctor."

"I pride myself in telling things apart sir. Now, if you will excuse me, I will go to the boy, with your permission." The nanny started to walk away when Jeff took a tight hold on her arm. "Sir, the little fellow should not be left alone after the sun drops and the shadows grow long. Their small imagination can build up monsters hiding in the room. Let me go to him now."

"That will not be necessary Mrs. Proctor. I will see to my son tonight."

"But sir, you must be tired. I really don't mind getting the little one ready for bed. He is such a good little boy." The nana tried to sound chipper even though just being around Jeff Wineworth made her nervous.

Jeff took a deep breath and spoke out sternly "I SAID I WILL SEE TO MY SON TONIGHT, MRS. PROCTOR! NOW, PLEASE RETIRE TO YOUR ROOM MADAM!" his grip grew tighter. "DO I MAKE MYSELF CLEAR?"

"Yes, of course, Master Wineworth." The nanny closed her eyes to avoid his stare, and the pain shooting through her arm. "You wish to take care of your son tonight. I understand and will retire to my room immediately." Jeff release her arm and she breathed a sigh of relief. "Have a good evening sir." Mrs. Proctor turned and walked quickly down the hall to her room and closed the door.

Again, Naomi stepped out from behind their bedroom door, only this time they had planned she wait there to listen to his conversation with the nanny.

"Jeff, what is wrong with that woman? Please tell me what is going on." Jeff took her hand lovingly.

"Come with me, my love. We must see to our son." Naomi wasn't sure what Jeff knew would be waiting, but she trusted the man she loved so dearly. They opened the door slowly and looked inside. Even though the bedside lamp was on, Teddy had the covers pulled completely over his head and his small body trembled beneath it.

Without hesitation, Naomi walked quickly by her son's bed and spoke softly. "Teddy, what's wrong? Why do you have your head covered up sweetheart?"

The small child held tight to the covers and he whispered "Go away! Go away!"

"Teddy, my son, it is your papa and mama. I said we would come to you tonight, I promised, remember?" Jeff spoke softly as he gently pulled the covers from Teddy's sweating face.

"Papa! Papa!" Teddy sat up and threw his arms around Jeff's

neck. "Don't leave me papa!" He looked up at Naomi, big tears rolling from his black eyes. "Mama! Don't leave me!" the little boy cried.

Naomi took his small hand in hers and kissed it, tears coming from her own eyes. "My baby, sweet child, please tell us what is wrong. Mama and papa would never leave you, never ever."

"Papa, Papa!" the young boy clung to his daddy's strong chest.

"Son, you will spend the night in mama and papa's bed. We will not leave you alone." Jeff gently lifted Teddy out of his bed. "You can get some well needed sleep there, son." Jeff carried the frighten boy down the hall as Naomi raced ahead to open their door and turned the covers. Lovingly, Jeff laid the tired child in the middle of their huge bed and kissed his forehead.

"Now son, say your prayers and go to sleep.

"Nana…Nana said, I should never say my prayers, Papa." Teddy's face was wet with tears. "She said I was a bad boy if I said my prayers."

"Mrs. Proctor should not have told you that, my son." Jeff looked over at Naomi as she joined him on the side of their bed.

"Teddy, darling, we all need to say our prayers to God before we close our eyes in sleep." She gently rubbed his wet hair back from his face. "Ted taught us to never forget our prayers. I will have a talk with Mrs. Proctor tomorrow morning."

"O.K. mama, papa, Teddy will say his prayers." He yawned and put his small hands together. "Dear Father in Heaven, thank you for my mama and my papa, for my Ted and Jenny, and my great big family on Goldsburg Mountain. And Jesus, please, send Nana far, far, away! I love you! Amen." Teddy laid his head down on the pillow and fell into a peaceful sleep.

Naomi looked down at their son as Jeff lovingly laid his hand on her shoulder. "Oh, Jeff, look how peaceful he looks." Tears filled her eyes. "I've been so worried about him."

"Yes, I know my sweet one." Jeff pulled her to her feet and wrapped his arms around her. "I have been worried as well, but that is about to change. I can see everything clearly now."

"Jeff, do you mean, Mrs. Proctor?" Jeff placed a finger over her lips and whispered

"Mrs. Mullican is more like it!"

"Marna Mullican? Jeff, she is dead. Your mother killed her! I was there, remember?" Naomi shivered under her husband's embrace.

"Yes, mother killed Marna, shot her in the chest but Lucifer uses these souls, brings them back in another form to do harm!" Jeff looked lovingly into Naomi's frightened face. "This demon has the power to destroy our son as we know him. My father wishes to turn him into me, the way I was."

"Oh, Jeff!" Naomi was totally devastated over this revelation. "I have been letting that woman read to Teddy, take him on long walks to God knows where, playing with him, and I am sure it was not games she learned in Sunday school, even teaching our little boy!"

"Yes, the books, the Three Little Pigs, Little Red Riding Hood, and her favorite, the Lamb and the Little Grey Wolf." Jeff took both her trembling hands. "All stories about mean wolves." Jeff pulled from his pocket what looked like a harmless child's story book and handed it to his wife. "Read the last two pages of the Lamb and the Little Grey Wolf, sweetheart."

Naomi nervously opened the book to the back and began reading softly as not to wake Teddy. "One day after the lamb and the wolf grew up, the wolf invited the lamb over to dine with him. As the wolf waited for the helpless lamb, he chuckled to himself and said, "My friend is coming over for supper, only, he does not know that he will BE SUPPER!" Naomi dropped the book, a look of terror on her beautiful face, "Jeff! I cannot finish this horrible story!"

Jeff reached down, picked up the book and continued. "The lamb arrived smiling, happy to see his best friend. The wolf smiled back, showing his very sharp teeth.

"Come in! You are here just in time for supper, my supper! Juicy lamb!" He laughed and moved toward the scared little lamb.

"No! No, please!" Begged the innocent lamb. "I am your friend."

"You were my friend, but now, I am going to EAT YOU UP!" and the wolf bit the poor little lamb's head off and enjoyed his juicy lamb supper! The End."

Naomi was crying uncontrollable and Jeff wrapped his arms around her and held her close as she spoke between sobs. "No wonder Teddy is so terrorized. If those hikes brought on more horrible things for our little boy, it will take a miracle to help Teddy get over this."

"Sweetheart, I am proof that miracles happen and I know, as well as you, Ted can help our son get back to being the Teddy we know and love."

"Of course, you are right, darling." Naomi reached up and kissed him thankfully. "What are we going to do about Mrs. Proctor, you know, Marna?"

"I will put an end to this demon! She has no power over me! That is why she is afraid of me!" Jeff's eyes grew dark. "That woman will not touch or see our son again! No one hurts my family! Not even my, pardon my word, my father. Lucifer took a chance by sending my old maid, thinking I would not recognize the hag but he forgot that I am just as cunning as himself. To outsmart the devil is hard for most men, sweet one, but I have always been one step ahead of my old man." Jeff could not resist a laugh as he added "Poor stupid Marna, she could not keep her old self's habits out of her conversations and insisting on calling me Master Wineworth, just slipped right back on her black tongue."

Jeff lowered his head and kissed Naomi tenderly. "Stay inside the castle my love, with our son. I shall return when I have finished my business."

"Jeff, please be careful darling." Naomi hugged him, always worried about the devil showing up to face off with his son. "I love you darling. I will be waiting here with Teddy."

"I love you too, sweet one. And do not worry about Lucifer showing up tonight. He will not be making an appearance just yet." One last kiss, Jeff silently walked out, shutting the door behind him.

Chapter Nine

Mrs. Mullican opened the door to Teddy's bedroom and peered inside and noticed the bed was empty. "Where are you hiding, Teddy Jeffery Wineworth? I know you are in here!" she moved slowly through the dark room calling softly "I will find you, you little brat! And when I do…"

"You will do what, Mrs. Proctor?" Jeff's voice came from the corner of the room where he had been hiding in the shadows waiting for the fake nanny.

"Oh! Master Wineworth, I did not know you were in here."

"Obviously, Mrs. Proctor." Jeff remained in the shadows, making the woman tremble with fear.

"It's just that, I thought it best to check up on the little fellow and make sure he was sleeping alright after his trying day."

"Just keep your voice down and come with me Mrs. Proctor." Jeff stepped out of the shadows and glared down at the frightened woman.

"Where are we going sir?" She felt his hand on her shoulder as he ushered her out the back door. "But sir, it is dark out here and the night air has a chill in it."

"You best soak the chilled air up for as long as you can, madam." Jeff whispered loudly as he pushed her down the path that led to the black forest. When they reached the overgrown tree in the swamp, they stopped.

"What have I done to upset you, Master Wineworth?" she swallowed.

"You can cut out the pretense, Mrs. Mullican. I know who you are and why you are here." Jeff stared down coldly as he watched her scrum.

"Mrs. Mullican? I beg your pardon sir, I can assure you, I do not know what you are talking about." The nervous woman stumbled on her words. "You know I am…"

"Marna Mullican! You know I can see through you, Marna, so stop pretending. You are wasting both of our time, Marna."

"You were always far too clever for me, Master Jeffery, but I was there when you needed me" her eyes grew seductive "Some of your needs made me feel good as well, remember?"

"Those days are gone forever, Marna, besides, I never needed you for anything. I just used you, like I did everyone around me. I was evil and full of lust, so when I had no one exciting around, I laid you! That was then, things are different now. My heart found someone I needed, someone I loved. I have changed but I am still capable of taking care of my family and my powers are just as strong as before, so I am sending you back."

"Master Jeffery, I guess you're still mad at me because I failed my job to watch that girl for you." Marna's voice shook as she looked into his serious face. "It was not my fault your mother would not return to her room. I was blocking her from taking Naomi, then she shot me in the chest!"

"That is not why we are here Mrs. Mullican, you bitch!" Jeff was consumed with anger over what this woman had done to his little boy and he could not control the hate that he felt for this demon as he yelled. "YOU HAVE BEEN SENT BY HIM TO DESTROY MY SON, YOU EVIL DEMON!!

"The master wants you back, master Jeffery. He prefers you over all his sons for you are more like him than all the others combined!" the demon laughed. "But if he cannot have you, then he WILL TAKE YOUR SON!"

"THAT, YOU EVIL WOMAN, WILL NEVER HAPPEN! Lucifer will not touch my son and HE will NEVER get me back! My mind is made up! I choose love over hate!" Jeff stared coldly.

"We shall see!" Marna grew a little braver, feeling the demon power given her by the devil. "The master has gifted me with powers of my own to use against you."

"I am completely aware if your pitiful powers, Marna, but they do not stand up to my powers. I can and will overcome anything you throw at me! Give me your best shot, bitch!"

"Then look and feel, Jeffery Wineworth!" Marna snapped her long fingers and evil came out of the woods and stood beside her. "Even now, your own wolf has been turned against you. It was not very hard, Master Jeffery, for you had trained him so well to be bad, it all came back."

"So, you turn my own wolf against me?" Jeff continued to stare, unconcern over her threat. "Turn him loose on me, then we shall see who is in charge here!"

"We shall see!" Marna drew her eyes away from Jeff's stare briefly to give the wolf her command. "Evil, ATTACK!"

Evil's lips rolled back over his sharp teeth as he made a plunge on Jeff, ripping into his arm. Jeff sternly gave the order, Evil, retreat or die!" The wolf coward away from his master's command. "Come boy, sit by my side!" the wolf obeyed and felt his master's hand rub his head lovingly. "Good boy, Eden!" His attention went back to the demon who had watched how quickly Jeff had recovered his property to its rightful place. Then Jeff's words took her by surprise.

"Well now, Mrs. Mullican, so you think Satan's pet serpent can kill me, do you?" Jeff's calmness sent chills up the woman's spine. "So, the snake, sent his giant killer snake to scare my son! Send down the big bully my old man's been bragging about for years!"

"Yes, you can read my thoughts and future actions! You have been gifted by many special strong powers! I should have remembered, but you are no match for your father or his special pet retile." She tried to sound brave against this man she was petrified of. "Phantom, most trusted and loyal servant of the master, come down from your perch and choke the life out of your master's undeserving son and send his evil soul down where it belongs, for all eternity!"

"Nice speech Marna. Too bad you did not learn my example of living was wrong and save your own soul!" Jeff stood staring at the evil woman, unconcern about the huge red snake that slithered down the tree and moved its large body above Jeff's head. It slid down on his shoulders and began wrapping its body around Jeff's neck and chest, then began squeezing the breath out of his victim. Jeff easily grabbed the snakes over-sized head and held it directly in front of his face. The deep black eyes of Jeff stared into the beady eyes of Phantom and seared the serpent's very soul. In Jeff's deep trance, the evil snake loosened his grip and he was now at the mercy of Jeffery Wineworth. Wrapping his strong hands around the serpent's neck, Jeff smiled over at the shocked woman as he strangled the life from the evil serpent from hell. Death came quickly as Jeff slung the lifeless snake down at Marna's feet.

"The master will not be pleased you killed his favorite serpent!" Marna spoke bravely.

"Well, that is just too bad, Marna. If I were you, I would be getting nervous. Your master will not be please with your failure,

Marna Mullican." Jeff's stare was penetrating, "Marna, will you ever learn. Now, you intend to send all my wolves against me?"

"True, you can read my thoughts." The demon laughed wickedly. "All your wolves attacking at once! You cannot escape this time, Jeffery! You will die!"

"Marna, Marna, you, poor unfortunate woman." Jeff's anger melted away, knowing her future. "Your words have sealed your own fate!"

"Fane, led the pack and come by my side!" The evil demon gave the order and the pack of big grey wolves came from the tense forest. "Go, under the orders of your new master, Lucifer, and kill Jeffery Wineworth! Send him to the master! Attack!"

The loyal pack of wolves walked over, circled their master and sit down, obediently. Jeff never took his eyes off the evil woman who waited in horror.

"Now, Marna Mullican, Satan's demon, you will return to the place you came from!" Remaining still, Jeff snapped his fingers and his wolves rose to their feet and began walking slowly toward the frightened woman. "Send her back from wince she came! Back to her master, Satan!"

"Please Master Jeffery, do not send me back!" Marna pleaded. "He will punish me for failing my assignment."

"I cannot save you, Marna. You chose this path." For a brief moment, Jeff wished he had the kind of power to help this poor woman, but this was out of his hands. "There is nothing I can do to save you now. If I did not send you back, then he would come for you and your fate would be worse off. Dear lady, I shall never see your face again."

Jeff's stare fell on the ground behind her and the earth began to tremble and shake until it cracked opened. The wolves drove her backward until the lost soul fell in, leaving one last scream. Jeff looked on sadly as the ground swallowed her then closed. "Poor girl, I would have released her curse if she had not died."

Chapter Ten

Jeff walked back inside the castle then made his way slowly to where Naomi had been anxiously waiting. Hearing him just outside their door, she slung it open and immediately saw his bleeding arm.

"Jeff! Oh, Jeff, my love, you're hurt!" then her attention fell on his red burse neck. "Oh, my God! What happened to you out there?" Naomi grabbed his arm and pulled him to the bathroom and had him sit down. She grabbed a clean rag and ran some cold water to wash away the blood. Jeff watched her closely, feeling his love for her explode inside him. He reached up and caressed her face, then closed his tired eyes.

"Marna is gone for good, sweetheart. I sent her back to Satan, where she belongs." Jeff gave a tired laugh. "She put up a good fight but she was no match for me."

"Jeff, there are times when your powers scare me." Naomi looked lovingly into his black eyes. "But this time your powers saved our little boy. I love you so much." She kissed him tenderly, Jeff returning it with warm passion before lending back, to stare at the ceiling. "What is it, Jeff? You still seem upset. Is Teddy still in danger?"

"Our son is safe, we will never leave his side. Teddy needs our love and help in order to start healing." Jeff squeezed her hand, his eyes serious. "But there is more, evil around, I can feel it. Ted can feel it too." Jeff touched her face lovingly as he said softly "He wants me back, darling. Satan wants me backs and he is ready to fight for me!"

"Well, he cannot have you! We must fight that devil!" Naomi felt her own need to protect her love ones. "Ted always says, 1 percent of good can conquer 100 percent of evil, and he is right, my love. Look how love changed you."

"I will fight Lucifer with everything I've got, my dearest one." Jeff pulled Naomi in his arms and held her tightly. "I WILL NOT let my father destroy our family. This is something I must do alone. Ted will be there to support me, but as before, this situation will be out of his hands. I know my father wants me back, but he is not the only one. God is testing me, my true faith in Him, to see what my choice will be."

"Oh, Jeff." Naomi buried her face in his strong embrace. "This evil you spoke of, do you know where it will be and who it is?"

"As of this moment, I do not know the many sources the demons will be placed. I know, because I can feel the strong presence of evil on Black Mountain and down in the valley, where all the citizens of Goldsburg live. Only on Goldsburg Mountain will you find complete safety from anything evil. Ted, through the power of God, has place a protective shield around its borders to keep evil out." Jeff gently lifted her face to gaze into her eyes. "My love, we must be alert at all times and beware of any strangers in town." Jeff kissed her forehead. "My sweet one, we must pray for everyone we know and God to give me strength. Satan's blood runs through my veins, and sweet one, it runs through little Teddy's too."

"Jeff, no one must be let inside our home again we do not know and from now on, we will be with our son. I have learned my lesson, no more nannies!" Naomi clung to Jeff.

"Until this nightmare is over, my love, we will 'never' leave our sons side." Jeff kissed Naomi tenderly, knowing this night he would be papa, instead of the husband, needing the sex every night. "One of us will be with him at all times. Now, let us go to bed darling. Teddy has rolled over to the end of the bed." He kissed her with passion after they laid down. "I will hold you in my arms until morning kisses your sweet face. Passionate love making must be placed aside this night, so we shall sleep as loving parents watching over our baby boy."

"I love you." Naomi smiled and closed her eyes, feeling safe in Jeff's strong arms and knowing that Teddy was going to be alright.

Jenny lay sleeping soundly, dreaming about Ted rubbing her face. Watching lovingly, Ted bent over and kissed her lips tenderly. A smile came to Jenny's lips, as she thought, "That kiss felt so real." When she opened her eyes, she could see Ted lowering his head to kiss her again. Jenny looped her arms around his neck, as she returned his kiss.

"Jenny, my darling Jenny." Ted's face was lit with total love and passion as he looked down. "You are awake, my love." His lips found hers again in a burning kiss.

Jenny felt her heart pounding in her chest and she could tell by Teds heavy breathing that he wanted her as much as she did him. In the dark room, she suddenly realized that Ted was unclothed when he gently pulled her blue gown over her long hair. His hand moved tenderly over her firm round breast as he whispered.

"Oh, my sweet beautiful Jenny." Ted pulled her body up to meet his and joined them together in a fiery embrace. The passionate love lasted for several minutes until at last it exploded to pure pleasure.

They lay quietly, wrapped in each other's arms until Jenny broke the silence.

"Ted, darling, what a wonderful way to get awakened."

He smiled over at her. "I woke this morning and gazed over at you. How beautiful you looked, lying there dreaming. I just had to have you, my darling, so I kissed your smiling lips to wake you and make love."

"You can feel free to wake me like that every morning, my sexy husband." Jenny touched his handsome face. "That was some kind of hot sex, most remarkable."

"Jenny?" Ted blushed.

"My sexy husband blushes." Jenny laughed and kissed him. "And after making love to me with such fiery passion."

"Jenny, my Jenny." Ted laughed softly as he caressed her face. "You were dreaming about me, so I decided to make it real."

"Ted Neenam, are you telling me, you even know what I am dreaming?" Jenny sat up, shaking her head. "Is there nothing I can hide from you?" she thought to herself, will you still love me the same as today years from now?"

"I will love you for as long as I live, Jenny." Ted's eyes twinkled with delight from her surprised face, never getting used to his reading her mind. "And that, my beautiful wife, is for all eternity. That is the reason I will never let you out of my bed ever."

"Now, my sweet innocent husband, I intend on being in the same bed with you every night, sleeping or making love." Jenny smiled when he sighed. "Except of course when our babies are ready to be born and it's off to the hospital's delivery room."

"Not even then Jenny. You will have our baby girls right here, in our bed." Ted laughed again at her questioning expression.

"Right here? A home delivery? By who, are you capable to perform childbirth, Doctor Ted Neenam?" Jenny gazed at his smiling face. "I know it won't be Kathy, she would faint and Miriam is too much of a baby herself to go around delivering infants!"

Ted laughed and pulled her into his warm embrace. "No, my angel, not Kathy, never Miriam, nor I will be delivering our precious babies. I have sent for my mother who has delivered many babies and she is more than happy to come."

"Your mother is coming here?" Jenny almost got choked before Ted rubbed away the feeling. "Your mother is coming…to deliver our babies right here, in this bed?"

"Yes darling. She knows I need her. I have written her and now mother is on her way here to Goldsburg Mountain." Ted took Jenny by the hand to calm her down. "Darling, you will love her."

"Ted, she is your mother. I know I will love her." Jenny swallowed, knowing her next question had to be asked. "Sweetheart, is your mother's name…Mary?"

Ted responded by laughing out loud before answering. "Jenny, my wonderful woman, you would think that." He continued to laugh as he spoke. "You really brighten up my day, Jenny Neenam. My mother's name is Hannah and my father, is name Peter. They run a children's home in Bethlehem."

"Oh." Jenny quickly climbed from the bed and pulled out some clothes. "I must get up and get busy. There's cleaning to do, preparing a room for Hannah, grocery shopping, after I plan what meals Kathy and I will make while she is here." Jenny started to the bathroom when Ted grabbed her arms.

"Jenny, mother is arriving at the train depot in a few hours."

"Ted! Why didn't you tell me sooner? There is so much to do!" Jenny stood still in Ted's loving arms, waiting for the next bomb shell.

"Everything has already been made ready for my mother's arrival. I knew you would be a nervous wreck, so I had it all finished, down to the full pantry of food." Ted smiled when Jenny relaxed. "Now, darling, all you have to do is get dressed so you can go pick her up later."

"Get dressed?" her hand ran through her tossed her as she stared down at the work clothes in her hand, tossing them back inside her closet. "Oh darn, what can I wear? It will take me hours to pick out the right outfit and I need a shower to wash this hair."

"Calm down sweetheart. I picked you out something to wear

and it is laying out across our white love sofa." He laughed at her wide eyes when she slapped his hand lightly.

"Ted Neenam! You know all my habits!" she stared up at him for a moment before looking over at the loveseat and spotted the blue dress, complete with underwear and shoes. "I see you thought of everything, my remarkable husband. I must admit that dress does look nice on me and hides my baby bump."

"It is one of my favorites and besides, it doesn't show too much of my wife's bosom so you won't get as many stares."

"Thanks, precious. I'm glad you are concerned about other men staring at me. I promised to save that treat just for you, darling." Now, before I hop into the shower, what does your mother look like so I can pick her out at the depot."

"My mother is slim, very attractive, with a warm brilliant smile." Ted pictured his mother in his mind as he remembered her and how he can see her looking now. Hannah has long black hair and she usually wears it pulled back." He laughed softly, knowing Jenny next question. "And no, Jenny, mother does not look anything like me. For that matter, my father, Peter, looks completely different too."

"Oh, Ted, how did you…" Jenny shook her head as she turned to walk to the bathroom, calling over her shoulder. "What am I saying, mind reader!"

Ted laughed and walked at the door to peek in while she ran water to get the shower ready. She turned when he called her name and she noticed right away, he was already dressed, and his hair looked perfect.

"Don't ask Jenny. I was going to tell you to get ready while I go check on the family. We have a busy day ahead."

Jenny watched Ted disappear out their door as she shook her head. "Just where did you get those angelic looks, Ted? I will be alone with Hannah for the long drive, maybe I can at least find out something about his childhood from his dear, sweet mother." Jenny winked at herself in the mirror and climbed in the warm water.

Chapter Eleven

Ted walked Jenny out to the white station wagon and gave her a loving hug. "You look beautiful, Jenny. I have written mother many times about you, so she will know you the minute she sees you."

"I have no doubt." Jenny smiled, anxious to get the meeting over with. "Ted, can I…may I?

"Yes Jenny, you may ask my mother about my childhood if you like." Ted laughed at her surprised expression. "Go ahead, I know you have been dying to find out since we met."

"Thanks, dear." Jenny narrowed her eyes up at his smiling face as she pulled her keys from her bag. "You will make up this little Jenny picking tonight in bed, husband! Make it memorable, lover boy." Now it was Jenny who laughed when Ted blushed.

"Jenny, behave yourself." Ted lowered his head and kissed her tenderly before opening her car door. "Be careful driving down the mountain."

"I will be extra careful darling. I'm carrying around precious cargo wherever I go." Her smile was genuine when she touched his lips.

"Yes, you are Jenny. You carry the love of my life and my two little girls." Ted squeezed her hand before helping her inside the car. "Oh, Jenny, watch out on the corner of Elm Street, 85-year-old Margaret Spencer will tip over her flower cart and spill her flowers while crossing the road. Just stay in your car after you have stopped. Some men will help her."

"Alright! Stop for Mrs. Spencer on Elm Street." Jenny made a mental note as she said, "Is that all?"

"No darling. Little 5-year-old Emily Clover will chase her ball out on Mable Ave." Ted looked serous as he added "Slow the traffic down behind you before you stop and wait for Emily's mother to see her and help her out of the street."

"Alright. Is there anything else to warn me about before I am late picking up your mother?"

"Yes Jenny. Please tell mother I will see her at supper. I will be tending the sheep for Matthew." Ted reached through the car window to kiss his wife. "Kathy and Matthew will be watching the children."

"O.K. Ted darling, I will tell your mother." She returned his kissed. "We will see you at supper."

"You may take mother to the rose garden for wine after she has settled in." Ted smiled before adding "And you can finish your talk you start on the ride home. Jenny, remember, wine for mother, lemonade for you, little mama."

Jenny gave a chuckle, blew him a kiss and headed the station wagon down the mountain road.

As Jenny drove to the depot, she remembered the letter she had received from George a few months earlier. It read: "My dear friend, Jennifer, I am so happy you found and married Ted. It is indeed a beautiful relationship and you my sweet beautiful friend, deserve all the happiness only Ted can give you. It was a joy to learn from your last letter about the wonderful news that you and Ted would soon be parents, and twins at that! What a nice surprise! I am sending you two new station wagons, your choice of color, although something tells me it will be white. I won't take no for an answer. It is a gift, to friends from a friend. That little sport car you have is much too impractical with a house full of children, and more on the way. You also wrote me that the children would be attending public school in town and I know you and Kathy can drive and perhaps Matthew can learn. Holly sends her love. She is doing remarkable at her job and she has met a good Christian man from the church she has been attending with me. I think there will be wedding bells in the near future. As for me, the business has prospered and the workers are all treated like family, so it's a pleasure for the workday to start, for everyone. It seems, the more I give away to charity, the more I make. I never knew, doing the will of our Father in heaven could bring so many blessings.

Dearest Jennifer, if ever, and I mean, 'ever', you and Ted, or the home, need anything, do not hesitate to call me. I mean this, with all my heart. No amount is too much. I know it is hard to take charity, at least an overwhelming amount, but please Jennifer, let me help if there is ever a need, no matter how small, no matter how large. Ted saved my life, Jennifer. The man literally saved my life and my soul. I owe him and my Lord all that I have, and will gladly give it. Please, don't forget, your dear friend, George."

"Speaking of miracles." Jenny smiled to herself as she turned off Mountain Road and turned toward town.

"Saving George was certainly a big miracle." Jenny gave her signal and made a turn on Elm Street and she quickly remembered Ted's warning. "O.K. Margaret Spencer." Jenny slowed down when she saw the 85-year-old woman start across the street pushing her flower cart. The cart tire hit a patch of loose gravel and started weaving. "She is losing it!" Jenny immediately stop and put on her emergency signal, to warn the cars behind her and those approaching on the opposite side of the street. Seeing Jenny stopped and her warning signal, the traffic stopped, then three men rushed out to assist the worried women rescue her cart and place fallen flowers back on. Before stepping away, Mrs. Spencer gave Jenny a grateful smile and silent, "Thank you!" Jenny smiled and waved, then continued down the street.

Making a turn on Mable Avenue, Jenny slowed down as she scanned each neighborhood house for a small 5-year-old, playing ball. Spotting the girl, Jenny spoke to herself.

"Alright, there is little Emily Clover playing ball in her front yard and I see no sign of her mother." Jenny slowed her car down even slower, causing the man behind her to lay down on his horn. Jenny gave him a big smile and waved at him through her mirror, keeping her mind focused on Emily Clover who had suddenly dropped her ball and began chasing it down the hill where it had rolled across the busy street. Jenny had quickly stopped the car and switched on her emergency signal.

The man behind Jenny had stopped and noticing the little girl dash out into the road, his mouth flew open in total surprise. He rolled down his window and called up to Jenny. "Wow lady, how did you know that kid would run into the road?"

"An angel warned me!" Jenny called back to the man, then smiled at the mother as she ran quickly to retrieve her daughter. Hearing Jenny's comment, the mother thanked her and her special angel for watching after Emily and walked the little girl back to their yard.

Jenny waved and drove away, after checking her watch, she found that time had seemed to slow down too, because she drove into the train depot right on time. After parking the white station wagon, Jenny made her way inside the terminal and noticed the passengers had just unloaded and were walking in. Several strangers came through and stared at her before passing by, giving her uncertain feelings. Before she could figure it out, Jenny spotted Ted's mother walking toward her with obvious recognition.

"Jenny, how very nice of you to come and pick me up. It is a pleasure to finally get to meet the girl who stole my Ted's heart." A warm brilliant smile covered her beautiful face, just as Ted had described.

"Mrs. Neenam, I have been looking forward to meeting you." Jenny hugged the loving mother of her Ted.

"Jenny, my dear, please call me Hannah. Or, if you will, please call me mother, like Ted does." Hannah's smile was genuine. "It would make me very happy, darling."

"Then I shall, mother." Jenny started to pick up Hannah's suitcase when Ted's mother patted her hand lovingly. "Mother, I really do not mind helping you with your luggage."

"I know dear, but you must not be picking up anything this heavy, Jenny. Those are my grandbabies in there and they are soon to be delivered." Hannah picked up her small overnight bag and handed it to Jenny. "Here Jenny, you may carry this for me."

"But..." Jenny stopped short, knowing Hannah was only thinking of her welfare. "Alright mother, you know best. Ted tells me you will be delivering our twins."

"Yes, and I am so excited, Jenny!" she laughed softly, showing real joy on her face. "Over my years in Israel, I have delivered many babies, but these little angels will be my sweet Teddy's and yours, Jenny darling."

Jenny knew in her heart she already loved and admired Ted's mother very much. Filled with emotions, Jenny could not wait until they were on the road back to the mountain, so she could ask Hannah about Ted's childhood. She smiled when she spotted her car in the parking lot.

"There is the station wagon. Let's get your things loaded up and take you home."

"Sounds wonderful! Any home where you and Ted live, will feel like home." Hannah got in and shut the door. She smiled out the window as Jenny drove slowly through Goldsburg. "What a beautiful, quaint town. It has been years since I have seen an American town." Hannah took in the town, then let her gaze go up to the two high mountains towering over the small town. "Oh! That green mountain has to be Goldsburg Mountain, and…my son is up there."

"Yes, mother, that is Ted's mountain, and like him, it is very beautiful. I know you must have missed him all these years, but you can see him now." Jenny drove her car passed her grandmother's house and slowed down. "This lovely farmhouse belongs to my grandmother, Bessie O'Donnell. I am sure grams would love to meet you. I will invite her and Aunt Kris up for a visit soon. Like you, they cannot wait to see those babies."

"Ted wrote me about your family, Jenny." Hannah smiled at the Christmas card house as they passed by. "I look forward to meeting them both."

"They are both very special to me, mother." Jenny drove past Maple Avenue and mumbled to herself, Emily Clover, safe and…" she passed Elm Street. "Margaret Spencer, safe and sound, no loss flowers."

"Jenny, dear, is everything alright?" Hannah glanced over, confused, making Jenny laugh softly.

"I was just remembering the almost accidents on Mable and Elm that Ted had warned me about. He saved an 85-year-old flower woman and her cart of flowers on Elm and A little 5-year-old Emily Clover, who chased her run-away ball into the busy Mable Avenue. It all happened just as he said it would and I followed his orders to the letter."

"That is just like my Teddy. He has always been special." Hannah reached over and patted Jenny's shoulder. "You love Ted very much, I can tell."

"Oh, mother, I love Ted completely and there are not enough words to describe my love for him, and I am a literary major, a teacher of English and literature." Jenny's eyes danced with love. "Ted is my life mother and I would give up everything for him." Jenny turned onto Mountain Road. "What was Ted like as a child. He never speaks about his childhood and I long to know everything about him, past and present."

"Where to begin. Oh, Jenny, Ted was a brilliant child." Hannah smiled as she reflected back to happy days with her young son. "But let me go back a little further. My parents were missionaries and they had been sent to Israel on a building team. My father, Franklin Summers was over the building team of six men, along with my mother, Vivian. Their mission was to build an addition on Saint Andrews Children's Home in Bethlehem. The couple in charge of the orphanage were Peter and Elizabeth Neenam. They took in unwanted children, homeless, just like those Ted took in. I decided to go along with my parents on their mission before beginning my career as a nurse working at Duke Medical, right here in North Carolina. I had helped on missions before and wanted to make one last mission with my parents. I had just graduated the nurse's academy and had the summer off before starting a fulltime career.

We arrived in Bethlehem at the home of the Neenams and Peter had come out to greet us. My heart skipped a beat when our eyes locked. He was so handsome, standing there in the door, dark hair with brilliant green eyes that seemed to caress me. I remember my father clearing his throat, obvious with our attraction for one another. He commenced to making introductions. First, mother, the six workers, then himself. Peter acknowledged each person politely, then turned his gaze back on me. I could hardly breathe and I knew, without a doubt, I was falling in love with this stranger and him a married man.

Then Peter's voice came soft and tender when he asked my father "And who is this lovely young lady accompanying you?" I could feel my feet moving uncontrollable toward him and I politely put out my shaking hand and said, "My name is Hannah, and you must be Peter."

"The same, dear Hannah." Peter smiled and it melted my heart. I could feel my parents observing our actions so father spoke up quickly. "Hannah, wouldn't you like to meet Elizabeth, Peter's wife? You will be working along beside her as well, sweetheart."

Peter gave a cheerful laugh as he called Elizabeth to come out and meet the new missionaries. "May I introduce my sister, Elizabeth." I remember Peter smiling at my parents as he added "I assure you Mr. Summers, I am quite single."

From then on, Peter and I became very close. We both knew it was love from the beginning. We were married a year later, then my parents, finishing the mission, return to the states, and I stayed with Peter, where I remained. That is until Teddy sent for me. Peter and

I knew our son really needed me if he asked. It is the first time he has needed us since he left. I felt like I had to come and to be honest, I really wanted to come to be with Teddy. So, Peter stayed behind to help Elizabeth watch the children. She never got married and stayed with us."

"What a beautiful love story." Jenny's heart felt warm all over. "It was love at first sight for me and Ted, too. I just could not get enough of him." She blushed when Hannah smiled over.

"I understand dear, more than you know." As Jenny pulled in the drive, Hannah looked out at the huge white farmhouse. "This is the Christian Home for Children! Ted described it perfect."

"Yes, mother, this is home." Jenny got out and retrieved the small bag while Hannah grabbed the large one. "I will show you to your room first, mother, and help you get settled in. You and Peter are the two things that have been missing around here. Now, our home feels complete." Jenny opened the door to the beautiful bedroom and looked around, seeing it for the first time. "Ted has done a wonderful job in here!"

"It is an exact copy of our bedroom at Saint Andrew's. Remarkable and Ted has never seen it."

"That sounds like Ted. He seems to know everything." Jenny helped Hannah put away her clothes before walking to the door. "I will let you settle in, then we can go to the rose garden for refreshments and resume our talk about Ted." She quickly remembered Ted's comment and shook it off, closing the door behind her.

After Hannah had refreshed herself, Jenny showed her to the rose garden where she had laid out wine, lemonade, and cheese.

"I know you would like to try Ted's wine, mother. In my opinion, it is far better than expensive bought wine." Jenny graciously poured Hannah a glass and offered the cheese plate. "Ted makes this wonderful cheese too. He simply amazes me all the time."

"Yes, Ted is extremely good at anything he touches." Hannah sampled the cheese, then drank down some of the rich red wine. "You are right, Jenny. He makes wines far better than me or Peter. Now, you were asking about Ted's childhood. Teddy was born two years after Peter and I were married. We knew there was something special, something different about our baby from the day he was born. He had long blonde curls and looked very much like a little angel.

We homed school him, teaching him only the basics like reading, writing, and a little math. He never seemed very interested in learning those basic skills. Teddy preferred learning about sheep, growing grapes, fruits and vegetables. He would watch us, everything we did. Peter make wine, me in the garden, the older boys tending sheep. The young genius knew enough though at two-years-old, to teach older children their reading, writing, and math or other problems they might bring to him. He could speak very plain and grown up for one so small. He began singing at one, and his voice matched his appearance, very angelic.

Teddy would climb up the hill behind the home, where he would stay for hours. That child knew the Bible by heart at the age of four." Hannah took another sip of the great wine, then looked as though she were far away in thought.

"On Ted's 16th birthday, he went up that hill and stayed later than usual. Peter called me to the back door. We saw our son walking back down the hill, a glow around him, from being in the presence of God, Himself. The jeans he had worn up were no longer on him. Ted wore a white robe, and it seem to blow gracefully around his sandaled feet. His sandy blonde hair seemed to have grown, along with a beard and mustache. Forgive me Jenny if this startles you, But Ted looked so Christ like, my knees buckled and Peter had to hold me up. He smiled at us with that brilliant smile of his and told us the Father was sending him to America, to a mountain called Goldsburg." Hannah's eyes searched the hills above them.

"Ted was grown up for his age. He knew so much. He stood there and told us what this place would look like, never seeing it. Ted said, sheep would need tending, there would be seed for planting, grape vines for harvesting, and lots of children, lost, alone, unwanted, forgotten.

He packed his few possessions and kissed us goodbye. Our son told us he loved us dearly and promised to write. We saw him walk away. He never asked for money, for a plane ticket, in truth, Ted simply disappeared."

Jenny felt the need to take around Ted's mother and give her a loving hug, as she spoke softly. "Ted, my darling, we all love you so dearly. We are so blessed to have you in our life."

Chapter Twelve

Jeff left Naomi and Teddy resting while he made his way slowly down the path that led to the tense forest. His dark eyes stared straight ahead, for he knew who was waiting for him to come. Jeff had felt the evil presence for some time and after discovering what Marna Mullican was doing and knowing who had given her the orders, Jeff was now aware the evil plan had begun.

This strong handsome man was not afraid to face Satan. Jeff had done it many times before, but after two years of silence from his father, he thought he was rid of this evil being for good. He knew his so call father, wanted him back. Back to do the monstrous evil things Jeff had done before he fell in love with Naomi. Lucifer would tempt him to return totally to him and do his bidding instead of the Almighty's.

Jeff's strong powers led him to the revelation that Lucifer was not the only one after his soul. The Almighty God Himself was testing Jeff's faith, to see if he would choose good or evil. All Jeff knew for certain was the fact that he was deeply in love with Naomi and life without her was not excepted.

Sensing his father's presence just ahead, Jeff stopped for a brief moment and closed his eyes, then whispered "Lord, give me strength to face Lucifer." He continued down the path and stopped when he spotted him, standing with his back turned to him. A light smile came on Jeff's face when he noticed Satan wore black clothes, from head to toe and his hair was long, an exact copy of his own. Jeff's powers let him know Lucifer was well aware of his presence.

"Jeffery, my once devoted son, at last you come to your father." The devil turned slowly to face Jeff and the resemblance was remarkable. Without moving or blinking, Jeff answered in his deep voice.

"You have changed your appearance, Lucifer. So, you dare come looking enough like me to be my father."

"I AM YOUR FATHER, JEFFERY! YOU BELONG TO ME!" Lucifer spoke loudly. "YOU ARE MY FAVORITE SON, WHY DO YOU TURN AGAINST ME?" A hint of seriousness fell on his face. "Jeffery, You, were perfect! You always carried out everything so evil and wicked. Your hate son, was beyond wonderful and you did everything to please me, not my enemy, not HIM!"

"No Lucifer, my life was hell!" Jeff stared unafraid. "With Naomi and my son, my life has just started. The old me is dead and that is where it will remain."

"This woman you speak of, this Naomi, you did lust for her, unlike all the others." Satan laughed. "She would not fall into your perfect web and give in to her desires for you so you took her, you raped her!"

"I LOVE HER!" Jeff shouted. "She is my life now and there is NOTHING you can do about that! It is my choice!"

"You forget who you are speaking to, son. I can easily take Naomi and hurt her, like I did your little boy." He smirked. "Although, the boy's blood is half mine, Jeffery. Perhaps, if I cannot win you back and can claim my grandson, Jeffery Jr."

"It is me you're after, Satan! Leave my family alone!" Jeff's anger was growing. "Finish saying what you came to say and leave me!"

"I will leave in my own good time, son!" the devil took a step closer to where Jeff stood firmly. "Listen to my warning. You chose to stay with this mere woman, then not only your family will be in danger, but also the ones you care about on Goldsburg Mountain!"

"You have no authority there!" Jeff stared coldly into his father's eyes. "There is NOTHING you can do on that mountain and you know it! The Almighty Himself shines on that high place!"

"Yes, God, the powerful!" Satan growled. "I knew Him well! I should have ruled heaven, I had more power!"

"Is that a fact?" Jeff gave a sarcastic laugh. "Is that why he 'kicked' you and your followers out of heaven and down into the deep? Is that why you rule down in a place called hell instead of the glory of heaven?"

"And you, my son, will be right there with me! Like it or not."

"As long as I am with my true love on this earth, I will be happy." Jeff continued to stare, making Lucifer feel uneasy. This one had never been afraid of him like everyone else. "As for living in hell with you, old man, I shall strive to find a way not to. If I can reach heaven and be with Naomi throughout eternity, I will seek it.

If not, then my soul is better off not to exist at all."

"You are a fool, Jeffery!" Lucifer shouted. "I can make your life a living hell! Those so call friends on your neighboring mountain come down to that stupid town all the time. I have nothing but time to wait for them and I can see them there!"

"Yes, I am sure you will try, but I will be watching and waiting for your demons, just like poor Marna Mullican!" Jeff was wanting to return to the castle before Naomi missed him and came looking with Teddy. "I will spot them easily now that I know they are here!"

"It will be hard to be at so many places at the same time." The devil remained calm, knowing he had the upper hand. "I am sure Naomi and young Teddy will be your first priority."

"Naomi is always my first priority! I will give my life for her!" Jeffery focused his attention on the path leading to the castle.

"Die for her? YES! OH, YES, YOU FOOL! YOU WILL SURELY DIE FOR THIS MERE WOMAN!" the devil turned his back to him. "You had your chance to return! I could have made you even more powerful! I could have made you my anti-Christ!" he spoke softly, regretfully. "You could have been immortal Jeffery, having anyone or anything you ever desired."

"I have got everything I could ever desire, Lucifer. Naomi is my very breath." Jeff's eyes glistened with tears. "She is all I need or want. Naomi is what makes me happy."

"Then you are indeed a fool!" the devil was growing tired of this useless talk. "Good luck on the fight that is coming, son. But in the end, you are sure to lose."

"That is where you are wrong, father. I have already won." Jeff smiled, making his devilish father feel strange, a reminder of something long past. "Besides, Ted will be fighting with me. You mess with any of his family and he will come down on you with the aid of Heaven."

"Heaven? I am in control down here, you idiot!" The devil looked up at the sudden darken clouds and gave a smirk. "I will take my leave for now, Jeffery. I chose the wrong mother for you. Her beliefs were mixed as was that husband of hers. But you fixed them when they tried to destroy you by taking away their perfect little Billy. I was so proud of you, my son, the way you controlled your family and everyone you met." He shook his head in discussed. "Your mother should have been packed to her soul with lust and evil! Damn your mother's soul! She suffers plenty now for her short comings where you were concern!"

He touched Jeff's face, almost tenderly, and said softly "When next we meet, my son, I 'will' be taking you home." Then in a flash, Satan was gone.

Chapter Thirteen

Jeff turned when he heard Naomi coming toward him and tried to smile, but it felt shaky. Naomi reached for his hand, concern written on her beautiful face.

"Jeff darling, you look like you just saw a ghost." Little Teddy peeked around his mother, looking sleepy.

"Much worse, my dearest." Jeff whispered in her ear, then lifted his son in his strong arms and carried him over to a bed of clover. "Sit down here, Teddy and rest. You still look tired." Jeff led his wife to a spot where they could talk without upsetting the boy. Naomi searched his eyes as she replied.

"Jeff, what could be worse than a ghost?"

"It was him, my father." Jeff returned her stared. "It was Lucifer. I felt his presence and knew he was waiting for me."

"Oh, Jeff! My sweet love! Are you alright?" her eyes fell down his body. "Did he hurt you, threaten you?"

"Father is angry, very, very angry and he seeks revenge, my darling Naomi." Jeff wrapped his arms around her trembling shoulders. "The next few weeks, we must be alert at all times. We or someone we can trust, must always be with our son. Lucifer will stop at nothing, even murder, to get what he's after."

"Who all is he after, Jeff, besides our family?" Naomi held tight to Jeff as she kept her attention on their sleeping little boy.

"It could be anyone we care about. Do not trust any stranger, no matter how friendly they appear. Even sometimes a demon can take the form of someone we do know personally. Just like Lucifer did for me, coming as an exact copy of myself." Jeff lovingly caressed her hair as he continued. "Satan's demons are very cunning, just like Marna. They can appear to be one thing but something completely different."

"Jeff, darling, I think we should…" before Naomi could finish her thought, Jeff did.

"Should go and talk to Ted." Jeff smiled at her bewildered expression. "Can't get use to your husband's mind reading? Poor baby. The fact is, our son needs his help and Ted wishes a word with me as well."

Jeff stood up and pulled Naomi up and into his strong arms where he parted his lips over hers in a tender kiss. "I will not let anything happen to you, my sweet one. You and little Teddy are my life now and I will protect you until my dying breath."

Jeff scooped his son into his arms and taking Naomi by the hand, turned to the path that led to Goldsburg Mountain.

Ted looked out the window when he felt Jeff and Naomi approaching from the woods. He had been expecting them and he knew what he must do. Jenny, thinking his mind was pre-occupied on another matter, slipped up behind him, hoping to surprise her gifted husband. Ted smiled to himself as he said softly

"Sneaking up behind your husband, Jenny?"

"Oh! Ted Neenam, I can never surprise you!" Jenny laughed as she grabbed him around his waist. "You, sexy darling man!"

"Jenny! My mother might hear you!" Ted joined in her laughter "Just you wait until later, Mrs. Neenam."

"Oh? I cannot wait!" Jenny kissed his smiling lips.

"Ted, are you expecting guest, sweetheart?" Hannah walked over for a hug from her son. "My boy, I have missed your warm loving hugs." Ted smiled as he gave her a warm embrace.

"Yes mother, I am expecting someone, but I would not exactly call them guest, more like family." Ted closed his eyes and said softly. "Naomi, Jeff and Teddy are at the door now." Just then the bell rang out and Jenny shook her head, then smiled at Ted's mother.

"Hannah, your son always knows before they ring the bell. Every single time!"

Hannah smiled, admiring her special son as he opened the door and smiled at his extended family. Knowing the small boy's trauma, Ted got down on his knees and motioned for the child. Jeff lowered their son and he ran swiftly into Ted's arms and burst into tears.

"Please, my Ted, make it go away!"

"Teddy, you are frightened, I know, but soon you will find laughter again, I promise." Ted stood up, and picked the frightened boy up in his arms, then carried him from the house. Naomi and Jeff looked out of the window as Ted disappeared down the path, tears filling their eyes. Jenny walked up and placed a hand on each of their shoulder as she spoke words to comfort them.

"Ted will help Teddy. He is the best one for the job and he really loves your little boy very much." Jenny smiled, thoughtfully. "Jesus said, bring the little children unto me, for thus belongs the kingdom of Heaven. You both know Ted is an instrument of God so Teddy could not be closer to God than he is right at this moment."

Naomi took around Jenny, finally giving her a beautiful smile. "Yes Jenny, I do know. Our Ted is very close to the Father in Heaven. Teddy will be fine soon."

Ted sat Teddy down beside him on a log and stroked the boy's dark hair. "Speak what is on your heart, son."

"I love my papa, but…papa was bad, he hurt people. He hated people."

Ted placed his hand on Teddy's trembling shoulder and the child calmed down, his big black eyes on Ted's face. "That is true Teddy. Sometime back, your papa was very bad and he did do evil things. But then something good happened to your papa. Something so good it saved your papa. He found love, he found your mama. Before knowing your mama, the only thing your papa knew was hate." Ted took Teddy by his small hand, his blue eyes shining with pure love.

"Teddy, do you know where love comes from?"

"I think so, my Ted." The boy lit up and declared "Someplace good, like…Ted's mountain!"

Ted laughed softly and hugged the young child. "Yes Teddy, you are right. There is good on this mountain, but it's not just here, love is everywhere. Love lives inside your heart and it comes from Heaven, from God, our Father."

Little Teddy sat up and clapped his hands, then hugged Ted. "Papa met mama! Papa found love! Love is in Papa's heart and God, our Father, gave it to him!"

"Yes son! Love is stronger than hate." Ted stood and lifted Teddy to his feet. "Your papa loves you deeply and he will always love and protect you Teddy."

"Thank you, my Ted! You made it go away and I feel much better now!" The young boy laughed out and waved up in the sky. "Thanks God for loving us and putting love in my papa, for me and mama!" Teddy grabbed Ted by the hand. "Let's go down, my Ted! I want to kiss my papa and tell him I love him!"

Ted's eyes twinkled with thanksgiving as he laughed along with the happy boy. "Well then, what are we waiting for, lets go! There's a lot of love waiting for you at that home!"

Jeff stood at the back door, his mind on his little son, and he had felt Ted and Teddy coming from the mountain path. Jeff glanced over at Naomi, who sat chatting with Jenny, Kathy, and Hannah, and called softly "Sweet one." Naomi turn to see him standing in the open door as he said, "They are coming back."

When Naomi joined Jeff at the door, she saw Ted and Teddy come into view around the wooded path. She noticed that they were holding hands as they made their way toward them.

"Listen sweetheart!" Naomi laughed softly, feeling relieved. "They are singing! And look how happy Teddy is, he is beaming with joy."

Ted stopped so the young boy could see his parents waiting for him at the back door. Teddy laughed out and took off in a run, calling their name.

"Mama! Papa!" Teddy stopped at Jeff's feet and smiled up at the man towering over him. "I love you, papa!" his small arms went up to Jeff, who scooped him up in a warm fatherly embrace.

"My little son! My sweet little boy!" Tears filled Jeff's eyes as he buried his face in Teddy's black hair. "I love you too, Teddy, very, very much!" Teddy pulled his head around and kissed Jeff on the lips, causing the big strong man to laugh and return the sweet innocent kiss.

Teddy smiled and patted his father's cheeks lovingly as he said "Can I play with Ruth now?"

"You certainly may!" Jeff laughed and lower his son to the floor. "I am so happy you are feeling better, Teddy."

"Yeh Papa, just like new!" Teddy smiled over at Ted. "Thank you, my Ted!"

"Go have fun, little friend. Ruth is waiting in the den." Ted smiled as the group watched the happy boy dash off to find his playmate. Ted laid his hands on, Naomi and Jeff's shoulder. "You have got a special little fellow there."

"He is so small and innocent, Ted and we knew what that demon put him through was almost more than our son could take. Thank you, from our heart, Ted." Naomi read Ted's serious eyes and added "For…a doing God's work through you."

Ted hugged Naomi and whispered, “That’s my angel.” Then his attention fell on Jeff, who stood silently, observing the closeness between Ted and Naomi. “Jeff, it is time we have that talk now.”

“Yes, I know you are right.” Jeff walked out the door beside of Ted and they walked silently up the path. Naomi smiled to herself as she watched from the big living room window. “There goes my two favorite men, my devoted loving husband and my beautiful angelic Christian brother.” She lowered her head in prayer. “Dear Father, Blessed Lord Jesus, Holy Spirit, my constant friend, please give Ted the right words to help my beloved.”

Naomi felt Jenny’s hand on her arm, opening her eyes, she noticed Jenny’s beautiful smile.

“Naomi, if anyone can help Jeff, it’s Ted. I am living proof!”

Chapter Fourteen

Ted and Jeff walked up to two chairs in the rose garden and sat down. As they sat facing the top of Goldsburg Mountain, Ted reached over and patted Jeff's arm.

"You are troubled by many nightmares, my brother. They are all your past demons that used to live within your heart and soul."

"I have not spoken all the truth to Naomi." Jeff turned to stare at Ted. "I just don't want her to worry so much about me. She already had a lot on her mind, worrying about our son's sudden change. You are right. It is the nightmares, they have returned and come to me every night. All my past evil sins keep reliving over and over in my mind!" Jeff placed his head in his hands and mumbled "Only when I am awake, and with my sweet one, can I feel a little peace."

"I know, my friend, of all the evil deeds you have committed and only by God's gracc you have not been found guilty to serve a life sentenced or be electrocuted for those acts of murder. The hate you had for everyone and anything beautiful, the way you could control their minds and bodies so they could do your bidding to please Lucifer." Ted's blue eyes were warm and kind, not filled with judgement. "But God permitted you to find love and although you find it hard to believe, love can and does blot out all transgressions, even yours, my brother."

"How Ted? How can all the evil I had inside me and the terrible things I committed through mind control, be forgiven?" Jeff stared up at the mountain. "How can God forgive me?"

"The same way He has forgiven all men, Jeff." Ted stood up and a soft glow illuminated around him. "No one can be forgiven on their own, Jeff. All men fall short of salvation, all men sin." Ted's smile was brilliant as he declared "That is why God, the Father, sent His son, Jesus, our Lord, to die on the cross and save all the world from sin."

"Even me?" tears came to Jeff's dark eyes as he repeated quieter "Even me?"

"Tell me Jeff, when you sent Marna Mullican back to

everlasting torment, what did you feel?" Ted knew the answer but needed Jeff to say it.

"At first, I felt hate for the demon, that woman sent to destroy our son." Jeff's eyes remained closed as he remembered sending his departed housecleaner back to Satan. "That woman, who had made my dearest, my Naomi, anguish over what had happened to Teddy. But suddenly, I started feeling sorry for Marna. My hate turned to pity, knowing she could never undo what she had done while she lived. If only she could still be alive and see the change in me. I would have released her, as well as my mother, from the curse I placed upon them." Jeff's voice grew softer. "But Marna was going back to Lucifer, to that place of eternal punishment, to be tormented even more for failing him."

"Jeff, your love is growing stronger every day. You felt compassion for that woman, even after what she had done to your little boy. You showed love and not hate, allowing God to give the final judgement to Marna Mullican, when our Lord Jesus returns." Ted waited for Jeff to open his eyes before adding "The Lord has great plans for us, Jeff. Greater than anyone living today. But first, He must be sure of your sincerity and true faith in Him."

Ted moved in front of Jeff and stretched his hands out over his rich black hair. "Jeff, you ask me earlier if God could save even you. All you have to do is to believe in Jesus, the Christ, who died for your sins, many though they are. You have come a long way, my friend, and there is much love waiting to grow inside you, but for now, you are heading in the right direction." Ted dropped his hands, on top of Jeff's head and declared

"Your nightmares will cease to be! From this day forth, you will have peace and rest, my brother, through Him who gave His life for you."

Jeff felt a calming peace fill his very soul and simply whispered "Thank you, my Lord." Jeff gazed up to find Ted smiling down at him, bringing out a smile of his own. "Ted, how can I thank you? You made me well inside and I felt the heavy burden lifting from my body."

"I am only my Lord's vessel, His hands, His voice." Ted lifted Jeff up "You were right to thank the Lord, Jeff. It was God who has made you well, Not I."

Jeff laughed softly as he placed his arm down over Ted's

shoulder. "Well, Ted, I shall try harder with this faith, this belief you have. But for now, we have got many demons to battle. Satan is very angry with me and he is taking it out on everyone I care about."

"Yes, I have felt their presence, both on Black Mountain and down in the village. We shall fight Him together!" Ted looked serious as he stated "But you, my friend, will have the final battle with your father, this round. You will be on your own, remember that." Ted smiled warmly and added "But I will not be far away when the battle takes place."

"Thank you, my friend. I guess I have come a long way Ted, calling you my friend. Before, you were my despised Bible thumping neighbor who kept getting in my way. My calling was to win you over to evil while all the time, you were winning me over through the love of my dearest Naomi." Jeff looked up at the house, then down at his companion.

"Yes Ted, I read your thoughts and you are correct. We do have love ones waiting for our return."

Chapter Fifteen

Jeff gazed down at Naomi while she moved beside him in bed and opened her eyes slowly, giving him her beautiful smile.

"Good morning, darling. You sure are awake early this morning. Sleep well?"

"I did! I had a very good night sleep, little wife, after all that love making last night." His canine teeth shone from his big smile when she blushed a deep pink. "But this time, I slept all night long. Not a single nightmare!"

Naomi sat up and hugged him. "Oh Jeff, that's wonderful! I just knew Ted, with the Lord's help of course, could make you feel better!"

Jeff lovingly pushed her bangs from her eyes and smiled. "Speaking of feeling good, how have you been feeling lately?" with a twinkle in his black eyes, he added. "Have you been having any morning sickness lately, my sweet dove?"

"Why that is a funny question to ask me." Naomi laughed "This little 'bird' has been feeling just fine, well just a little queasy this morning, but I am just hungry for breakfast."

"My dearest, you feel queasy because you are with child." Jeff climbed quickly from bed before she could slap his arm. Naomi threw her cover off and slung her feet around to face him.

"Jeff Wineworth, are you telling me that I am going to have a…a baby?"

"Another son, to be more exact, my pregnant little wife." Jeff laughed at her innocent expression as he slid into his clothes. "Remember that wonderful sex we had the night Mrs. Proctor came?"

Naomi slid back under the covers and hid her face, bringing out Jeff's loud laughter, then he walked over and sat down next to her as she spoke softly from under the sheet. "How could I forget that night."

"I recall you liked it very much, darling. I remember you telling me how rewarding it was."

"Yes, oh, yes, very rewarding." Naomi peeked out and Jeff

smiled down at his shy bride. "I think I must be the luckiest girl alive to have you for my husband. You really know how to make a body come alive." She squeezed her eyes shut, still seeing her husband's big smile from her true confession. She wondered why she was saying all these things to Jeff. She was sure he must be enjoying her little speech. Jeff surprise her when he simply said.

"I am enjoying your little speech." Jeff bent over and kissed her serious lips. "But you must remember, my love, I too love every moment with my sexy wife. I can't seem to get enough." His hand moved gently over her body and came to rest on her breast. "If only little Teddy weren't up already and making his way down the hall to our room."

"Jeff Wineworth!" Naomi jumped from the covers and grabbed her clothes. "Before she could say another word, Jeff pulled her into his arms and kissed her with passion. Naomi could feel herself melting in his embrace as she whispered "Jeff, we are going to have another son?"

"Yes, my darling, but you are just a couple weeks pregnant." He took around her. "We will tell Teddy about his new brother when the time gets closer. I am sure he will have lots of questions."

"If it gets too hard for us to find a way to tell him, I know we can ask Ted to explain how things work." Naomi smiled sheepishly.

"Oh? Push the burden on poor old Ted?" Jeff laughed "I think I am pretty capable of telling my son just the things a small mind can understand. It won't be that hard, my love. Teddy takes after me, he will catch on fast."

"That is what I am afraid of." Naomi said thoughtful as Jeff opened the door for her.

"I will tell Teddy all the facts when he is older, sweet one. Stop worrying. Now, let's go down for a family breakfast." Jeff lifted his son in his arms as they met him in the hall.

Jeff pulled his silent black car to a stop in front of the Christian Home. He reached over and patted Naomi on the knee, then got out to retrieve their son from the back seat. The little boy smiled happily as he marched up to the front door.

"I can stay here all morning and play with Ruth?"

"That's right, son, so be a good boy." Naomi brushed his hair back from his eyes. "Never have I seen hair grow that fast. Maybe

I'll trim it when we return home."

"No mama! My hair looks like my papa's and I don't want it cut!" Teddy reached for the rope to ring it when Ted opened the front door. "Hi, my Ted!"

"Hi, my little friend. You are just in time to play with Ruth." The young girl peeked out around Ted, a big smile covering her face. Ted turned his attention on Naomi and he smiled brightly as he added, not looking away. "Run along kids, Matthew and Kathy are waiting in the kitchen with the other children, to take you on a fun hike."

Naomi watched Teddy grabbed Ruth's hand and take off to the kitchen, then looked back up into Ted's smiling eyes.

"So, my angel, you are with child." Ted reached down and kissed her as she shook her head and said

"Not you too?" bringing out laughter from both Ted and Jeff. "And, I suppose you know its…"

"Another boy? As a matter of fact, even at only two weeks, I do. What a blessing."

"Another little boy?" Jenny walked up next to Ted, shaking her head. He slipped his hand lovingly around her waist as she gave Naomi a weak smile. "Are these men telling you, you are going to have a baby?"

"What can I say, Jenny. Who needs a doctor with these two around?" Naomi hugged Jenny, glad she was not the only one with a gifted husband. "Do you think we will ever get use to them?"

"No, not likely." Jenny squeezed Ted's hand. "But as long as they good in bed, who cares."

"Jenny?" Ted blushed, causing Jeff to laugh and reach over and pat Ted's shoulder.

"Jenny, it would seem you are not as shy as my sweet Naomi. Just enjoy her Ted, my good fellow." He looked into Ted's eyes and smiled. "Oh! I see you do, very much!"

"A…yes, well…" Ted mumbled "So, you are on your way to town to see Doctor Ward, Naomi. I am sure my mother wouldn't mind taken on anther delivery here."

"Ted, that is very thoughtful and I know your mother has had a lot experience when it comes to childbirth, but I think Hannah will have her hands full with your and Jenny's new arrivals, not to mention all the other children here. Doctor Ward did a wonderful job with Teddy's delivery, so I know I will be in good hands."

"Whatever you want, angel." Ted took Jeff to one side to have a word before they left for town. "Jeff, stay with her, close by at all times. There is something not quite right here."

"I agree. I have felt it too." Jeff's eyes grew dark. "I just cannot put my finger on it as yet."

"You will, but for now, there is nothing we can do until they make their move." Ted grew serious as he whispered. "What do you know about a Doctor Raven?"

A frown clouded Jeff's face as his voice came low. "A Doctor Raven was the one that recommended 'Mrs. Proctor' for our nanny. That name is very familiar. Someone from my past memory. I feel he is close by."

"Very close. Warn Naomi again about strangers. She must know and be extra careful if she encounters a Doctor Raven."

"Do not worry about Naomi, Ted. I will guard her with my life." Jeff looked down at his wife when she walked over, looking concerned.

"What are you two talking about over here so serious?" Her attention went from Jeff to Ted. "is there something I need to know, besides the fact that I am two weeks pregnant with another little boy?"

"Jeff will fill you in on what you need to know, Naomi." Ted gave her a loving hug, making her feel relaxed. "Now, be off you two and do not worry about little Teddy."

"That, my friend, is the least of my worries." Jeff gathered Naomi's hand in his as he patted Ted's arm, then they walked to their car.

Chapter Sixteen

Jeff pulled the car to a stop in front of the office of Doctor Thomas Ward, one of only three family doctors in the small town. He stared for a moment at the white brick building, then climbed his tall frame out to help Naomi and through the front door.

Those waiting in the reception room looked up to see the handsome couple walk inside and followed their movements to the front desk. The receptionist, Mrs. Mason, had been with the good doctor for many years and smiled up from her paperwork.

"Good morning, Mrs. Wineworth, Mr. Wineworth. The doctor will be with you shortly."

"Thank you, madam." Jeff pulled Naomi over to a private sofa and whispered. "Listen sweetheart, there is a stranger in this building, I can sense it. Someone or something we cannot trust. Be extra careful and tell me everything you see and hear." Jeff took her hands lovingly. "If you need me, just whisper my name. I will hear! I will come!"

"Jeff, who could possibly be here with Doc Ward, besides his usual helpers?" Naomi saw her husband's deep concern and she laid her head over on his shoulder. "Very well, Jeff, I promise to be extra careful and keep my eyes open for anything or anyone suspicious." She looked up and smiled. "I will whisper your name if I need you to come."

Mrs. Mason walked over to tell Naomi the doctor was ready to see her. "Please follow me."

Jeff stood to help his wife up and said softly "I will wait right here in the waiting room, darling." His eyes spoke volumes of love as she reached up and kissed his waiting lips, then handed him a short list of items.

"Sweetheart, could you run across the street to the drug store and get these things for me while Doctor Ward is examining me? I will be alright, Jeff. Besides, it will take the doc awhile."

"Very well, but I shall not be gone long." Jeff kissed her, then smiled at the receptionist, who had been observing the loving couple. "Take good care of my wife for me." He turned and walked from the white building. Mrs. Mason stood staring dreamingly after the tall mysterious man with the penetrating eyes.

Naomi touched her shoulder, causing her to snap out of her dreamy state. "Excuse me, Mrs. Mason, but you said the doctor was waiting."

"Yes, yes I did!" the woman blushed with embarrassment as she led the way to the center examining room and had her take a seat on the exam table. A rap came on the door before Doctor Thomas Ward stepped in smiling, followed by a stranger, apparently a doctor as well, from his white coat.

"My dear, Naomi, what brings you in today? Not feeling well?"

Naomi laughed softly, then said "I feel great, Doctor Ward. Jeff tells me we are going to have a baby. I'm here to confirm his diagnosis."

"A baby?" the doctor chuckled, remembering Naomi's moody husband, then patted her arm. "So, when did Jeff become a doctor, my dear."

"Oh, my goodness! Jeff is hardly a doctor, as I'm sure you are aware." Naomi joined him in laughter. "Let me just say, Jeff is special and he just...knows things."

"Young lady, your husband sounds like a mind-reader to me or perhaps a fortune teller." The stranger had been silently listening to Naomi's description of her husband. "Perhaps it would be wise to leave such predictions on pregnancy up to us professionals, my dear."

Doctor Ward turned red when he stated "Where are my manners. My dear, this is my new assistant, Doctor Luther Raven. He and his wife have just moved into Goldsburg and he is seeking to start a practice here."

"Goldsburg is a lovely town to work in, Doctor Raven. If I might ask, where did you live before making our fair town home?" Naomi felt unusual uneasiness around this man with a too familiar name.

"My wife Hazel and I moved here from Salem, Mass. After the children grew up and left home to start their own careers. The Mrs. and I decided to downsize and move to a small town, away from tourist, seeking to learn all the gruesome history connected to Salem." Naomi had a sudden chill when he stepped closer and looked down. "Your beautiful little town is exactly what we had in mind, so here we are."

"Doctor Raven might decide to go into business with me since I have taken on all of Jim Carter's patients. He just suddenly retired." Doctor Ward took some blood samples from Naomi's arm. "Jim's patients are starting to trickle in and I can see I will be overwhelmed by the increased number."

"I am sure you and Hazel will like it here, Doctor Raven." Naomi was busting with questions for this man, but she knew she must be careful with her words. "I wish you much success in your practice here, doctor." Naomi smiled at her old doctor, as she added "But as for me, I am very happy with Doctor Ward. He made my first son's birth very easy for me."

"Of course, my dear." The stranger's tone was polite enough as he continued "I never intend to take any patients away from my new friend and college. The way I see it, these new patients of Doctor Carters are more than enough for my part time option."

"Doctor Raven will be a nice addition to our practice. But now, let me go and check these blood samples and see if your clever husband is correct about you being pregnant, young lady." Her old doctor patted her hand. "If it is alright with you, I will leave Doctor Raven to check your blood pressure and listen to that good heart of yours. Nurse James, you may come with me." The doctor smiled and walked from the room, the nurse right behind to take notes and record findings.

Naomi felt more nervous being left alone with this Doctor Raven who had pulled his chair up next to her and strapped the blood pressure sleeve around her slim arm.

"Now, young lady, let me check that blood pressure." After reading the numbers, the stranger peered over his black rim glasses to state. "My dear, it is a little high. According to your records, it usually runs perfect."

"I'm sure it is all the excitement over having another baby, Doctor Raven." She tried to keep her voice calm. "It's not every day my husband announces I am with child, two weeks long."

"Two weeks? How can your husband be so sure? Even doctors have some difficulty when the baby is only two weeks." His dark eyes stared into hers. "Your husband, Jeff, is absolutely sure you are with child? We shall soon know. The blood test is the science way to be certain."

"I do not need a blood test to prove my husband is telling me the truth. I am sure. I am going to have another baby. Two weeks shy of nine months." Naomi glanced over at the closed door, hoping Doctor Ward and Mrs. James would come back in. "I never doubt anything my husband tells me."

"Whatever you say, Mrs. Wineworth." He smiled and started listening to her heart as he laughed. "It must be love."

"Doctor Raven, you said you had older children." Naomi tried to sound normal as he stood behind her listening to her heartbeat. "You must remember how excited you were when you found out about having babies."

"Oh, my yes! Some of my fondest memories." The doctor casually walked around to fill out her chart. "They just seem to grow up too fast and fly off to college, then find jobs in other towns, other states."

"Doctor Raven, forgive me if this is too personal, but you seem like a very respectable man, I was just wondering, with this being my second child, my first one just two-years-of-age," Naomi smiled warmly, thinking her words through. "You wouldn't know of a nanny I might get to help me out, just in case I ever need one?"

"As a matter of fact, I know the perfect nanny for small children." His smile looked real enough when he reached for his wallet and pulled it open. "The dear lady was with us for over eighteen years. The kids adored her and Hazel and I thought the world of her." The doctor thumbed through his billfold until he found the photo he was searching for. "I thought I still had her picture with the children, in here." He handed it over for Naomi to look at. "Her name is Mrs. Proctor. She was like family to us, but we had no use for a nanny after the children moved out."

Naomi stared down at the woman in the picture and ask softly "Did you say, Mrs. Proctor?" As she looked at the happy group, she knew this woman was unfamiliar to her and not the Mrs. Proctor who showed up at her doorstep.

"That's right, Irene Proctor, but the children called her Nana." The horrible demon's face came into Naomi's mind at the mention of Nana. "Let me write down her address and phone number for you." He quickly scratched it on a notepad and handed it over, taking back the photo of the stranger's face. "I am pretty sure the nanny has not taken on another position yet, but you might want to give her a call if you're interested."

Hearing the door open, Naomi smiled over, relieved, as she watched Doctor Ward walk in shaking his head in dismay.

"Well, my dear, you can tell 'doctor' Wineworth, that his prognosis was correct! There is no doubt, you are most certainly pregnant. How Jeff could tell at just two weeks is beyond me." Her doctor took her hand. "After you get dressed Naomi, stopped out front and make an appointment in two weeks or if you want to know if it's a boy or a girl, you'll have to wait a while longer to find that out, unless your gifted husband finds out first."

"Yes, Doctor Ward, let Jeff look into his crystal ball to find out!" Raven chuckled at his jesting.

"There is no need, Jeff has already informed me about the sex of our child." Naomi gave her old doctor a wink. "We are going to have another son and Ted has confirmed it."

"A…yes. You just take care of that little bun growing inside you." Doctor Ward headed for the door, turned and added "And do your old doctor a favor, please ask your husband not to open a practice beside me. I cannot compete with that genus." He motioned for Doctor Raven. "Coming Luther?"

"Yes, of course, Doctor Ward." He turned back with a cold stare and said "Take care, madam and tell that husband of yours to 'watch over you'."

As he closed the door, Naomi jumped from the table and pulled on her skirt and top. She could feel her heart beating wildly in her chest. Looking around the windowless walls, she whispered

"Jeff, where are you?"

Chapter Seventeen

Jeff had just stepped out of the drug store and started across the street when he heard Naomi's plea. Without hesitation, he darted across the road, oblivious to traffic.

A car came speeding around a curve, trying to make a caution light before it turned red, and didn't see the tall man dashing in front of him until Jeff stopped and calmly held up his arm, killing the motor and stopping the car with a jerk. The shaken driver could only stare in total shock at Jeff's dark serious eyes. Jeff made his way to the sidewalk and lowered his hand. The car motor roared back to life, and shaking his head trying to make out what had just happened, the man drove away slowly.

Jeff flew inside the waiting room and straight to the front desk, getting the attention of everyone in the waiting room and those behind the desk.

Looking up startled, the receptionist tried to sound calm as she spoke. "Is there something wrong, Mr. Wineworth?" she instantly noticed his cold dark eyes, staring first at her then the door leading to the examining rooms. "Your wife should be walking through that door any second now." To her relief, the door opened and Naomi stepped quickly out and looked relieved to find Jeff waiting.

Jeff was next to her in a flash and took her hand, squeezing it lightly. She smiled down at the speechless receptionist.

"Doctor Ward wants me to come back in two weeks."

"Yes, of course." She checked the openings and said "Is two o'clock alright, the same day two weeks from today?"

"Yes, thank you." Naomi took the appointment card from her shaking fingers and pulled Jeff out the door.' She breathed a sigh of relief when the bright sunshine hit her. It was far better than the closed in exam room.

"Naomi, what happened in there? Why did call me sounding panic?" Jeff pulled her into his protecting arms. "I was scare out of my mind!"

"Jeff, darling, your feelings about a stranger being near by was correct. It appears Doctor Ward has taken on a new doctor to help him. Doctor Carter retired, for no apparent reason, and gave doc all his patients."

"And this new doctor just happened to be here in our small town looking for an opening! How convenient for him!" Jeff said sarcastically.

"Exactly! I thought the same thing. Doctor Carter is ten years younger than Doctor Ward." Naomi lend in close as a couple past them on the street. "And darling, you are not going to believe this, the new doctor's name is…"

"Raven!" Jeff went white as he blurted out "And that monster was in the same room with you! I can see it all now! Did he harm you, sweet dove?"

"No, but I was pretty frightened by the way he was looking at me." She looked into Jeff's concerned eyes. "And, there's more."

Before Naomi could continue, Doctor Luther Raven walked out of the office and smiled their way. Without hesitation, the doctor, now in a black suit, walked over, a smirk on his face.

"Well now, you must be Jeff Wineworth. Your wife has been telling us some very interesting things about you."

"Please, do not keep me in suspense, doctor. What sort of things are you referring to?" Jeff's stare was cold as ice, causing the cocky man to back slightly away from the man towering over him. "That I informed her that she was having another baby and it would be a boy, now only two weeks in her beautiful belly."

The man stood speechless for a moment, then cracked a smile. "You had me going for a minute there, young man, but now I can see your wife just told you what we talked about inside."

"I assure you, sir, I do not know what you are referring to. We never discussed what she might have said, just what Doctor Ward had to say about the baby!" Jeff spit the words out with fire.

"Jeff, Doctor Raven and his wife our new to Goldsburg." Naomi placed her hand behind Jeff's strong back, a sign to take a breath and relax. "We hope you like it here, doctor. Don't we Jeff, darling?"

"But of course. It is a far cry from Salem, Mass." Jeff's attention never left the stranger, who stared back with suspicion. "Tell me, Doctor Raven, have you found a church yet?"

"A church? We did notice your town had two churches in town, Shady Grove Baptist and Maple Wood Methodist. I am of the

Catholic faith and unless there is a Catholic church close by, I might have to decline going." Raven looked over his glasses at Jeff, and asked sarcastically "Do you attend church Jeffery Wineworth?"

"I do, Luther Raven! But you may never go to our church. Before you inquire, it is a private church service on the mountain, for family only." Jeff smiled at the sour face and added. "But nothing should keep you from stepping inside of St. Andrew's Catholic Church, located on Elm Street. You must have missed it." Jeff opened the car door for Naomi and helped her inside. "Good day, sir." Without another glance at the doctor, Jeff walked around, got in and drove away.

After driving out of town, Jeff reached over and took his wife's hand. "You were going to tell me about asking Raven about his grown children."

Naomi glanced over at her husband and sighed before saying "Yes and I ask him if he knew any nanny's he might recommend for small children, should I have the need for one."

"Smart little wife, playing detective." Jeff winked at her and brought on her beautiful smile. "And of course, the man said yes, a Mrs. Proctor, right?"

"Exactly!" Naomi grew excited. "Then he showed me her picture and it was not the same woman who showed up for the nanny position." She took out the slip of paper Raven had given her. "Doctor Raven gave me her address and phone number!"

"Do you think this woman really exist? Raven knew you wouldn't call her and if you had written, he would have conjured up another Marna, looking like the woman in the picture. I can assure you darling, those children in that photo were not that mans!" Jeff found a pull off and drove over to park. Turning toward his wife, he draped his arm around her. "Perhaps I will give the 'good' doctor my business. Suppose I make an appointment on the same day you are going in."

"What would you say is wrong with you Jeff?" Naomi took his hand and kissed it. "You are never sick! Actually, you are very perfect!" she smiled when he laughed and kissed her.

"I can tell Doctor Quack, I've been having nightmares, even though we both know they are gone, thanks to Ted. I will ask for something to help me sleep at night."

Naomi sat up, looking uneasy. "Jeff, that could be dangerous!"

Jeff gathered her up in his warm embrace and kissed her with tender passion. “Sweet one, do not start worrying about me. He will give me some pills but I won’t be taking them, only pretending.” He laughed softly. “If I really needed any help, I would just call my good friend, Ted.”

“Alright Jeff, I know how smart you are.” Naomi scooted out of his arms and moved back to her seat when she saw a police car driving down the street in their direction. “Start this car before that officer pulls over to check on us. Let’s go pick up our son before he wears Ruth out.”

“Ruth?” Jeff laughed and pull away, waving at the passing police officer. “More like Kathy and Matthew.” He gave her his handsome smile, showing his sharp canine teeth. “After we put Teddy to bed, I will be taking you to our bed and make love, my darling. That is the only medicine I require.” Smiling at her flushed cheeks, Jeff patted her legs and sped up the mountain road.

Chapter Eighteen

Ted had been to the mountain and had meditated for an hour before returning to his bedroom. He walked over and smiled down at Jenny, deep in peaceful sleep. Her deep breathing made her chest move up and down under the cotton sheet. Ted reached down slowly and lowered the cover, revealing Jenny's perfect round breast. Letting out a deep breath, he pulled the robe over his head and climbed back into bed. His fingers gently moved over each breast, then his kisses moved over them, as he remembered their night of love making. He could tell he was growing excited as he climbed over on her and slowly started making love to her.

Jenny smiled and opened her eyes as her arms draped around his back. Their kisses grew with each movement until they both moaned in ecstasy. Ted, breathing heavy, remained on top of Jenny, as sweat dripped from his shag hair.

"Oh Ted, just when I think it cannot possibly get any better, you rack up another win."

Ted looked into her eyes as he kissed her, then rolled over and slid to a sitting position. "Jenny, my beautiful Jenny, I am the luckiest man alive."

"Well, I am the luckiest person alive, Mr. Neenam!" Jenny reached over and pulled him back down for another kiss then rubbed his tan chest. "Sweetheart, do we have to get up so soon?"

"How about right now, Jenny Neenam. Have you forgotten it is the first day of school?" Ted smiled when she sat straight up. "My girl has got a big day."

"The first day of school!" Jenny jumped from bed "How could I have forgot, after Leah has talked about it for the past two weeks." She ran her hand through Ted's hair. "I'll miss seeing you there, though. Two years of school and you passed with flying colors, straight A's." Jenny looped her arms around his neck and kissed him before adding "Your wife gives you an A+ in love making!"

Ted laughed as he stretched. "The Lord provides, darling. I will get my shower first. Better not take one together, we might never get ready and Leah will be pounding down our door."

"God forbid we upset Leah." Jenny laughed and added "If you think a separate shower is safer, my sexy husband, I'll wait and pick out my teacher's clothes." Jenny watched Ted walk into the bathroom, admiring his body when she heard him say

"Do you like what you see? Does your husband suit your taste?" Ted knew she was watching and used her same words to him on their wedding night.

"Yes, I certainly do!" she smiled and walked to her closet as she whispered, "He remember me saying those very words to him, that heavenly little stinker!" When she pulled out a skirt and blouse, she said to herself. "Jenny Neenam, you are the luckiest person alive."

"No Jenny!" Ted called from the shower. "I am the luckiest stinker alive!" he laughed as Jenny grabbed a pillow off the bed and threw it at the door, laughing along with him.

Jenny and Ted walked down the steps, followed by most of the children. Kathy and Hannah stood at the bottom of the steps, admiring the handsome group. The children lined up, smiling at Kathy when she gave them a wink and said

"What a smart and great looking bunch of kids!"

"I am not smart, Kathy, but I am real pretty!" Leah yelled out happily."

"Leah?" Ted touched her lips. "You are smart and pretty, but you talk too loud."

Leah blushed when the children laughed and looked up at Ted shyly. "I'll try to do better Ted."

Hannah reached for her hand and motioned for the other children. "Alright children, your breakfast is getting cold. Everyone, take you seat and wait for Ted to give the blessing."

"Alright children, after I give the blessing, I need to tell you a few important things before you leave for school." Ted motioned for Kathy and Jenny to have their seat. "This includes you ladies as well."

"What is it, Ted?" Jenny gave her husband a serious look as he took her hand, then bowed his head to give the blessing, then told the children to start eating.

"First of all, children, I want you to study real hard so each of you can get good grades, like you did last year. I am very proud of all of you. Remember you are Christian boys and girls and you 'must' take God in your hearts every day." Ted smiled and looked over at his wife, who sat listening carefully. "Listen to Jenny and Matthew." Then Ted grew very serious. "Now, this is very important, so listen carefully. Beware any strangers you see, whether they be a new teacher or a new student. If something happens and you are afraid, go find Jenny or Matthew at once." Ted looked deep into Jenny's eyes before adding "You must be extra careful, extra watchful. You must never be afraid because, I am just a call away. You do remember that Jenny, I know."

"Ted, what on earth is going on? Are you sensing some sort of danger?" Jenny got up and pulled her special husband to one side. "Is there something you need to tell me, darling? You are scaring me here!"

"There is danger nearby, Jenny, but nothing bad will happen today, my love." Ted took her hands in his and she relaxed. "I will tell you everything you need to know tonight." He felt her hands shake again. "Darling, I promise, everything will be alright. Jeff and I both know what is going on and we are ready for the fight that is coming."

"Fight?" Matthew walked in the back door and overheard the couple talking quietly. "It sounds all mysterious to me. Care to fill old Matthew in."

Miriam came twisting down the staircase, the last one to descend. Ted noticed her heavy make-up immediately and stopped her before she stepped off the last step.

"Miriam, do you care to explain why your face is all painted up like a show girl!"

"Teddy, Jenny wears make-up, all the time." She smiled innocently at Ted. "besides, I feel real pretty with make-up. After all Ted, I am nineteen-years-old and I am capable of making my own decisions."

Matthew laughed. "Miriam, Jenny looks great in make-up, just like my Kathy, but miss boob, you, look like a circus clown."

"Matthew, that will be enough." Ted frowned at him, then gave Miriam his serious face. "The fact, young lady, is that you do not need that much make-up on, especially at school."

"Yeh, Ted is right, madam movie star, all the boys will think you are a hooker and start hitting on you." Matthew heard Ted clear his throat. Matthew walked quickly next to his wife, where she placed her hand over his mouth and whispered.

"Husband, you had better keep those sweet lips zipped tight. You are making Ted mad."

"Matthew, grow up!" Miriam noticed Ted shaking his head and walking away. Quickly, she stepped from the stairs and raced over to him. "Teddy, I've been thinking about school. Since I am eighteen, I really don't think I need to return to school this year." the blonde reached out and touched Ted on his shoulder, making Jenny's eyebrow fly up in anger. "Can't I stay home and help you, Teddy dear. With everybody at school, you need someone."

"Miriam, you need to go back to school." Ted, knowing Jenny was getting upset with Miriam's actions, he draped his arm around his wife and smiled down at her, receiving her smile in return. "You need at least one more year to graduate, if you make better grades than last year."

Miriam's attention flew over to Jenny and noticed Ted caressing his wife's shoulder. Feeling instant jealousy and envy toward this woman that stole her Teddy's heart, Miriam yelled

"I guess 'Jenny' told you I needed more school!"

"No dear." Jenny said calmly. "I never had to say a word about you. Your grades told Ted you needed more school."

Matthew just could not keep still another second as he laughed mockingly. "Yeh goofy, crack them books more and stop flirting with boys so you can study!"

"Matthew, I don't see your grades any better!" Ted frowned over at Matthew, bringing out Miriam's laughter. "It would pay you to get certain subjects off your mind." Ted nodded toward Kathy. "If you do not want to fail another year, crack your books and concentrate on your studies. If you keep flunking school, you may find yourself graduating with Leah."

Andrew walked in the back door, carrying a bucket of seeds and smiled at Ted. "I have everything ready for planting, Ted. I will get the hoes out and wait for you outside by the garden wall." His attention went to all the children ready for their first day and smiled at the young happy faces. "Good luck, my sisters and brothers. Remember, if you want to move up a grade next year, or graduate this year, you must study real hard and make good grades."

"Hey, wait just a minute, Ted, Andrew is a year younger than me!" Matthew looked from Andrew to Ted. "How come he don't have to go back to school?"

"Because genius, he studied hard the first two years and passed with A's and B's." Ted laughed and patted Matthew's drooping shoulders. "You do not see me going back, do you? Again, two years of hard study making straight A's and you and I are the exact same age, my brother."

"Oh sure, Ted! You probably knew everything before the teachers got their words out!" Matthew jumped and yelled ouch when Kathy punched his arm and laughed.

"Ted, you know my sweet Matthew. Always the joker."

"As a matter of fact, I do know that, Kathy. That is the reason 'your sweet' Matthew might really find himself graduating with Leah." Ted laughed and clapped his hands. "Alright everyone, out to the station wagons and we will place you inside."

"I want to ride with Jenny!" Leah shouted and instantly grabbed her mouth. "Woops, sorry."

Jenny tossed her bag over her shoulder and smiled at the young red head before taking her hand. "Why don't you want to ride with Matthew?"

"You drive better and he is always joking with me! Matthew is a pest!" Leah made a face at Matthew before opening the car door.

Matthew frowned over at the outspoken girl. "Listen kid, I will have you know I passed my driver test with perfect grades and I am getting my butt out of that school this year. It will be a cold day in H-E-double L toothpicks before I walk up for my diploma behind you!"

"Matthew, just study hard and graduate this year. It will make Ted proud of you and your devoted wife will be cheering you on the day you walk up for your diploma." Kathy reached up and kissed him. "Drive safely and I hope to be back home when you return from school."

Matthew let his eyes wonder down Kathy's dress suit before returning to her made up face and hair. "Why are you so dressed up beautiful? Are you going to volunteer again at school this year? I thought you were staying here to take care of Ruth."

Kathy noticed she had everyone's attention. "Well, sweetheart and family, I am going into town for a job interview this morning at 9:00 a.m. I have an appointment with good old George Claremont at the law firm of Claremont & Williams. You remember George, Jenny? The gentleman you sold produce to from Ted's wagon and talked him into donating money to help with the children's education?"

"Good old, free giving George! It's hard to believe that was over two years ago." Jenny smiled at her best friend. "Good luck pal, you are a great secretary. Tell George I said hello." Hugging her friend, Jenny took out her car keys and handed them to Kathy. "Take my M.G. You can't walk and it needs driving."

"Thanks friend! I am looking forward to the drive." Kathy noticed everyone was still staring at her and instantly she assumed they thought she was forgetting her responsibility. "Oh, Hannah ask if she could watch Ruth and take care of the cooking and cleaning so I could bring home some much needed money to help buy things we cannot grow or raise."

"Kathy is right, everyone. With extra mouths to feed and more laundry and bath products needed, it only made sense that Kathy apply for the secretary job opening in town." Hannah smiled down at the chubby little girl holding her hand. "I will love watching Ruth and I'm tired of being treated like a guest. I am part of this family too and we all do our part."

"Well mother, you are family and we love and except all the help you can give." Jenny hugged her mother-in-law causing Ted to smile to himself, knowing Jenny and his mother were growing close. He walked over to join them and gave his mother a hug of his own.

"You are a sweet beautiful lady, Hannah Neenam. Thank you, mother."

"That is what mothers and grandmothers do, darling." Hannah winked at Jenny who had laughed softly.

"Well, enough chit-chat, folks! Let's get going! We can't be late on the first day of school! They will give us all a F to A on F D!" she called loudly and noticed every staring confused. "Come on kids! F-Failure to A-Arrive on F-First D-Day!" her eyes grew wide. "I am serious here!" Leah grabbed Jenny's hand. "Let's go!" she shouted.

"Leah?" Ted walked over and knelt down at her level. "Listen young lady, if you yell out like that in school, the teacher will put a pointed hat on your head and make you sit in the corner, facing the wall."

"WHAT!" Leah quickly grabbed her mouth, her eyes wide as

she spoke softer. "My teacher…will…turn me…into…a witch?"

Everyone laughed at the notion of Leah being turned into a witch, then Jenny took her hand.

"Sweetheart, just learn to speak softly, especially in class and in the library." She smiled over at Ted. "And I wouldn't worry about your teacher putting you in the corner with a pointed hat. I don't think teachers turn children into witches anymore."

"Now that Jenny has settled Leah's problem, besides Leah riding in the front car, you six can climb in with Jenny, the rest take seats in Matthew's car. We do not want the Christians to be the only children late on the first day of school, so it is time to leave." Ted and Matthew helped the kids in their seats before Ted opened the door for his wife. "Drive careful sweetheart."

"Should I be expecting anything to worry about on my way to school, any more children running across the road or old ladies dropping their belongings?" Jenny remembered her trip to pick up Hannah and Ted's warnings coming true.

"No, my love, I see nothing to slow you down today." Ted reached his head inside the door and kissed Jenny, getting giggles from the girls. "You take the lead and hold Matthew back. Drive careful going down the mountain." He took her hand and spoke softly "And Jenny, remember everything I told you and you will recognize the ones you need to beware of. I will fill you in tonight on the rest."

"Alright Ted, I will be aware of my surroundings and look out for strangers." Pulling his head back down, she returned his kiss, and there were more silly giggles. "I love you." Jenny started the motor and motioned for Matthew to follow.

Kathy had kissed Matthew goodbye and told him to be careful and pay attention to his teachers. Miriam watched from the front seat, where she sat between Matthew and John. After blowing Kathy one last kiss, Matthew started his motor as Miriam placed her hand on his knee and smiled back at Kathy, waving when they drove off. Kathy heard Miriam's whinny voice through Matthew's open window.

"O.K. hotshot, let's see what you got!"

Putting her hands around her mouth, Kathy yelled as the white station wagon pulled away, Miriam looking back with a smirk. "Hey Miriam, if you plan using your 'piano' hands, you will keep them to yourself and off my husband!"

Ted walked over and took Kathy's hands down and turned her around to face him. He gave her a beautiful smile before saying "Kathy, you've got nothing to worry about where your husband is concern. You have Matthew's heart, totally and completely. Miriam just likes to upset people with her flirting. She is really harmless where me and Matthew are concern. We both are very loyal to our woman."

Andrew had been standing back watching the excitement of going back on the first day of school. He stepped up next to Ted, still holding the seed bucket, hoes propped up against the garden gate.

"Wow, it sure did get quiet when those cars drove away. Do you think we can get used to it being so quiet around here?"

"We will stay so busy, Andrew, those precious children and my adorable Jenny will be back home before we know it." Ted noticed Kathy walking from the house, purse hanging off her shoulder and swinging Jenny's car keys. Andrew watched Kathy as she opened the car door and throw her purse inside. He was still thinking about the quiet day ahead.

"I guess we could sing while we worked or something." Andrew waved back at Kathy when she waved.

"Well guys, I am off for my interview. Wish me luck." She smiled.

"You will do find, Kathy. You have worked in a law firm before in Chicago and Jenny tells me you were the lead attorney's secretary there." Ted opened the driver's side for her. "Since Matthew's not here to assist you, I will offer my services."

"Thank you, sir. You are quite the gentleman." She pondered the fact that he knew where she had worked in Chicago, but Jenny could have given him that information as well. "Jenny and I met in Chicago and became the best of friends. I guess that's why she told you so much about me."

"Jenny only told me what position you held as secretary, which you shared just moments ago with the entire family. I just know it was in Chicago and you worked in the law firm of Hancock & McBride for seven years before you met Jenny, then another three years before her accident and you moved here with her to Goldsburg."

"Wow! You don't say? I mean, you are spot on, Ted." Kathy laughed nervously. "I tried to tell Matthew several times when we were alone, but his mind was always on something else, if you know what I mean? Night, bedtime!" she noticed Ted had turned a bright shade of pink from embarrassment. "Gee, I've made you blush." Kathy couldn't resist her laughter as she slid in the driver's seat. Reaching up, Kathy playfully patted his cheek. "I'm sorry."

"Kathy, remember the warning about strangers. Our small town has been invaded with beings posing as ordinary people. They could be teachers, doctors, a new neighbor, a school child, or a lawyer. Always be aware of people you do not know and a few you do know and probably trust." Ted had succeeded getting off of Matthew and Kathy's sex life and back to more serious matters. "Pray that the Lord will guide you to always know the truth."

"O.K. Ted, now you are scaring me." Kathy looked up worried. "What exactly am I supposed to be looking for. Someone new working for George?"

"You will know, Kathy." Ted took her hand and she suddenly drew strength from his heavenly warm touch. "Do not try to be brave and take on this evil being all by yourself. You cannot know the power and strength you will be up against. Just come home immediately and call my name."

"Well, I have visited Mr. Claremont on several occasions and have met everyone working in his law firm, so if there is a stranger there I will know it at once."

"Not necessarily Kathy." Ted squatted down to get eye contact with her. "These evil beings have a knack of taking over a person's body and using it for their means." He noticed her frightened unsure expression.

"Kathy, just use the gift the Father has given all women. The gift of a woman is the ability to sense things that are not right. Just use this gift Kathy, and you will know the one who seeks to do you wrong." Ted stood and took both her hands. If you are unsure, whisper my name and I will come to you. This is another kind of warning I give you, Kathy. Do not drive this car too fast. It could prove dangerous as well and you have plenty of time to make your appointment."

"Whatever you say Ted. You always know best, so, slow is the word!" Kathy smiled and started the sports car. It roared to life and she quickly checked her watch. It appeared to be the exact same time she and Ted started their conversation. This was one mystery she would leave unsolved for the time being. George had made it clear that he liked his staff to always be on time and thanks to Ted's magic, she had plenty of time. Kathy patted the steering wheel and waved as she said "It feels like old times being in this little car. So many good memories coming up this mountain to pay you and the family visits."

"Kathy?" Ted looked at her serious. "Just remember what I said."

"Yes Ted, I know. Nice and slow and be on the lookout for any suspicious characters." Kathy waved when Ted stepped away, a signal he had finished his speech. She drove out the driveway and creeped down the mountain road." Kathy mumbled when she was a long distance from the farmhouse.

"That Ted, making me crawl all the way to my appointment. This baby can move around these curves and once I pull out on the main road, it's smooth sailing. I had to go slow in that station wagon when I drove those kids to school before Matthew got his license, now I am in this fast little M.G. and…" Kathy felt Ted's frown as he said her name, bringing out a guilty grin. She stopped the car when she came to the end of the mountain road. She looked up toward the green mountain and whispered

"Slow like a turtle! Creeping like a snail!" Kathy made a face at herself in the mirror. "Driving like Aunt Kris, all the way to town! I pray I do not get ran over by 90-year-old Clara Martin!"

Chapter Nineteen

Kathy reached a long straight stretch and noticed she was the only car in sight. Giving herself a wink in the mirror, she switched gears and took off, letting the wind blow in her hair.

"This is more like it! Let's see what this baby will do!" Kathy pressed down on the gas pedal and flew off down this road. She dropped her eyes momentary to check her speed, 85 miles per hour, then back on the road, just in time to see an old 62 Ford was pulling out slowly, directly in front of her. Kathy squeezed her eyes shut and slammed on the brakes, sending the small sport car into a spin. She loss count of the number of times it, spin around before it came to a complete stop, jerking her up. Still strapped in her seatbelt, Kathy finally opened her eyes and noticed right away she was facing the right way.

A little woman was standing beside the Ford, shaking her fist at Kathy and yelling. "This is not a racetrack, young lady! Slow down before you kill somebody!" the woman climbed back inside her car and drove away, leaving Kathy mumbling to herself.

"It was your fault, granny! If you cannot see a car heading right at you, you need damn glasses!" Kathy stopped complaining when she realized she was not hurt anywhere. Pulling the sport car over, she climbed out and check it over, not a single scratch. Her attention went to the mountain.

"Oh, Ted Neenam, why are you always right!" Kathy got back in the car and started the motor, then drove slowly down the highway, shaking her head. "I'm just glad he did not witness this little incident. That heavenly man would never let me forget it."

Ted was waiting in the big den with his mother and Ruth, when the group of school goers came running in.

"WOW! WHAT A FUN DAY!" Leah quickly found Ted's frown and she bit her lip, looking sheepishly. "I'm sorry Ted. Me and my big mouth!"

Ted laughed and gave her a warm hug. "You were a very polite young lady at school, Leah. Besides, it's alright to get excited over your first day at school." His attention went to Jenny as she pushed her way through the door with an armload of books. Matthew walked close behind her, carrying his own arm load. Ted retrieved the heavy books from Jenny and placed them on a coffee table. "Children, from now on, bring your own books inside, They, are your responsibility." He gathered Jenny in his arms and smiled down in her tired eyes.

"How's my girl? You look worn out." Jenny gave him a smile when he brushed back her hair and whispered in her ear "I have missed you darling."

"Sweetheart, If I could be with you 24-7, it still would not be enough time with my man." Jenny took Ted's hand and led him to the sofa, and flopped down, kicking off her heels. Ted reached for her feet and started rubbing them as he called the children over. All fifteen walked over and sat down on the floor.

"Alright my darlings, after we have eaten our supper, I want everyone to remain at the table so I can hear all about your first day at school." Ted motioned to the stairs. "Now, run up to your rooms, put away all your books, and wash your hands for supper."

"Alright Ted." The group said happily in unison as they jumped up, grabbed their schoolbooks, and dashed up the steps. Hannah watched them disappear in separate doors, then she put down her knitting and stood up, smiling.

"My, what a nice bunch of kids. You have done a wonderful job raising them, Teddy." She noticed Jenny starting to get up to help her and she place a gentle hand on her shoulder. "You just relax and enjoy your husband dear. Everything is ready and all I need to do is set it out."

"She's right Jenny, you looked exhausted after driving up with Leah." Matthew walked up next to Hannah. "I'll give this pretty lady a helping hand with those dishes." He winked at Ted. "I'm sure you would like to give Jenny a proper welcome." Matthew's smile was genuine when he added. "I know I will when my girl gets home." He started for the kitchen when Ted called after him

"You had better hurry then, Matthew. Your girl is driving up mountain road right now."

"Yips!" Matthew dashed through the kitchen door and raced back out carrying two serving bowls of mashed potatoes, then retraced his steps for more.

Ted took around Jenny and pressed his lips on hers, gazed into her eyes, then returned for a more passionate kiss. "Tonight, cannot come fast enough, my love." He whispered breathlessly. "But for now…" he sat back and ran his fingers through his long hair. "I must behave myself. The children will be down soon."

Jenny laughed softly and hit his arm playfully. "That's right, my sexy husband, turn me on and move away! Tonight, is pay up, buster!"

Ted gave her a smile as he placed his arm around her shoulder, pulling her over to him. "I will force myself." he teased and turned toward the door. "Kathy is coming in now." Instantly the door opened and Kathy stepped inside whistling, until she spotted Ted and Jenny watching her.

"Caught me! Whistling while I enter!" she tossed her bag down in a big chair and flopped down next to her bag. "I didn't see you all hugged up over there. What a day!"

"I take it you got the job and dear old George had you start work immediately." Jenny stood up and stretched before walking over to join her friend. "I never doubted for one second that George would get you for his personal secretary. You are the very best, in my book."

"Oh, yes! Getting that position was a piece of cake. George was really impressed with my fast typing and perfect shorthand. By the way, old George ask me to tell you hello." Kathy laughed, keeping her focus on her friend to avoid looking at Ted. "The dear man kept asking about you. He went almost boggle when I told him you were expecting twins."

"You don't say." Jenny smiled over to Ted who was frowning. "That George is so sweet. He hasn't changed a bit." Ted walked over and looked down at Kathy seriously.

"Anyone new working at the firm, Kathy?"

"As a matter of fact, there is." She relaxed, thinking Ted had no clue about the car incident. "I had seen him in there on my previous visit to set up this job interview with George. His name is Phillip Tucker, a hot shot lawyer from New York. He claims to be sick of the rat race in the big city and needed a quieter, smaller town to work. The man seems to be pretty brilliant. Ten of his old clients have already flown here with their cases." Kathy smiled at Matthew as he made his way across to the sofa and stopped behind her, rubbing her shoulders. He could tell from experience, Ted had more to say to his wife, so he knew to remain quiet until he had finished.

"Keep an eye on him, Kathy. Sometimes things are not what they seem, no matter how many legal looking licenses he might have."

Jenny and Kathy noticed when Andrew walked in the room quietly, he, like Matthew, remain completely still as he watched Ted. It was obvious to the two friends that these young men knew something they had not learned yet about Ted, so they too thought it best to listen and only speak when spoke to. The whole time, Ted had not taken his eyes off of Kathy and she was beginning to think she had misread his not knowing what happened on the highway. At the moment, his words came out soft, yet stern.

"Where you afraid after slamming on you brakes going 85 miles-per-hour when that slow car pulled out right in front of you? Where you afraid when Jenny's little sports car started spinning around uncontrollable?"

"Oh, shit!" Kathy bit her lip as she squeezed Jenny's hand. "It was a straight stretch and there was not one car in sight. I had poked all the way down that mountain and I felt like an old silly turtle. I wasn't going to go fast for very long, I just needed to move." Kathy swallowed, feeling everyone watching her and she noticed Matthew's fingers seemed to freeze to a stop as she confessed. "How was I to know some silly old woman was going to crawl out right in front of me and me speeding down the highway directly toward her?" She glanced at Jenny who looked back sympathetically but knew to remain silent. Kathy looked up at Ted's serious face and blinked. "Ted, you were up here, on this mountain, hoeing in the garden with Andrew. Or, so I thought."

Ted did not take away his stare as he spoke softly. "You thought I was up here too busy working and had my mind totally on Jenny and I would not know what you were up to. So, you went ahead, after all my warnings and drove that car fast!"

"Well, I…survived." Kathy gave a weak smile. "I had closed my eyes when the car started spinning and when I opened my eyes, the car was headed in the right direction. After checking the car, I was amazed there was not one little scratch." Her attention fell on her friend. "Honest, Jenny, The M.G. is as good as ever."

"That is because I saved you Kathy." Ted's voice grew serious.

"I can tell you true, you would have been killed, along with Mrs. Arlene Moore, that 87-year-old lady who pulled out in front of you, late for her friend's funeral, if I had not been there!"

"Kathy, sweetheart! My Lord! Don't you know Ted is always right!" Matthew had grabbed her shoulders, his heart sinking with the close call his wife had.

Jenny reached out and hugged her friend, tears filling both their eyes. "Kathy, thank God, Ted was there to save you and that poor old woman!" Jenny reached for her husband's hand as she smiled lovingly at him.

"Ted, I…never saw you!" Kathy sniffed her nose. "How…how did you know?"

"Kathy!!!" the unison voices of Jenny, Matthew, and Andrew sounded at once. As though a revelation switched a light on in Andrew's mind, he snapped his finger.

"Oh! I remember! Ted and I were busy pulling weeds and talking when suddenly, Ted grew silent." Andrew looked thoughtful. "I stopped weeding to look at him and noticed Ted had just vanished, disappeared, his hoe and bucket sitting right where he had just been standing. I checked my watch and it was almost 8:30."

"8:30? That was the exact time on the car clock…" Kathy looked at Ted sadly. "when I glanced down at the speed, I saw the time. Will you ever forgive me, Ted, for not listening to you?"

"Kathy." His voice was soft and full of love, his eyes were warm with forgiveness. "You were forgiven before you ask." Ted reached out and took her hands. Kathy could feel his powerful love flow through her as she took a grateful breath. "Beautiful Kathy, you are a part of our family, Jenny's best friend, Matthew's loving wife. To have loss you would have broken each heart here. We love you." Ted finally smiled and added. "I think you have learned your lesson."

"I have, most certainly!" Kathy stood up to hug her rescuer. "Thank you for being there, Ted. We are so blessed and lucky to have you!"

"We are blessed and lucky to have you too, Kathy." Ted looked down at Jenny and smiled. "And, by the way Kathy, I was thinking about Jenny!" he pulled her up from the sofa and hugged her. "Jenny is never far from my mind."

Matthew and Andrew seem to let out a relief breath as they

watched the children making their way down the stairs. Miriam followed behind them and smiled down at Ted.

"Everyone is ready, Teddy. Got the little kids all clean and ready to eat their supper."

"Thank you, Miriam." Ted patted her arm then added. "But I think you forgot to wash your face."

"I think Miriam likes being a clown." Matthew quickly took Kathy's hand after seeing Ted's eyes flash, then made tracks for the kitchen table, changing his subject in case Ted was still listening. "Now Kathy, about you driving that sports car…"

The rest of the family followed and ate their supper as they spoke quietly. Ted would wait for everyone to finish eating before asking the group about their day.

Chapter Twenty

Ted looked around the quiet group of children and youth, knowing they were nervous about answering his questions, but he knew they all loved him just like he loved them.

"Dearest ones, you have nothing to fear by my questions, I merely wish to know how your first day of school went." The smiles showed they were ready to share their day with the man they admired and looked up to. "Alright, let us begin with the youngest in our group." Ted reached and patted Ruth's chubby knee, causing her to giggle with delight. "So, tell us about your day, sweetheart."

"It was a real goodie day, Ted. Hannah and I had lots of fun, playing games and reading my books. We enjoyed a swell walk in the rose garden and picked some grapes off the grape vine to eat, then we made cookies!" Ruth pointed at the empty dish and giggled again. "See, they're all gone!"

Everyone laughed as Ted winked at his mama. "That just means, you and my mother can make terrific cookies, Ruth." Another giggle from her chocolate cookie lips. Ted turned his attention on Leah, James, Sarah, and Rebecca.

"My 2nd and 3rd grade children, which teacher did you get this year?"

James spoke up for the group, being the only boy. "Our teacher is Mrs. Collins, the same one we had last year."

"Yeh, she's real nice, a real smart lady." Leah tried to speak softly, knowing the room was quiet.

"The classmates are the same as last year too, Ted." Sarah smiled shyly. "There were no new kids."

"You remembered my warning about strangers, good girl." His attention fell on Rebecca, too shy to look up. Ted reached over and gently lifted her chin and softly ask "How was your day, Rebecca?"

Rebecca blinked her big brown eyes and stuttered "It…was good, Thank…you."

Ted touched Jenny's hand under the table and brought out her beautiful smile in return. After exchanging smiles, Ted turned to the next group.

"Alright, Paul, Elizabeth, Rachel, and Peter, my 4th and 5th graders."

"Our teacher is Mrs. Rains, and she is real sweet." Elizabeth smiled.

"Peter and Rachel had her last year." Paul's voice shook nervously as he tried to speak up. "Elizabeth and I just moved up to the 4th grade and have her this year. They said she was a good…teacher." His eyes dropped, happy to be finished.

"Thank you, Paul, that was very good." The shy boy smiled at Ted's praise for him. "Rachael, I believe you have news about a new student in your class?" Ted took her by surprise, causing her to sit straight up and stare at him in wonder as her voice came out softly.

"That's right Ted. There is a new girl in our class. Her name is Molly Darson and the teacher put her next to me."

"She's kinda cute, too." Peter grinned silly.

Rachael looked down shyly. "Mrs. Rains told us Molly was new in town and we need to help her feel at home. So, I walked her to the playground and sat with her during lunch." Her eyes met Ted's as she said sweetly "She didn't laugh at our bag lunches like some of the other students did last year and she seems to be real nice, but I will watch her, being a stranger and everything."

Ted smiled and reached over to pat her head. "That's a good girl." He looked over at John, Thomas, and Ester. "O.K., 9th and 10th graders, let's have your report."

"Our teacher is Mr. Cobb." Ester's eyes lit up looking at Ted. "He was there last year. The only difference, he is wearing glasses this year because he had a hard time seeing the black board."

"He really needed glasses then, if the poor man could not see his own black board, the biggest thing in our classroom." Jenny tried not to laugh at the serious girl.

John laughed, then lend on his elbows as he announced, "There's no new students in our class, but I must admit, the girls are looking better this year."

Thomas hit his arm and mumbled "I'm sure Ted is not interested in that, John, but I think you might be interested in the new guy in Matthew's room, Robert Perkins."

Everyone heard Miriam sigh, causing Ted to clear his throat. "Go on Thomas, what about this Robert Perkins?"

"Robert Perkins was standing at his locker with Tommy

Fletcher and Billy Smith, when he noticed me and John, removing books from our lockers across the hall. He motioned for us to come over and showing brotherly love, we walked over, knowing the meeting couldn't be good."

"Tommy and Billy are pretty rough characters and a couple of real bullies at school." John looked serious. "Well, this Perkins guy said he had a really cool joke to share and we looked like we could use a good laugh."

"Then the foul mouth Perkins told us a very nasty joke, bringing out loud laughter from the two bullies." Thomas looked up at Ted and noticed a nod to continue. "I told Robert Perkins we did not care to hear such trash and started to walk away, when Fletcher grabbed me by the arm and his buddy Smith took a hold on John's arm."

"And, the entire time they held on to us, they kept putting us down in front of the new guy. They called us a couple of goodie-two-shoe Christians, living on Goldsburg Mountain, being raised by…" John couldn't bring himself to say their words, not wanting to hurt the man they all loved. Ted's eyes reflected true love and understanding when he said softly

"Go ahead son, it's alright to say his hate filled words about me."

John's eyes filled with genuine tears as he spoke softly, recalling their hurtful words. "being raised by a Bible thumping weirdo, who talks to some God who doesn't even exist."

"How utterly mean!" Jenny's eyes flashed, angry that someone could speak so ill of Ted, God's special gift. "Someone needs to sit them two brats down and give them a good talking to!"

Kathy nodded and frowned. "I think those boys could use a good thrashing! Of all the nerve!"

"Jenny? Kathy?" Ted remained untouched by the boy's hateful remarks directed at him. He felt only sadness for their misguidance and never learning about the one and only God in heaven, who could and would turn them around if someone took the time to reach out in love. He turned back to the boys. "Go ahead boys, then what happened?"

"John and I told them we felt sorry for them and that we would pray that they learn the truth." Thomas' eyes dropped as he added softly "They just laughed at us."

Ted took Jenny by the hand and squeezed it lovingly, then spoke softly "Go ahead."

"We told them we forgave them." John teared up. "We then let them know the young man, not much older than ourselves, took us into his heart and home and taught us how to make something out of our life, told us about our Father in heaven and His great love."

"With the fear all swept away from us, we told them Ted is the best thing that has ever happened to us, every single child living on Goldsburg Mountain!" Thomas wiped away his tears. "And that this town has been greatly blessed to have him among us!"

"My brave sons." Ted reached across the table to place a hand on each, young men and he could read their next words as he said, "Then this Billy and Tommy looked down in shame but this new boy laughed in your face."

John and Thomas looked at each other as they realized Ted knew what had happened even before they told him. Ted's attention fell on Miriam, who was listening while checking out her fingernails. She felt Ted watching her and looked over with a smile.

"Remember what I said about strangers, and think on this, I have never said anything like what I am about to say, keep watch children. If something does not sound or feel right, tell me at once, understand?" positive nods from each child and youth, then he smiled and added "Never forget, your heavenly Father sees all and will guide me as well." Ted looked seriously at Matthew.

"Alright Matthew, it is your turn, along with your fellow classmates, Simon, Philip, and Miriam, 11th and 12th grade. Fill me in on your day."

"We have a new teacher, Ted." Simon's eyes lit up.

"Yeh!" Philip smiled sheepishly, recalling seeing the 'hot' teacher for the first time. "Her name is Angela Rayfield. Quite a dish, don't you agree, Matthew?"

Matthew instantly shook his head in a diffident no, toward a frowning Kathy, who punched his arm when his face grew red.

"Well Matthew, is this Miss Rayfield a 'dish'?"

"Kathy honey, I wouldn't know, I barely noticed her." Matthew heard Ted grunt and turned to see him frowning at him. "Gee wiz Ted, come on, man! I'm a married man, and a very happy one at that. Just let me tell Miss Rayfield that I'm married!"

"We discussed that Matthew, remember?" Ted continued to frown "As long as you are going to public school, no one needs to know you are married, got it?"

"Got it!" Matthew looked back with discuss. "I remember you kept your marriage silent at school for two years. The only difference is, when the girls would flirt with you…" Matthew looked at Jenny who was taking it all in, "and there were lots of love-struck girls, Jenny, old Ted here would just block their minds so they would forget what they were going to say or do."

Ted felt Jenny's eyes burning on him, filled with questions from his school days, she had insisted he attend.

"Jenny, nothing happened and trust me, those girls do not remember liking me. Matthew is just stalling for time by changing the subject to me. I think Miriam has something to say. She has been anxious to fill us in on this teacher."

"Well, it's obvious Miss Rayfield has an eye for the boys." Miriam gave Matthew a knowing smile as she added with a slight giggle. "Anyone can see, our teacher mostly has her eyes on Matthew

Kathy slid her chair back and stood straight up. "That little bitch! I will…" Matthew gently took her arm and pulled her back down in her seat, pointing under the table at Ted. Kathy tried to laugh as she sought out the right words to say, for this 'holy' man. "What I meant to say, before my loose tongue anger took over, was, this woman is supposed to be there to teach students, not flirt with them."

"What does Miss Rayfield look like?" Jenny came to her friend's rescue, knowing how she felt over some woman flirting openly with her husband. You four top graders describe her as, a dish with an eye for boys. How does she look and what kind of clothes does she wear? I haven't got to meet her yet."

"Oh, you cannot miss her when she comes around the other teachers, Jenny." Philip punched Matthew's arm and winked. "Rayfield has got long blonde hair, amber brown eyes with really long eye lashes, and very large, very round…" Philip jumped when Ted cleared his throat and nodded a negative. Feeling the tension, Matthew kicked his shin under the table. Miriam laughed and took up the teacher's description.

"Miss Rayfield's clothes, what there are of them, are really cool! They really flatter her shapely body." Miriam smiled at Ted, then gave Kathy a fake grin. "But her blouse is very low cut and I am sure when she bends over in front of dear old Matthew, he must see clear down to China."

"Wow! See all the way to China, from a blouse?" Leah asked, wide eyed and stared at Matthew. "Did you see any of those really fat wrestlers wearing nothing bathing trunks down in that blouse, Matthew?"

"Leah, Miriam did not actually mean old Matt could see China, just the teacher's belly button." James chuckled until Ted stood up and walked over beside Miriam.

"Miriam, remember there are impressionable children at this table."

"You are absolutely right, Teddy. Forgive my bad manners." Miriam smiled down, pretending to be shy as she continued. "Well, the teacher's tops are low cut and her skirts are very short. Let me just say, Angela Rayfield clothes makes the way Jenny dresses, look like a virgin, next to her." The blonde smiled to herself when Jenny stood up and stormed out.

"What? Miriam, so help me, if these children weren't down here, I would..." Ted placed his hand over Jenny's mouth and turned sharply on Miriam.

"Miriam, do you remember the warning I gave you about speaking about my wife like that!"

"But Teddy, I never meant anything by it. I was only trying to describe..." Ted cut Miriam off as he said sternly.

"Just go straight to your room, young lady! I do not want to see you until you leave for school!" his blue eyes shot fire as he pointed to the door. "Now go!"

Miriam burst into tears as she turned and raced up the steps to her room.

"Ted, sweetheart, I really don't think..." Jenny stopped abruptly when Ted turned and stared down at her for a moment then walked back in front of the group, who waited quietly.

"We've had enough excitement for one day, so off to bed, my angels, and sleep well." Ted walked around helping the younger children up, then gave them a hug. "Say your prayers."

"Alright Ted." They said in unison, hugging him as they filed by and made their way up to their rooms.

Kathy pulled Matthew toward the kitchen after loading his arms with plates. "Let's clean this mess up sweetie and give Hannah a rest. We've both got a busy day ahead tomorrow so it's clean the dishes, then go to bed and go to sleep!"

Before they went through the kitchen door, Matthew made a face back at Ted, who watched them smiling. "Get me in trouble with my wife, huh!"

"Just behave yourself at school, Matthew and don't get yourself involved." Ted continued to smile, bringing out a slight grin from the young man. "You've got enough love to get you through this temptation."

"Yes, you are absolutely right there, Ted. I love my woman and she is crazy about me, a little mad at me right now, but she will come around." Matthew took a breath of relief and carried the heavy load through the door whistling.

Ted moved toward Jenny and took her hand, then pulled her up the steps as he spoke softly. "Alright, Mrs. Neenam, you and I are going up to our room, first to discuss your day."

Jenny took in his perfect body as they walked up slowly and thought to herself. "I bet Ted has forgot about telling me what is going on."

Ted smiled to himself as he pulled her gently inside their bedroom and shut the door. He turned and looked down at her beautiful face, then smiled. "No Jenny, I have not forgot about telling you what is going on, at least what you need to know for now." He smiled mischievously. "And, I have not forgot what I promised to give you, when we go to bed." Ted's fingers gently touched her lips. "My girl is in for a spectacular night."

The butterflies once again invaded her stomach as her heart beat with anxious passion. "I can hardly wait, Mr. Neenam."

Chapter Twenty-One

Ted and Jenny sat on the side of their bed holding hands. "Alright, Jenny, it's your time to report on your first day."

"Oh, I see! You start with Ruth, the youngest, and end with me, the oldest." Her eyes twinkled with mischief as Ted shook his head smiling.

"Alright Jenny, you got me." Ted laughed softly. "Now, my beautiful, 'young' wife, may I hear about your day?"

"We have a new principal, a Mr. James Morgan, from Salem, Mass." Jenny frowned as she recalled asking several teachers what made the old principal retire. No one seem to know the exact reason. "I never got any straight answers about why Mr. Vernon quit. He was well liked and seemed to enjoy his job here. The devoted man had been with Goldsburg School for twenty-five years. The first five years as a high school history teacher, then promoted to the principal's position after Harold Fonda retired after 50 years." Jenny looked over at Ted, who was taking in every single word. She laughed softly. "I don't know why I am telling you all this. I'm sure you already know."

"Jenny?" Ted's voice was low but stern, his face filled with sudden seriousness. Jenny glanced down quickly and whispered.

"Ted, sweetheart, I'm truly sorry." Jenny glanced up and noticed he was still very serious, so she forced a weak smile. "I'm bad, aren't I? I never should have said that." To avoid his stare, Jenny gazed out at the night sky, twinkling with stars. "But I said it because…I really did think that." When she looked back over at her husband, she found him smiling.

"Jenny, who could stay upset with you for very long? How was Mr. Vernon doing toward the end of last year?"

"Clarence seemed very healthy and completely happy. He spoke about plans for this year and how he looked forward to getting back after the summer." Jenny thought back to conversations in the teacher's lounge and at staff meetings. I remember at one meeting, Mr. Vernon discussed wanting to work another 25years and said that would make him 75 if the good Lord gave him that long." Jenny frowned, confused. "He seemed really sincere and happy."

"Then, all of a sudden, Mr. Vernon had to resign and move his family out west, to Arizona." Ted stood up, the revelation coming to him. "He had gotten word that his parents were in danger of losing their home and land of 65 years and they needed him to come out at once to look after things."

"That poor man." Jenny looked thoughtful as she tried to reason with the facts. "I wonder why Clarence didn't just send for his parents to live with him here. He had spoken of bringing them back here to live with him and his wife so he could take care of the elderly couple. Clarence and Elene had a quest house fixed up for them and he had a job here he loved."

"Mr. Morgan, what is he like, Jenny?" Ted stood quietly, looking at his beautiful wife.

"He seems nice enough, I suppose." Jenny gave him a warm smile. "But he is a stranger and because of what you said about strangers, that bothers me, somewhat."

"You feel bothered because of Mr. Vernon's sudden retirement and the fact that this Morgan just happened to be here looking for a principal's job." Ted walked over and pulled Jenny to her feet and looked down, a serious expression on his handsome face. "You remember I told you I would tell you what you need to know for now, darling. The devil is angry Jenny, he is very angry and has returned to claim his son back and Jeff has refused him."

"Good for Jeff." Jenny's hands trembled in Ted's steady grip. "The love Jeff has for Naomi is holding strong." Suddenly the reality hit her. This was not just some angry human that lost what he had. She swallowed back her panic fear as she whispered. "The devil, himself?"

"Yes, my love, Lucifer, the Father's arch angel who betrayed his very creator and lives to destroy God's perfect plan and win over as many of the Father's children as possible before he is stopped forever. Now one of his own has been taken away from him because of love, so he seeks revenge on anyone connected to Jeff." Ted remained calm as he stroked Jenny's hair. "There is nothing more-evil on this earth Jenny and the strength of Lucifer is far greater than all his many demons who obey his will, willingly. So, he has unleashed many of his demons on our little town and is focusing on anyone Jeff cares about."

"That mean all of us, does it not?" Jenny squeezed Ted's hands, fear lacing her alluring eyes. "Oh, Ted, all these poor children, the innocent citizens in town." Her hand touched her stomach, her mother's instinct to protect her babies. "Our innocent little girls."

"Jenny, my dearest love, the devil is strong, even powerful" Ted's voice was tender and calm as he took his wife into his arms. "but God is many times more powerful and stronger than Lucifer. The Almighty uses his arch angels and warrior angels to fight and defeat Lucifer, just like they did in heaven. The Father's great love extends to all his creation, including his fallen angels, even though their fate is sealed for all eternity and they can never again enter into the rhymes of heaven. The power of the Almighty God is unmatched and with just a thought or a blink of His eye, he could utterly destroy Lucifer and his demons, but he has even given them a fighting chance. But in the end, Love will prevail! Love will win! Do you remember what I told you, Jenny, about love and evil?"

"That 1% of good can win out over 100% of evil, every time, anytime, anywhere; because, God is love!" Jenny smiled when she could read on Ted's handsome face he was very proud of her answer."

"Now Jenny, this is very important so listen carefully to what I am about to tell you." Jenny felt her heart race as she nodded a positive, then waited for his words. "Not 'if' Jenny, but 'when', something happens in the school, and it will, you must whisper my name and I will come quickly. You and the children will be safe, my darling, no matter how bad things seem to appear."

"Yes Ted, that much I do know. I can depend on you to hear my softest whisper, wherever I am and you will come to save me and all who are in danger."

Ted gently took Jenny's face in his hands and lowering his head, he parted his lips over hers in a tender kiss. His fingers slowly started unbuttoning her blouse. Without taking his eyes off her face, he pulled his robe over his long shag hair. With madding slowness, he undid the zipper on her skirt and it fell to the floor where he gently scooped it up and placed it neatly across the chair. Reaching around her, Ted quickly unsnapped her bra and lowered his eyes to her perfect breast. With his slim fingers, he massaged each breast, as he closed his eyes and smiled.

Jenny grew hotter with each move Ted made and helped him

slide his boxer shorts to the floor, where he kicked them to one side. With his eyes still shut, Ted reached down and with a smooth motion, pulled Jenny's panties to the floor. Given them a kick on top of Ted's boxers, Jenny took a deep breath and thought

"I don't see how this can get much better, but something tells me it will."

Ted laughed softly as he pulled Jenny into his arms. "Oh yes, darling, it's going to get a whole lot better." Ted lifted Jenny off the floor and carried her to the bed and laid her down gently. Once again, he began moving his hands down her neck to her breast, feeling the harden nipples, smiled and continued his movement down until his hands came to rest between her thighs, stroking her tenderly for a few minutes until Jenny felt like she was going to explode. Feeling her getting close, Ted climbed on top of her and resumed kissing her passionately. Jenny could feel his erection pressing up against her and she managed a breathless whisper as she pleated

"Oh Ted, Ted...please...take me now!"

His eyes spoke compassion, his lips love, as he entered with a fiery connection that sent her reeling, not once, not twice, but three spectacular times until at last he released himself. Ted lay quietly on top of Jenny, sweat dripping off his long locks as well as the sweat connecting their bodies as one. He slowly rolled over beside her, kissing her gently and with his handsome smile, said

"Tell me my darling Jenny, did I deliver a spectacular night of love for you?"

"Yes, yes you certainly did, sweetheart!" Jenny sighed. "Again, and again and again!"

"I know." He smiled when she blushed, then he placed his arm across her naked breast and fell asleep, exhausted.

Chapter Twenty-Two

Jenny opened her eyes and saw Ted walking from the bathroom after having a shower and retrieving a pair of clean boxers from his dresser drawer. He climbed into them and reached for his robe.

"Jenny, are you just going to lay there all day staring at your husband?" Ted turned and gave her a beautiful smile.

"Well, I do enjoy watching my husband walk around butt naked." She glanced over at their bedroom door when she heard someone walking passed whistling. Noticing the lock was unlatched, Jenny quickly pulled the covers up over her.

"Jenny, relax darling. No one will be coming in through that door, when it's closed or open, unless they have my permission." Ted walked over and gave her a kiss. "I have never locked that door. I have no need to."

"Gave everyone orders, huh?" Jenny laughed and climbed out of the bed to shut his dresser drawer as he slipped into his sandals.

"Jenny, I will only say this one time, I have never given anyone the order to stay out of my room, the angels do not allow anyone entrance unless I invite them in." Ted noticed Jenny's attention was on his underwear. "Now what, am I running short on boxers?"

"No! That's just the mysterious problem, Ted Neenam! This drawer is filled to the top with brand new boxers and there is never a trace of the ones you take off!" she turned to look at him, questions filling her eyes. "That applies to your robes and a few other clothes you come down in, like perfect fitting jeans and white sweaters." Jenny walked over and stared down into his innocent face. "How can I ever go shopping for you when you always seem to have everything you need?"

"The Lord provides, Jenny." Ted stood up, smiling. "Besides, you can have more time to shop more for yourself, beautiful."

"Ted Neenam, are you telling me, you get your clothes, undies, robes, jeans and other things from God? How can that be? Does he have a sewing machine or something?"

Ted chuckled loudly and patted her behind. "Jenny, never question where things come from when they are heaven sent." He picked the white Bible off Jenny's dressing table and held it up. "Like this Holy Bible you cherish, You, do not know how it came to be in your beautiful hands on our wedding day, but you must know it was heavens sent."

Jenny moved over and took her most treasured possession, then pulled it to her chest. "So, you admit it! Well, husband, if God gives you everything you need, how can I ever give you a gift?"

Ted walked over and pulled her down on the bed, then turned her to face him. "My darling Jenny, You, are giving me the very best gift any woman can give her husband."

"I…am?" She took his hand and kissed it. "What Ted, besides my everlasting love?"

"You are giving me two beautiful little daughters." Ted bent down and kissed her, "That, dearest Jenny, is the best gift I could ever receive."

"You helped me, my love. I could not have done it without you." She smiled when Ted laughed.

"I just willingly planted the seeds, but you are feeling them grow into the beautiful little girls their daddy will love forever, my darling. They will be a part of our love for all eternity." Ted stood up and lifted Jenny to her feet. "Alright, my beautiful wife, up with you and get ready. You don't want to be the one responsible for everyone here being late for the school bell, do you?"

"Oh, gosh! What am I thinking?" Jenny dashed to the bathroom, mumbling all the way. "What in the world am I going to wear today. My plans for laying it out last night went to bed games!

Ted laughed softly as he made the bed in a flash with fresh clean sheets that just appeared and replaced the dirty ones. Looking over at the closet, the door opened quietly as a royal blue pant suit floated across the room to his waiting hands. He laid it gently on the bed and smiled at the matching underwear that appeared. Looking at the invisible being, he winked and slipped out the door, returning with a breakfast tray of sweet rolls, coffee for Jenny and milk for himself. Now he would wait for Jenny, who he knew would be full of more questions as to where the new outfit came from and how Ted managed to get that tray of food so fast.

Ted and Jenny stood at the top of the stairs looking down at the many smiling faces waiting below them. A big smile fell on Ted's handsome face as he greeted his family.

"I see everyone is ready for school. Such bright happy faces!"

"Yes, we are Ted and I can see you had your breakfast in bed this morning." Matthew gave Ted a wink as he asked, "What else did you do to keep you upstairs in your private bedroom so long?"

Kathy noticing Ted's frown, she slapped her husband on his arm. "Matthew, are you trying to get started on the wrong side of Ted this early in the morning?"

"That's quite alright Kathy. Matthew will be Matthew." Ted simply replied as he walked down the steps carrying the tray in one hand and holding Jenny's in the other. Avoiding Matthew, he smiled down at the happy children. "Little darlings, you've had your breakfast so it's time to load up for school.

"Boy, there is going to be a lot of tension to go around." Philip looked down to avoid eye contact with Ted. "But I'm glad to see you and Jenny so…relaxed and…happy."

"Yeah! There's a certain glow on Ted's face this morning." Matthew teased as he smiled down at Jenny. "Jenny, I'm sure you got a lot of sleep last night after that long school day."

"Matthew, you are pushing your luck!" Ted stared at him angrily as he spoke sternly. "Now, get that stupid grin off your face and pull both cars around." Their eyes locked for a brief moment. Instantly Matthew grew serious, his hands shaking. "Now, Matthew!"

"Got sha!" Matthew grabbed Kathy's hand and raced out the door. Ted's smile returned to his face as he spoke to the gang of kids.

"Be on your best behavior, keep your eyes open and remember Ted loves each and every one of you." As the children told him they loved him too and would be good and watch for unusual things, Miriam walked down the steps quietly, with make-up just on her eyes and cheeks. Ted smiled and held out his hand to her. A big smile stretched across her face when she ran over to him and stopped at Jenny.

"Jenny, I was out of line yesterday and said some nasty things about you. I had no right to behave that way. We are family now and I know Teddy loves you dearly, so if you can forgive my childish behavior, I will try to be more understanding and loving." Miriam appeared serious enough to Jenny, so she would except her apology just as graceful.

"Miriam, I will except your apology if you will except mine, for anything I might have said or done in anger toward you." Jenny smiled down at her outstretched hand. "Miriam, like you said sweetheart, we are family, so that calls for a sisterly hug, wouldn't you agree?"

Miriam laughed softly as she ran into Jenny's arms. Ted closed his eyes, and silently thanked God, then took around both young women.

"My family has really made me happy this morning, except for cut-up Matthew, who just might grow up one day when he becomes a daddy."

"Ted, are you saying Kathy and Matthew…" Ted laughed and hugged Jenny.

"Not at this moment darling, but I see another little baby coming very soon and I'm not speaking about us."

"Did someone mention my name?" Kathy stuck her head inside the front door.

"You came in to tell us the cars are outside waiting, Kathy." Ted lined the children up. "Kids, just ride in the same car you rode in yesterday and Leah, keep your voice down in the car too." Ted winked at the little red head when she giggled. "Remember, today is Friday so there will be no school tomorrow or God's Sabbath."

The children clapped happily and ran out the door to load up in the waiting station wagons. Ted and Jenny followed, and seeing Matthew looking his way, he motioned him over. Matthew made his way over slowly, looking down.

"Matthew?" the young man looked up to see Ted's warm loving smile. "Remember what I said about temptation? That woman has powers that can seduce you into desiring her with lust."

"Knowing she has that kind of power Ted. I will keep my guard up. That sexy teacher means nothing to me." Matthew placed a hand on Ted's shoulder. "You know how much I love Kathy. I got all the woman I want or need." He turned and started to walk to the car but turn to look back at the man who gave him strength. "But it wouldn't hurt for you to say a little prayer for me, Ted."

Ted reached over and pulled the serious young man into his arms, giving him a brotherly hug. "I love you, my brother, now go kiss that perfect wife of yours goodbye and drive safely. I keep you in my prayers always."

"Thanks Ted, I love you too." Matthew threw Jenny the front car's key, kissed his perfect wife goodbye, then called to Jenny when she opened the car door. "Ready Jenny? We bus drivers better be headed down the mountain to school!"

Ted and Jenny laughed, then kissed before she climbed behind the wheel. "As before sweetheart, you're in the lead car to hold Matthew back." Ted lend in the open window and kissed Jenny tenderly, causing all the little girls to giggle with delight. "Now, take off before I decide to keep you here with me all day."

"I would stay gladly darling, but someone has to take these darlings to school and kids need teaching." She pulled his head back inside for a final kiss before departing, and another round of giggles came and James mumbled

"Silly girls!" Jenny laughed and gazed into Ted's heavenly blue eyes. "Goodbye, darling. When that time comes you spoke of, I'll call your name and wait for you."

Ted rubbed her cheek gently, stepped back and watched them drive away.

Chapter Twenty-Three

Jeff pulled his car to a stop across from Doctor Thomas Ward's practice and switched off the silent motor. His dark serious eyes found Naomi watching him and moved over to collect her hands in his.

"This is it, my love. I will go in to see if I can find out what Raven is doing here."

"Jeff, please promise me you will be careful." Naomi squeezed his strong hand. "If he is a demon, he might be capable of reading your thoughts, same as you and Ted can read all of ours!"

"My sweet innocent dove." Jeff caressed her face and smiled, revealing his sharp canine teeth. "I have far more powers than any of these demons. They are mere shells of lost souls Lucifer has won and now claim, like Marna Mullican. He uses them to suit his needs, then sucks them back down to Hell. These are not his powerful demons, the fallen angels. Father is saving them for future dealings with me and Ted."

"Then I am glad Lucifer did not set loose his powerful fallen angel demons on us, darling and I trust you can fight these lost soul demons much like you did Marna." Naomi smiled "I can go inside, a little more relaxed now, knowing you are more powerful." Naomi knew if she didn't ask now, she would worry and wonder about future dealings with Lucifer. "Jeff, do you have any power at all over the fallen angel demons?"

"Dearest love, worry not for your life or our babies, I have the power to protect all of us from the great demons but...there are those who are stronger than I." Jeff knew those words drove deep within his beautiful wife heart as she whispered nervously.

"Who, Jeff? Who is stronger than you?"

"Satan, the Almighty God, and...Ted!"

"Ted? His power is greater than you own?" Naomi ask, wide-eyed, convinced both men were equal in gifts, strength and power.

"Ted is more equal to the strength of my father than that of me, sweet one, but when we join forces, Ted and I, or if I had picked Lucifer and myself, the pair would prove stronger than all mankind.

This is the reason Lucifer wants me back. I have proved to be the blood son he has been waiting for and he will not give up until he makes me his Antichrist!"

"Jeff, the choice is and has always been up to you, just as it was with Jesus, who chose to do the will of His Father and die on that horrible cross to save us all from sin, set upon all God's children by your father!" Naomi's eyes pleaded. "Jeff, my dearest darling, Satan cannot make you choose him, choices are out of his control, they are freely given and freely chosen!" her small hand touched his strong handsome face. "Jeff, no matters what happens, even if Lucifer tries something with me, you will 'never' trade your beautiful soul to that beast! Please Jeff, promise me, my darling!"

"My beautiful, loving wife, I promise." Jeff kissed her tenderly, sending warmth through her body. "Even if it meant giving up my life for you, dearest one, I would, but to give up my soul and loose the chance of ever seeing you again, is not excepted!" Jeff's eyes flashed fire as his father's sneering face came into focus. "I swear, if that devil ever touches you, my dove, I will fight his bloody heart to the end."

Naomi grabbed around him. "Jeff, we must be extra careful and never give that devil the chance to find me alone! I would die if he took your life for saving me!"

"My sweet dove, how precious you are to me and I can feel your great love pouring into my deepest part of what and who I am and wish to be. Your devoted husband and lover forever. The love we share for one another, will get us through what dangers lies ahead." Jeff turned his attention across the empty street. "It is time for our appointments, my dove." He kissed her, got out of the car, then walked around to open the door for her. Naomi placed her small hand in his and he helped her out.

Across the street, inside the supply closet, Nurse Abby Powell and Nurse Melody Penrose watched the loving couple in envy through the small window, just above the medicine filled shelves. Sighing at the tall, dark, handsome man, as he opened the car door and helped her out, then repeating his hot kisses while holding her very close to his manly body, made both women grow flushed with desire.

"That girl is so damn lucky to be married to Jeff Wineworth. That is one hot stud!" Melody held on to the shaky step stool as she drooled, staring out at the couple.

"Yeah! And, he is such a gentleman. So tall, so muscular, so handsome, so damn sexy!" Abby Powell took a deep breath and shook her red ponytail. "Can you believe they have been married for almost two years and still cannot keep their hands off each other."

"What I would give to have that stud instead of my Alvin." She suddenly lost sight of the couple and made a dive off the stool. "Oh shit, they are on their way inside! To your post girl! Talk later!"

The excited nurses made their way quickly out of the supply closet, just as Jeff and Naomi came through the entrance. Martha Mason looked up to see who had entered, expecting the Wineworth's. Her attention went straight to the tall handsome man and she gave him her brightest smile.

"Good morning, Mr. and Mrs. Wineworth. You are right on time." The receptionist looked down to check them off as she thought to herself. "Damn, he's one hot stud!"

Jeff watched her closely as his voice came softly. "Do you bet on the races, Mrs. Mason? I bet you put your money on the 'hot stud' instead of the cute little filly, don't you?"

"Horse Races? Hot…studs?" she swallowed nervously "A…yes, sometimes, I enjoy betting a small amount for the winning racehorse." The upset woman turned her attention on Naomi, to avoid looking at him. "Doctor Ward will be ready for you soon, my dear. Just take a seat and…" she found the courage to look back up at Jeff, who had not taken his stare away from her. "Your appointment should be right on time too, sir. So, just have a seat next to your pretty wife. They will call you."

Martha relaxed when they stepped over to have a seat. Bravely, she peered over her glasses at the handsome man. "I wish that hunk would come in sometime without that little wife tagging along." She jumped when Jeff looked up and stared coldly directly into her eyes. She could feel the burning spread through her and she quickly swirled her desk chair around to the file cabinet behind her and pretended to be looking up a file. "What sort of man is he, anyway? It's as if he can read my thoughts!"

Naomi had looked up to notice the friction between Jeff and the receptionist. She smiled and took his face and pulled it around.

"Jeffery Wineworth, what are you doing? Is that receptionist having thoughts about my husband?"

Jeff smiled down and gave her a wink, then whispered. "I'm use to women having hot thoughts about me, Naomi. It's just that some of their thoughts rub me the wrong way, that's all."

"Then, just turn your thoughts to me, right now and stop ease dropping in their fantasies, my wonderful sexy husband!" she gave him a kiss, hoping the flirty woman would see it.

"I like my girl saying I'm a wonderful sexy lover. It turns me on!" he smiled and pinched her nipple.

"Jeff?" Naomi laughed nervously when she heard the lady near them clear her throat. She was relieved when Doctor Ward's nurse opened the door and called her name.

"Naomi, the doctor is ready for you." Melody Penrose watched Jeff walk his wife to the door and give her a kiss.

"See you out here in the waiting room, darling."

"See you, sweetheart and good luck." Naomi stood on her tip toes and whispered in his ear. "Try to behave yourself with the nurses." She winked and heard Nurse Powell's voice call Jeff's name.

As Naomi went off with Melody, Abby ushered Jeff down the hall.

"Just follow me, Mr. Wineworth." Nurse Powell made it a point to twist her hips as she made her way slowly down the hall in front of Jeff, her mind going a mile a minute. "Oh, yes handsome, you can follow me anywhere."

"Is anywhere the name of Raven's office, Mrs. Powell? Jeff smiled to himself when the nurse stopped short. "Do not tell me you have lost your way to 'anywhere'." His eyes twinkled with mischief when she twirled around.

"I beg your pardon?" she swallowed, then opened the door, motioning him inside. "Please remove…your shirt." The flustered nurse picked up his chart as she thought with a smile. "You can remove those damn pants too, as far as I'm concerned."

"But the doctor wants only the shirt, correct, Mrs. Powell? Since this is not a complete physical, my black underwear would come off as well…" He laughed softly seeing her surprised expression. "that is, if I wore black underwear. I find no need of the silly things." Jeff pulled his black shirt over his long black hair as her eyes followed it moving over his head revealing his muscular tan chest. "I may call you Mrs. Powell. It is on your name tag."

"Why certainly sir, but if you prefer, you may call me Abby. Last names are so formal, don't you agree, Jeff?" the nurse reached for the blood pressure pad and walk up, staring down at his manly chest. Her fingers started to tremble as she placed the band around his arm and switch on the machine. "Just…a breathed normal."

"Why, Abby, you're shaking." Jeff's dark eyes smiled mockingly. "Too much caffeine this morning?"

"Ah…yes! That is exactly what it is, Jeff. Way too much coffee! I really must cut back!" Abby Powell undone the strap and wrote down the perfect pressure numbers. "Your blood pressure is perfect, Jeff." She smiled nervously as she though. "Everything about you is perfect, Jeff Wineworth! Perfect chest, perfect lips, and I'm sure what lies inside those black, well-fitting pants, is extra perfect!" she glanced up and froze looking into his black piercing stare.

"Abby, if I'm not being too personal," he noticed her eyes light up. "Are you married?"

"Married? Yes! Yes, I am, Jeff." She gave a nervous laugh "To my wonderful husband Al, short for Alvin. Been married for 18 years." The nurse let her mind wonder, never realizing Jeff could read all her thoughts. "But if I had been married to you, Jeff Wineworth, instead of those three kids I had with Al, I would have had six or more with this hot stud! And gosh, the sex while conceiving them would have been hot and spectacular!"

"Abby, you seem to be far away, perhaps dreaming about all that hot and spectacular sex you had with your hot stud, Al" Jeff smiled broadly, revealing his canine teeth. Seeing her eyes grow wide and backing away, he added. "And only three kids. I would have guess at least six or more with that incredible sex!"

"Dear Lord! Is it hot in here to you!" the nurse grabbed a folder and started fanning herself.

"Tell me Abby, how old are your children?" he continued to smiled broadly at the hot, stunned woman.

"A…Chuck is fifteen, Martha is sixteen and Annie is seventeen." She laughed nervously and thought "But if my Annie was your baby, she would be eighteen, I'm sure. I would have had to have you before I said I do."

"So, by the math, you and old Al held out until after you got married, unlike me and my hot little woman!" Jeff had to turn his head to keep from laughing at her wide mouth gasp. The hotter she got, the redder her face grew. The frazzled nurse hoped she would cool down before the doctor came in.

Doctor Ward smiled weakly up to Naomi, as he sat down slowly. His appearance showed he had lost a lot of weight since she was in to see him two weeks ago and he showed signs of fatigue.

"Naomi, my dear, you are looking lovely as always and your report is excellent today." when he took her hand, she noticed his grip was very weak as was his once strong voice. "Just continue to do what you're doing and this will be another strong little Wineworth."

"Doctor Ward, are you feeling alright?" Naomi's eyes and voice held concern for her dear friend and doctor. "Have you been feeling ill?"

"I assure you, sweet girl, I will be fine." He gave her a weak smile. "I think I'm just a little tired, that's all. Too much overtime lately, what with all these little babies coming into the world. The little ones don't always choose the perfect time to be born."

"Thomas, you have been delivering babies at all hours for years and it has never bothered your health before." Naomi laid her hand on his pale cold one. "Your complexion is white and you have lost so much weight. You must be coming down with something. Have you had any really sick patients that could have past their virus over to you?"

"My dear, it does my heart good to know someone as young and as busy as yourself, cares about an old man like me." The doctor's smile was warm and genuine.

"Thomas Ward, you are not an old man! You are only 50-years-old." Tears formed in her loving eyes. "You will be a doctor for many more years."

"I hope so, Naomi." Doctor Ward placed his weak hand on her shoulder. "Your Jeff is a lucky man to have you, young lady."

"That is very sweet, Thomas, but let's get back to you. Have you seen a doctor?" Naomi stood up, worried about her doctor and friend. "I really think you need to have a doctor check you out."

Doctor Ward laughed weakly, giving a little cough. "My dear, I am a doctor." He teased. "Perhaps I will ask Doctor Wineworth for a diagnosis. He seems to be pretty sharp when it comes to knowing things."

"Thomas Ward, I am serious!" Naomi placed her hands on her hips and frowned down. "I could ask Ted..."

"Dear girl, that won't be necessary. If it makes you feel better, Doctor Ravin has given me some medicine to help me feel better. He said it just takes time and a lot of rest." The weak doctor walked Naomi to the door. "I'm certainly glad I hired him. He has offered to see most of my patients until I am feeling better. Luther is a great guy and I'm glad he came knocking."

"Then, let's hope and pray the man knows what your problem is, Thomas." At that announcement, Naomi really became concerned about her friend's wellbeing. "Doc, just be careful and make sure that this medicine is really what you need."

"Thank you for caring, Naomi." He took her hand. "That young man, Ted, has done wonderful things on that mountain of his, especially the day he took you in."

"Ted can do wonderful things for you too, Thomas." She just got a sweet smile from her doctor. "God be with you Thomas." She hugged him, afraid to walk away and leave him in Ravens care. "I will inform Ted of your illness and have him pray for you, as will I, dear friend.' Naomi turned and walked back into the waiting room to find Jeff had not returned yet. Checking her watch, she walked up to the front desk to give the receptionist a message for her husband.

"Mrs. Mason, would you tell Jeff I have gone next door to the children's store to buy Teddy a new pair of jeans." Naomi smiled and took her appointment card. "That little fellow is growing out of his old ones and he insisted that I buy him a black pair this time, just like his papa wears."

"You got a real cute kid, Naomi. Spitting image of his daddy." The woman smiled as Naomi walked to the door.

"Tell Jeff I will meet him at the car." Naomi smiled and walked outside, thinking about her doctor's trust in Luther Ravin.

Chapter Twenty-Four

Jeff could not help but laugh at the red-face nurse, sweating through her uniform. She was still fanning her face when Luther Raven stepped in and immediately took in the situation.

"My dear Mrs. Powell, you look as through you might catch on fire any second. Hot flashes?" his mocking eyes stared at Jeff. "Or, does your bare chest always do this to women, Jeffery?"

"The name is Jeff, and I can assure you sir, I do not know what you are talking about. The lady admitted to drinking too much coffee this morning and it seems to have disagreed with her blood pressure." Jeff caught her staring at him and added. "But she told me that my pressure was perfect, right Abby?'

"Right Jeff, you are perfect!" she blushed when the doctor cleared his throat.

"Nurse Powell, please excuse yourself. Go splash some cold water on your face and try and cool down!" Raven opened the door and gently pushed the hot nurse out. "I can truly say, I have never seen that happen to one of my nurses since I've been in practice."

"You don't say. I seem to see it all the time." Jeff could not wipe the smile off his handsome face. "Women just seem to heat up whenever I am around. The entire staff of ladies working here must be coming down with the same illness."

"Interesting, but let's get to you and why you are here." Luther Raven read over Jeff's chart. "Perfect blood pressure, strong heartbeat…" his eyes fell on his perfect body. "and, by the looks of all those muscles, I'd say you must work out to stay in such great physical shape."

"I work out occasionally, mostly in my bed games with my wife." Jeff smiled when the doctor's head jerked up, mouth gasped open. The smile on Jeff faded into a serious expression as he stated: "What about my problem?"

"Your problem, oh yes. Not quite perfect." The doctor rolled his eyes slowly up to Jeff's face. "You said, you were having trouble sleeping at night. Is that correct?"

"Yes, I'm having nightmares! They wake me up in the middle

of the night and I cannot go back to sleep!" Jeff's dark penetrating eyes stared into Raven's cold steel eyes. "Bad dreams! Evil dreams!"

"Jeff, have these nightmares always been with you, even as a small child?" he sneered.

"No sir, only the past two years." Jeff noticed Raven blinked nervously and looked down to avoid Jeff's stare.

"Two years? That is the same amount of time you've been married, I recall. Has it been every night since your wedding night, Jeff?"

"Not every night at first, but then my son Teddy was born and suddenly the bad dreams returned every night." Jeff remained unmoved. "My best sleep comes after passionate sex with my wife, then I rest soundly for two straight hours."

"How often is that, when you have sex?" Luther gazed up over his black glasses, a wicked smile on his face.

"Every single night, except when my sweet dove has her monthly." Jeff's cold stare was giving the doctor the shakes, but Jeff ignored them as he added. "Now that Naomi is expecting our second son, I can have her every night, until Ward tells me to back off."

"Interesting. Most men don't have the endurance to make love every night. You must be from special genes to acquire so much sex. How does the little woman make out with you on her all the time?" Luther Raven had sat up, the topic seemed to please him greatly.

"I am not here to discuss my sex life, doctor!" Jeff all but growled. "My sleepless nights are getting the best of me!"

The doctor smiled and sat back. "Then tell me, where you a bad boy, Jeff? Did you do evil things?"

"I did! I was a very bad and evil boy, Raven! And a far greater evil man!" Jeff smiled, revealing his canine teeth, causing the doctor to back away as Jeff finished saying. "Be glad you did not know me then!"

"Good Lord! Has…has your eye teeth always been more canine, like a…wolf! Or maybe…a vampire?" Doctor Raven could not take his eyes off Jeff's teeth and Jeff forced a laugh.

"A vampire? Luther Raven, there are no such things as vampires. Mere fiction! My mother always swore it was because I hung around with wolves too long."

"Wolves? So, you had wolves as a child." Raven's hand shook as he wrote down his words. "Were your wolves evil too, Jeff?"

"Only when I ordered them to be. They are very loyal to me and obey my every command." Jeff looked closely at Raven and adding coldly. "Even now, they obey me over things from beyond. Simple demons have no power over me, should I run across one."

"You said, even now they obey you. By that, I assume you still have your pet wolves?" Raven swallowed hard, obviously shaken. "When did you stop being evil Jeff? Or…did you?"

"I stopped being evil when I fell in love with Naomi." Jeff's expression softened at the sound of her name. "She saved me from evil."

"I see, this girl saved you. Were you converted to some kind of religion?" Raven stood up and walked to the window,

"Not just some kind of religion, doctor! The only true religion. I am learning to be a Christian, to follow the teachings of Jesus, the Christ." Jeff thought he noticed Ravin tremble at the name of Jesus.

"Then you had one child. Now, your wife is giving you another son."

Jeff sat up, suddenly the true identity of Luther Raven filled his mind, recalling just who and what this man was and why he seemed so familiar. Doctor Luther Raven was gaining big points with Jeff and his father when he was alive. Jeff's voice came out firm.

"Can you do something about these damn nightmares? Enough small talk about my past and my personal affairs!"

"Very well, Jeff. I had to ask those questions to get to the root of your problem so I could prescribe the right medicine for you. Now, I admit I'm not a physiologist, but I know what you need now to help you get the sleep you need. These pills will put you in a deep relaxed sleep without dreams and you will wake up renewed with more energy than you can imagine." Raven all but snickered. "Poor girl, might even be in for day time sex!" hearing Jeff's grunt a warning, the doctor continued as he opened his black bag and pulled out a bottle of red pills. "I get these samples to hand out to be sure this is what you need before you have to pay for a prescription. They can get pricey." He handed Jeff the bottle. "Now listen carefully, before you go, you must know these pills are strong and they do have some side effects so you must follow the correct dosage. They can be habit forming. Do you understand?"

"Yes sir, if I am not careful, I could get hook on the drug inside the pill, take the correct dosage and never take too many!" Jeff stuck the bottle in his pocket and pulled his shirt over his head. "I will be careful, Doctor Raven." Jeff took a step toward him, causing the doctor to stumble backward. "I assure you, I know exactly what to do." Jeff walked to the door. "If you are finished doc, I have a wife waiting."

"There is one more, small thing you must do while you're on these strong pills, Jeff Wineworth. You 'must' cut back on sex while you are taking them." A smile formed on his lips.

Jeff grew still, his eyes cold and dark as his words came out sharp "I will have sex with my wife whenever and wherever I want to and no pill pushing doctor is going to tell me otherwise! Do I make myself clear, Raven!"

"Just be…careful!" the shaken doctor ran from the room past Jeff. When Jeff stepped out in the waiting room, Naomi was nowhere around. He slung his head to the front desk and stared into the receptionist's startled eyes.

"My wife, where the devil is she?"

"Your wife is safe, Mr. Wineworth. She asked me to tell you she was going next door to buy your son a pair of black jeans." She tried to smile while looking into his cold eyes. "She promised to wait by your car if she finished before you."

"Thank you!" Jeff gave her a slight smile. "I'm sorry I got so mad. I will go to her now." He turned and walked out as the woman stared after him.

"Oh, to be loved like that!" she sighed "and by him!"

Naomi had finished buying Teddy's jeans and was headed for their car when out of the blue, a young punk came up behind her and grabbed the purse off her shoulder, then gave her a push toward the hard street pavement in front of her. In a flash, Jeff caught her in his arm, while his other hand grabbed the young man by the collar and lifted him over his head. Naomi caught her breath and took back her handbag as she watched Jeff's eyes turn red as flames, showing his teeth at the frightened young man.

"Who…who are you?" the boy's voice shook with fear. "And…where did you come from?"

"It would appear I was just in time to save my wife from falling and from losing our baby boy, you little thief!" Jeff stormed out. "Just who do you think you are stealing from innocent young women? If you need food, ask for it! If you need a place to stay, that also can be arranged, but if you steal, you will get your room and food in jail! Is that what you want?"

"No sir." Sweat rolled off the boy's long hair. "I just needed money to buy my mama some medicine, sir." Tears came to the youth's eyes. "I tried to get a job, but no one would hire me. They said I was a no account because I live on the other side of the tracks."

Jeff lowered him to the ground and watched him take a deep breath. "How old are you boy?"

"I'm twelve years old sir, the oldest of six children in my family sir." The lad looked at Naomi and noticed she had tears in her eyes. "You look real nice ma'am, I'm very sorry I stole your bag."

"I won't judge you son for stealing my bag." Naomi took his trembling hand. "I was once like you, when I was twelve."

"I can say one thing for you, 'boy', you are a good actor." Jeff narrowed his eyes as Naomi stared up at her husband, not understanding why he was saying such mean things to this poor boy. Jeff just smiled down at her and tightened his grip on the stranger's arm. "Did you really think you could fool me, Mister."

"Mister?" Naomi blinked, confused at Jeff's words. "Jeff, what are you talking about? This is just a young boy, not a man."

"See how you have fooled my wife, Chucky boy." Jeff had recognized the midget he used to use to deliver telegrams for him on his bike. "I bet you remember taking a letter to my wife when she lived at the children's home on Goldsburg Mountain, don't you, Chucky boy?"

"The letter from your mother?" Naomi turned to have a closer look at the person who tried to steal her purse. "Yes, I can see now, it was you. But that was over two years ago and you haven't change a bit!"

"Midgets usually don't, sweet one, only until they get old." Jeff motioned for a street cop walking by. "Looks like you will get a place to stay and something to eat, Chucky boy."

"Wineworth, you are just plain mean!" the midget finally used his real voice. "You should be the one locked up, not me!"

"Did I try to steal your shoulder bag, Chucky boy?" Jeff stared deep into the thief's eyes.

The midget lost all knowledge of Jeff's past deeds. "I…you…" Chuck teared up for the police officer. "Please sir, these people are accusing me of stealing and I am just a small boy. I would never do anything that mean."

"Not just a good little actor, Jeff, your ex-mail carrier is an expert liar." Naomi shook her head. "And to think I felt sorry for you."

"That just goes to show you're a bad judge of character, lady!" he laughed "Married to Jeff Wineworth!"

"Chuck, I certainly misjudged you, but I knew perfectly well I wanted to marry Jeff! He is my life!"

"Thank you, Mr. Wineworth, for catching this guy. He has been grabbing lady's purses and shopping bags for some time now." The officer strapped the hand cuffs on him. "He hit them from behind so they cannot identify him and leaved them on their face." After reading the midget his rights, he added "Chuck Briggs, you'll be locked away for a very long time." The officer took him away as Jeff wrapped his arms around his wife.

"That little jerk singled you out darling, hoping to push you down on your stomach and kill our baby."

"Jeff? Why…why would he want to hurt our innocent baby?" Naomi realized just how much danger she really was in. "Oh darling, if you had not been close by, he could have succeeded!" "Sweet dove, Chuck was paid to hurt you. My guess, one of my father's demons, maybe even Raven."

"Raven?" Naomi slipped inside the car seat as Jeff walked quickly to the driver's side and got in.

"I know what Raven is now, Naomi. I remember everything." He took her hand. "At ten-years-old, I already had knowledge on who was followers of my father. Some of these followers were extremely evil, hoping to win big points with Satan, true atheist. One such man was Doctor Luther Raven, a famous baby doctor. Behind closed doors, this insane man would abort babies for women, up to full term. The worse thing he did, that made him pure evil, was when he would deliver a perfectly healthy baby to mothers would really wanted them, he would wrap the umbilical cord around its neck and kill it, then tell the unsuspected mother her baby was still born.

Tears stun Naomi's eyes and she began shaking her head in

disbelief "Jeff, surely no one could be that mean and cruel! Be that evil, to kill an innocent helpless little baby!"

"Dearest love, I can see now just how evil men like this really are. Falling in love with you and having our own precious baby, soon to have another son." Jeff placed a loving arm around his wife's trembling shoulders, his expression reflecting her sadness. "Please forgive me, my sweet one, for the words I am about to confess. At ten-years-old, I was even more evil than Raven. I not only cheered his work but enjoyed laughing at the suffering mother's loss."

"No Jeff! No, I cannot believe it! I refuse to believe it!" Naomi pushed him away and turn to stare out the window. "You were just a child! How could you have such hate in your heart at ten?"

"How? I am the devil's son, Naomi! His foul blood runs through my veins and it is filled with pure hate!" Jeff's voice cracked up as tears welled up in his dark eyes. "Dearest one, it is a miracle I've come this far to the right and it's because of you. My loving you and needing you."

Naomi turned slowly and saw the tears, the love written on his sincere face. She reached over and put her arms around his neck.

"Jeff, my darling, I am so sorry! I love you so very much, I guess I just blocked out your evil pass. You cannot help who your father was, no more than you could help knowing only hate and the need to hurt people, to win souls to please the only father you knew." She, lend back, and gently touched his handsome face. "Jeff, please forgive me."

"Forgive you?" Jeff parted his lips over hers in a tender kiss. "Sweet dove, I owe my life to you, my very soul! It is I who needs constant forgiveness."

"Only if you continue to sin, dearest." Naomi remembered saying those same words to Ted and she never forgot the answer she received from this great man of faith. "If you sincerely ask the Lord to forgive your sins, all past and present, and believe that Jesus died for your sins, the Lord in His mercy will forgive them and bury them in the deep sea, forgotten for all eternity."

"So, that's what Ted meant in his sermon last Sabbath, when he said: The Lord will blot out all your sins and you will become whiter than snow." Jeff smiled when Naomi smiled and nodded a positive. She turned her attention back across the street to Doctor Ward's practice.

"Jeff, you said that Raven could have paid that midget off to get rid of our baby. Is Raven here to kill our baby?" Naomi turned and took Jeff's hand. "What happened in his office and what did he say to you?"

"Raven ask me a lot of personal questions. Questions I'm sure he already knew what the answers would be. My childhood, being evil, wolves as pets, and acted surprised that my nightmares began after I got married, after I changed." Jeff reached in his pocket and pulled out the bottle of red pills. "Then, the 'good' doctor gave me these so call samples to try, told me to follow the dosage carefully because they can be habit forming and have serious side effects." Jeff rolled his dark eyes back as he snarled. "Then the jackass, after hearing my desire for a lot of sex with you, had the damn nerve to tell me to cut back on sex while taking this drug!"

Jeff smiled at Naomi's blushing face as he winked at her. "I let that no count jerk, know, and not in a nice way, that I would have sex with my wife, when and where I wanted to and no pill pushing doctor was going to tell me otherwise!" Jeff laughed, recalling the fear and panic on the cocky doctor's face. "The 'good' doctor practically ran out of the room."

Naomi had not taken her eyes off the red pills and her face reflexed worry for her husband. "Jeff, what exactly are those 'red' pills? Please tell me you're not planning to take them, are you?"

Jeff put his arm around Naomi for comfort as he spoke softly "You and I both know I do not need any stupid pills to help me sleep. Ted has already fixed that problem." Jeff smiled at Naomi's bright relieved smile. "You ask what the pills are? I can assure you, without a doubt, these red pills are poison!"

"What? Poison pills?" Naomi's eyes grew wide as her heart began to race with fear. "Jeff, I think Doctor Raven has Doctor Ward on those same red pills!"

"Are you sure, sweetheart?" Jeff took her hand as his attention went on the medical building. "Naomi, did Doctor Ward tell you that he was taking pills prescribed by Raven?"

"Yes, he did and that Doctor Raven told him he should get some rest to get over this sudden illness that has struck him." Naomi swallowed, fear racing through her veins. "Oh, Jeff, Thomas is pale and extremely weak. The dear man has loss a considered amount of weight and I fear he might die if he doesn't get real help." She blinked back her tears. "I offered to let Ted help him but the dear soul trust Raven!" Naomi grabbed Jeff by his strong shoulders. "I think Raven is killing doc, slowly, so he can take over his practice! Doctor Ward said Raven offered to look after his patients until he got well! Jeff, Raven could end up as my doctor? Doctor Ward is in immediate danger! How can we help him?"

"Just try and calm down sweet one and listen. I can get Raven's briefcase, where he keeps those poison pills, and switch the poison pills for sugar pills, made by Ted!" Jeff started the car. "We will go by the castle and grab a few things and head over to our neighbor's mountain. Ted will agree that it will be safer for you and little Teddy to spend the night there in the farmhouse while I go and swap the pills."

Naomi grabbed his arm. "Jeff, what if Raven catches you? Then what?"

Jeff smiled tenderly and patted her face. "My sweet Naomi, you keep forgetting that I am no ordinary man. Raven may be a demon but he is in human form, so he gets tired just likes humans. So, when the creep lies down to night, I will be waiting in the shadows and with my powers, I can put him into a very deep sleep, one without dreams, one of total darkness."

Naomi shivered. "Spare me the details, Jeff, just do it!"

The loving couple gathered a few overnight things and headed for the children's home.

Chapter Twenty-Five

Ted saw Naomi and Jeff making their way to the house and opened the front door, holding two-year-old Teddy in his arms. Naomi smiled and took her son and gave him a big hug.

"Two of my favorite men greeting us at the door! My goodness, son, you are getting heavy!"

"That's cause I'm a big boy now mama! I am big brother!" Teddy padded her stomach. "You carry my little brother too."

Naomi frowned up at Ted. "Ted, why did you tell our son I was having a baby? Jeff and I were going to let him know closer to delivery." Ted and Jeff looked at one another and laughed causing Naomi to stare from one to the other. "What is so funny?"

Ted put his arm lovingly around the girl he had taken in a few years back and had turned her life around.

"Angel, I never told your son anything about your baby. It looks like your little Teddy is going to take after his father."

"Are you saying, my innocent son can read thoughts?" She hit Jeff's arm when he continued laughing. "Jeff, can't you do something?"

"I could possibly slow it down for a while." His dark eyes twinkled. "Or even block it out if necessary."

"Then you must block it!" Naomi took his arm. "There are things little ears should never hear, darling. Like, talk about Santa Claus things, our private bedroom activates." There was another round of laughter from the two men and Naomi just shook her head, blushing.

"You know what Teddy asked me earlier today, while strolling through the rose garden." Ted seem to glow with merriment when he chuckled. "That little rascal said: My Ted, if I choose Mary can my brother get Martha?"

"Oh, for heaven sakes!" Naomi looked up at Jeff, then Ted and both men were trying hard not to laugh. "What, might I ask, did you tell Teddy?"

"I told your sweet little boy he had to wait and grow up before he could find a girlfriend." Ted almost glowed as he continued.

"Then your boy simply said, O.K! I'll just play with Ruth till I'm all big."

Ted took Naomi and Teddy's hands and headed for the kitchen for a nice cold glass of lemonade. "My dear mother made enough for 50 people."

While Teddy and Ruth sat quietly rolling the young girls red ball across the kitchen floor. The four adults enjoyed small talk and lemonade at the big harvest table. Hannah got up to removed two long pans from the oven, each holding fresh baked yeast rolls. Naomi glanced over and started to get up when Ted's mother waved her back down.

"Please let me help you, Hannah. I'm rather use to feeding this bunch."

"That's very sweet darling, but it's all finished, except last minute things, nothing I cannot handle."

Naomi looked around the big house as she spoke softly. "My goodness, it's quiet around here."

"It won't be for long, Naomi, when that school bunch returns any minute now."

As if right on cue, Leah opened the kitchen door, a wide grin spread on her freckled face and announced their arrival loudly. "We're home!"

Ted looked over a Jeff, who had covered up his ears at the first sight of the redhead. Naomi returned Ted's smile as she consoled her husband then whispered to Ted.

"Leah never out grows her mouth, does she?"

"Let me see what I can do." Ted stood up and patted Jeff before stepping over in front of the little girl as Jeff mumbled.

"I feel sorry for the man she marries"

Ted laughed softly and ushered the young girl into the big den. "Alright young lady, I have asked you to speak softer and you still cannot control your volume, so go straight up to your room and do your homework!"

"Gee whiz Ted, I'm sorry. I never meant for it to come out that loud." Leah looked down, knowing she was being punished. "Me and my big mouth." She turned slowly and climbed up the stairs to her room.

Ted made his way back to the kitchen door and watched the rest of the children file in, Jenny dragging at the end of the line. Smiling,

Ted walked over and gave her a warm hug.

"There's my girl. Did you have a hard day, darling?"

"The day went alright, sweetheart. Driving up that mountain with the none-stop talking of Leah can be nerve-racking." Jenny smiled over at Jeff and Naomi. "It's good to see you both. It feels like home when you're here."

"It always feels good to be back home with my family." Naomi got up to hug Jenny.

"They are spending the night with us, darling." Ted's arm rested over Jenny's shoulders. "Jeff has got some shady business to take care of tonight and he knew his family would be safer here, with us."

Naomi lend in to Jenny and whispered. "It's Doctor Raven, he is a demon."

"What's a demon, mama?" Teddy got off the floor and walked over as Jenny stared down at the young boy.

"Naomi, Teddy could not have heard you whispering to me. He was on the other side of the kitchen, playing with Ruth. What is going on?" Jenny looked up at Ted when he and Jeff laugh out softly, while Naomi frowned at them.

"You two, cut it out!" Naomi got down and took her son by his hands. "It only adult talk, sweetheart, so go back and play with Ruth and stay in the kitchen. We are going into the den to talk."

Teddy shrugged his shoulders and walked back to Ruth. Naomi grabbed Jeff and went to the den.

"Jeff, you had better do something right now!"

"Would somebody tell me what is going on?" Jenny's voice grew tense, as she followed Naomi.

Ted laughed and took her hand. "Teddy is able to read minds just like his papa."

"Oh, good Lord!" Jenny looked helplessly at Naomi. "It was bad enough having our men read our mind." Her attention went to her husband. "Ted, will our girls be able to read minds as well? Is there nothing left for me to teach them?"

"Jenny" Ted tried to keep a straight face. "I am certain you can teach our daughters things I could never teach them." He gently took her hands in his. "And besides, we cannot be sure they will have the gift to read minds."

"I can tell you this much!" Jenny pulled her hands away and sat down. “When I was dating men, I could always read their thoughts and believe me, if I chose not to deliver what they wanted, I did not!” She looked up at Ted seriously. “But not with you, oh no! I never know what you’re thinking or what is on that beautiful mind of yours!

“But I do believe you enjoy what I give you in our bedroom, Jenny.” Ted bit his lip to keep from laughing at his wife’s shocked expression and all she could say was

“Ted?”

“Well Jenny, I can tell I really make you happy in our bed.” Ted gazed down, trying not to laugh.

“Ted Neenam!” Jenny’s face flushed a bright red, causing Jeff and Matthew to burst out laughing. Jeff reached over and gave Ted a pat on his back.

“I never thought I’d see the day that Jennifer would blush! Delightful!”

Ted pulled Jenny’s hands away from her face and smiled. “Jenny, darling, I can see my ideal worked.”

“Ideal? What Ideal?” Jenny searched his eyes and only saw love.

“By changing the subject and get everyone minds off of demons.” Ted responded innocently as Jenny tried to keep her serious face, but she started laughing with everyone else and said

“The truth is, Ted is absolutely correct.” Jenny’s eyes twinkled with mischief. “Ted is great in bed! He is the sexiest man I’ve ever known and the sex he gives me is the most rewarding I have ever had!”

“Jenny!” Ted felt his face growing hot as he blushed a bright red. Once again, Jeff laughed out.

“Looks like Jenny has turned the tables on you, my friend.”

Matthew was bent over double laughing as he spoke between breathes. “Wow! Ted! I never would have guessed! I hope my Kathy thinks that of me!”

Jenny put her arm around Ted’s neck, feeling bad for embarrassing him in front of the family. “Ted, sweetheart, I’m sorry darling. I just could not help myself.”

Ted pulled her up close so he could whisper in her ear. “When we go to bed tonight, I will be going to sleep.”

Jenny pulled away and looked up sadly. “Ted, sweetheart, I was only kidding around, same as you." She felt relieved when she noticed a big smile spread across his handsome face.

"Like I said, darling wife, I am going to sleep after I have had my way with you."

Jenny smiled brightly and said softly, "I am all yours, Mr. Neenam."

"Yes, I know, Mrs. Neenam." Ted suddenly realized that everyone had grown quiet and was watching them. "Matthew, stop staring and go get the children. They have done enough homework." He patted the young man's back when he walked past him. "Mother has the lemonade set out for all of them."

Matthew looked at the closed kitchen door but knew not to question Ted about how he knew the glasses were poured and waiting.

"What about Leah? Does she get to come down for lemonade? She was really loud today. Jenny had her window open coming up the mountain and I could hear Leah all the way back in my school bus. It had to give Jenny a headache. I know it did me."

"The little trumpet gave me an earache coming through the door announcing they were home." Jeff looked at Ted. "Maybe she doesn't deserve a treat. It might make her think twice before screaming out every word she says."

"It is just a bad habit I hope she out grows." Ted smiled and gazed up the stairs. "Leah has been very quiet since I sent her up to her room. I hurt her feelings and I know she really tries. Leah has earned her lemonade."

"Alright Ted, you know best. I'll call the little critters." Matthew walked over to the bottom step and looked up.

"Matthew? Do not yell for those children!" Ted had been watching while placing his arm lovingly around Jenny. "Go up and bring them down, then you can get you and Jenny a glass when you return."

After the children were settled in the kitchen drinking cold lemonade, Ted, along with Jenny, Matthew, Naomi, and Jeff, followed Ruth and Teddy out to the rose garden. The two energic kids dashed for their favorite tree swings as the two couples settled down in matching love seats. Matthew flopped down in a single yard chair and mumbled.

"Seeing you guys all hugged up, I wished my Kathy would

hurry home." He shuffled his feet through the grass. "This, nine-to-five job is stealing my time with her."

"It's almost five Matthew. Kathy will be home soon." Jenny was glad to see this young man was crazy about her dearest friend. She laid her weary head over on her husband's strong shoulder after having a sip of the good lemonade. "Ted, how many demons are there, sweetheart?"

Ted lifted her chin to kiss her, then smiled, tasting the lemons on her sweet lips. "Mum, lemon lips." She returned his smile and repeated

"How many, darling?"

"We do not really know yet Jenny. They have only begun their invasion." Ted and Jeff exchanged serious faces when Jeff added.

"Satan is starting the demons slowly at first, but he is very cunning and will add many more in time." Jeff's eyes locked on Ted's. "Soon, my friend, the count will be too great for you and me to handle."

"Jeff, my brother." Ted remained relaxed and calm as he reached a handout to him. "It's true, the devil has released many demons on us, along with lots of innocent people and children. But you must never believe we are in this fight alone, Jeff. Lucifer has his many demons, but we have God's Holy angels, many of which are warrior angels." Ted looked around at the three listening as he stated: "As I always say, 1% of good will always conquer 100% of…" Jenny, Naomi and Matthew finished in unison.

"Evil, every time! Good always wins, because, God is good! God is love!"

Chapter Twenty-Six

Jeff looked at his watch, 1:00 a.m., time for his mission. His attention fell on his sleeping companion and a smile escaped his lips as he watched her breast moving peacefully in the moonlight. Brushing his hand over one breast, he bent down and kissed her, then started to leave when her slim hand reached for his arm.

"Jeff, darling, are you going now?" she looked up, trying to awake from dreaming. "Why didn't you wake me so I could send you off with love."

"My dearest one, you were sleeping so peacefully, I did not want to disturb your sweet slumber." Jeff ran his long fingers through her short black hair. "I will be back before you know it, into your arms again, so get your rest." He read her worried thoughts and gave her a reassuring smile. "Nothing is going to happen to me, I promise."

Jeff parted his lips over hers in a tender kiss and pulled the sheet over her breast. "I will exchange Raven's poison medicine to Ted's magic sugar pills, then pay a visit to Doctor Ward and exchange his pills, along with a magical dose of Ted's healing medicine I will personally inject in the good doctor's arm. He will not feel a thing." Jeff walked to the window and opened it.

"Jeff, sweetheart, we are on the second floor." Naomi sat up, but he only smiled and waved her back down. "But darling, you could get hurt jumping down from this high!"

"Naomi, my sweet dove, I will not be jumping out this window. Trust me when I say, I will simply be gone in a 'flash' and find myself in the Raven's nest!" he blew her a kiss. "I love you!" he whispered then simply disappeared into the darkness outside as the window lowered slowly by itself.

Jeff stood in the shadows of Doctor Luther Raven's bedroom, on the out skirts of Goldsburg. As expected, there was no Mrs. Raven to be found, just the demon, back in human form. The tall dark figure moved with cat-like swiftness over to the bed and stared down at the sleeping demon. Placing a hand over his brow, Jeff made a few strange sounds and whispered unknown words of this world as the sleeping man fell deeper and deeper into slumber.

Jeff's swift motions had the brief case open and the pills exchanged with seconds, then he replaced the evil man's brief case back on the bedside table, where he thought it was safe.

After his visit to the sick doctor's house, Jeff returned to Goldsburg Mountain and his watched showed he had only been gone less than one hour. Naomi was sleeping soundly, feeling safe and at home here with Ted and the family. Jeff removed all his clothes and climbed into bed beside his wife. As not to wake her again, he gently removed her gown and tossed it next to his own, then pulled her over into his strong arms and fell asleep.

Kathy walked quickly across the street to the law firm, trying hard to be on time. She and Matthew had awakened, feeling the need for one another and they had stayed in bed a little longer than they had intended. Kathy could not help the grin on her face though as she remembered how her Matthew had made her feel so wonderful, so early in the morning. She was still smiling when she ran into her boss as she entered the building.

"There you are, Mrs. Christian." Kathy jumped when Mr. Claremont called her name. "I am sorry if I frightened you my dear."

"You didn't exactly frighten me, George." Kathy felt her face flush. "I was, well, daydreaming sir. I didn't see you walk up."

"There's no need to explain to old Claremont, Kathy. I was young once." He patted her shoulder and walked with her to the elevator. "There's nothing wrong with happy thoughts." She smiled as he continued when they reached his office. "I have a case today in court, nothing big, so I have asked Miss Conner to assist me. Mr. Tucker wanted to switch secretaries today Kathy. He thinks Miss Conner does an excellent job for him, but since you are faster with shorthand and typing, it will really come in handy for him today." Kathy's boss peered over his glasses. "Do you mind the switch dear? Just for today."

"Of course, not George, if you feel you can get along without your girl Friday." Kathy laughed softly as her boss patted her back.

"It will be difficult, but I will force myself this one time. Alright then, you can go on into Phillip's office and I will grab Miss Conner and head for the courthouse."

Kathy smiled and nodded as she knocked softly on Mr. Tucker's door.

"Come in, Kathy!" the friendly man peered over his black rim glasses. "Please take a seat. Thank you so much for your assistance today." his chubby hands held up a stack of papers. "These reports must go out today and they…well, simply slipped up on me."

The new lawyer walked over to a small bar and poured himself a glass of tea then took a long drink.

"Now, that it is refreshing!" his attention fell on Kathy, who was observing his actions carefully. "Let me fix you a glass of this great tea, Kathy. Miss Conner made it early this morning and I must admit, that little lady knows how to brew tea."

"You say, Miss Conner just made it, this morning?" Kathy remembered Ted's warning about trusting strangers, but she had known Miss Conner about as long as she had George. Kathy watched him take another big sip and noticed it didn't bother him and it did look refreshing, since she had missed her coffee before leaving for work. "Thank you, Mr. Tucker, tea sounds wonderful." Kathy took a small sip and found it extra tasteful, so she took a bigger drink, then sat the glass down and picked up her shorthand tablet. "You are quite correct about the tea, Mr. Tucker. Miss Conner makes great tea."

"Well, good! We agree on that." He placed his glass down and picked up the first sheet of paper off the high stack. "Alright! Miss Christian, if you're ready, I will began reading the first letter. 'Dear Mr. Jamerson, in regard to the case of Rogers verses Baker, I would like…to…" Tucker looked up and smiled, seeing Kathy's limp body slumped over the desk.

"Good work, Tucker!" Lucifer stood behind Kathy, smiling down at the helpless woman. "It is time to start hurting the family." He laughed. "Perhaps, it will even be rewarding for Katherine here. She has always had a lusting eye for the male body." His hand ran over her head, then he made his way in front of her. "Do your thing, Tucker!"

"Kathy, you can hear my voice! You are now in my trance and everything I tell you, you will believe it to be true. Your marriage to this mere 'boy' is not going to be enough to satisfy your sexual needs. Only one man, Kathy, can do this! You will not worry about whom you hurt to get this man! You will lust for him, constantly!

You will desire his body so much, you will not be happy until you make lustful love with him! When I ask you to open your eyes, you will see him! You will feel the hot passion swelling up inside you and you will try to reach out to touch him, but you cannot move. Katherine, open your eyes and look upon your sexy man!"

Kathy slowly opened her eyes, the room was spinning around, and through her blurry vision she could see a naked man in front of her. His tall body was perfect, tan, strong and he stood ready, his manhood in full display. Kathy tried to move but she seemed frozen, except for the hot desire that was moving swiftly through her body. She could feel herself throbbing, getting closer and closer to ecstasy, until she finally exploded with the most powerful fireworks she had ever experienced, and at the exact moment, the man's face came in clear view, Jeff!

Kathy's naked body fell to the floor and she lay unconscious under Lucifer's feet. Satan smiled wickedly down at his victim as Tucker laughed out in delight.

"The poor girl looked up at you and saw Jeff, your beautiful, sexual son."

"Yes, and perhaps my son will regain some of his lust when she seduces him. The lucky boy, is weak when it comes to a naked woman." The devil smiled mockingly. "Pool, stupid Christian girl he married will see he still has weaknesses and desires she could never fulfill." Lucifer easily lifted Kathy up off the floor and laid her across Tucker's desk. His long fingers moved over her exposed breast, then he ran his hand down between her legs and smiled at her wet thighs. Taking a deep breath, his lips parted over the still woman's lips and he moaned "So tempting lying there. What a shame we must put her clothes back on before she wakes up."

"You, my master, are always right. The girl is more beautiful this way. If this were really my office and she was really my secretary, I would insist we both wear no clothes while working, and I could have her whenever I desired." Tucker grinned wickedly. "Never-the-less, this one's soul will be yours soon."

"She will be mine! Her lust and adultery will condemn her to Hell!" Satan looked down at her one last time and vanished, leaving Kathy sitting back at her seat, pad and pencil in her hand.

Chapter Twenty-Seven

Ted and Jenny made their way down the steps, smiling at each other and holding hands. A soft sob drew their attention to the sofa in the den, where Matthew sat alone, his head in his hands. Without hesitation, Jenny dropped Ted's hand and made her way to the upset young man, Ted close behind her. Jenny fell down beside him and wrapped her arms around his shoulders. Matthew looked up slowly, tears racing down his handsome face.

"Matthew, darling, please tell us what's wrong? Is something wrong with Kathy?" Jenny thought her heart would break watching the happy-go-lucky Matthew so torn with grief. "Please, let us help you."

"Yes Jenny, it is Kathy." Ted took a seat on his friend's other side. "Son, it's alright, please tell us what is troubling you."

"I…I think Kathy has fallen out of love with me." Matthew brushed away his tears. "She pushed me away this morning when I tried to hug her. She refuses to let me touch her and if I try, she just keeps pulling away from me." Once again, his tears began to roll down his face.

"Matthew, what is she saying to you?" Jenny took his trembling hand. "Did she give you any reason for pulling away from you?"

"She said she was tired and needed to rest." Matthew glanced down, looking lost. "Kathy has never been too tired for me before, Jenny. I think…my girl has found someone else. Someone who can give her more! More things! More…fulfillment, than I've been giving her."

"Nonsense Matthew, Kathy is madly in love with you! I am her best friend and I know her better than anyone!' Jenny looked into his sad eyes. "Kathy and I are very close, Matthew and believe me, I know she is very happy with you and what you give her. Like me, finding true love at last in our life, material things mean nothing to us anymore." Jenny took his trembling hands. "Kathy has told me that you are the very best thing that has ever happened to her, besides our friendship. She told me, Matthew, her life is now complete with you." Jenny glanced over at Ted who had been silently taking in her comforting words, and she smiled weakly. "Forgive my next words darling, but I think Matthew needs to hear this part." Ted smiled and nodded a positive so Jenny turned back to the unhappy young man. "Kathy told me that you gave her the best sex she has ever had and it was because of the love you both share together."

Matthew seemed to be more relaxed, with Jenny's revelation, but he still couldn't understand her sudden behavior toward him.

"Then, what could be happening to Kathy?" his attention fell over on Ted. "You know, don't you Ted?"

"Yes, Matthew, a least enough at the present to know we must stay very close to Kathy at all times." Ted's attention went up the stairs to the young couple's bedroom. "Kathy is not herself right now. I am afraid Kathy has been put in a deep trance from a demon, most likely Mr. Tucker, the new lawyer at Claremont's Law Firm. She is so deep into this trance she believes everything the demon told her is true."

"Ted, sweetheart, you have the gift of reading minds. Could you look inside that trance placed in Kathy's mind and see what it is? Then you can snap her out of this demon's trance." Jenny was suddenly afraid for her best girlfriend.

"It is not that simple Jenny. There is more involved here than just a demon. Satan himself has made a move on Kathy." Ted reached over and took his wife's hand. "Do not start worrying about your friend being sexually molested by either Lucifer or this demon, although the devil physically touched her with his hand. They have set her up to lust for someone we know. Someone who can make our family hurt if she completes her orders from Lucifer."

"Who Ted? And why, for what possible reason?" Matthew looked heartbroken as he asked quietly.

"Who? I have my suspicions and soon will know. Why? Lucifer wants Kathy to commit adultery with this person, through temptation, and that is a sin against the Almighty God. Satan wants Kathy's soul." Ted stood up and walked over to the stairs and gazed up. "Well, we will not let that devil get it! Matthew, it is for the best that you go and tend the sheep at this time. Pray continual and think positive thoughts. We will save Kathy!" Ted pulled Jenny to her feet. "Jenny, I want you to stay here and wait for Kathy to come down. The family has just finished their breakfast and I will send them all outside to work in the garden so you and Kathy can be alone for a little girl talk. Understand, sweetheart?"

"Yes, darling, I will not let Kathy out of my sight." Jenny looped her arms around her husband's neck. "What will you be doing while I am catching up on 'girl talk'?"

"I will be paying Jeff a visit. I think he is the only one that can help us with Kathy." Ted kissed Jenny tenderly, then patted Matthew's arm. "And Jenny, do not bring up sex. Leave that to Kathy. I will see Matthew and a couple of the other boys off to move the sheep back out to the mountain slopes." Taking Matthew by the hand, Ted went to the kitchen to collect the group of children and youth, then headed out the back door.

Jenny looked up from her book when she noticed Kathy making her way dreamily down the steps. She closed the book and laid it on the coffee table, then stood up smiling.

"There you are, sleepy head. I was beginning to think I was going to have to come up stairs and throw a cold rag on your face, pal."

Kathy finally looked around the big empty room and noticed Jenny was alone. "Where is everyone this morning? It's usually buzzing around here on Saturday mornings."

"After having their breakfast, they all filed outside to work in the garden, then have some play time." Jenny looped her arm around her friend's shoulder. "I stayed behind to wait for you to come down, so we could have some one on one time to get caught up. I thought we needed some girl talk and besides, I missed our times together for chit-chat. Right, best friend?"

"I think that is a wonderful ideal, Jenny." Kathy joined Jenny on the large sofa. "You're right, we don't have much time alone together, just the two us. This will be like old times." Kathy smiled. "I suppose Ted and Matthew are out busy with those stinking sheep, or maybe hoeing weeds in the 'hot' garden."

"Yes, those wonderful fellows were out early this morning." Jenny placed an arm around Kathy's shoulder. "Matthew said you were tired this morning and needed a little more sleep. Did dear old George work you too hard yesterday?"

"No, not really. I actually helped Mr. Tucker yesterday with a pile of papers he needed to get out. I think I'm just tired because it was a very long week." Kathy glanced over on the side table and saw the photo of Naomi and Jeff. Her focus was only on the tall dark handsome man. "How's things going at school. Any new teachers this year besides Ragsdale?"

"Just the same ones. I assume Miss Ragsdale has been behaving herself around Matthew and the new principal has been keeping up a good appearance. That new student in Matthew's class is starting to act up and Matthew thinks he is hitting on Miriam. Unfortunately, Miriam seems to be enjoying all the attention." Jenny noticed her friend had not taken her eyes off the portrait of Naomi and Jeff. "My job is really pleasant there and my students are very polite. I must admit I feel a little nervous when I go to the teacher's lounge for coffee or a drink. I usually play it safe and have bottled water. With these demons around, you never know when someone might slip something in your drink, like Raven handing out poison pills."

"I know my coffee is safe at work because I make it myself." Kathy laughed. "Now, Mr. Tucker has his secretary, Miss Conner, make everything fresh each morning. From coffee to tea and probably lemonade, when he's not entertaining a client and opens his bar."

"Have you ever had any of Miss Conner's coffee or tea?" Jenny asked casually. "I was just wondering if it is as good as we make it."

"Her coffee I would not know anything about, but I do recall having her iced tea once and found it surprisingly delicious. I recall drinking all of it..." Kathy wrinkled her brow in thought. "or, at least most of it. I remember, it really pepped me up after I missed my morning coffee."

"Did Miss Conner offer you the tea?" Jenny tried not to sound pushy. "It just sounds like she might be happy to share her great tea with others."

"Actually, Mr. Tucker offered me the refreshing glass of tea, when I was doing him the favor that George ask me to do, for just the day."

"I see. So, you feel safe being alone with Mr. Tucker, being a stranger to Goldsburg and all." Jenny reached for the photo as Kathy sat up.

"Phillip is harmless, just a big teddy bear." Her eyes remained on the photo in Jenny's hand.

"I noticed you looking at this picture of Naomi and Jeff. I've always admired it too. You can just see the love they share with one another, can't you?"

"I suppose." Kathy took the picture and slowly traced Jeff's lips with her finger, then ran it down his strong chest and between his legs. "I wonder if that girl knows how lucky she is having a hot stud like Jeff?'

"Kathy!" Jenny reached over and snatched the photo out of her hands. "Such talk about your friend's husband! You are a married woman and many women would consider you very lucky to have someone as young, handsome and sexy as your Matthew!" Jenny draped her arm around her friend's shoulder. "Kathy, I know we are nowhere near over the hill yet, but you and I have landed two young, hot studs of our own. Men who are madly in love with us and we with them! Ted is my life, now, my entire world resolves around him and I love him beyond words. I know you feel the same way about your Matthew."

"Matthew is great for his young age and I'm sure with time he will mature into a real man." Kathy closed her eyes and pictured Jeff standing before her, naked. "But there is something about Jeff Wineworth that turns me on. He makes me hot all over, just thinking about him" She gazed out the window, in a daze. "After the kid left the bedroom, I fell back to sleep and dreamed about Jeff. When I awoke, I was having a wet dream. It seemed so real and I felt so sexy."

"Kathy! For the love of God! There can 'never' be anything between you and Jeff! You have got to stop dreaming about him! If thoughts were actions Kathy, you would already be an adulterous!" Jenny pulled Kathy to her feet. "Naomi is one of our best friends! I am taking you in that kitchen for a good strong cup of hot coffee, a little breakfast, then we are going outside for a nice long walk! You need some fresh air!"

"Jenny, where is that old girl's imagination?" Kathy laughed as she followed her friend to the kitchen. "Don't you know when I am kidding, pal?"

Jenny gave her a smile, then observed her fixing a very small breakfast, instead of her usual large breakfast. As Kathy ate slowly, gazing from the window, Jenny folded her hands in her lap as she thought

"That's just the problem, dear friend. I do know you and the person I'm looking at is not the same Kathy I know and love. She is lost somewhere inside herself!"

Chapter Twenty-Eight

Naomi and Jeff were busy working in their garden when Ted appeared behind them. Sensing his presence, Jeff gazed down at his wife, unaware of their visitor, then turn to face his friend and neighbor.

"What is wrong with Kathy, Ted?"

"Ted?" Naomi jumped up and bumped into her dear friend. "Is there something wrong with Kathy?"

"It was my father! Lucifer and Tucker, the demon!" Jeff pulled off his garden gloves and took hold of his wife's hand. "Sweetheart, we must go to the farmhouse at once. There's no time to delay. Gather Teddy and a few things for another overnight stay." He watched her race off before moving close to his special friend.

"It is me Kathy is after. She has been put in a satanic trance and now lust for my body."

"We must explain things to Naomi, so she will understand what you have to do. She won't except it easily, but when it happens, she must know." Ted placed a brotherly hand on the tall man's back. "Jeff, Naomi deserves to know why you will be doing what you know you must do, to save Kathy's soul."

"I will tell her what she needs to know and…" his dark eyes fell on the castle. "I will appreciate anything you can do to help make it easier on my fair one." Jeff watched lovingly as Naomi walked swiftly toward them, balancing two suitcases in one hand and holding tight to her young son with the other.

Jeff gave a low howl for the wolf sleeping under a shade tree. "Here Fang! Come boy and sit, stay with Teddy." Jeff lifted his son and gave him a kiss before placing him on the soft green grass. "I want you to sit right here with Fang and play with your truck while mama and papa goes over by the garden to talk."

"O.K. Papa! Then, mama said we could go to my Ted's and I could play with Ruth."

"That's right, my precious boy." Jeff retrieved the suitcases from his wife and motioned her over to where Ted waited. "Let's go out of Teddy's hearing range. His hearing is sharp like mine, but

I have blocked his mind reading for now."

"What is this about?" Naomi felt nervous, from the men's serious faces. "It cannot be good."

"Angel, now that we know what Satan is planning for Kathy, we can help save her."

"Is the devil trying to kill Kathy? Has he made her sick, like doc?" Naomi looked from Ted to Jeff.

"It is not to kill her, my sweet angel. Lucifer is after Kathy's soul and if things turn out badly, she will lose it." Ted glanced at Jeff, knowing this girl's salvation was in his hands.

"Ted, you said you and Jeff could save her! How? What do you have to do?" Naomi suddenly had a bad feeling about the answer she would receive. Somehow, her husband was involved.

"That is what we need to tell you, dearest one. I would look like I was enjoying what Kathy will be doing to me." Jeff searched his wife's confused eyes. "Sweet one, Kathy has been put into a deep dark trance, similar to what I use to do to my victims. She believes she has to have me, all my body." Naomi took a deep breath and looked at Ted.

"It is the only way we can intervene on this devilish plan, angel. To let her seduce Jeff and almost have…" Ted could not bring himself to say the sexual act, so Jeff glanced over at his son playing happily with the wolf, and whispered

"To let her go through the act of seducing me until we almost have intercourse together." Jeff could see Naomi's tears building in her beautiful eyes as Ted reached for her hand.

"Naomi, Jeff knows what he must do, but Jeff also knows when to stop. He will not commit adultery. He will not go that far."

"So, Kathy has been brain washed into believing she has to have you!" Naomi took Jeff's face in her hands and looked him in the eyes. "She will seduce you, probably come to you unclothed! Then, she will undress you, or maybe you will undress yourself for her! She will start touching you, all over, kissing you! How can you control yourself after that, Jeff? How can you not want her at that point?"

"Because, I will be there, angel. Just before the actual act, I will order the demon out of Kathy!" Ted pulled her into his safe arms and hugged her. "Jeff is extra strong, darling, and he loves you. Like I said, he would never commit adultery against you and return to Lucifer."

"Ted's right, sweet one. Before I fell in love with you, I could have any woman I wanted. I could turn my desires on or just as easily off, anytime, with any woman." Jeff pulled her into his arms. "Naomi, dearest, you are the only woman I cannot turn my desires off for. I need you constantly, only you, my love. This act will mean nothing to me. Please, trust me, my love."

Naomi looped her arms around his strong neck and kissed him "Jeff, my dearest love, I do know where your heart lies and I do trust you. I believe you could never make love to Kathy or any other woman, just like you know I could never desire another man." Naomi felt her tears falling as she looked up into Ted's heavenly blue eyes."

"Why did Satan choose Jeff's body for Kathy to lust after?"

Jeff turned her around and swept his hand through her short hair. "Sweet one, my father wants me back! He believes I am weak when it comes to lust and naked women. He had hoped that I would desire her and give in to the lust and we both would therefore commit the act against God and lose our souls to him. But I promise, this will not happen, dearest one."

"And angel, this will all take place tonight." Ted looked at Jeff, his thoughts penetrating Jeff's mind. "You tell her!"

"Naomi, you know this cannot take place at the farmhouse, around all the children." Jeff grasp her hands tightly. "It will happen darling and it cannot be there!"

"You…you want me to take Teddy to the home, so…" Naomi teared up. "So, you can bring Kathy here, to our home!"

"This is where it must take place, the castle." Jeff pulled her into his arms when he saw her tears falling in streams. "Sweetheart, please believe me, if there was any other way, I would gladly do it."

"Naomi, it would not stop with Kathy's soul, Matthew would…" Ted's eyes grew sad as he could see the future if they lost Kathy. Naomi grabbed Ted's arm.

"Please tell me! What would happen to Matthew?"

"Sweet angel, the upset young man would kill himself and lose his soul as well. We would lose them both, if we don't go through with this." Ted touched her face, calming her fears. "Kathy will go completely mad if she cannot have Jeff and end up committing suicide, followed by our Matthew, not wanting to live without her."

"No! Please, no!" Naomi grabbed her husband's arm. "Jeff, do it! Bring Kathy here! Do whatever it takes to make her whole! I trust you Jeff! I love you so much!" Naomi buried her face in his strong chest, weeping. "At least, I won't have to witness this…and Ted will be here, so, all will go well in the end!" she breathed a sigh as she whispered

"Promise me, when you come to me tonight, to our bed, it is me you're breathing heavy for and not all the sexual seduction you will be getting."

"That is an easy promise, my dove." Jeff kissed her with passion. "I speak the truth when I say, you are the only one that can turn me on."

Ted cleared his throat, feeling unconvertable from this personal, confessions of love. Naomi blushed, knowing Ted had heard them and Jeff just laughed, then patted Ted on the shoulder.

"Sorry Ted. We were lost in one another's affection. Let's get this demon out of Kathy and then we can wait for our next demon." Jeff bent to Ted's ear and whispered. "Aren't you glad Lucifer chose me for Kathy to have the 'hots' for, instead of you?"

"Just grab a bag and hand me one." Ted walked over and helped Teddy up. "Let's go find out where Ruth is at."

"Ruth is in the apple orchard with your mama, supposing to be gathering apples, but she is eating one while she watches Hannah." Teddy smiled back at his mama when she grunted and gave Ted a wink back, as they headed for the path to the green mountain.

Chapter Twenty-Nine

Jenny was waiting by the back door when Ted walked through. She instantly threw her arms around his neck and began sobbing. Ted held her tight as he spoke softly

"Jenny, darling, Kathy is not herself. She is under the devil's spell."

"Ted, it's Jeff! Kathy wants Jeff and she doesn't care who she hurts to get him!" Jenny gazed up into her husband's understanding eyes.

"Yes, Jenny, I know and so does Jeff as well as Naomi." Ted ran his hand down her wet cheeks as Jenny took his hands.

"Darling, what are you and Jeff going to do? Can you help her? Please, darling, please! I need my friend back! Matthew needs his wife back!"

"Jenny, my love, Jeff and I have a plan to win Kathy back and to heal her soul." Jenny smiled gratefully as she gave him a tender kiss. Ted took his wife's hand and led her to the big den. "Where is Kathy now?"

"She wanted to lie down and rest." Jenny choked up. "Kathy has been having sex dreams about Jeff. She cannot get enough!" Jenny looked up the stairs as she asked, "How is Naomi taking all of this?"

"Naomi knows who is responsible for Kathy's actions. She does not blame Kathy and she trust Jeff and what he has to do." Ted pulled Jenny down on the sofa, next to him. "Naomi and Teddy will stay here again tonight. I will have a talk with Matthew, and I need you and Naomi to stay with him while Jeff takes Kathy to Wineworth Castle. I will be there watching the entire time and step in at the moment of salvation."

"You can depend on me and Naomi to take care of Matthew." Jenny laid her head over on Ted's shoulder. "We won't let him out of our sight."

John and Thomas stood over behind the sheep talking about school as their eyes were glued on Matthew, who sat quietly on a rock, staring at his hands. Sadness showed in the young men's eyes as they watched their once joyful, joking friend, fiddling with his wedding band.

"Something is really wrong with Matthew. He is always joking around with us." Thomas shook his head. "Yeh, Matthew is always so upbeat, smiling and laughing." John had genuine tears in his eyes as he observed his Christian brother. "I feel like crying and…I'm too old to cry."

"My young friend, you are never to old to care about someone you love." Ted put his arms around John and Thomas. "Do not worry over your brother. Soon, he will be his old self again. Now, please watch the sheep while I speak to Matthew."

Ted laid his hand gently on Matthew's shoulder. He looked up, sadness written clearly on his handsome face. Without a word, the youth got up and followed Ted to the rose garden.

"Matthew, Kathy is not herself. She has been put in a deep trance by the devil and she has become obsess with Jeff's body." Ted looped his arms around a trembling Matthew. "Please trust me Matthew, we shall save Kathy tonight and break this spell that she is in."

"We?" Matthew asked weakly.

"Jeff and I, working together."

"You know I trust you Ted. There is no one I trust more," Matthew's voice came out shaky. But why wait until tonight? Why not right now?"

"Matthew, Kathy must be in the act of seducing Jeff before I can bring her back." Ted noticed Matthew tense up and he gazed deeply into his uncertain eyes. "Son, that is the only way Kathy can come back to you. I promise your devoted wife, will return to you without committing adultery with Jeff."

"Then do what you need to do Ted. I trust you with my whole heart and I have faith to believe Jeff will not let it go too far. I know how much he loves our Naomi and he would never hurt her." Matthew laid his head over on Ted's shoulder and wept.

While Jenny and Naomi were keeping Matthew busy in the kitchen, Jeff and Ted set their plan in motion. Kathy was sitting in front of her mirror brushing her hair, her attention was on the portrait of Jeff she had taken from the den. She had slipped into a long black night gown, knowing black was Jeff's favorite color.

Kathy picked up the frame and took the photo out, then folded it so Naomi could not be seen. She lifted it to her lips and kissed it, as she whispered, "Jeff darling, I need you." Sensing she was not alone, Kathy turned around and looked up into Jeff's alluring black eyes. As his dark gaze searched her body seductively, Kathy stood and made her way over in front of him. Taking her hands in his, Jeff willed her to close her eyes and when she opened them dreamily, she was standing inside of Wineworth Castle.

Jeff released her hands and stood back, his eyes still on her. Without a word, Kathy slipped the nightgown over her head and dropped it to the floor, revealing her naked body.

Feeling her desire growing hotter, Kathy moved over to Jeff and removed his black shirt, her kisses burning on his strong manly chest. Wanting him naked, she reached for his zipper and pulled it down, then pushed his pants quickly to the floor. Her eyes lit up with delight when she noticed he wore no underwear, revealing a hot and sexy body. Reaching out, the demon inside of Kathy gathered Jeff's erection in her hand.

At that very moment, Ted appeared and turned the dark room into a brilliant light. Kathy, lustful and burning with desire, turned angrily to face the one responsible for stopping her. Like a wild animal, she backed up against Jeff and hissed, claws posed for attack.

Ted held up his hands toward the possessed woman and froze her actions as he demanded "SATAN, COME OUT OF THIS WOMAN! HER SOUL IS NOT YOURS, BUT TOTALLY GIVEN TO THE ALMIGHTY GOD! IN THE NAME OF JESUS, THE CHRIST, LEAVE HER!" Lighting flashed across the sky and the heavy thunder shook the foundations of the sturdy castle, as Kathy screamed and fainted in Jeff's strong arms.

When Kathy opened her eyes, she instantly saw Ted and Jeff sitting by her bed holding her hands. For a moment she thought she might be dreaming, but somewhere in the distance she plainly heard Leah tell someone goodnight. She noticed Ted and Jeff exchanged smiles as they helped her sit up.

"What…what happen?" Kathy asked with a weak voice as she looked at each man confused.

"Kathy, do you remember having tea with Mr. Tucker?" Ted spoke softly.

"Tea? Mr. Tucker?" Kathy frowned down, trying to recall the last thing she remembered doing. "I was drinking tea when I helped Mr. Tucker with some, last minute reports. He told me his secretary had made it fresh that morning." Her gaze fell on Ted, then Jeff, wondering why both of these men were here in her and Matthew's room. "Did I mess up? Are you saying, Tucker is a…demon?"

"It is over with now, Kathy. You were lost from us for a while, but we have reclaimed you from the devil." Jeff felt the picture of him and Naomi in his pocket and pushed it further down, out of her view. "I believe you have a husband who loves you deeply, waiting downstairs."

"Matthew!" Kathy began crying as she looked at Ted. "Please tell me I didn't hurt my darling Matthew? Did I Ted?"

"Kathy, Matthew knows it wasn't you he heard and saw. Demons have complete control of the person they possess and that person is no longer there." Ted helped her up and down the steps. Her attention went to the kitchen door where Matthew walked out, surrounded by Jenny and Naomi. Noticing Kathy on the bottom step, Matthew stopped, tears feeling his eyes to match his wife's.

"Matthew, my darling, I am so sorry! I never knew what I was doing and if I hurt you in any way, please forgive me!" she cried. "I love you!"

"Kathy!" Matthew ran up to the stairs and grabbed around his wife. "Kathy, my Kathy! I thought I had lost you! I love you so much!" he reached over to touch Ted's arm as he smiled up at Jeff. "Thank God she has come back to us! Thank you both, from the bottom of my heart!"

"Now that you have Kathy back, Matthew, just take her on upstairs and show her how much!" Jeff patted him lightly on the back.

Matthew glanced up at Ted and received a loving smile from the man he admired.

"Go ahead Matthew. For a man and a woman who are one, the sure way to show how much you love someone is to connect in total romantic affection."

"In other words, you love birds fly off to your nest and make wild passionate love, fulfilling each other's desires." Jeff winked at Ted. "Come Naomi, sweet one, let us connect in total romantic affection!"

Chapter Thirty

Bessie O'Donnell sat talking on the telephone to her old friend, Bernard Evans. "I certainly understand, Bernard. You have managed that business by yourself for many years, but there comes a time when things get too overwhelming. God knows you need help, what with Mr. Honeycutt retiring, leaving you the only handy man in Goldsburg." Bessie sipped on her coffee as she listened to her friend. "I am sure Mr. Manning will work out fine. Just send him right over."

After the older woman hung up the phone, her old maid daughter glanced up over her glasses. "Mother, what was that all about? Bernard not feeling well?"

"Bernard is fine, Kris, he's just trying to cut back due to his age and now Lester Honeycutt has retired, leaving poor old Bernard with twice as many jobs so he has hired a helper." Bessie got the coffee pot to refill their cups before joining her at the kitchen table. "Like us, Bernard is not getting any younger."

"Tell me about it." Kristine O'Donnell picked up her coffee and walked to the big window and smiled up at Goldsburg mountain. "Who is Mr. Manning, Bernard's new helper?"

"Yes dear. Paul Manning seems to have a wonderful record and Bernard says he's a jack of all trades, the perfect handyman." Bessie got up and began clearing the breakfast dishes off the table. "He should be here shortly to, began working on those projects we got lined up, trimming the boxwoods, painting the potting shed, mowing the grass. Do you still have that meeting with the town board this morning, dear?"

Kris glanced at her watch and carried her cup to the sink. "Yes, mother, at ten o'clock, town hall." She checked her hair in the hall mirror. "The meeting has something to do about the new owners of First Peoples Bank on Main Street."

"Didn't you say those two men were from out of town?" Bessie had followed her daughter to the hallway.

"That correct Mother." Kris gathered her shoulder bag and matching hat from the hall closet.

"That is very interesting. There seems to be a lot of new faces in our little town." Bessie walked to the door when she heard a pickup pull up and stop. "Jenny told me there is a new teacher and a new principal at Goldsburg School, along with several new students, I think."

"You are right mother, she did tell us that, as well as a new doctor and lawyer working here now." Kris shook head. "But the strangest thing Jenny said was to beware of strangers and that sounded a little creepy to me." A chill ran down her spine, recalling Jenny's strange warning.

"Well, darling, I am certain Jenny meant every word of it. After all, Ted is probably the one who warned her and he would know."

"Of course, you are right mother." Kris looked out at the middle age man climbing from the black truck. "Do you think this Paul Manning is safe, Mother?"

"I do not think Bernard would send him over here to work for us if he wasn't." Bessie opened the front door and smiled up at the seemingly friendly man with a bright smile. "You must be Mr. Manning. I am Bessie O'Donnell and this is my daughter Kris."

"So nice to meet you both." He looked around and smiled warmly. "You have a beautiful place here, Mrs. O'Donnell and I hope to stand up to Mr. Evan's excellent work. Bernard has told me some lovely things about the both of you and I can see that you are dear friends."

"I am sure you will do a fine job, Mr. Manning." Kris smiled warmly at his fairly handsome face. "As you know, the grass could use a good cutting, the bushes need to be shaped and the potting shed's paint is waiting just inside, with brushes."

"Very good Miss, mow, edge, then blow off everything after I trim the boxwoods. The adorable shed will be a pleasure to paint." The new handyman looked down when their cat rubbed up against his leg. He bent over to rub its soft fur "What a cute cat. What kind is it, if you don't mind my asking."

"Milly is a tabby, Mr. Manning." Kris blushed when he looked up and winked at her. "I have had the sweet thing ever since she was a wee kitten. She is the sweetest, lovable little cat I have ever owned, right mother?" she couldn't pull her eyes away from this stranger with green eyes and Bessie had never seen her daughter take on so, in front of a total stranger, much less a man.

"My yes, Milly is adorable. All the neighborhood children love to come over just to play with her."

"You don't say. Then I will give Milly all the room she needs." The handyman reached down to rub her head "You will be the queen of the yard, sweet lady."

Kris laughed giddy. "Oh, Mr. Manning, it is such a pleasure having you work here." She heard the old grandfather clock chime ten. "Oh drat! I've got a meeting in town and I am already late!" she reached out and shook his hand. "Welcome to Goldsburg, Mr. Manning. But I must run."

"If you must, but I really wish you lovely ladies would call me Paul." He laughed shyly. "Mr. Manning sounds so formal."

Kris giggled, causing Bessie to stare up at her daughter. "Then, 'Paul', I insist you call me Kris." She kissed her mother on the cheek, grabbed the car key from her bag and walked swiftly to her car.

"Well Paul, you really impressed my daughter and her approval doesn't come lightly." Bessie picked up the tabby cat and rubbed it furry head. "You may go about your work. I will take 'Queen' Milly inside with me." The friendly lady smiled and left the handyman to his work.

Kris O'Donnell walked quickly into the meeting room and everyone turn to stare at the woman they had just been discussing as always prompt, never late.

"I am truly sorry for being fifteen minutes late this morning, but we had a new handyman coming this morning and I would never allow mother to have to meet someone new alone." She gave them a beautiful warm smile, which they still had trouble getting used to, but found her attitude a nice change. "Have you started the meeting yet?"

"No Kristine, we would not dare dream of starting without you." The overweight mayor shuffled through a few sheets of paper and waited for her to take a seat before beginning. "It appears we have a new banker at First Peoples Bank who likes to show his authority. A Mr. William Cashton and his partner, his personal lawyer from upstate New York. It is obvious these two gentlemen are true northerners who have no intention of continuing our old southern banker, Mr. Shelton's traditions."

"Just what has Mr. Cashton done, Mr. Bradley?" Kris carefully removed her hat and straightened up her twist. "Should we be concern?"

"As of this moment Kristine, I'm afraid we really do not know what Mr. Cashton or his lawyer, Mr. Tucker have up their sleeve but they have been going over all the bank's records with a fine-tooth comb, according to Mr. Shelton's old secretary that is still employed at the bank." The mayor cleared his throat, looking over the silent group nervously. "Friends, my instincts tell me, we cannot trust these two men."

"This sounds serious, Joseph." Mr. Davenport, the pharmacist at the corner drug store spoke up. "I have been told, the man has hinted about taking over a large track of property belonging to the city."

"The city owns several large tracks of land, Joseph." Kris O'Donnell sit up, suddenly feeling anxious. "The town park, the school, the ten-acre lake and playground." Then it dawned on her what these men could be after as she slid her chair back and stood up, eyes wide with a new kind if fear. "Goldsburg Mountain!"

"We gave that mountain to that young man, Ted Neenam, remember? For his children's home and all the dedication of raising and caring for unwanted kids. Such a fine young Christian man and the children are so happy and polite!" Ginger Gray spoke up excitedly "He just can't possibly mean that property!"

"I am afraid we will have to wait. There is nothing we can do." The mayor stood up and joined Kris. "I'm sorry Kristine, for now, I don't see any other solution but to wait and see what he's up to."

"Mr. Bradley" Kris pleated "Perhaps we don't have to wait. Then, it might be too late to do something! Dear friends, please, just listen to me before you decide waiting is the best course to take!" Jenny's aunt took a deep breath as the town council looked around at one another, hoping she had the answer to this problem. "As you all know, Jenny, my precious niece, is married to this wonderful, special, young man, Ted Neenam. I believe with all my heart, that if I could speak to Ted about this, he would know what these men, Mr. Cashton and Mr. Tucker, intend to do. I know, without a doubt, he can tell me which property we need to worry about and hopefully fine a way to stop any action they plan to make."

"What is this Ted, fellow? A mind reader? A prophet?" Mr. Davenport laughed. "Surely you can't be serious?"

"I am very serious, Clarence." Kris noticed Ginger walking up beside her, the red head's attention on the owner of Walgreens Drug Store.

"Wait just a minute, Clarence! I've heard some pretty remarkable stories concerning that young man! I have witness for myself one of his miracles. We all know little Cindy was born blind and one visit to that mountain, that child came back seeing for the first time in her life!" Genuine tears came to the local shop owner's eyes. "The only medicine that young Christian man used was his strong faith in the one and only Father in heaven!" Ginger placed a loving hand on Kris's shoulder, as she declared "I too believe in Ted, so go to him Kris and tell him everything you know about this banker and his lawyer! It could involve him; he needs to know." The red head turned to face the group, who had been listening closely. "I move that we send Kris O'Donnell up to see Mr. Neenam and find out if he can help us."

"I second the motion!" the town librarian called out and smiled up at the two ladies as Kris looked around the table at the remaining nine members.

"Well, do I have this committee's blessings? I am asking for a yes response as your, friend. For our town, for our citizens, and for that wonderful young man who turned this bitter old woman into a warm, gracious, lady."

Without hesitation, Mr. Davenports spoke up loudly. "I vote: YES!" and it was followed by a unanimous yes from the entire group. Kris could not control her tears of gratitude as she gave a weak, "God bless you all!"

The mayor smiled and stood up, feeling a small glimpse of hope. "Let us know if you find out anything, Kristine. Until then, this private meeting is close.

Kristine O'Donnell walked out to her old '75 Chevrolet and climbed in behind the wheel. Her attention went to the two mountains. Black Mountain once again had an eyrie appearance as the green trees and undergrowth seem to die away, while the green mountain looked alive with God's radiance and love. Kris smiled at the peaceful mountain her new nephew lived on and whispered

"Alright Ted, it's up to you now. The only way we can help you is to know which property those strangers are after and why they want it so badly."

Chapter Thirty-One

Ted had sensed Kris's need to speak to him and he knew it had something to do with the mountain they called home, so he had Jenny to drive them down for a visit, along with Ted's mother, Hannah. Calling earlier to let Bessie and Kris know of their arrival, the gracious grandmother had insisted on having them for supper.

"Hello grams, Aunt Kris, we're here!" Jenny called as she walked inside the familiar surroundings.

"Coming, Jenny darling." Came the sweet loving voice of Bessie O'Donnell, followed by both women coming from the kitchen, both with cheerful smiles of welcome. "I am so glad you all could make it for supper." Bessie gave Jenny and Ted one of her good hugs and as Jenny kissed her grandmother's cheek, she took her hand and led her over to meet Ted's mother.

"Grams, Aunt Kris, I would love to introduce Ted and my beautiful mother, Hannah Neenam. Hannah, Bessie and Kris O'Donnell, my dear grandmother and sweet aunt."

"How nice to meet you, Hannah. Jenny has told us you have come to help with the newborns." Bessie gave her one of her special hugs, followed by Aunt Kris.

"It is so wonderful to meet one of Ted's parents. He is so very special to us and I know our Jenny is overjoyed to finally get to meet you. I do believe the dear girl has wondered about Ted's family for some time now." Kris kept looking over at Jenny's special husband and could feel him almost reading her thoughts as she heard Hannah's friendly warm voice.

"Jenny and I had a long talk when I arrived and she was filled with many questions about Teddy. Mostly about his childhood. Who could blame her? Certainly not I, my son is not like anyone else on this earth." Hannah laughed softly and caressed her son's face. "There are many times, I too have a difficult time understanding Teddy, but never doubt my belief in him. His strong faith in God and our Lord, Jesus, is unwavering and pure as the winter snow. I cannot express the amount of love and the deep affection Ted has for your Jenny, but never have I witness so much love between a man and his woman."

"Isn't she a darling, grams? A true blessing to me and our children." Jenny truly felt close to Hannah and she wanted to shout her joy to the world. "When my own mother walked out on me and daddy, I felt lost and heartbroken. Hannah has filled that empty place in my broken heart and once again I have someone I call mother and with Peter, Ted's father filling in for daddy, after he moved to Heaven, my family circle is complete. Grams, you and Aunt Kris round up the family circle with my beloved Ted taking the highest place, second only to my Lord." Jenny's attention was drawn to Ted's smiling, loving face as she added "My love for Ted is like an eternal flame, always burning in my heart."

Ted moved to Jenny's side and gave her a warm hug, then smiled at the three admiring women and gave a soft laugh "Ladies, you make me feel like I have a fan club." Then, just as quickly, he became serious, his eyes falling on Jenny's aunt. "You have something to ask me, Kris, about a large track of property?"

"I told the committee you would know." Kris could only stare, while the other three women stopped speaking to hear what they were talking about.

Bessie, absentmindedly ask everyone to have a seat as her attention remained focused on her daughter. "Kris, my dear, what are you talking about? Tell us, please. Was it something to do with your meeting with the town council earlier this morning?"

"Yes! Yes, it was." Kris snapped out of her shock and swallowed. "I am truly sorry about my reaction. I admit I was just taken back for a moment. You're right Ted, it does have something to do with a large parcel of land that the city owns. There is a new banker in town, a Mr. William Cashton, and he has hinted that he has plans to do something on one of the cities big property." Her eyes remained on the young man, who remained quiet as she spoke, polite and respectful. She turned to look at those listening. Knowing her next statement would no doubt upset all three women, like it had her. "I remembered Goldsburg Mountain had belonged to the city and was given to Ted for his orphanage, but unfortunately the deed is still in the city of Goldsburg's name."

Jenny could not sit still, and flew to her feet, hands on hips, ready to defend her husband's rights and her new home. "Aunt Kris, surely this Mr. Cashton cannot be that cold hearted! These are children who have finally found a place to call home and the most loving person on earth to raise them in a Christian way of living!" Jenny walked up next to her aunt, ready for battle. "Aunt Kris, surely the city council will not go along with this man's plans!" Jenny was feeling anxious when she added "Those sweet children feel safe and loved, by that man!" Jenny pointed at Ted. "He has devoted his life to them, asking nothing in return!"

"Jenny, darling, we are on your side, yours and Ted's." Kris took around Jenny's trembling shoulders. "I have come up with a solution to this problem and we will be ready for Cashton if it is the mountain he's after! I will advise the council members to have the deed made over to Ted, for Goldsburg Mountain, full and complete, then Mr. Cashton or any other greedy rich man will never be able to get their hands on it!"

"That is a wonderful ideal, Aunt Kris, thank you!" Jenny reached for her aunt and gave her a thankful hug as Ted watched silently. He stood up and looped his arm around his wife's shoulders.

"Ladies, it will not be that easy." Ted's gaze was warm and loving as he continued. "This Mr. Cashton, from New York, is a stranger in our town and he was sent here to do one job. He knows he must succeed or he will have all hell to answer to." Without warning, Ted was suddenly drawn away into a world of his own, eyes fixed straight ahead, his head cocked, as he appeared to be listening to an unseen being. Slowly he closed his eyes and opened them just as quickly. His voice grew serious as he announced, "Mr. Cashton is seeking the mountain and he will not be stopped until he gets it."

"No, Ted! Darling, he could never take our home! Our life is there, our family is there and God is there!"

Ted smiled down at her before kissing her to show his approval for her loving answer. "You are correct, sweetheart, God is there and that is why Mr. Cashton wants Goldsburg Mountain, but the devil will never have it! God will show me the way, Jenny, and we will get the help we need when Cashton makes his move."

The four women felt better, knowing Ted knew who and what Cashton and his lawyer, Mr. Tucker, was and what they were after, so they all enjoyed the fine meal Bessie had prepare and their visit together. After a long goodbye, the Neenam walked out on the front porch to find darkness had fallen and there was a cool feeling of Fall in the air.

Ted helped Jenny behind the wheel and his mother in the back seat, then made his way around the back of the station wagon. He paused before opening the car door. His attention was drawn to the freshly cut grass and trimmed boxwoods. A warm draft of air blew past him slowly and immediately Ted knew a demon had been here. He would watch over Jenny's love-ones closely, but in her condition, she already had enough demons of her own to worry about at school. Ted finally climbed inside the car and felt Jenny touch his leg.

"Ted, what's out there?"

"Trust me Jenny to watch after your family. They are my family too!" he took her hand and squeezed it lovingly.

"I do trust you Ted, with my life." She smiled, switched on the motor and started home to their mountain.

Chapter Thirty-Two

Matthew followed behind Jenny and her carload as she drove up to the school entrance and let all the children and youth out riding with her. After waiting for Matthew to unload his group, the disciplined children walked in an orderly straight line to their classrooms. Jenny and Matthew made up the rear of the line after parking the two white station wagons.

Jenny smiled over at the handsome youth as they made their way down the high school corridor. "At least we're on time this morning, Matthew. Neither one of us stayed up in our bed too long this morning with our mate." She chuckled softly when Matthew blushed.

"At least the morning you and Ted enjoyed a little bed fun, we all made it here before the final bell. I admit it was our fault for being late last Friday. We just couldn't keep our hands off each other. You know, you just get deeper and deeper until…" he stuttered "well…you gotta do it or die!"

Jenny couldn't control her laughter as she patted his back. "That is a feeling I know all too well. Trust me Matthew. I understand."

"I was really sweating explaining the reason for being late." Matthew's eyes fell on Jenny. "If I came out with a little white lie to the principal, Ted would have known I lied, and believe me, I would rather be honest with that new principal than upset Ted."

"I guess we should be happy about your sudden flat tire before we left for school." Jenny stopped at her classroom. "I guess we could call it a miracle."

"Jenny? Don't you know Ted by now?" Matthew smiled. "Ted had asked me to tell the truth about why I was late and after promising I would, he gave me another reason for being late, so I could keep my marriage a secret."

"Ted gave you the flat tire?" Jenny whispered, then laughed, remembering it only took her darling husband a second to fix it. "So, you said we were late due to a flat tire, then you had the rest of the day to smile about the real reason."

"True." Matthew grew serious. "A dream in the morning and a nightmare that night."

Jenny touched the youth's hand. "We have Kathy back now, Matthew, and she's safe on the mountain, where she will remain until those demons are gone. George has given her some time off at work, at least until Tucker goes back to hell where he belongs."

"Amen!" Matthew opened the door for Jenny, then checked his watch. "I'm off to home room." He made a face. "Then, it's history and Miss Rayfield."

"Just keep a close eye on her Matthew." Jenny walked inside her empty classroom to lay down her briefcase then rejoined her handsome friend. "I am off to the teacher's lounge before my first class starts. See you after school." She waved and walked into the small room, where three female teachers were having coffee and enjoying a conversation. Jenny refrained from speaking until the ladies stop talking to have a sip and smile up at the pretty English teacher.

"Good morning, Mrs. Collins, Mrs. Raines, Mrs. Smithers. How is the coffee this morning?"

"Pretty much the same as every morning, Mrs. Neenam. If I were you, I'd stick with your usual bottle water." Mrs. Raines gave Jenny a friendly smile and turned to see who had walked in.

"Good morning ladies. Isn't it a beautiful day?" Mr. Morgan, the new principal smiled over at Jenny. "Mrs. Neenam, my secretary informs me, you have most of your classes filled up this year. Most astounding for a town as small as Goldsburg." His stare seemed to take in her entire body, even though his words came out normal. "You are to be commended, my dear. Reading some of your student's entry forms, many of these students are from neighboring towns."

"If you permit me sir." Doris Collins carried her empty cup to the sink. "Our Jennifer is an excellent English Teacher and her method of teaching these students are second to none. Parents, living outside our school zone, is happy to pay the extra funds to get their son or daughter in this lady's class." Doris walked over and patted Jenny on the back. "My daughter, Tracy is taking English Two this year under Mrs. Neenam and she made straight A's last year and loved every second in her class."

"Thank you, Mrs. Collins, for that fine testimony." The principle walked over to fix his coffee as the teachers picked up their bags to leave.

"Mr. Morgan, the only reason all my classes are so full is because Goldsburg School is the only school for the town and surrounding rural communities." Jenny drank down her bottled water and checked her watch. "If you will excuse me, I must be off to my room."

As Jenny started to leave the room, the principle gently took a firm grip of her arm and smiled. "There is still ten minutes before regular classes start, so if you're not in too big of a hurry, Mrs. Neenam, I'd like a few minutes of your time." He waved the other teacher away with a smile. "You may go now, if you need to ladies."

They all set their empty cups down and said their goodbyes to Jenny and the principle, then left, leaving Jenny alone with Mr. Morgan. He casually poured himself a cup of coffee and took a small sip.

"Like mine black! Not the best coffee in the world, but it will do." He laughed and smiled when Jenny checked her watch again. "Relax Jenny. I hope it's alright to call you Jenny. I always considered my school staff as one big happy family, so feel free to call be James." Mr. Morgan sat down at the round table and pulled out a doughnut, taking a big bite. "Not the best breakfast, but I didn't have time to eat before I left home. I like to be prompt." He noticed her gazing out the door, looking for students exchanging classes. "I won't keep you long dear. I know you cannot keep those students waiting. Tell me, how long have you lived in this fair town?"

"I made Goldsburg Mountain my home over two years ago. Before I decided to stay, I lived with my grandmother and Aunt, who have called Goldsburg their home all their life." Jenny glanced back down at her watch, only three minutes had passed. She thought, time was really crawling by. "Tell me Mr. Morgan…I mean James, do you like our little town?"

"Like it? I love this town, Jenny." The principle stretched. "It is everything I have dreamed of." He rolled his eyes up slowly toward her and said, "Sort of, picture card perfect, wouldn't you say, Jenny?"

"Yes, that describes our town perfect sir." Jenny could sense this man knew about her grandmother's house. She noticed the students starting to come down the hallway. "I really have to run now sir. The students are changing classes."

"Very well Jenny. I mustn't keep our best teacher waiting!"

James Morgan stood up and took her hand. She noticed how cold it felt, almost like a corpse, causing her to shiver. "If you ever need my help for anything, feel free to ask."

Jenny tried to smile naturally as she pulled her hand free, thanked him and raced from the room, her heart pounding in her chest. She knew, without a doubt, that James Morgan was a demon.

Chapter Thirty-Three

Matthew walked to his seat in the back of Miss Rayfield's classroom and slid in, taking out his history book. The handsome youth had picked out this desk because it was the furthest from his sexy teacher's desk.

The flirty blonde had noticed Matthew enter her room and followed his movements to the back of her class. She smiled to herself as she lightly hit the top of her desk with a ruler. Her attention remained focused on Matthew as she spoke to the class.

"Alright students, please turn to chapter 7, page 171 in your books." Miss Rayfield noticed Matthew open his history book and keep his eyes down on the pages. "I want you to begin reading and read the entire chapter, then we will discuss it."

All the students began reading, except Robert Perkins, who exchanged smiles with the teacher before training his attention on Miriam, two seats up from him. Angela Rayfield made her way slowly down the center isle until she came to Matthew's desk. She spoke softly.

"Matthew, I need a word with you." The teacher reached down and closed his book, but he continued to stare down, answering lowly.

"Yes, Miss Rayfield?"

"You and the other Christian students were late for classes on Friday, Matthew." She gently placed her hand on his shoulder. "I haven't asked you to give me a written excuse but I would appreciate it if you would tell me the reason for being late. I do not buy the flat tire excuse, young man. Those tires are almost new."

Miriam looked back at Matthew and smiled, overhearing their conversation and knowing the real reason they were late. Matthew and Kathy had stayed upstairs longer making love. Hearing Miriam's soft chuckle, Matthew glanced up at her and made a face before saying.

"I…a…overslept, Miss Rayfield." Matthew narrowed his eyes at Miriam before looking back down. "It won't happen again, ma'am."

The brazen teacher, lend over, facing him. Her low-cut dress revealed her amble bosom. "Matthew, please look at me when I am speaking to you."

Miriam glanced back and giggled softly. Philip reached over and hit her arm before whispering

"Miriam, get quiet and turn around!"

"Philip Christian, would you and Miriam tell me what is so funny?" The history teacher stared coldly at the pair. "No one told you to stop reading, have they?"

"No ma'am. Miriam must have read something she thought was funny. Girls are like that when it comes to soldiers and war history." Philip tried to cover for Miriam's mockery.

"Miss Christian, I really do not see anything funny about Washington crossing the Delaware River! Kindly restrain yourself from laughing in this class! Do I make myself clear?"

"Yes ma'am. I'm sorry." Miriam twirled back around in her seat and looked down at the history book, feeling completely embarrassed.

"Now, where was I? Matthew..." Miss Rayfield noticed his head was still dropped, so she took her ruler and hit him over the head. "Do you have trouble following my command, Matthew? I said LOOK up at me, NOW!"

Matthew turned his head slowly and looked up, right into her huge breast. He managed to moved passed them and find her smiling eyes watching his reactions. He swallowed back the nervous lump in his throat, knowing this woman was deliberately hitting on him.

"Now, that is much better, my dear." She reached out and caressed his face. "Mr. Morgan informs me that you and Mrs. Neenam bring your big family down that mountain in two station wagons."

"That is correct, Miss Rayfield. We divide the group up."

"I have spoken to the school board about having a school bus sent up your mountain to get you and the other students." She licked her red lips and took a deep breath, rising her breast, causing Matthew to drop his eyes briefly before looking back into her mocking eyes. "Of course, Mrs. Neenam would have driven herself to school, school rules, you know."

"That really isn't necessary ma'am, Jenny and I know that

mountain road like the back of our hand." Matthew kept his eyes focused on her face. "Besides, I don't think Ted would approve a school bus picking up his kids."

"Are you a good driver, Matthew?" Angela moved around where the rest of the class could not see her hands. She gently let her fingers brushed away his hair from his forehead. "Beautiful eyes should never be hidden under hair." The teacher whispered next to his ear.

Matthew nervously brushed his hair back into place and sit straight up. "I consider myself a very good and safe driver, ma'am, when it comes to transporting my family to school. I take my responsibility serious."

"I bet you are good at a lot of things, Matthew Christian." The words came softly to his ears as her attention wondered down his body. Without turning away from the handsome youth, the teacher reached behind her and tapped Simon on the back. "Is Matthew a good driver, Simon?"

"Matthew is an excellent driver, Miss Rayfield, as well as a good shepherd." Simon turned around to answer his teacher, but only saw her back to him. "Besides, Matthew is right about that school bus, ma'am, Ted chose Matthew to take over for Kathy, who got a secretary job. Ted only agreed to let his kids go to public school if his wife, Jenny and Matthew drive them to and from school."

"Kathy?" Miss Rayfield looked deep into Matthew's eyes. "Is she an older orphan that has already graduated, Matthew?"

"Kathy graduated high school around the same time as Jenny, her very best friend." Matthew swallowed, and thought to change the subject from his wife. "Thank you for the offer ma'am, but we Christians do not won't or need a school bus coming up that mountain road to pick us up."

"Very well, dear. I wouldn't want you to get upset over it. I was merely trying to help you out." The flirty teacher moved in closer until their legs were touching. Robert Perkins smiled as he watched her in action and was taking in all their words. "There is one way I can help you, Matthew. I've noticed you are still behind on a few subjects in school and I know how much you wish to graduate this year."

"I will try harder, Miss Rayfield." Matthew felt uncomfortable from her closeness as he wiggled back around and looked down. Taking his face in her hands, she lifted it slowly, stopping briefly at her breast before moving up to her face.

"I will be more than happy to help tutor you after school." Her smile was seductive as she continued speaking softly, just for Matthew to hear. "Sometimes, extra help does a lot of good, to boost up your sagging grades. It could be lots of fun, learning, just the two of us."

"Thank you, but I've got all the help I need at home, Miss Rayfield." Matthew could feel the sweat running down his neck. "Jenny is an excellent teacher and Kathy has already helped me with many of my subjects."

"Kathy? There is that name again." The teacher moved his hand so it would rub along her hip. "Do you like this Kathy, Matthew? Is she your girlfriend or something more?"

Miriam had overheard that statement and she had to cover her giggle in, wondering what Matthew would come up with.

"Of course, I like Kathy a lot. Everyone in the family loves Kathy, she's a beautiful, funny person." Matthew moved to the far side of his desk and stood up. This time, he was looking down on her. "We are all one big happy family on that mountain, Miss Rayfield." He picked up his books and started to walk away when she reached out and grabbed his arm.

"Matthew, just where are you going?"

"I need to be excused, please." He looked down at her, feeling a little braver on his feet. She relaxed and smiled, giving him a wink.

"I understand. You may go, but your homework is to read chapter 7. The bell will be ringing shortly anyway. There will be questions tomorrow." The teacher watched Matthew walk swiftly out the classroom door. She smiled down at Robert Perkins and whispered, "He has got a sexy rear end!"

Robert returned her evil smile then looked up where Miriam was packing her books away in her book-bag. She felt him staring and glanced around only to receive a wink from him. Quickly she turned back blushing, and resumed packing her books away.

Robert folded a note and handed it to the boy sitting behind Miriam. He passed it to her and she opened her trembling fingers to see her name written on the top. Giving the busy teacher a quick glance, Miriam opened the note and began reading its contents.

"My dear Miriam, I find you to be the prettiest girl in the entire school. I would love to know you better. Will you sit with me in the lunchroom today? If yes, turn and just nod. Mad for you, Rob."

Miriam slid the note in her pocket, took a deep breath, then turned and locked eyes with Robert Perkins. Her serious face melted into a sweet smile as she nodded yes. Robert smiled broadly and blew her a kiss. He had passed test number one! Miriam liked him!

Chapter Thirty-Four

Miriam walked into the lunchroom and looked around for Robert, but couldn't see him among all the many other students filing in to eat. Suddenly, a pair of hands covered her eyes as a male voice spoke softly in her ears, causing her heart to speed up.

"Guess who beautiful?"

Miriam smiled and turned to gaze into the new student's handsome face. "Rob, I was just looking for you. You scared me!"

"Did I? I am truly sorry, sweetheart!" the fresh boy laughed. "I confess, I saw you standing over here looking around for me and I just couldn't help myself." he gently slapped his own face as punishment. "In my defense, I can only say, shame on me for scaring you. I really do like you, a lot! I hope you like me too, Miriam."

"I do like you Rob, very much." Miriam glanced down shyly, always the one flirting, but now, she was the one being flirted with. "I guess I never dreamed you ever notice me, with all the rich, popular girls going to this school."

"Then, that just shows you do not know me at all." Robert Perkins smiled and caressed her cheek. "I do not go for girls with a lot of money, who think they can hook any guy they desire on campus. I admit, most of them have already tried to grab me, but all of them put together do no hold a candle to you, Miriam." The youth moved in close to her lips as he whispered. "I want you, Miriam. You're the one I dream about at night. You're the one I want to spend my time with.

Miriam gave Robert Perkins a big, beautiful smile. "Oh Rob, nobody has ever said those things to me before, not ever!"

"How about a date Saturday night? We can swing by the diner, then take in a movie?" Rob took her hand in his, her other handheld her lunch bag containing her un-eat sandwich and apple from home.

"It sounds wonderful Rob, but I will have to ask Ted first." Miriam felt like she was on cloud nine. "Ted let my Christian sister, Naomi go out with Jeff Wineworth, so I am certain he will agree to you taking me on a date."

"Jeff Wineworth?" Robert rubbed his forehead, recalling how his family all but praised this man's name. "Isn't that the powerful man who lives up on Black Mountain?"

"Exactly, the same!" she studied the handsome youth. "You seem to know Jeff."

"Jeff Wineworth is a household legend in Salem, Mass." Robert raised his eyes brows in disbelief. "According to the old town citizens, this dark knight is as evil as the witches burnt at stake years back."

"I can say this much for that tall, dark, handsome man, with hypnotizing black eyes and very sharp teeth, he is not considered a knight!" Miriam looked down, feeling nervous from Robert Perkins constant stare. "The fact is, Ted knew Jeff when he permitted Naomi to date him. He does not know you at all, Robert."

"Of course, he does not know me, Miriam, how could he? We just moved here from Salem at the first of the school year, sweetie." Rob took her hand again. "This fellow, you call Ted, Is he like a father to you?"

"Ted? My father?" Miriam laughed. "Ted is the same age as I am. He lives up on Goldsburg Mountain, where he took all us unwanted children in and raised us as one happy family. Ted gives us love and faith. He is the very best person I have ever known and I love him." Miriam's eyes met Robert's "I've always loved Ted. If he could have loved me the same way I loved him, I would have married him, someday." She blushed. "You needed to know this."

Robert Perkins shook his head. "Wow! What an honest confession!" his hand slipped from her fingers to caresses her face. "I'm glad you didn't marry this Ted, Miriam. Didn't that glamorous sexy English teacher, Jennifer Neenam, marry your Ted?"

"Yes Rob, Jenny and Ted are married and expecting twin girls." Miriam gave him a sweet genuine smile. "And, it's not, My Ted, Rob, Ted and Jenny are very much in love and I am not jealous of Jenny anymore. I have grown to see what Ted sees in her and I love her very much!"

"That's a relief! So, I have a chance to become your boyfriend?" Robert grew serious. "Can you ask Ted about us dating?"

"Yes, and yes!" this time, she gathered his hand in hers, "If we are going to eat our lunch, we had better find a seat."

Robert looked down at her bagged lunch. "Brought yours, I see.

You find us a nice private table and I'll grab my food and your drink." He let go of her hand and pointed to a corner table, then smiled, "What will you have?"

"Milk, thank you." Miriam pulled her milk money out to hand to Robert Perkins, just to get it waved away.

"My treat, Miss Christian! Just grab that table." He bent over and kissed her hand. "I'm going to buy you a lot of beautiful things! My family is loaded!" he turned and broke into line, bought the milk, one iced tea, and two pieces of chocolate cake. He placed the items down and smiled as he took his seat. "I would bet there's no dessert in that bag on yours, right?"

"Just a healthy apple." Miriam licked her lips as her eyes feasted on the rich chocolate icing. She opened the milk and handed Robert half of her egg salad sandwich. "Since you are sharing with me, please eat half of my sandwich. It's quite good! Kathy made them this morning."

"Kathy? Matthew's Kathy?" Rob took a bite of the sandwich and noticed Miriam staring at him.

"Miss Rayfield was really giving Matthew a hard time during History class."

"You seem to be enjoying it, Miriam." He chuckled and took a sip of his tea and made a distasteful face. "I'd say, our sexy teacher, has the hots for your Matthew."

"Well, the big flirt is just wasting her time." Miriam pushed the half-eaten sandwich away and pulled the tempting cake in front of her. "Matthew's wi…, Matthew will not give in to Miss Rayfield's advances. Ted has taught us how to avoid temptation." Miriam bit her lip, as she stared at her plate, hoping Robert had not picked up her close mistake.

Robert Perkins smiled to himself as he thought. My innocent Miriam almost let the word, wife, slip from her beautiful lips. So, good old Matthew is a married man! I really don't think that will matter to Angela. She desires Matthew's body, so it just a matter of time before that sexy little demon has him.

Molly Darson pulled Rachel by the hand as they ran quickly to the last two swings. A couple of boys dashed around them, causing Molly to narrow her eyes toward their legs. The boys suddenly took a spill just before they reached the swings and the girls flew passed them, grabbing a swing a piece.

"Gosh! Did you see that, Molly? Those boys always grab the swings first!" Rachel watched them get up and look around for whatever made them trip and found nothing but smooth flat ground. "I wonder what made them fall."

"Our guardian angels most likely!" Molly giggled as the boys drooped their shoulders and walked away. "Maybe that will teach the bullies to stop passing us." Molly watched their teacher, Mrs. Rains clapped her hands to get the children's attention.

"All those wanting to play kick-ball, please follow me."

Elizabeth stepped up to the swings, tossing the white kickball. "Aren't you two coming? You love to play kick-ball, Rachel."

"Not today, Liz. I'm hanging out with my friend Molly."

Elizabeth looked confused by Rachel's remarks and shrugged her shoulders. "Suit yourself. See you later." She raced off to catch the rest of the class, leaving Rachel with Molly.

Molly laughed and pushed her swing higher. "I told you that cool talk will get their goat every time!" as the wind blew through their hair, Molly asked casually "What kind of candy do you like, Rachel?"

"Candy?" Rachel thought for a moment, then glanced over at her new friend. "I can't recall ever having any candy, Molly. Ted gives us fruit for treats. He says they are better for us."

"Boy, you don't know what you're missing!" Molly slowed her swing down and stared at her friend. "Have you ever had chocolate?"

"Oh yes, every Christmas!" Rachel laughed as her eyes sparkled, remembering their Christmas Eve tradition. "Ted makes us hot chocolate! It tasted heavenly and he calls it our special treat for being good all year."

"Once a year?" Molly shook her blonde curls. "I simply cannot believe it! I would absolutely die if I did not get my chocolate fudge candy!" the girl smacked her lips. "My mama makes the best fudge I have ever eaten!" Molly's eyes lit up with an ideal. "Rachel, I will ask mama to make some of her great fudge and bring us a big piece tomorrow for lunch! You best not tell Ted. This can be our little secret dessert!"

"It sounds wonderful, Molly!" Rachel's mouth watered just thinking about the special treat. "I guess Ted wouldn't mind if I had one small piece."

"Of course, he wouldn't care, Rachel, but you must not tell Ted or anyone our secret!" Molly jumped from the swing and pulled Rachel off. "This is our secret, Rachel, yours and mine! We must make a pack, never to tell anyone! A secret between two best friends!" Molly smiled. "Our little gifts between each other will be our secret, yours and mine! You are my very best friend Rachel!" the little blonde held up her pinky finger. "Let's give the pinky shake! I won't tell my mama and you won't tell your Ted!"

Rachel hooked her pinky finger to Molly's and folded it around tight. "Our secret, Molly, yours and mine!"

Chapter Thirty-Five

Ted was waiting for the school group when they walked through the front door. His attention fell on Jenny when she came in last. He walked over and draped a loving arm around her. "I know everyone has something they need to say to me." His hand went down and brushed over Rachel's head. She glanced up shyly and smiled. "Little lady, you and your friend Molly had a big day, didn't you?"

"Yes, Ted." She looked down nervously. "Molly is my very best new friend and we like to swing and talk together."

Ted lifted her face to him and spoke softly. "Did you talk about anything I need to know, dear one?"

"We just talked about things girls like to do." Rachel looked down, "I really like her."

"I know you do, sweetheart." Ted knew Rachel was hiding something out of friendship, so he wouldn't press her just now. He dropped Jenny's hand to hug the sweet child before turning to Miriam, who stood daydreaming about Rob.

"So, Robert Perkins wants to date you. A dinner, then the movies!"

"Huh?" Miriam's jaw dropped. "Ted? How did you…" Miriam shrugged her shoulders and Jenny walked over and patted the girl's arm.

"Miriam, we all forget Ted's powers sometime, darling." Jenny moved next to her husband and took his arm. "If they go to the drive-in, you and I can double date." She smiled up mischievously.

"One date at the drive in with you, Jenny Neenam, is quite enough. Although the station wagon would give us more room, I prefer to do those things behind closed doors." Ted winked at his wife, then looked down seriously at Miriam.

"Miriam, you cannot go anywhere with this Robert Perkins! He is not to be trusted!"

"Ted, please! I really like him!" Miriam begged. "I like him a lot, Ted, and he likes me!"

"Miriam, you are a very likable and lovable young lady and trust me, I know what you are feeling." Ted took her hand and led her over to the sofa. "I said, you cannot go out with this boy, but you may invite him to have supper with the family, if you like. I will give you the space you need to get acquainted, but remember everything I taught you about how to behave around the opposite sex."

"Oh, I will behave, I promise! Thank you, Ted!" Miriam reached out and hugged him. "Can I invite him this Saturday or Sunday to eat with us?"

"He will come Saturday, after you tell him I gave you permission and I would welcome him." Ted smiled at Miriam's confused look as he added "He will not except your invitation to come on Sunday, this I know for a fact!"

"Ted, what's wrong with Robert?" Miriam suddenly felt apprehensive. "What are you not telling me?"

"Just be careful, Miriam. Do not put your full trust in this young man." Ted stood up pulling her up with him. "Just watch him. I know who he is. Now, you must learn who he is." He gave her a brotherly hug, then turned to the room of children. "Now, please take these children to the kitchen for their afternoon snack. Mother is waiting for you."

Ted watched as Miriam rounded up all the children and went inside the big kitchen before turning to Matthew, whose attention was on his wife walking over to stand beside him.

"Matthew?" Ted looked deep into the young man's eyes. "Miss Rayfield made her move on you today. I am very proud of you Matthew. Under the circumstances, you proved to be strong and loyal."

"She pressed me almost the entire hour of class, after having the rest of the classroom read a long chapter." Matthew glanced over at Kathy and noticed she was wearing a frown on her beautiful face. "It's obvious she wants me!"

"Well, the big flirt cannot have you!" Kathy spoke up, obviously upset over the situation. "I think I need to volunteer down at old Goldsburg School again! To keep an eye on the little bitch!"

"Kathy?" Ted said sternly. "You cannot let that woman upset you! That is what she wants!"

"Not to mention, she also wants my husband!" Kathy tried to calm down."

"Then Rayfield knows I'm married?" Matthew took around

Kathy. "I never let it slip Ted. How could she possibly know?"

"You didn't Matthew, but Miriam same as did when she was eating chocolate cake, instead of her apple, and sharing her lunch time with Robert Perkins. She almost let it slip after Robert set her up." Ted gazed at the young couple holding hands. "Robert knows you're married to Kathy and he is good friends with Angela Rayfield." Ted looked toward the kitchen. "Miriam has really fallen for this Robert Perkins. He knows her weaknesses and enjoys flirting with her, making her feel special." His attention fell on the three listening "We all need to watch her closely."

"That Miriam and her big mouth!" Matthew stared at the kitchen door. "She laughed when the teacher was flirting with me! Philip almost got into trouble by telling her to get quiet!"

"Miriam tried to cover up her slip of the tongue, but Robert Perkins saw right through her." Ted looked around seriously "This Perkins boy is one of them." He touched Matthew's shoulder. "You need to stay strong, my brother. This so-call teacher is one of them too."

"Rayfield is a demon? What can I do, Ted" Suddenly feeling panic, Matthew grabbed Ted's arm "She is getting worse! I have no doubt what that broad wants from me, Ted! How can I fight her power over me?"

"So, she will stop at nothing until she has you in her control. Her goal is to have sex with you, so that is what must happen so we can stop her and send her back." Ted stated coolie.

"What? Let that over-heated teacher have her way with me?" Matthew pulled Kathy over closer in his embrace. "Well, I won't let her! Kathy is my wife and she is the only woman I will touch!"

Ted could not resist smiling as he patted the upset young man on the back. "Relax Matthew. It will never go that far, trust me. She wants you to commit adultery so the devil can claim your soul, but believe me, it will never happen." Ted placed his hand over Kathy's mouth as she was about to speak out.

"Kathy, I will be with Matthew the entire time and stop her and most likely send her back to where she came from." Without warning, Ted turned to Jenny.

"Mr. Morgan spoke to you alone, after sending the other teachers away."

"And I'm sure you know everything that demon said to me."

Jenny smiled at Ted's serious expression. "I'm sorry darling, it's just that I know you already know everything before I can tell you."

"Jenny Neenam!" Ted grabbed her around her waist. "I got a good notion to take you up to our bedroom and give you a spanking."

"I suppose I deserve one!" Jenny smiled up into his beautiful blue eyes "Should I remove my clothes first?"

"Jenny!" Ted blushed as Matthew and Kathy joined Jenny in laughter.

"I guess it's a good thing the day is still young and we haven't had our supper yet." Matthew patted Ted on the back. "The way I see it, you had better hold off that spanking until all the wee ones have gone to bed tonight."

"Outside Matthew!" Ted walked toward the door. "There's plenty of afternoon sun left to gather vegetables so grab a bucket on your way out!" He glanced over his shoulder at Jenny and smiled. "As for you, baby doll, I will take care of your back side later!" he walked out, leaving Jenny speechless.

Chapter Thirty-Six

Jenny looked at Ted as he walked down the mountain path, the sun setting behind him. He looked up when he sensed her presents and speeded up his steps to reach her side, then draped his arms around her.

"Jenny, why are you out here? It grows dark soon. I thought you would be inside waiting for me."

"I just had something weighing heavy on my mind, darling." Jenny looked up in his heavenly blue eyes. "I really need some answers."

"You want to know why Lucifer waited this long to unleash these demons on us." Ted took her hand and headed toward the house.

"Yes, I do." Jenny gazed down at her feet as she walked, feeling safe with her angelic husband. "That devil knows Jeff has chosen love, so why can't he leave him alone and find another lost soul to torture?"

"I'm afraid Lucifer does not see it that way, my love, and he never choses the simple way out. Jeff is the devil's favorite son and he will not give him up easily."

"But why? There has got to be more sons of Satan out there, just as evil as Jeff was!" Jenny stopped and looked toward Black Mountain. "Naomi and Jeff deserve to have love for one another."

"Jenny, do you really want to know all the truth?" Ted's stare was intense. "Are you absolutely sure you want me to tell you? Once spoken, I cannot take it back."

"Surely it cannot be that bad. I am a big girl, Ted, and besides, I really want to know." Jenny pulled him down on a near-by rock. "Tell me, I can handle it. I lived in Chicago, remember."

"Chicago will seem peaceful after I tell you the cold hard facts!" Ted took Jenny's hands. "You are aware that Jeff is Lucifer's son, but what you don't know is, Jeff has been chosen, by Lucifer, to be the Antichrist."

"The Antichrist? Spoken of in the book of Revelation?" Jenny swallowed.

"Lucifer has produced thousands of evil sons over these many years, but from all the thousands, Jeff Wineworth is his favorite. Jeff was becoming everything Satan desired in the perfect son. He was by far the most handsome and tempting. Jeff lived evil, he lusted for it, he craved it, night and day. Jeff was becoming as strong as Satan himself!" Ted lifted Jenny dropped head and waited for her to open her eyes. "My dearest, are you sure you want me to go on."

"There is more?" Jenny blinked before speaking softly. "Yes darling, I have heard this much and I know it must get worse, but go on."

"Jeff has done everything perfect in his father's eyes, on his own, without any aid from Lucifer. Jeff has already received two of his three sixes, branded on him permanently." Ted stopped for Jenny's reaction, when she jumped up.

"The 666, the mark of the beast! My God! Ted, are you saying, if Jeff receives one more six, he will become the…Antichrist?"

"Yes Jenny, and we would lose Jeff forever. The only thing standing in Satan's way is Jeff's love for Naomi."

"Oh, my Lord!" Jenny grabbed her husband. "Ted, will that be enough? I know that 1% of love can win over 100% of evil, my darling, but…what if the devil tries to destroy Naomi and takes away the only reason for Jeff feeling love?"

"Remember I said, Jeff is almost as strong as his father, so he will protect Naomi from Lucifer." Ted took her hand and started back to the house in the growing darkness. "It won't be easy to fight Lucifer, an arch angel is powerful, and this one is evil, more, evil than anything you have ever known." Ted reached the farmhouse and turned to gaze at the neighboring mountain. "It's Jeff I worry about. Not only is Satan trying to win his soul back, but an even higher power is testing him. Our Heavenly Father is testing Jeff to see what he will choose, good or evil, and if he will believe in that which is true."

"I should have listened to you. I wish I hadn't asked." Jenny's eyes filled with tears. "Are you sure Naomi will be alright, Ted? Does she know about Jeff?"

Ted squeezed his wife's hand lovingly. "My beloved, I will let no harm come to my angel. Naomi is aware Lucifer is Jeff's father, but she does not know about the two sixes. Jeff choses to keep those marks invisible to her."

"Ted, what can I do?" Jenny buried her head in his strong chest.

"Pray, my darling. Pray for Naomi, pray for little Teddy, pray for Jeff." Ted pulled her face up and gave her a kiss. "Just pray for everyone in our town."

Jeff drove his car up in front of the doctor's office, then reached over to take his wife's hand, his dark eyes gazing into hers. "You do not need to feel frightened my dove, I will not leave your side."

Naomi smiled and relaxed. "Let's get this over with. I just hope that man does not have to touch me too much."

"If he wishes to keep his hands, he will restrain from touching you at all." Jeff climbed from the car and walked around to help her out. Martha Mason looked up when the door opened. She gave Jeff a big smile when they walked over.

"Good morning, Mr. and Mrs. Wineworth. You're right on time. Doctor Raven is almost ready for you." The receptionist could not pull her eyes away from Jeff's handsome face. She thought "Naomi, I hope you know how lucky you are."

"Mrs. Mason, not feeling lucky this morning, like my little wife?" Jeff's tone held mischief as Naomi smiled shaking her head when the receptionist blushed.

"We will just wait over here, Mrs. Mason." Naomi took Jeff's arm and pulled him over to the sofa near the window. "Bad boy." She whispered. "Mind reading!"

The door opened and Nurse Vernon looked out, holding a chart. Her eyes fell on Jeff as she said, "Doctor Raven will see you now, Naomi."

Jeff lifted his wife easily from the sofa and followed behind her. After the nurse took Naomi's blood pressure and checked her heart, she recorded it on the chart. Luther Raven came in smiling, and noticing Jeff sitting in the corner, his smile faded.

"Mr. Wineworth, you're looking…" he paused in disbelief. "well rested. Did you…finish all those pills I gave you."

"I did and they worked like a charm! I feel like a new man, doc." Jeff's cold dark eyes stared into Raven's.

"Do you need more?" the doctor's eyebrow went up. "I've got plenty of samples. I'll be glad to give you more."

"I am sure you would, Raven." Jeff never drew his stare away from the demon. "But you see, I do not like medicine. I feel like it 'poisons' my perfect body."

That statement brought chills to the already cold doctor, as sweat ran down his face. He turned to Naomi and cleared his throat.

"Let's see how the little mama and baby is doing. Mrs. Vernon, pass me the chart." He glanced over at the nurse, staring up Jeff's perfect body, her mind in a trance. The upset demon clapped his hands loudly, causing the nurse to jumped back into reality. "Mrs. Vernon, snap out of it and hand me the chart!"

"Oh! Certainly doctor." With shaky fingers, the nurse handed the chart to him and forced a weak smile for getting caught caulking at the patient's husband. Doctor Raven nodded to the nurse before smiling down at the chart.

"Very good report, young lady." Luther Raven started to reach over to touch her stomach when Jeff stood and cleared his throat. The demon doctor smiled. "Your husband doesn't approve of another man touching his wife, does he, my dear? And yet, he seems to have our staff of women, have shall I put it, desiring him."

Naomi laughed softly as she smiled up at Jeff. "Yes, I can see, Doctor Raven. Jeff has a way with the ladies. My husband is a fine specimen of the perfect male, but I know his deep devotion to me and innocent flirtations do not bother me, sir."

The doctor started to feel the baby bump, then smiled at Jeff. "I just want to check the little one's process, Jeff. I can assure you, I am not hitting on your sweet trusting wife." He gently touched her rounded belly. "This seems to be a fine baby boy. By the looks of things, I'd say, Jeff has a way with you too, young lady."

"I'll not deny it doctor, but in my case, I enjoy it as much as Jeff does." Naomi heard Jeff laugh softly.

"Well said, young lady!" Doctor Raven gave an earie smile as he placed the stethoscope on her chest, then moved it down to her belly. Removing it from his ears, his fingers began to move slowly over the unborn baby, causing Naomi to tremble with uncertain fear.

Jeff walked over and put his hands on her shoulders, his eyes blazing down at the doctor. Luther Raven's hands began to shake as he nervously pulled them away and picked up the chart, scribbling something down.

"My dear, everything looks normal." He made his way toward the door. "You should have a healthy baby." His eyes met Jeff's, and they stared at one another for a brief moment before the doctor broke away and said. "Stop by the desk, my dear, and make your next appointment. My nurse will assist you with your clothes."

Nurse Vernon started to pick up Naomi's clothes when Jeff reached for them. "I will help my wife get dressed, Mrs. Vernon." The nurse had tried to avoid looking his way, but his smooth voice saying her name, drew her attention toward him. "I'm used to dressing and undressing my wife, Nurse Vernon."

"I am certain." She picked up her supplies and headed for the door to wait on them, her mind racing with thoughts. "You can dress and undress me, Jeff Wineworth, anytime, anywhere!"

"So, you need help with your clothes, Mrs. Vernon?" Jeff smiled down at the flustered nurse as she raced out the door.

"Jeffery Wineworth, hand me my clothes!" Naomi stood up laughing. "You do enjoy reading all those silly women's minds, don't you?"

"It is very amusing!" Jeff helped his wife down from the examining table as he chuckled. "The whole lot are sex starved! Maybe a word with their husbands could help."

"Jeff, stop it!" Naomi laughed and took his hand, pulling him to the waiting room. Jeff continued to laugh as she whispered before opening the door to the crowded lobby. "Jeff, please stop laughing. It's hard to keep a straight face." Jeff was so cute trying hard not to laugh, Naomi couldn't resist her own chuckle when she stopped in front of the flirty receptionist.

"Mrs. Mason, I need to make an appointment in two weeks."

"Yes, it came across my screen. I have it ready." As the woman handed the appointment card to Naomi, she gave Jeff a note. "A Mr. Ted Neenam called and ask me to pass along this message to you, Mr. Wineworth. He said you would understand."

"Thank you." Taking Naomi's hand, Jeff walked out and got in his car before opening the note. "Jeff, I need you to come and see me as soon as possible. It is alright to take Naomi by the castle first before you come over. I have already sent Andrew to stay with her while you are here, so she won't have to be alone. Teddy is still playing with the other children, so you can pick him up before you leave. Hurry."

"What do you think, Jeff? Ted hates to use that new phone and he usually lets Jenny do the calling." Naomi looked puzzled. "He must really need to speak to you. Maybe he has found out about more demons in the school and what they're planning."

"I cannot understand Ted using the phone to send me a message when he can just appear wherever I am." Jeff drove up the mountain road, still trying to make sense out of Ted's message.

"I'm sure there's a good reason he cannot leave the farmhouse darling. I will be fine with Andrew with me."

"Forgive me dearest, but young Andrew is no match for my father or his demons. I will make my visit brief and return to you quickly." Jeff reached over to rubbed Naomi's baby bump. "Hang in there, son."

Naomi smiled, seeing how Jeff loved his boys. "I hope Doc Thomas is getting better so he can deliver our baby. Doctor Raven gives me the creeps and I am afraid his thoughts will turn to killing our perfect son."

"Over my dead body!" Jeff eyes shot fire as he stared straight ahead. "I'd deliver that boy myself before that demon tried. Your doctor will take some time before he is well enough to return to his practice. We cannot let on to Raven that he is recovering. Ted and I will send that demon back before he returns, to keep him safe."

When Jeff pulled up in the courtyard, Andrew was already there, waiting by the front door. He walked to the passenger side to help Naomi out.

"Hi Jeff, Naomi! Ted sent me over to stay with you for a little while." Andrew patted her short black hair.

Jeff stared at the young man as he helped his wife out. "We know you won't let anything happen to Naomi and you will keep her in your sight at all time!"

"I will stick close beside my sister, Jeff and defend her with my life if need be. You can depend on me!" Andrew smiled. "Better run along now, Jeff. Ted is waiting and it must be important."

"Then I will go." Jeff got out to kiss his wife and got back inside the car to head for Goldsburg Mountain.

Chapter Thirty-Seven

Naomi hugged her young friend. "Did you walk over?"

"You walk over to see us all the time." Andrew kicked at a rock. "Besides, Ted said it would do me good to walk."

Naomi laughed. "Ted knows best, Andrew. I bet that long walk made you thirsty. How about some cold lemonade to cool you down?"

"I'd never turn down your lemonade, Naomi. Can we have it in your garden?" Andrew followed her to the kitchen and looked around. "This place still gives me the shivers."

"It's my home now, Andrew, and I feel safe here with Jeff." She placed the pitcher of freshly made lemonade on a tray with ice-filled glasses. "But if it makes you feel better, let's go out to the garden. It's quite lovely out there under the big shade trees." Naomi sat the tray on the garden table and poured two glasses, handing one to her Christian brother. "Let's sit on that bench facing Jeff's vegetable garden."

"Wow! Jeff has become a real family man!" Andrew took a big sip and smacked his lips. "Mum, that's as great as I remember. We all sure miss you at home."

"So, how are things with the family?" Naomi felt relaxed here in her beautiful garden.

"Everyone is about the same. Leah is still loud!" Andrew and Naomi laughed. "Kathy and Jenny tried their hand at cooking, but nobody cooks as good as you."

"That's sweet Andrew." Naomi patted his knee. "I bet Hannah can cook very good. A lot of the recipes I used Ted said he got from his mother."

"I admit that woman can cook real swell!" Andrew reached for Naomi's hand. "But nobody can bake banana pies as good as you!"

"Andrew, let me know when you can visit again and I will bake you a banana pie." Naomi smiled and stood up, getting the empty glass from her young friend. "I need to rinse these glasses out, so I will be right back. You can wait out here. It won't take long. Jeff thinks I can't get out of his sight for one second, these days."

Andrew stood up and took the tray from her hands and set it back on the table. "You are not going anywhere, young lady!" Naomi noticed Andrew's tone had taken on a demanding sound. "Let's play a little game."

"Andrew, what on earth is wrong with you? These glasses need rinsing out, then talking is just fine with me!" she turned to get the glasses when the young man pulled her around in his arms. "I said, you are not going anywhere, Naomi!"

"Who…who are you?" she swallowed, as he stared down at her, a sick smile forming on his lips. "You're…not…Andrew."

"That is very perceptive, my dear!" his cold eyes burned on her. "Who-do-you-think-I-am?" he spoke every word sharply.

"I know who you are now!" her heart pounded with fear. "You…you are Jeff's father!"

"You, my dear, are a very clever young lady!" Lucifer squeezed his fingers tightly around her slim arms, causing Naomi to flinch in pain, so severe, she blacked completely out.

Jeff drove up to the children's home quickly and jumped out. Teddy had seen his father drive up and ran out the front door and into his father's strong arms.

"Papa? Papa?" he cried. "Where is mama? Mama in danger?"

"Son, your beautiful mama is waiting for you at home." Jeff looked around for Ted and felt the small hand pulling his sleeve.

"Papa, you left mama at home by herself?"

"No Teddy, Andrew is with your mama." Jeff saw fear fill his little boy's eyes as he began crying.

"Andrew? No papa!" Teddy pointed his little hand toward the milk barn, where Ted and Andrew were walking back to the house, carrying filled buckets.

Fear swept through Jeff's veins as his eyes locked with Ted's. Instantly, Ted threw down his milk bucket and raced toward the father and son. Andrew had stopped when the over-turned milk bucket sent milk all over the ground, splashing everywhere. Andrew glanced down at the overturned milk bucket, then quickly sat his bucket down, whispering to himself

"Oh God! This can't be good!" he chased off after Ted.

When Ted reached Jeff, he grabbed him by the shoulders. "It's him, Jeff! It's Lucifer and he has Naomi!"

Jeff stood, frozen in his spot, his eyes blazing. "He tricked me!"

"There's no time to waste! Go Jeff! NOW!" Ted yelled loudly and stared in his dark eyes. "Leave the car and take flight!"

Without a word, Jeff just simply disappeared, leaving Andrew rubbing his eyes in disbelief.

"Where…where did he go?"

Without looking at the confused young man, Ted simply patted his back and took Teddy's hand. "Andrew, go back and get those milk buckets and bring them to the kitchen. I'm taken the scared boy inside." Ted walked away, leaving Andrew staring after him. He mumbled to himself as he retraced his steps to the two buckets.

"Bring the milk buckets to the kitchen. Sure Ted, after you threw yours down and spill every drop in your bucket. I guess I'm supposed to go back to the barn and milk those goats for more…" he stopped short, and stared down at the two milk buckets, sitting upright and filled to the brim with fresh milk. His eyes scanned the ground where the milk had spilled and found it dry, with not a trace of milk stains. "Darn! I see it but I be dang if I believe it! I do not get it! I just don't understand how that empty bucket got a fresh refill, all by itself." He nervously looked around him as he picked up the filled buckets, not sure what he was looking for. Unseen angels? Maybe!" Andrew shook his head and walked on up to the farmhouse.

The devil had picked up Naomi and laid her on the garden bench. He reached out and stroked her breast, and smiling, began slapping her face until she opened her eyes and sit up quickly, still in his strong grip. "No, my dear, it was not just a bad dream, I am very much real."

"Let go of me!" Naomi struggled to free herself from his deadly arms.

"Is that any way to talk to your devoted father-in-law, sweet one. Just relax. You might learn to like my touch better than my undeserving son." Lucifer mocked and sniffed the air. "Jeff is near, I sense his presence." Jeff became visible, just an arm's length away from them. Satan stared into his son's dark, serious eyes. "Jeffery, my son."

Naomi couldn't take her eyes off the perfect resemblance between Jeff and his father. She thought, how could two men who looked so much alike, be so completely different. Both Jeff and the devil had read her thoughts as Lucifer smiled down at her.

"We are not so different, Christian girl. It wasn't very long ago my son was exactly like me, in every beautiful horrible way." His face moved up close to hers. "Then you came along and ruined my perfect plans! But not for long! I will show my son I can give him so much more than one simple girl, who will grow old and wrinkled, with breast that sag,"

"That is enough!" Jeff moved up closer. "Leave her alone! Leave me alone!"

"You see, I cannot do what you ask, son. I am the one in charge here, not you." The devil said calmly.

Naomi looked up at Jeff. "Jeff, darling, don't let him confuse you! I love you, Jeff, something your father is incapable of doing."

"How touching." Satan laughed loudly. "Jeff, my favorite son, I will get you back! It's just a matter of time!"

"You will NEVER get me back, father!" Jeff's eyes blazed with anger. "Now, let her go and get lost!"

"Son, you WILL come back!" Lucifer's eyes were mocking. "The Holy One will never have you, yours will be a wondering soul! Come back and be young and handsome forever. Your strong sexual body can have as many sensual women you choose, all the virgins your lustful body requires. You will be the ultimate evil being, my son and your powers will be as great as mine."

"Jeff, please do not listen to him!" Naomi pleaded. "You know him Jeff, how cunning he can be to get his way. The Almighty God will never let you down, Jeff! He will NEVER turn His back on you unless you chose to follow your father! Jeff, darling, don't believe any words Satan says, they are false, all lies!"

"Listen to this pathetic girl begging Jeffery. Almost amusing." He sneered. "All my other offspring were weak on their own. It was I who gifted them with power, but not you Jeff. From the moment you were conceived by that bitch, you have been evil. Even inside her womb you scratched and kicked to be set free." Lucifer rolled his eyes toward Naomi. "I recall little Jeffery doing that too while he was still trapped inside you, small one."

"Leave our son out of this! Just say what you came to say and go back to hell!" Jeff kept his focus on his evil father. But I'm warning you, you are wasting your breath."

"You never needed my help at anything son, every bad thing you accomplished you did by yourself. A satanic work of art!" Lucifer laughed and showed his sharp canine teeth, "I just sat back and watched you perform, and it was pure pleasure drinking your victims' blood with you in celebration." His attention fell on Naomi, who had grown white. "And it was a pleasure indeed to watch you rape this sweet innocent little Christian girl, Ted's angel, even though that was the only act you did for your own enjoyment..." Lucifer stared at his son angrily. "because you NEEDED HER? A MERE HUMAN?"

As fast as he became mad, he flipped back to lustful, and smiled as his hand moved up Naomi's leg as she tried to squirm away.

"GET YOUR DAMN HANDS OFF MY WOMAN, YOU DEVIL!" Jeff yelled as he gave him a push, sending him to the ground. "LEAVE HER ALONE AND GO! NOW!" Jeff shook with anger.

"Yes Jeff, show me that beautiful hate that still lives within you!" Satan's smile gave Naomi the chills as her focus was on the two men in front of her. "Tell me son, did you tell this girl about your marks, how you have already received two, branded on you for life. And with the third and final mark, which is only a whisper away, you shall be the greatest being on the earth?"

"Shut up, Satan! She need not know about them; they mean nothing to me now!" Jeff seem to be unmoved by his father's bold statement as he continued to stare at him coldly.

"Oh? I think different on this important matter. It could be the one thing that might change her simple mind about you." Lucifer moved back to Naomi and rubbed her head, much like a child. "There must be a reason my son is hiding those marks from you, my child. He knows you will find him repulsive, perhaps..." He turned to Jeff. "she might even hate the sight of you after she knows WHAT THEY ARE!"

"No, Jeff darling, don't listen to him! I could never hate you! You know my heart Jeff, just as I know yours! This thing he speaks of happened before you found love, my darling!" Naomi called out loudly. "Do not listen to his ravings!"

"It's me you want, damn it! Leave her out of this!" Jeff shouted.

"Well, you see son, she is the reason we are having this conversation, so I have three choices for you. Two of the choices, she loses, one, she gains you for life." He snarled "If she gives me her soul, you may have her just as she is now, young and sexy forever. You may be free to lust after one another throughout eternity, while you rule the world!"

"You devil! She will NEVER SELL HER SOUL TO YOU! Not even for me!" Jeff grew loud. "NAOMI BELONGS TO GOD! THAT IS WHERE HER SOUL LIES!"

"Then, just give her up and come back to me. I will permit her to live and go back to that Bible thumper, as you use to call him so nicely."

Jeff turn to see Naomi's tears and hear her soft plea. "Jeff, please, don't listen to him, darling. Lucifer can only give you empty riches and lustful things, evil power and hate, I come to you with pure love, Jeff! Ted and the family, along with your little sons, shower you with love and a chance to find real hope, real peace, real joy! It is something you cannot buy; it grows inside your heart."

"Jeff, you will NEVER be excepted by 'her' God! NEVER! You are my son!" Lucifer shouted. "HE KICKED ME OUT OF HEAVEN AND I SWORE I WOULD WIN AS MANY OF HIS SON'S AND DAUGHTER'S SOULS AS POSSIBLE!" The devil's eyes blazed with flames of fire. "He has His own, Son! HE WILL NEVER HAVE MINE! Jeff, this GOD knows the great sins you have committed! You have already won more souls for me than all my many sons combined. You are a part of me and your sins are unforgivable! Come back and be my number one son! Receive that final mark and you shall reign as king!"

"NEVER! I LOVE NAOMI AND I CHOOSE HER!" Jeff grew loud as he stepped forward. "NOW, LET HER GO!"

Lucifer smiled coldly. "The second choice you have, I kill your precious Naomi, the only thing standing in my way. With her out of the picture, YOU WILL BE BACK!" Satan's loud voice echoed across the mountain.

Jeff eyes shot fire. "KILL ME, DAMN IT! LEAVE NAOMI ALONE!"

"No Jeff, please darling!" Naomi struggled to free herself. "Lucifer can never kill my soul! Learn about salvation, Jeff and we shall never be separated!"

Satan lend back his head and laughed out loudly. "Priceless! The great fallen angel's son learning about salvation from the very one who threw His most beautiful, not to mention, smartest angel, out of heaven down into the dark stinking deep!" Lucifer grew serious, as he looked from Jeff to Naomi. "The third choice, my grandson has your good looks and already he shows some strong powers. If I cannot get you back, son, perhaps young Teddy Jeffery is my best choice."

"NO! God, No! Jeff?" Naomi could not control the flood of tears that started falling down her face.

"That will be enough, Lucifer! Leave me alone! Leave my family alone!" Jeff bawled up his fist, feeling the need to strike this evil being.

"You want me to leave? Then tell her about the damn marks, Jeffery!" Satan smiled, noticing Jeff's reluctance to speak. "Very well, then I will tell her, you, ungrateful son! On a spot of Jeff's own choosing, he has already earned two of his number six." The devil smiled when Naomi sink to her knees after Jeff dropped his head, not disputing this terrible revelation. "You should have witness him, my dear, when I burned then into his flesh. His erection was so great he went out and took a virgin's virginity and soul after each perfect branding."

Naomi trembled with fear as she searched Jeff's eyes, hoping for denial, but got none. "The mark of the beast? The 666? Jeff, you…you will be the…antichrist with one more mark?" she dropped her head, sobbing.

Jeff pushed the devil away and kept jabbing him in the chest with his finger. "YOU BASTARD! YOU ARE LOWER THAN HELL, ITSELF! NO WONDER GOD ALMIGHTY THREW YOUR ASS OUT OF HEAVEN! YOU DO NOT DESERVE TO BE IN HIS BRILLIANT PRESENSE!"

In his anger, Satan slung around and ripped Naomi's blouse off and wrapped his long fingers tightly around her throat, strangling her as she struggled to breathe, then pulled off her bra with his teeth.

"NO!" Jeff lunged down on his father and lifted him up over his head. Switching his hands swiftly to the devil's neck, Jeff tightened his fingers, cutting off his air. Jeff slung him through the air until his body slammed into a big rock. Jeff continued to pick him up and sling him down on the hard rock, until he lay stun, staring up with his evil eyes. Lucifer finally managed to stand up on wobbly legs.

"Yes, you are very strong son! The hate is still there, this I see.

I am not finished with you, by no means! I will return, Jeff, and when I do, this WILL BE SETTLED!" he yelled and vanished.

Jeff walked quickly over to Naomi. She looked up into his dark eyes, fear clearly showing on her sweet face. He reached down and pulled her to her feet and Jeff could hear her heart pounding in her chest. The sky over head was growing dark and her head was spinning as she said

"Show me, Jeff! Show me the marks you've been hiding from me."

"Naomi, my sweet one," his voice came soft. "I have kept them hidden from you, dearest one. I did not wish to worry you with their presence. I love you, my one."

"Jeff" her eyes searched his. "show me, now!"

Jeff pulled his shirt over his head and dropped his pants to the ground. He stood before her completely naked. His attention was on her bare breast and he instantly became aroused as her eyes grew as big as his erection. Then they appeared, just above his great erection, two sixes, perfectly spaced, leaving room for one more. With a third six branded on his perfect middle lower abdomen, Jeff would become the Devil's Antichrist.

Naomi's head was spinning as she tried to keep standing, but her knees began to buckle as darkness consumed her until she fainted in Jeff's strong arms.

Chapter Thirty-Eight

Jeff had carried Naomi inside the castle and laid her across their big king size bed. His dark eyes gazed down at her angelic face, still in deep sleep, then his attention dropped to her perfect breast and he could feel himself still aroused from outside. With expert skill, Jeff removed the rest of his wife's clothes and let his hand glide slowly down her neck, over her breast, then move between her thighs. Jeff smiled to himself when Naomi let out a soft sigh and opened her eyes to see her husband standing over her slowly rubbing her until he brought her to full ecstasy, then climb in the bed, gathering her in his strong arms. He climbed over her and filled her with his manhood and began bringing his woman to pleasure, again and again as well as himself. After feeling Naomi reach her tenth climax, Jeff knew to let go his strongest and most powerful ending, sending them both into exploding fireworks.

Jeff rolled over and smiled up at the ceiling. "My sweet one broke a record, this time! I felt you go ten times, then one last blast, along with mine!"

"Jeff, that had to be the best sex any woman has ever had!" Naomi smiled over at her husband, lying there cool, like he hadn't just been making incredible hot love for over an hour." She said breathlessly. "Aren't you exhausted, darling?"

"I never grow tire when I am fu…making love." Jeff reached for her hand and kissed it. "It gives me far too much pleasure."

"I love you Jeff. You are my life now, you and our family." She sat up to kiss him. "Please forgive my reactions outside. I just felt so frightened by the mean things Satan was saying and doing. Then, to find out you are his chosen one!" Naomi swallowed, recalling staring at the two six marks on her dearest love.

Jeff was sincere when he took both her hands. "Sweet one, I choose not to be his anymore. I never wanted you to see those marks on me, branded there for the rest of my life. After falling in love with you, to gain that third six is out. I have no more desire to become Lucifer's chosen son. After earning the first two on my own, I will admit, I was looking forward to earning the third six, then I would have been as strong as my father. I would have lived forever."

"Yes, forever in torment as you burned in a fiery hell!" Naomi put her head on his strong handsome chest. "And in the mist of those flames, you would never see me, my darling." She looked up, her eyes serious with love. "But Jeff, there is another forever place, free from torture, free from a lake of fire. A place far more beautiful than anyone living on this earth can imagine. Happiness grows there like the streams of living water. Hope grows there, like the total gift of peace, Beauty grows there like a fresh bouquet of colorful flowers and love grows there, because it is God's Holy Throne!" her eyes held perfect love as she spoke softly. "And we will be together, forever young, in this perfect home of love." Naomi reached for his hands and gazed deeply in his dark eyes. "My most loving Jeff, I cannot show you, Ted cannot show you, but that which can, is within your reach, my darling. It is the one beautiful thing that can help you find that road to salvation, I told you about."

Naomi climbed out of bed. "Now, I am going to get a shower. By myself." she smiled. "We will never get back to the farmhouse and pick up Teddy, if we take a shower together. I know that child is worried sick and Ted is waiting for us, I'm certain." She ran her hand through Jeff's black hair. "You can look for that one thing that will help you, darling, right here in our room. Just use that genus mind of yours and think, look around, the answer lies within your reach." Naomi walked quickly through the bathroom door.

Jeff sat up on the side of the bed and spoke softly "Just in reach." His dark eyes scanned the room until they came to rest on Naomi's Bible. He got up to retrieve it off the end table. "The New Testament! Salvation must lie in the New Testament." Jeff opened the Bible and found "The New Testament of Our Lord and Savior, Jesus Christ" Turning the page, he spoke the first books title out loud "Matthew!" then Jeff began his speed reading and as he flipped the pages over, his quick special mind processed each word, much like a memory chip in a computer, storing every word for recall later.

Jeff had just finished reading the entire New Testament when Naomi came out and slipped in her clothes. Within minutes, Jeff had showered, was dress and ready to leave as he watched Naomi brush through her short hair.

"I hope Ted don't ask why we're running late." She glanced at her husband in the mirror. "But he might just think, fighting the devil would take a long time and that's why we're late."

Jeff chuckled. "My sweet innocent girl, Ted knows exactly why we are late." He patted her blushing face. "He knows every single little, or should I say many times, details!"

"Jeff, please tell me you're kidding, please! Ted could not possibly know how many times I…" Naomi's eyes grew wide when Jeff continued to laugh and knew he must know the truth. "Oh, my Lord! You're not kidding! How can I face him? What will he think of me?"

"Naomi, sweetheart" Jeff pulled his worried wife out the front door, shaking his head. "Ted will not judge you for making love to your husband, believe me. Sporting between a man and woman is biblical! Why King David was believed to be one of the best lovers in his day. Who knows, good old Ted might even get some ideals to use on Jenny."

"Jeffery Wineworth! That is no way to talk about Ted!" Naomi playfully slapped Jeff on his arm. "Besides, even if he did get some ideals from us, do you actually think Ted could hold out as long as you did or go as many times as you do?"

"Naomi Wineworth!" Jeff playfully slapped her back side and swept her up in his arms. "Such talk from my shy, little dove and Ted's sweet angel!"

Before Naomi knew what was happening, Jeff whisk her away and in a blink of an eye, they were standing on the farmhouse porch.

Ted had been waiting at the big kitchen window with young Teddy, when they spotted the couple appear on the front porch. Teddy hopped down off the cabinet and raced off to open the door, Ted right behind the excited young boy.

"Mama! Papa!" Teddy threw himself in his mama's arms. "Mama! Mama is safe! Papa save mama!"

Naomi locked eyes with Ted as she whispered.

"Ted, what did you tell this boy? How did he know I was…you know…in danger?"

"I did not have to tell your son anything, angel. Your little Teddy is very smart and he just knew about your danger, all by himself." Ted gave her a reassuring hug. "I know it doesn't seem natural to you Naomi, but your son takes after his father and will continue to grow stronger."

"I'm sorry Ted. I guess I just keep forgetting my little boy is different from most boys." Naomi closed her eyes, the long drawn out afternoon finally catching up with her.

Jeff reached for his son and gave him a kiss before sitting him back down on the floor. "Teddy, go find Ruth and tell her goodbye. We are taking your mama home and put her to bed."

"Alright papa, I can see mama is tired. You better stay off mama tonight, papa and let her rest." Before Jeff could set him straight, the little boy giggled and raced off to find Ruth. Jeff noticed Naomi giving him a hard look and just shrugged his shoulders.

"Relax sweet one, boys will be boys." Before his wife could comment, Jeff turned to Ted who was watching Naomi with wonder. "Just say it Ted, go ahead. Naomi knows you know what we've been up to." When Ted laughed, Naomi looked down, blushing.

"It would appear I'm not the only one that knows what happened. I am glad you took care of Lucifer first, at least for now." Ted took Naomi's hand. "My angel had quite a time in bed. Maybe it's a good thing young Teddy doesn't grasp what you were doing in bed. In his innocent mind, he saw it as a game between you both. Much like his games with Ruth, like chase and tickle." Ted smiled when Naomi grew white, then blushed red.

"Please tell me our son cannot see what we do in our bedroom! And all the way from here?"

"Teddy can sense what we are doing, my love, but the boy cannot actually see us doing it." Jeff remembered knowing exactly what his parents did together and their son was starting to be like him.

Naomi tried to look at Ted when she asked "Oh, Lord! You do know, everything!" Naomi covered up her eyes with her hands. "How can I ever look at you?"

Ted and Jeff laughed at her innocence as Ted gently lowered her hands and kissed her cheek.

"My sweet angel, the passion you and Jeff have for one another is tremendous! Many couples would love to have what the two of you have." Ted looked over at Jeff, amazement in his eyes as he said "Eleven times, for the both of you?"

"Eleven beautiful 'hot' times! I could have gone on longer but my dear little wife was wearing out." Jeff walked over to hug his blushing wife.

"Do you think I could wear Jenny out like that?" Ted ask seriously as Naomi's mouth flew open.

"What? Am I dreaming?" Ted ask innocently.

Jeff squeezed his wife in his embrace before reaching over to give Ted a pat on the back. "Sure, you can, Ted. With a little practice, you can do things close to the way I fu...make love. Although, once you get going, holding back to please her will take some concentration." Jeff stopped talking when he noticed Teddy running toward them. "Well, this conversation must come to a close." Jeff picked up his son and taking Naomi's hand started for the car, Ted right behind to see them off. "Good luck, Ted. Better make it Friday or Saturday night though. You cannot wear Jenny out the night before school."

"What is my Ted and Jenny gotta do, Papa?" the boy's big black eyes looked up innocently. "Pulling weeds or hoeing in the garden? Maybe, climbing all the up the high mountain?"

"Defiantly something like that, Teddy." Ted laughed at Naomi's shocked face. "Angel, go home and get some rest. You have had an exciting day."

"Goodbye Ted." Naomi finally smiled, knowing at least, their little boy had no clue what they were talking about. "And Ted, good luck holding out." This time it was Naomi who joined Jeff in laughter as Ted's face went red. To Naomi, it felt priceless as she waved and road away with her clever boys.

Chapter Thirty-Nine

The following afternoon, Ted was waiting just inside the door as Jenny and Matthew drove up to a quick stop. He heard a car door sling open and the sound of running footsteps as Leah dashed in the door out of breath.

"Ted! Help Ted!" the red headed child yelled with excitement, bringing Kathy and Hannah running from the kitchen, followed by an excited Ruth. They saw Leah standing there, her face white with fear. Kathy could tell Leah was upset, so she asked.

"What in the world is going on here?"

Ted knelt down to the very upset little girl, who could not stop shouting at the top of her lungs. He draped a loving arm around her trembling shoulders as he spoke softly "Leah, sweetheart, please calm down and tell me what is wrong with Rachel?"

Hannah and Kathy looked at each other and shrugged their shoulders, then turn to hear what Leah had to say.

"Rachel is fast asleep, Ted!" Leah started crying, concern for her sister filling her with dread. "She won't wake up!"

At that moment, Matthew came through the door carrying the limp girl. Jenny and the rest of the excited school group raced in behind him. Jenny's eyes found Ted's.

"Sweetheart, Rachel's teacher came to get me. She said Rachel was acting up in class, laughing and talking back to her." Ted could see his wife was frighten as she spoke. "I immediately left my class reading, and followed her. I found our Rachael standing on the window seal, yelling: 'I am a bird! I am a big black scare crow! Caw! Caw! Caw!' Ted, I instantly race over, praying all the while, and made it just as she gave a leap."

"Then when you caught Rachael, she suddenly passed out and has been in a deep trance ever since." Ted calmly took Rachael from Matthew, where he noticed the red lipstick on Matthew's neck. "Matthew, you can come with me. Jenny, did you see Molly Darson in that classroom?"

"I'm sorry darling, I was so frightened about what Rachael was about to do, I did not look around at any one else." Jenny felt like she had let Ted down.

"My dearest, you have not let me down. Your choice to help Rachael was all that mattered and the fact that you prayed for help." Ted touched her face when Jenny shook her head, knowing once again, he knew her thoughts. "Molly Darson was sitting in the back of the classroom, the only child in class, smiling."

"Smiling? Seeing Rachael almost jumping from a window, and the kid was smiling!" Kathy walked over and looked down at the sleeping girl. "What is wrong with that kid? Smiling! I thought she was Rachael's new best friend!"

"Kathy, Molly Darson is neither a kid or a friend." Ted started up the steps, carrying Rachael to her room. He called over his shoulder. "Molly Darson is a demon!"

Everyone in the room stared at Ted, after he declared a child a demon. Matthew shrugged his shoulders at Kathy and followed Ted up the stairs. Less than five minutes, Rachael came down the steps, smiling at those waiting below. She suddenly realized everyone was staring at her with disbelief. She spoke up shyly.

"Why is everyone staring at me? Did I miss the refreshments?"

Jenny, so relieved to see Rachael being her old self, ran over to hug her. "No darling, you did not miss refreshments! You just happen to be right on time! Right gang?" the children sang out a happy, yes! Jenny took her hand and led her to Hannah. "Hannah, can you take all these darling children to the kitchen for their afternoon snack?"

"Glady! I can't imagine eating all those peanut butter and crackers all by myself, then washing them down with all those glasses of coke!" there was an exploding round of applause from the happy bunch of children as Hannah marched them inside the kitchen and shut the door, leaving Jenny to relax after her trying day.

Jenny walked over to the staircase and gazed up at the empty hallway. "I wonder where Ted and Matthew are? What could they be talking about all this time?"

"I think I know, but I'm not saying a word." Miriam walked over to the piano and started playing "Your Cheating Heart".

After sending Rachael downstairs, Ted smiled over at Matthew, who looked back confused.

"Matthew, are you trying to make your wife jealous or just want to get a fat lip from her?"

"Huh? I'm not sure what you're talking about, Ted." The young man looked innocent.

Ted chuckled and led his friend over to the mirror, then pointed out the red lipstick mark, the perfect shape of a woman's lips.

"Now, how the shit did that get there?" Matthew started rubbing it, trying hard to wipe it off.

"That's what I would like to know? I am certain Kathy will demand an explanation when she spots it." Ted pulled Matthew to the edge of the bed. "Didn't you feel Rayfield kissing you on the neck? By the looks of it, she got you, real, good and with permanent lipstick."

"Permanent? Holy cow! I guess I'd better start at the beginning." Before he could utter another word, the door flew open and Kathy and Jenny walked in. Kathy walked straight to her young husband and pushed his head to one side to clearly see the lipstick mark.

"Don't let us stop you, Matthew! Let's hear this 'innocent' little story, starting at the very beginning! Leave NOTHING out!"

"That Miriam! She had to go and run her big mouth!" Matthew started to stand up, but Ted and Kathy lowered him back on the bed. "Look, it had to be Miriam! She has a way of stretching the truth! You all know how she is!"

"Miriam didn't come out and tell us anything, Matthew! All she had to do was hint that she knew something, then go over to her piano and start playing her give away song! Your Cheating Heart! Believe me, it didn't take Jenny or me long to figure it out and get her talking." Kathy patted his knee, a little harder than just playful. "Start talking!"

"The truth is, I thought if I changed seats in Rayfield's class and moved to the front of the class, she would not try to hit on me where the entire class could see her!" Matthew swallowed. "It didn't work! The shifty flirt just instructed the class to read the longest chapter in our history book, then threatened everyone by declaring, if she caught anyone looking around instead of reading, she would give them an F!"

"That bitch!" Kathy regretted her remark as soon as it flew out and she silently whispered, "I'm sorry." To Ted. "I guess that flirt made her move on you why everyone was reading."

"Yeh, something like that, sweetheart." Matthew looked at Ted for help and just heard his, 'go ahead'.

"I was trying hard to concentrate on my reading when I felt the teacher brush up against me and whisper in my ear. She said my name soft and seductive, then stated we were close to the same age and she would like to get to know me better." Matthew heard Kathy grunt and looked up to see her frowning at him. "Gosh Kathy, I don't want to know her better! You know that!"

"Kathy, if you do not keep making Matthew feel unconvertable, I will have to ask you to leave the room." Ted reached over and patted her shoulder. "Do you think you can behave?'

"Sure Ted, I'll put forth my best effort." Kathy force out a smile. "Do go on Matthew, darling."

"This is not easy for me to say in front of all of you, especially you, Kathy. But you must believe me, I did not start it and I never wanted anything she was offering me." Matthew sat up, sweat trickling down his face. "Miss Rayfield bent over, showing me her well-rounded bosom, and smiling she said,

"Matthew, darling" Matthew began speaking in a woman's sexy voice, as he mocked her. "I can teach you a lot more than old history. I think you and I could be great together, two sexy bodies making fiery love."

I remember shaking as I tried to stand up and flee from her spider web but she held me down with her hands, powerful strong hands, not a delicate lady's hands, like yours, Kathy." Matthew noticed his wife blinking, trying not to throw out a few choice words. "Gee, wiz, I felt so helpless! I just could not move. That woman had the strength of a…"

"A demon!" Ted stood up. "The kiss, Matthew?"

"Like I said, I could not move, not one muscle. It was like she had me in a trance, cause my eyes were glued…" Matthew looked helplessly at Kathy, dreading the next words, as she tried patiently to remain calm, replied

"Matthew, do go on. Your eyes were glued on what?"

"Her big breast! I just could not pull away. I swear guys, her clothes had just vanished, disappeared! Rayfield was standing very close to me, very naked!" Sweat ran down Matthew's face, knowing things just got worse. "Then I realized, I was naked too! Do not ask me how! All I recall was, one second I was fully clothed, the next thing I knew, I was as naked as Adam!"

"I will kill that hussy! The very nerve of that witch!" Kathy jumped up and started for the door when Ted and Matthew grabbed her. "Fellows, turn me loose so I can go strangled that bimbo! Seducing my husband and in front of a bunch of impressible kids! Say your prayers sister, because I am coming after you!"

Ted gently turned her around to face him, then his words came softly. "Kathy, for starters, You, cannot kill Angela Rayfield. She is one of Satan's demons, highly trained in her skills of seduction, a high price prostitute by trade when on earth, but she had a faddish for chaining up her clients while having sex and got turned on by tightening the chain around her lover's neck until he could not breathe. Demons are not only very strong, they can block out their actions so others cannot see what they are doing. Those students never saw anything going on between Miss Rayfield and Matthew." Ted took Kathy's hand, feeling her calm down. "The only thing real that happen between Miss Rayfield and Matthew was that kiss, and she is the one who put it there."

Ted watched Matthew walk back over to the mirror to examine the lipstick mark. He made his way by his side and laid a loving hand on his shoulder.

"Tell us about the kiss."

"The kiss." He closed his eyes as he recalled what had happened. I remember Angela Rayfield pulling me up, out of my seat, then she led me to an empty room, that appeared next to her classroom. I could not control my feet as they followed her. She had me to lay down on the floor and she climbed on top of me. I felt her kiss my neck, then she started to rape me when somehow I managed to say: "Stop! I'm married!". Matthew opened his eyes and gazed into Ted's loving ones. "She stopped suddenly, her face seemed to be detached from her head for a brief moment. It was the weirdest thing I've ever seen. I heard chains rattle and she was staring down at me. I managed to say: "I love my wife, you devil! Do not touch me!" Matthew trembled recalling how her eyes turned red when she stood up. "Rayfield smiled and hissed out these words:

"I hate that lovely sexy body has to burn."

"Then she disappeared and I found myself back in my desk, completely dressed, and that teacher was sitting behind her desk staring at me."

"I guess Miriam noticed your neck and saw where that demon

had kissed you!" Kathy made a fist behind her back.

"Well, little Miss Noisy Miriam was picking with me about the lipstick when Rayfield stopped her to inform our dizzy blonde sister, the lipstick on my neck would have to wear off, but it was just a harmless kiss." Matthew made a face. "Then Rayfield told Miriam she hoped that innocent kiss did not make Matthew's girl mad. So, Miriam could not wait to rub it in."

"Did Robert Perkins hit on Miriam today?" Ted thought it best to change the subject before Kathy grew upset again. "Did she spend any private time with him?"

"They did walk hand-in-hand to the lunchroom." Matthew was glad someone else was in the hot seat. "He had her blocked, but I think Perkins kissed her at the lockers and I heard him tell her, he couldn't wait for their date. Miriam told him she was looking forward to it." Matthew's eyebrow went up when he added. "Rob, which Miriam calls him, thought he was speaking too low to be heard, but my sharp ears picked up his words and his meaning, being a guy."

"Tell us what she said after 'Rob' told her he hoped they had some alone time, so he could show her how much he cared about her." Ted smiled at Matthew's dropped jaw. "That is what he said, right?'

"You know it!" Matthew frowned over at the two girls when they giggled. "Our sweet 'innocent' Miriam just gave a big sigh. It was obvious, she fell for his flattery, hook, line, and sinker!"

"For someone that don't pay much attention, you sure know all the details." Kathy laughed and walked over to give her husband a hug. "I love you, sweetheart." She pushed him to the door. "Now, go and get in our shower and wash that woman off of you! I will scrub your neck for you!"

Ted took Jenny by her hand and led her back down to the quiet den. "Alright my darling, I believe you have something you need to tell me about being alone with Mr. Morgan again."

"Ted, do I really need to waste my breath telling you what happen? I'm sure you already know every little detail." Jenny glanced up and noticed Ted's serious stare, so she took a deep breath. "Whoops, I am truly sorry, darling. James Morgan sent a message to me just as my first class was ending, asking me to drop by his office when I had a few spare minutes." She looked up helplessly. "Ted, I really did not want to go, but what kind of excuse could I use? He knows my class schedule, what else could I do?" Jenny got up and started pacing the floor. "Morgan gave me a big smile when I walked in and stood up, then ask me to have a seat. I sat rigid as he made his way to the door and closed it, then came up behind me and gave me a pat on the back. Casually he stated, it's hard to talk with all that noise out in the hall. He went on about how much he loved kids, but sometimes they could be too loud, especially on Fridays." She shivered. "Then he gave a deep laugh and said Friday the 13th was his lucky day! I ask him why Friday the 13th was so lucky to him? I just could not imagine what he was after."

"The man was after you, Jenny!" Ted stood up, his eyes growing angry. "That dirty man tried to kiss you!"

Jenny gave Ted a playful slap on his arm. "Ted Neenam, I told you, you already knew everything! So, why don't you tell me what Mr. Morgan did?" Jenny suddenly noticed the hurt look on Ted's handsome face, making her feel bad for her comment. "Forgive me, darling. I will continue. I just came right out and ask Mr. Morgan why he wanted to see me and reminded him I had a class that started in ten minutes." Once again, Jenny felt chills race up her spine, causing her to shiver. Ted pulled her in his warm embrace, calming her nerves. "He said, I know this will sound strange, but I cannot seem to get you off my mind. You are the most beautiful woman I have ever seen and even though I know that you are a married woman, the truth is, I love you, Jenny." Jenny could see the emotions rolling around on Ted's usually peaceful face as she continued.

"Ted, I tried to move but I couldn't, just like Matthew. I wanted desperately to get up and run out, but my feet could not move! His eyes stared into mind and I knew if something did not happen fast, that man would be on me!"

"That creep!" Ted made a fist, feeling the need to strike out at the man hitting on his woman. That demon did come over and touch your breast! I will send that low life back to hell where he came from!"

"Ted Neenam, call me down for getting angry!" Kathy walked over, hands on her hips. "It's a different story when it's your lover that some jerk is groping!"

"You are absolutely right, Kathy, I did get angry!" Ted took a deep breath to relax. "Thanks to Morgan's secretary walking in, the spell he had on Jenny was broken."

"That's exactly what happen and James Morgan, like magic, was sitting behind his desk, looking innocent!" Jenny shook her head. "That demon was slick. The secretary never saw a thing and had no idea that jerk had groped me!"

"They will be making their final move soon, so, please Jenny, remember what I told you" Ted hugged her and whispered in her ear "I'm only a whisper away."

Jenny gave him a hug, then ran her hand up his leg. "Until then, my dearest, it's Friday and our weekend has started."

"Excuse us Kathy." Ted took Jenny hand and pulled her out the door. He led her to a bench as the late afternoon sun was dropping behind the mountain. "Supper will be soon and the children will expect to stay up a little longer because it's Friday." He looked into her eyes, love reflecting from his. "Darling, I know we need to make the most of our night together, especially the weekends when you don't have school the next day. Soon, we will have to slow down. The girls will be growing bigger inside you and for their sake, we must cut back."

"That is the only thing about being pregnant I hate!" Jenny laid her head over on Ted strong chest.

"What? Getting fat?" Ted asked innocently, causing Jenny to chuckle.

"No, sweetheart, not being able to make love."

"We have a little time left for fun and games, Jenny. As a matter of fact, I have something special planned for you Saturday night." He gave her a winning smile and a hug. "I am certain it should please you greatly."

Jenny sat up excited. "Oh? Now you have my curiosity up! Please tell me!"

"Let's let it be a lovely surprise." Ted pulled her closer and kissed her with passion as he thought "I hope and pray I can pull it off."

Ted had everyone go to bed early because Saturday would prove to be a full, busy day. He had insisted that his beautiful wife get some much-needed sleep because he would be keeping her up late on Saturday night, plus the fact that he had to get up at four a.m. to relieve Thomas and Phillip with sheep duty. Knowing Ted had promised her he had something special planned on Saturday night, she agreed sleep sounded sensible, so she did not try to tempt him when they crawled under the covers.

Jenny opened her eyes and glanced at the bedside clock, seven a.m. Ted had been quiet getting up at four, because she didn't hear a sound from him. She sat on the side of the bed, stretching, then patted her growing stomach.

"Girls, your daddy is so good to me!" After a quick shower, Jenny got dressed in a pair of stretch jeans and a cotton pull over, then made her way down the hall, hearing her best friend calling her name at the foot of the steps.

"There you are, sleepy head." Kathy had a serious look on her face as she spoke softly. "Jenny, your Aunt Kris called this morning and sounded very upset. She said that both she and your grandmother had gotten very sick and have taken to their beds." Kathy took Jenny's arm. "Kris wants you and Ted to come down as soon as possible!"

Chapter Forty

"My God! Kathy, what do you think they both caught?' Jenny grabbed her car keys and bag. "Have you seen Ted? Phillip and Thomas are probably already in bed asleep after sheep duty till four a.m. I have no way of knowing where Ted is watching those sheep!"

"Jenny, just relax and take a deep breath. You know Ted. I am sure he will know you will need him." Kathy hugged her friend and walked her to the sportscar. "I'd go with you, pal, if I hadn't already promised Matthew I would help him in the vegetable garden."

"You are right about Ted. I am sure he already knows and will catch up with me, unless he's already there waiting!" Jenny tried to sound cheery as she climbed in and jumped when Ted tapped on the window. He opened up her door and helped her out.

"Jenny, you are sitting on the other side, I'm driving."

Kathy stared up at Ted confused. "Ted, what are you doing?"

"Kathy is right, darling! You can't drive a car! You don't know how, remember your bad attempt to drive on our first date?" Jenny held tight to the car keys.

"Jenny!" Ted led her around to the passenger side and helped her inside, waving the keys away. "I won't need those keys, darling. I will not be driving the same way you do! Now, close your eyes, sweetheart!"

Jenny looked at him like he had lost his marbles. "Believe me Ted, darling, if you are driving this car without keys, I will have to close my eyes!"

Ted gave her his beautiful smile as he laughed. "Just close those beautiful eyes, my love, and trust me." In a flash, the sports car, along with Ted and Jenny, had vanished from the courtyard.

Kathy rubbed her eyes in disbelief. "Damn! Where did they go? They just simply disappeared!"

Matthew had walked out to witness the car disappearing and laughed softly as he took around his wife's shoulders. "Kathy, when you have been around Ted for as long as I have, even though you cannot explain what the heck happened, you just except it. Ted has powers we could never understand, but he uses them for good."

Matthew handed her a bucket and hoe. "A little garden work with your sexy husband will make you feel better." He pulled her to the garden.

"Jenny, you can open your eyes." Ted was standing outside her opened car door. Jenny saw the 'Christmas card' house in front of her and knew somehow, they had arrived. As Ted helped her from the sportscar, Jenny thought to herself

"He didn't even start the motor and yet, here we are!"

Ted smiled and took her hand as they walked to the front door where Jenny knocked, calling her aunt's name. Ted reached down and opened the door.

"Jenny, the door is unlocked. Just go in and up to your grandmother."

Jenny made her way quickly up the steps to Bessie's bedroom. "Grams? It's Jenny." She walked over and sat down by the frail woman, who could barely lift her hand.

"Jenny, we need a doctor!"

Before Jenny could respond, Ted appeared and looked lovingly at his upset wife. "Jenny, go to your Aunt Kris now. I will stay with your grandmother."

"Whatever you think best Ted, darling." Jenny bent down and kissed her grandmother's hot forehead. "Grams, darling, Ted will help you. I am going to Aunt Kris."

"Yes, please see to your aunt, my dear. I'll be fine here with Ted." The old woman's voice came soft as she tried to sit up, but her sickness made her too weak. "I'm sorry, my son, that I cannot get up and fix you a nice cup of tea."

Ted took hold of her frail hands and said softly "Bessie, sit up."

"You are such a darling young man, Ted. I wished I could sit up but I am just too weak." Bessie's eyes grew pale.

"Bessie, sweet child of God, please sit up!" Ted looked deep into her eyes and new life filled them as she sat up slowly and blinked. "Now, slide your legs to the side of your bed and in the name of Jesus our Lord, stand up!"

Without hesitation, Bessie O'Donnell did as Ted instructed and stood up, her sickness completely gone. She grabbed her face and laughed. "Praise the Lord! Thank you, Jesus!" the sweet elderly lady hugged her grandson-in-law. "You are a blessing to this troubled world, my son. Do you know what made me and Kris get so ill?"

"I do, grandmother. You were poisoned, Bessie. Do not eat anything you have in this house. It must be throwed out!" Ted gave her the warning. "Now, have a good warm bath and get dressed. I will send Jenny to stay with you why I attend your daughter."

"Thank you, Ted and thank God, you came into Jenny's life." She returned the smile he gave her and watched him leave her room.

Ted relieved Jenny by Kris's bedside and sent her to stay with her grandmother as he helped Kris. He looked down at the sick woman and reached for her hand.

"Kristine, do exactly as I say, and you will be made well."

Kris gave Ted a weak smile, then said "I believe in you Ted. Just tell me what to do, and I will gladly do it."

"Hold tight to my hands and slide to the side of your bed." He waited until she sat on the side of her bed before saying "In the name of Jesus our Lord, stand up, sweet child of God!" He locked eyes with her as she stood to her feet, the illness completely gone.

"God be praise! I feel fit as a fiddle!" she wrapped her arms around Ted. "Thank you!"

Ted smiled, hugging her back. "Jenny and your mother are down in the kitchen throwing out all the food and drink inside this house. You were both poisoned!"

"Poisoned? Good Lord!" Kris looked shocked.

"Have a good bath and put some clean clothes on, then join us downstairs." Ted started to walk out the door just as another truth hit him "Kristine, I am truly sorry about your cat. I just realized the sweet innocent thing is dead. It was Paul Manning! He must go!"

Kris' jaw dropped, realizing the man she had been flirting with was the one responsible for her sweet tabby cat getting killed and worse, poisoning her and her mother.

"It was Paul? He seemed so sweet and always helpful." Tears filled her eyes. "He…he poisoned us? Why? I don't understand?"

"Why? He is evil, Kristine, that's why. Paul Manning is not human!" Ted tried to remain calm. "Now, just listen to me, after you have dressed, you and Bessie must get in your car and leave this house until late this evening. He will be gone by then and he will never bother you again, I promise."

"You said Paul was not human, Ted. Please be careful." Kris looked genuinely worried over this young man's welfare. "Would you like us to take Jenny along with us."

"That is most thoughtful, Aunt Kris, but Jenny will stay with me. She will be safe. Now, move quickly, there's no time to spare." Ted left Jenny's aunt getting ready to depart, then went straight to the kitchen. The two women had already filled up several large trash bags with contaminated food when Ted walked in, Bessie pocketbook in hand.

"Bessie, Kristine is taking you into town for a few hours. She can explain things to you, but you must leave to stay safe until I get rid of the one that tried to kill you." He took Jenny's hand. "Jenny, you will stay with me, but you must stay inside this house. I am going to find Manning!" Ted walked out the back door.

Within minutes, Aunt Kris and Bessie had left their home, leaving Jenny upstairs, looking out the window in the hallway, down in the back yard for any sign of Ted. Ted had easily found Paul Manning lurking inside the garden shed. Ted's voice rang out loudly

"Manning, your evil has been found out! I am sending you back to hell!"

"Ted! The angel's son!" the demon gave a gruesome laugh, meant to send chills up any attacker's body, but it failed to bother Ted. "I am strong, good man! My evil is powerful and I can destroy you easily!"

"You have no power over me! Like your master, YOU ARE A LIAR!" Ted's stare held his. "I can and I will send you back to where you came from, you, demon!"

"It will not be easy! I will fight you and with the power the great Lucifer has given me, I will rip you to pieces!" his evil eyes wondered above Ted's head "Or better still, I will mash you like a cockroach!" a large rock dangled just over Ted, just waiting to be released by the evil demon.

Without looking up, Ted knew what waited above his handsome head, so he yelled "DO YOU ASSUME TO DROP THAT ROCK THAT WAITS ABOVE MY HEAD? THE VERY ROCK YOU PLACED THERE FOR THAT VERY PURPOSE! YOU REALLY DO NOT KNOW ME OR OF MY POWERS! YOUR MASTER, THE DEVIL, THE CREATOR OF ALL LIES, MIS-INFORMED YOU, DEMON! DROP THAT ROCK AND YOU WILL FEEL WHO SHALL GET MASHED LIKE A COCKROACH! IT IS

YOU, WHO WILL BE DESTROYED, NOT I!"

The demon hesitated, not as sure about his plan to drop the heavy rock on this small man. He jumped when Ted called out loudly

"DROP IT!"

Jenny heard Ted's angry voice and knew he was facing something very evil, so she dropped to her knees to pray, the one thing she could do to help him.

"Father, I know you are with Ted, Lord, but please, keep him safe. I need him! The family needs him as does the entire town." Her fingers felt movement in her belly and she closed her eyes and added "Our daughters need their daddy. I believe with all my heart, that you will keep him safe."

Jenny jumped when she heard a very loud crash coming from the garden shed, followed by a horrifying scream. Jenny covered her ears to block out the continuing painful screaming. "It couldn't be Ted! Please, let Ted send that demon away!"

Ted stared down at the heavy rock pinning down the evil demon, who continued to scream in severe pain. "This was your punishment in hell, wasn't it, Paul Manning? While you lived on this earth, you delighted in mashing your victims to death slowly, didn't you? You would tie them down and lay a strong sheet of steel across the length of their body, then began stacking up heavy squares of rock on top of them until you mash their insides out! You undeserving demon!" Ted's attention fell on the ground between him and the demon, then pointed his finger straight to the ground. It began to tremble and crack open, as fire shot up. "I have the power to send you there, Paul Manning, or I can send you back to hell." Ted spoke calmly. "But your master wants you back. You failed him, Paul Manning! He will get you back!"

"I'd rather not go to either place, angel's son. To be tortured in hell by Satan is horrible, but to be thrown into the lake of fire, sounds even worse!" the demon moaned in pain. "Have mercy, I'm in great pain! I cannot move!"

"Now you know the fate of each of the men and women you tortured on earth, Paul Manning!" Ted looked down on the demon, seeing only hate. "Tell me truthfully, if you can, would you have had mercy on me if it was me under that rock? Did you have mercy on two trusting women who gave you a home and a job? Did you have mercy on that innocent cat you ran over deliberately with that push mower? Ted looked at the rock and it moved off the demon's broken body. Paul Manning managed to stand up on wobbly legs as Ted continued. "You don't know the meaning of the word! You are already doomed, Manning! You lost your rotten soul when you were hung, one-hundred and twenty-three years ago!" Ted yelled "GO BACK!"

Instantly, the demon's body flew into the second whole, as he was fighting the air, trying desperately to escape his fate. Both wholes trembled as they closed, then disappeared, along with the big heavy rock. Ted brushed off his anger and walked back to the house.

Stepping inside the kitchen, Ted looked around at the bags filled and the remainder of the poison food still to be throw away. Without a sound, Ted put out his hand and all the bags and leftover food and drink simply vanished, leaving the kitchen spotless.

Jenny came down after hearing Ted come in and found him in the clean kitchen, looking drained and tired. Walking over by his side, Jenny looped her arms around his waist.

"Sweetheart, that mean demon wore you out."

"I will snap back, I always do, Jenny." Ted pulled her to the front door. "Jenny, the bags have been taken care of. They're all gone."

Jenny shook her head, knowing Ted was aware of the question she was about to ask. "I guess the kitchen is…"

"Clean and spotless, as is the rest of the house." Ted open the driver's side and helped Jenny in, then went around to the passenger side. "You can drive home, Jenny. Please put the top down. I need some fresh air." Ted laid his head against the headrest and shut his eyes. "You can drive up the mountain slowly, my love. I think I need a little nap." Within seconds, Ted fell into a peaceful sleep as Jenny pulled away slowly and made her way home, grateful for God's healing and Ted's safety.

Chapter Forty-One

Jenny and Ted came down the stairs dressed and ready for Miriam's guest, who'd be arriving for supper with the family around 5:30p.m. Miriam was already dressed and waiting for Robert Perkins, in a cute red dress with matching red shoes. Kathy had taken her shopping at the Goodwill Store where they found the dress and shoes, still new, tags attached. Knowing Ted's thoughts on too much make-up, Miriam had asked Kathy to help her with her hair and make-up, keeping it light for Ted's approval. He stopped to admire her fresh new look.

"Miriam, I see you are all ready for your supper date with Robert. You look very pretty tonight, wouldn't you agree, Jenny, darling?"

"You look beautiful Miriam. I hope Robert Perkins works out for you." Jenny did not really trust this outspoken young man, who had even given her a wolf whistle when she walked past his locker one day. "Robert is older than all the other seniors in school. His records state him as twenty-one years old, a little older than Ted and Matthew."

"I guess Robert has a hard time learning, much like our Matthew." Miriam was feeling a little nervous about Robert and Ted meeting. "He likes to cut up and he's really a lot of fun." She walked to the hall mirror to check her reflection. "As for my dress and shoes, Kathy was sweet enough to take me to a discount store in town. She helped me picked this dress out and it was a perfect fit." She twirled around. "I really love it and it makes me feel wonderful. I hope Robert likes it."

"Just be careful with him, Miriam." Ted took her hand and it made her feel special to be the one who had everyone's attention. "You know what I told you about strangers."

"I'll be careful, Teddy." Miriam's heart beat heavy at Ted's touch. He would always be her greatest love. "I really think Robert is alright. I certainly hope so Ted. I really like him, very much."

Ted stared into space for a moment, then walked over to the door and stated "He is coming. The young man is halfway up the mountain road. It would appear, he is going to be right on time. At least, one good trait." His eyes fell on his wife. "Jenny, sweetheart, please have mother set the dining room table for six and see that the children eat around the big table in the kitchen."

"I'll see if mother and Kathy need help arranging the seats." Jenny kissed Ted and walked to the kitchen.

Ted, Jenny, Matthew and Kathy had all gathered in the living room with Miriam when Ted opened the front door and exchanged looks with Robert Perkins, who had just picked up the rope to ring the bell. Robert dropped the rope and looked away quickly, then walk in looking around. Spotting Miriam, he smiled at the beautiful vision and tried to avoid looking toward Ted's glamorous wife, afraid he might involuntarily make a pass at her. Miriam smiled down shyly.

"Rob, you made it, right on time." She took his hand and began making introductions. "I think you know Mrs. Neenam. This is Jenny, Ted very pregnant wife.

Robert tried to force back his laughter as he managed to say "So, I assume you are Ted." He looked from Jenny to the man wearing a religious robe. "And you are having a baby, with this very beautiful woman?"

"Ted and I are having babies, Robert." Jenny reached out to shake his hand and was surprised to find it warm. "We are expecting twin girls."

"Really?" the brazen young man smiled at Ted. "Who would guess?" Robert's attention fell on Kathy. "And who is the lovely lady, Miriam?"

"She is my lovely lady, Robert! Her name is Kathy." Matthew put his arm around Kathy. "Now that you've met everyone, old chap…oh wait, you haven't formally met Ted. You just seem to know him. How's that Perkins?"

Robert looked around nervous, giving a shaky smile. "How could I know him? I guess it's just…the way he dresses…" he swallowed. "Kind of Holy."

"Matthew, stop making Miriam's friend feel unconvertable." Ted walked over to take Jenny's hand. "We don't wish to make you feel unwanted, Robert. I teach my children and youth to beware of strangers. If you have nothing to hide, you have nothing to fear here. We have our supper right at six, Robert, so if you and Miriam would just follow us. Come along Matthew and Kathy, mother is ready to serve us." Like a gentleman, Ted pulled Jenny's chair out for her, then walked to the other end, facing his wife. The two couples, flanked both sides of the long table.

After Hannah brought in the four plates of food in front of each person, then made sure everyone had bread before returning to eat with the children. Robert picked up his fork and started to eat when Miriam reached over and touched his arm, whispering in his ear.

"Rob, we say grace first before we eat."

"Sorry. I guess I'm hungry and this homemade meatloaf smells great!" He gave Miriam a smile, then rolled his eyes over at Ted and watched him bow his head as he folded his hands in front of him.

"May we all bow our head in prayer." Ted spoke softly. "Father, we thank you for all good gifts. For food, for friends and family." Robert glanced up as Ted continued to pray, and yet, at the exact same time sent thoughts to Robert's head. "We know who you are." While aloud he was saying "We owe all to you, Holy Father. Amen," Ted opened his eyes on Robert and they stared for what seemed like a minute, but the young man quickly glanced down at his plate, to escape the love reflecting from this holy man.

Robert looked around at everyone's filled plates, meatloaf, mash potatoes and green beans with corn. He chuckled softly and began eating, talking at the same time.

"I've never had my food already placed on my plate like this. No passing food around this place?"

"Robert, this is a home filled with children. We have to do things a little different, for their sake." Jenny glanced across the table at her husband, who's attention stayed on their rude guest.

"Perkins, I guess you grew up in a big house with servants to bring you each course. From the expensive car you drive, you're not hurting for money." Matthew didn't care for the fellow's attitude and he was certain from the looks he saw, Ted did not trust the creep. "The truth is, you just don't pass heavy bowls of food around the table with a lot of little fingers grabbing for it." Matthew looked over at Kathy and Jenny, then laughed. "Can you imagine Leah and James fighting to pass the same dish?"

"You certainly would hear it!" Miriam laughed along with Matthew. "Leah would loudly proclaim I had the bowl first!"

"Everyone just eat your supper while it's hot. Mother did not get it hot so we could eat it cold!" Ted reached for the big decanter on homemade wine and poured out five glasses then passed two glasses to Miriam and two to Kathy. Miriam thanked Ted, then passed one to Robert.

"I guess we do pass something at our table, Rob." She gave a big smile as she held her glass. "I don't get your wine very often, Teddy. Thanks again."

"You don't get wine, beautiful? Perhaps, I can take you to a fancy restaurant and get you some expensive French wine, if 'Teddy' allows it." Robert noticed Jenny was drinking what looked like, lemonade. He smiled over at her. "What, no wine for the glamourous lady?"

"It's milk, water, or lemonade for me, Robert." Jenny forced a smile as she continued. "I've got to keep these little girls healthy. That's a mother's duty."

"Having a wife as sexy as you are, if you were mine, you would never get to have wine." Robert stared at Jenny's breast. "I'd have a bun in your oven all the time."

"Robert, stop speaking to my wife like that!" Ted pushed his chair back and stood up. "You are in my home and if you want to remain here, you will show some respect!"

"Hey man, I was just fooling around." Robert put his arm around Miriam's shoulder. "I've got my own beautiful girl. I wouldn't dream of wanting yours."

"Please Rob, be careful. Ted is very protective where his wife is concerned." Miriam touched Ted's hand. "He will behave, Teddy. Please, sit back down and enjoy your supper."

They all ate in silenced until Hannah walked in carrying a tray decked with slices of peach cake. Robert watched her pass the plates around and when she sat his down, he looked up and smiled.

"So, you are Ted's mother. You are an excellent cook, Mrs. Neenam." His eyes searched her body as he added. "Have you seen any angels lately, Hannah?"

Ted jumped up and took the tray from his mother's shaky hands. He touched her face gently and spoke softly. "It is alright mother. Go back with the children." Ted watched until she closed the door, then he turned angrily on Robert Perkins. "EAT THAT DESSERT AND IF YOU CAN BEHAVE YOURSELF, YOU MAY VISIT A LITTLE WHILE LONGER WITH MIRIAM IN THE SITTING

PARLOR! THEN GET OUT!" Ted stormed out the dining room, then walked out the front door. Jenny excused herself and followed Ted to the rose garden, where she found him pacing back and forth. Jenny gently reached for his arm and he looked down.

"Ted, what just happened in there?"

"Please Jenny, not now." Ted sat down on the bench and buried his face in his hands. "I do not have all the answers yet. When I do, I will share them with you."

Miriam led Robert to the sitting room and frowned up at him. "Rob, what is the matter with you? First you say those horrible things concerning Jenny, then you come out with this outrageous statement to Ted's mother. I just don't get you!"

"Come on, Miriam, they both were jokes, nothing more! Boy, you people don't have a sense of humor around here!" Robert Perkins shook his head, laughing. "I guess I read you wrong, Miriam. I thought you were into me, sweetheart."

"I do like you Rob. That is the problem! I want Teddy to like you too!" she glanced down, not sure she could win this argument. "Don't you see, I need his approval to date you and the way you're acting, he'll never let me see you again!"

"Holy crap! Does 'Teddy' own you, Miriam?" Robert lifted her head, seriousness showing on his handsome face. "Or do you want to own him?"

"Robert Perkins! Teddy is married!" Miriam walked over to the piano, her place of refuge, and played a few notes as she talked. "I was hoping you and I could have something."

Robert walked up behind her and pulled her into his arms, kissing her passionately. Being caught up in his hot kiss, she didn't resist when he slipped his hand down her dress and caressed her breast. She took a deep breath, suddenly feeling somewhat hot as she managed to ask.

"Rob, what…are you…doing?"

Between his kisses he would whisper, "I'm kissing you, baby. I'm kissing you and feeling those, beautiful, sexy breast. Miriam, I want more of you, my darling. I want all of you, my Miriam." Robert's kisses burned on her lips and she felt something happened deep inside her body. She knew she had to push away before Robert had her down on the sofa.

"Robert, please stop! There are…children here! Teddy is here! I can't…" she pulled away and pushed him back. "Not here Robert!"

"I agree beautiful, this is not the place for romance. That Ted fellow would kill me if he saw me showing you how much I care about you!" His fingers pulled at her nipples, "I need these, baby. I need to kiss them!" Robert kissed her, holding her tight. "Go out with me Miriam. I have my own apartment. Just the two of us, alone."

"Teddy might say no, Rob. You haven't been on your best behavior this evening and he seen very upset when he left the house."

"Then make something up, sweetheart. Lovers do it all the time." Robert ran his hand down her back then rubbed her shapely butt. "I think you need me to too, don't you, baby." He knew he had Miriam turned on. "Or maybe you don't feel the same way I do."

"I do Robert! I have never felt like this before." Miriam grabbed his arm when he turned away. "There was something happening inside me Rob, when you kissed me, when you touch me."

He smiled to himself, then turned around and pulled her in his arms, laying another kiss on her. "Then, we can enjoy one another completely, Miriam, if you come to me." Robert felt her tense up. "Something is bothering you?"

"Ted will know, Rob. Teddy can read my thoughts!" Miriam looked concerned. "He will see right through anything I tell him that's false. I could never lie to him."

"You are right about this guy's mind reading. Listen to me, I am aware of what Ted can do, Miriam. Don't ask him anything, darling. Keep your mind blank when he is around you, then slip out tonight. I will be waiting at the edge of your driveway." Robert Perkins took her in his arms. "Can you do this for us, darling?"

"Yes, Rob. I love you!" Miriam held him close, and could feel him hard against her, a new thing for her.

"I knew you did, darling." He gave her another kiss, then pulled her to the door, hoping to get away before Ted returned. "I'm so damn lucky! Make some excuse to go to bed early, then wait for Ted to take his wife to bed. That should keep him occupied awhile." His face lit up with laughter. "Shit! Ted with a woman in bed! Damn!" he tried to picture them in bed and smiled. "Then, slip out and meet me. I will take you to my place and show you just how much I love you, baby." He gave her a last kiss and slipped out the door, unseen by anyone.

Ted saw that everyone had gone up to bed when he and Jenny finally came back inside. The first thing he had noticed, was Robert Perkin's car was no longer sitting in the driveway, but he had a feeling the boy hadn't gone far. Making sure Miriam was in her bed, Ted took Jenny to their bedroom and closed the door.

Ted lend down to kiss her tenderly, while his hands easily pulled her top over her chestnut hair. Without taking his eyes off of hers, he slid off his robe and out of his briefs. Jenny smiled down at his erection as his fingers ran down her back to undo her bra, then gently rubbed her breast. His tan muscles seem to glimmer when he lifted her in his strong arms and placed her on the unmade bed. With ease, Ted removed the rest of Jenny's clothes and looked down on her with passion. His words flowed from his lips as his hands moved over her body.

"I love you, my dearest Jenny." Ted's kisses burned on her lips as he moved next to her, his hand moving between her legs and began rubbing her, bringing her to total joy. Before she could relax, his hand brought her to fulfillment again and again, until finally, he climbed over on her and started moving. By this time, Jenny found herself having repeating orgasms and she could tell Ted was having one every time she did. If it had not been for the incredible feeling she kept having, she might think she were dreaming.

Then after losing the number of times they came, Ted began moving with madding slowness, as he deliberately held back both their final release for what seen like ten minutes, Ted gave a powerful thrust, sending him and Jenny into the most incredible ecstasy either of them had ever experienced.

They lay exhausted in each other's arms as Jenny whispered breathlessly "Ted, I cannot begin to explain how I am feeling right now! It is as though I have just been living a wonderful, romantic dream! I know I have stated, I cannot see how it can get better, but darling, it just did!" Jenny propped up on her elbow and traced his lips with her fingers. "Sweetheart, you promised me something special and you delivered something spectacular! I lost count at the number of times you brought be to fulfilment, not to mention how many times you went!" she fell back on the bed and stared up.

"I never knew men could go that many times! You are the first!"

"No, Jeff is the first, darling." Ted smiled when she sat up. "He is still the champion when it comes to sex. But I think I did pretty good for a beginner."

"Pretty good?" Jenny gave him a kiss. "I was completely satisfied, darling, again and again."

"And again, twenty times!" Ted laughed when she hit him.

"You knew all this time?"

"I knew! I can feel you even when I am not inside you, Jenny." He closed his eyes, feeling the tiredness taking over.

"I'll let you rest now, hot daddy." Jenny wrapped her arm around him. "Just tell me how many times you went first."

"What do you think, Jenny?" Ted peeked his eye open.

"Well, you caressed me with your fingers through five of mine, so I would say, you went fifteen times!" she laughed softly, then heard Ted's quiet breathing and knew her wonderful husband and lover had fallen asleep.

Jenny snuggled up to him and within minutes was sound asleep, neither one of them realizing that Miriam was about to get herself into trouble.

Chapter Forty-Two

Miriam had waited until everyone had gone to their rooms, knowing that Ted and Jenny had come in late and looked in on her before closing themselves behind their bedroom door. When things grew quiet, she pushed her covers back and climbed from her bed, still dressed in the new dress. Slipping on her shoes, she made her way quietly down the stairs and out the front door, closing it slowly behind her. She had had time to think about what she and Robert was about to do, and Miriam knew she couldn't go through with. Ted had taught her it was wrong to have sex before marriage and she did not want to do anything to upset Teddy.

As soon as Miriam reached the edge of the road, Robert saw her and jumped from his car and pulled her into his arms.

"There's my girl! I was beginning to think you changed your mind about coming with me, darling."

"Rob, I have changed my mind about us going all the way, you know, have sex." Miriam looked down shyly as she reached for his hand. "I'm sorry if I mislead you into thinking I would make love to you Robert. I really, truly, care about you. I just can't go through with this. For me, it's wrong."

"I understand sweetheart, truly." Miriam was surprised by his remark, but grateful. He gave her a gentle hug. "Couldn't we just go to my place and talk? Find out more about one another? I promise I won't force myself on you. I really care about you too."

As he gave her another hug, he smiled to himself behind her back and continued his sweet talk. "I'm new in town and all my family are miles away. I could use a friend. The right friend, you, Miriam."

"I suppose it couldn't hurt for us just to sit and talk a little while." She gave him a beautiful smile, feeling safe with the boy she liked. "If you promise to bring me home in about one hour. I have to get up early for church tomorrow. I play our small organ during our worship service."

"And I know you play it lovely." Robert Perkins helped her in his fancy sports car. "Don't worry, I'll have you back in no time.

I'm sorry I don't feel convertible talking here, but I get the willies being around your Teddy."

"Rob, I know Teddy is different, but if you get to know him, you couldn't help but love him, like the rest of us." Miriam watched the mountain fade behind them as Robert's Corvette swirled around the downhill curves. "Where is your apartment, Robert? Is it very far from here?'

"It's in the Stafford community, just this side of town. It's a five-star complex with three and four, bedroom apartments. Mine is a three bedroom with three baths and my own personal drive-in garage." The young man placed a card inside the private parking slot and drove in to park. "This is home! Pretty great digs, right?"

"A…it looks expensive." Miriam followed him inside a luxury apartment, with high ceilings and lots of marvel. "You have a lovely place here Robert."

"I like it. It took some getting used to the small space after growing up in a 100-room mansion, but I've grown accustom to it now. I'll put on some music and open a bottle of French wine. It's probably the very best wine in the world, although your Teddy makes one hell of a wine." He started for the kitchen, calling over his shoulder, "Have a seat beautiful and I'll be right back for our chat."

Miriam walked over and sat down on a black sofa and looked around at the empty walls. She made a face when the morbid music started playing, but it seemed to fit the room.

Robert poured two full glasses of French wine into black crystal wine glasses and reached inside a cabinet to get a small capsule containing a stimulating sex enhancing drug. He smiled as he emptied the contents into one of the glasses. Robert made his way over to the door and gazed out at Miriam, sating there, so trusting, so innocent. He thought to himself.

"You will be all over me sweetheart before you finish half your wine." Then he stepped back in the room and handed the laced wine to Miriam.

"Here you go sweetheart. Let me know how you like it." he joined her on the sofa and drank down a sip. "How do you like my music? I wrote it for my band."

"You wrote this?" She took a small sip and found it taste wonderful, so she had another bigger sip. "It is a most unusual sound

Rob. Now, at least that explains why did not recognize the music."

"It's new. I just wrote it and recorded it with my group in Salem right before I came here. It's called: The Devil's Virgin, spicy name, wouldn't you agree?" he noticed Miriam tremble and thought it best to change the subject before she caught on to his plan. "Tell me, Miriam, what do you plan to do with your life when you graduate Goldsburg School. Thinking about college?"

"I would love to teach piano lessons. That's a start." Miriam drank down a little more wine and began to feel warm and set her glass down to slow down. "College is out. Ted couldn't afford to send any of us to college so I guess for now, we must rely on our own talents. What about you, Rob? What are your plans?"

"I want to be a scientist, like my father and grandfather." He smiled and took another sip, knowing the drug was starting to work. "I know my grades are low, but I have a job waiting for me back home. A family business that's been active for four generations. I won't need college. Father and grandfather will teach me everything I need to know, and believe me, I already know plenty."

"That sounds very interesting Rob." Her words came slurry as she picked her glass back up for another sip. "What…is the name of this business?"

"The Perkins Institute of Science, located in Salem, Mass." Robert sat down his glass and got up to pretend he was checking the cooling thermometer. "Shit, is it hot in here to you, baby, or am I having a heat flash? I hope you don't mind, but I've got to come out of this shirt now." Robert pulled the black shirt over his head, revealing a tan chest. "Man, does that feel better! What about you Miriam, 'hot'?"

Miriam grew very dizzy and close her eyes, but the room still seemed to be spinning out of control.

"I'm…I'm burning up!" she opened her eyes and could see Robert's naked chest close to her and she could not control her hands when they reached out to touch him.

"Let's take that hot dress off and cool you down." He slowly lifted the red dress over her blonde head and laid her back on the sofa. "isn't that a lot cooler, baby?" Robert moved his hands over her breast as he removed her underwear. Miriam felt her passion swelling within her lower body as Robert placed his hand between her legs and started rubbing her.

Miriam did not understand what was happening, but she could not stop herself and kept repeating "Robert, Robert." Her mind struggled to fight it, pull away, it screamed, but she had lost all control and Miriam knew there was only one thing she could do to get help. She called, just above a whisper. "Ted! Please...please, help me!"

Ted sat straight up in bed and wondered, could he have been dreaming. The echo of Miriam's frantic call came again and he knew Miriam had called out for help.

Jenny had felt Ted jump in bed and sat up, rubbing his arm, after reading panic on his face. "Sweetheart, is anything wrong?" she glanced at the bedside clock, 1:00 a.m. "Did you have a bad dream?"

"I thought at first I awoke from a dream." Ted climbed from the bed and quickly dressed. "Miriam needs me, Jenny. I heard her cry out for help."

"Ted, we saw Miriam asleep in her bed. Are you sure you're not just dreaming about Miriam?" From the hurt expression on her husband's face, Jenny regretted her ridiculous jealousy.

"We saw Miriam in bed, but now I realize she was only pretending to be asleep, so please don't act jealous over nothing. There's no time for that!" Ted reached down and pulled her from bed. "Please put on your robe and come with me."

They walked quickly to Miriam's room and found it empty. Jenny checked out the bed and found the covers thrown back up.

"Ted, you're right, the bed hasn't been slept in!" Jenny looked around worried. "You don't think Robert? Miriam went with Robert?"

"I've got to go!" Ted looked into Jenny's eyes. "Get some rest, sweetheart. I might need you when I get back."

"I doubt if I can sleep, but should I go back to sleep, awake me." Jenny kissed him and saw him to the window. "Ted, be careful. Now, hurry!"

Ted caressed her cheek and disappeared.

Miriam tried to pull herself up, but it was hopeless and Robert Perkins was having his way with her. Just as the brass young man was about to insert himself inside Miriam, Ted yanked him off and threw him across the room. The young man slammed up against one of the marvel walls and lay stunned for a few moments before staring into his attacker's angry eyes.

"How dare you! Take a young innocent virgin and drug her!" Ted shouted, knowing Perkin's apartment was soundproof, another rich luxury, and no innocent dweller need not be woken up. "This girl has not done this of her own free will! You tricked her into believing you really cared for her!"

"So, what, holy freak? I'll take it any way I can!" Robert said with a smirk. "I could have had her in your house, without any drug to help!"

"You are a liar!" Ted pointed to him. "Miriam was weak for a short while, because she is young and she genuinely cares about you! You only used her! Believe my words when I say, SHE WILL HAVE NOTHING TO DO WITH YOU 'EVER' AGAIN!"

"We shall see, Teddy." The fresh young man mocked him. "Poor sweet Miriam loves me, now that she cannot have you."

"If she is in love with you, I will teach her different! Miriam listens to me and she will not ever trust you again!" Ted kept his attention on Robert Perkins as he tried to stand up.

"Tell me, why is it angel brats always think they are better than fallen angel brats?" Robert laughed out. "We are from the same Creator, are we not, Teddy?"

"Your words of tricks will not work on me, now or never!" Ted looked down at Miriam and helped her sat up, his attention never straying from the evil boy.

"Miriam, I will pull your dress over your head, just relax."

"There she is, Teddy! She has been wanting you for a long time and I am sure she is willing to give you herself, her virginity. So, sweet, so naked, and ready to lay. Go ahead, take her! Your Jenny need not ever know!" Robert Perkins smiled.

Ted leaped over the coffee table and picked the startled young man up by his neck. For the first time, Robert Perkins felt real fear from this holy man. Ted got right in Robert Perkins' face and said loudly. "How dare you speak my wife's name! You act out the part of a demon but for some reason, I know I cannot send you back! You have never yet been there! But you can feel my wrath!" Ted slung him across on the other side of the room and this time, Perkins hit his head and lay unconscious.

Miriam had watched as Ted yelled to Robert, then threw him

across the room, leaving him in a pool of blood. The room was spinning as she could see Ted walking back over to her. She still could feel the effects from the strong sex drug as she uncontrollably reached her hand under Ted's robe and between his legs. Within seconds, Ted had grabbed her hands and held them firmly until she calmed down. Then he commenced to putting her dress back on her. Blushing, Ted gathered up Miriam's underwear and shoved them in his robe pocket. He lifted her in his strong arms and his loving eyes met hers. Miriam felt her tears flooding down her face when she finally realized what she had been trying to do. In despair, Miriam covered her eyes, to weep and beg forgiveness.

"Teddy, I am so sorry! I am so very sorry!"

The look in his eyes only reflected his perfect love and not one once of blame. "Miriam, just close your eyes and rest, sweetheart. We're going home."

Feeling his perfect forgiveness, Miriam close her eyes and in a blink, they both vanished from the large room.

Ted gently shook Jenny, who had fallen asleep with a book in her hand. "Jenny, darling, wake up. I need you."

Jenny dropped the book as she sat up and looked around, trying to collect herself. "Did…did you find Miriam? Is she alright?"

"Come and help me, darling. I need you to put Miriam in the shower." Ted led Jenny to Miriam's bedroom and found her stretched out on her bed, still in that red dress. "Robert laced her drink with a date rape drug, then he played with her first and was about to rape her when I stop him." Ted spoke softly.

"She needs to wash that sin off her body and I need you to assist her. Miriam is still very dizzy and could slip in the shower." Ted looked at Jenny as he reached in his pocket and pulled out Miriam's underwear, then placed the bra and panties in Jenny's hand. "I put her dress back on her, but these, I could not."

Jenny reached up and gave him a loving, understanding kiss. "Ted, darling, you are the sweetest and most innocent man I have ever known."

"You really think that?" Ted gazed at her seriously and added "I practically killed Robert Perkins! Is that sweet and innocent, Jenny?"

"But Ted, you cannot kill a demon, remember? They're already dead." Jenny caressed his face. "You said so yourself. But you can send them back. Did good old Robert put up a good fight before you sent him back to his 'master'?"

"Jenny, I never sent Perkins back." Jenny gave Ted a puzzled look, knowing this demon would not give up. "Darling, he has not been to hell yet! Robert Perkins is very much alive!"

Chapter Forty-Three

Jenny tied her hair back for Sunday services and watched Ted brush his fingers through his hair causing it to fall perfectly in place.

"It must be nice to never need a brush or a comb for those handsome locks. Some days it takes me a long time to fix my hair."

Ted laughed softly as he walked over behind Jenny and kissed the top of her head. "You always look beautiful, Jenny, whether your hair is combed or simply tossed over your face. Like it does when we make love."

"You always know the right words to say, Mr. Neenam." Jenny stood and looped her arms around his neck. "You probably think this fat tummy looks beautiful."

"And you don't?" his smile was bright and almost shining. "That's our beautiful girls in there. Of course, it is beautiful!" Ted hugged her. "Every inch of my wonderful wife is beautiful."

"I know I have the most handsome man around!" Jenny pulled his head down for a kiss, then moved over to the chair to put on her low heels. "What do you make of Robert Perkins? I could have sworn he was a demon like the others."

"I thought so too at first, but he is defiantly human. Demons do not bleed nor can they be knocked unconscious." Ted looked out the window. "My guess is that the young man has been raised a devil worshiper. He is lost, even evil. I am afraid the devil has a hard grip on Robert's soul."

"Do you suppose there's any hope for Robert?" Jenny joined Ted by the window and gazed up at the peaceful mountain top. "If there was hope for Jeff Wineworth, surely there's hope for this kid."

"Robert has only known evil all his life, much like Jeff, only not near as powerful as our neighbor." Ted continued to stare up at the mountain. "He pretended to be a fallen angel's son, but Robert is from four generations of mad scientist who devote their time and resources to Lucifer" Ted looked down at Jenny. "Darling, there's always hope for salvation. If a person seeks the truth, they shall find it." Ted walked over and sat down on the edge of the bed, his stare miles away as he said. "It won't be easy for Jeff. It is an uphill challenge for him and it will be for years to come. There will be days when he will struggle to remain good, but that 1% of good can conquer any temptation he encounters. I will not fail him and help him through his many trials."

"I was hoping Jeff was already won over to the right side, especially for Naomi and little Teddy." Jenny joined her husband on the bed. "You don't think he will return to his father, do you?"

"Jeff wants to remain with us, Jenny, but it will be very hard. If he passes this next test, he will be one of us, but he must always be on guard. Lucifer's blood runs through his veins, as it does every child he and Naomi bare." Ted arose and went to the door. "Come, my love, I wish to have a word with Miriam before services. She must be warned."

Miriam jumped when the soft knock came on her door, but soon relaxed at Ted's loving voice, asking if he and Jenny could have a word with her. She opened the door and dropped her swollen eyes on the floor, to hide her tears.

"Oh, Teddy, I am so sorry! I should have never slipped away! I told Robert I did not want to have sex, I told him if we could just talk as friends, then I could go with him for a short while." She looked up, pleadingly. "He…he seemed so convincing. He talked about being lonely, a stranger in a strange town and just needed a friend to talk to. Robert pretended that he cared about me too and said beautiful things to me. I swear, he promised he would not force himself on me, Teddy. There is no way I would have gone with him if I had known what he really wanted!"

"Miriam, it's true, you should not have slipped out of this house. Pretended to be asleep, so we would think you safe, even though I felt Perkins nearby. I trusted you so I let my mind get preoccupied with my wife." Ted reached for Jenny's hand. She knew what time he was referring to, the sexiest night of her entire life. "But Miriam, in your heart, your trusted Robert's words. They know how to deceive you, sweetheart. Please believe me."

"Did…did you send Robert back, Ted?" Miriam wiped her eyes, wishing she did not have feelings for the young man. "He was a demon, wasn't he? One of those strangers you warned us about?"

"No, Miriam. Robert Perkins is as much a human as you are. He is just very evil."

Ted placed his arm around her trembling shoulders until she

relaxed. "Stay away from him Miriam. He cannot be trusted."

Once again, Miriam began crying and through her sniffles, tried to speak. "Oh, Teddy, I think I was falling in love with Robert. Why do I always fall for the men I can never have?"

Jenny walked over and hugged the upset girl. "Miriam, Robert is a very bad person, no fault of his own, really, but nevertheless, he has grown to enjoy his evil ways. But the fact that he is young and alive can shed a ray of hope for this young loss man." Jenny locked eyes with Ted, who stood back to listen what Jenny had to say. "You have learned from Ted, like the rest of us, that 1% of good can win out over 100% of evil, every time, isn't that right, Ted, darling?"

Ted smiled. "Yes, my love, we could bring Robert Perkins around to God's side, if he truly seeks it, but it might depend on Miriam. I will never sacrifice her for him."

"Of course not! Let the devil have him first! She must never be abused by that jerk again!" Jenny said so angrily that Ted and Miriam couldn't help but laugh.

Miriam gave Jenny a real smile of gratitude before turning to Ted. "Teddy, what would I have to do to help save Robert, and stay safe?"

"If I permit you to see Robert again, you must never be alone, have one of your Christian brothers with you at all times." Ted took her hands, knowing Miriam had to forget about anything ever happening between himself and her, and Robert Perkins could be the answer, if he proved he could change. "Miriam, if Robert has just been using you, he will give up and move on to another target. But if he cares for you at all, he will start to show it. That is when love will start to grow in his heart, little by little. It will be a struggle for Robert because the young man has never known love."

"That's so sad. I remember my life before you rescued me and gave me a home, filled with perfect love. I cannot imagine life without love." Miriam wiped her eyes when Jenny handed her a tissue. "If I can help save Robert, I will do my part. I really do care for him, even knowing the horrible things he had done to me. Is that sick? Is that wrong to still care, Teddy?"

"Do you think Naomi would think herself sick or wrong, because she gave her heart to Jeff?" Ted rubbed his hand playfully through her blonde hair.

"Jeff! Jeff Wineworth!" Miriam's eyes lit up. "Jeff changed, and all because of love! If Jeff can be saved, so can Robert!"

Chapter Forty-Four

Monday came and so did another day at school. Miriam was very nervous when she walked inside the History class, Matthew right behind her. He leaned over to whisper in her ear.

"Looks like Robert Perkins hasn't arrived yet. Maybe he gave up and quit."

"That would solve everything, except..." Miriam pulled Matthew down to whisper to him. "I won't have a chance to save him, then."

"You can't win them all, ducks." Matthew patted the girl's arm who sat beside of Miriam. "Excuse me, Jan, would you mind changing seats with me? I have orders to keep a close eye on Miriam for a while. Do you care if we switch?"

"Not at all, Matthew. That will be fine with me." Jan Williams blushed, having a crush on the handsome young man. "Anything you want."

"Thanks Jan, you're a real trooper! Ted will be please." Matthew helped the shy girl move her things to his old seat up front, then sat down next to his Christian sister and started putting his books away.

Robert Perkins walked in. When he walked past Miriam, he slipped her a folded note, gently touching her hand, then moved on to the back of the room. Miriam glanced around to see him looking back seriously.

Matthew straightened up from putting his things away and noticed Miriam had turned around and was watching Robert Perkins.

"Hey kid, what did I miss?" Matthew reached over and turned her around. "You have to tell me doll, I can't read your mind like Ted."

Miriam smiled and showed Matthew the folded note Robert had given her. He nodded for her to open it, then glanced back at Perkins and noticed he was reading or pretending to. Miriam began reading the note.

"Miriam, my darling, Miriam, I was a total jerk Saturday night to treat you like I did. My only excuse is that I really wanted you and I knew I could never wait until you were ready. I realize Ted has taught you not to have sex until after you are married. I also know that you are a virgin and that made me desire you that much more. I cannot explain to you why I am the way I am; the truth might drive you away. I'm pretty sure I have already ruined any chance to be with you again. There is something different about you Miriam. I cannot get you out of my mind, but if there is no hope for us, tell me, my love, and I will suck it up and go back home to Salem. Your Robert."

Miriam stared down at the words and felt tears feeling her eyes as she gazed back at Robert, who was looking back. Only this time, there was real sadness in the young man's eyes. He was asking for another chance and in his way, he was asking her to forgive him. She slowly nodded yes, as she thought,

"Perhaps you can be saved, Robert, and we can find a life together,"

Miss Rayfield arrive in her classroom and instantly noticed Matthew had switched seats again. This time with Jan Williams, in the middle of the class. The flirty teacher hadn't approached Matthew since the small room incident, but she could not resist the opportunity to speak to him, so she walked back to assess the situation.

"Matthew, is there a reason for your changing seats again?"

"Oh, yes ma'am, a very good reason. You see, Miriam is my girlfriend and I cannot leave her side another second. Boys just keep hitting on her, so I'm sticking close by her side." Matthew smiled over at a bewildered Miriam.

The evil teacher stared down at the girl Matthew claimed to love. Her jealousy raging inside her. "Is that true, Miss Christian? Is Matthew Christian your 'boyfriend'?"

Miriam looked up, wide eyed and a little frightened by Rayfield's angry glare. "Well, Matthew is a boy and I am his friend." Miriam gave Matthew a weak smile. "I guess you could say, that makes him my boyfriend. You've got to admit he is one handsome stud! Gosh, Miss Rayfield, what girl wouldn't want Matthew to be her boyfriend. I'm just glad he's mine!"

"Not in my classroom, you, blonde little flirt!" Miss Rayfield spoke up loudly, causing Robert Perkins to walk up the center row and stand behind Matthew and Miriam.

"Miss Rayfield, you are way out of line! Miriam is not a flirty little blonde! These two are friends, just like she said. They are very good friends, almost brother and sister. I think Matthew is sitting here because he is tired of you hitting on him!" Robert and Angela stared at one another coldly as the young man continued, unafraid. "Matthew belongs to someone else and he is very committed to her! As for Miriam, she is a wonderful, warm person, so back off!"

"And I suppose you're going to make me, Robert?" the teacher held her ground.

"You know I can! Don't push me, bitch!" he yelled and the class grew nervous and quiet as Robert Perkins took a step toward the teacher.

She stared backing away and pointed nervously to the back of the room. "Just, sit down Robert!" Rayfield's attention fell on her staring students, eyes wide with fear. "Alright, students, snap out of it! Now turn to page 30 and start reading! There will be a test tomorrow, so concentrate on the words!" she walked up quickly to her desk and sat down, knowing Robert had not moved back as she ordered.

Matthew smiled up, grateful for his intervention. "Thanks Rob. You really stood up for us."

"Sure thing, buddy. I'm starting to get sick and tired of this game." He looked down at Miriam, no more, flirty, mocking eyes, only serious ones. "If we could just have a date again." Robert nodded toward Matthew "You know, double date with old Matthew here and his wife…" he whispered as he winked at the handsome married man. "I just want a second chance to prove I really care about you, Miriam. Just you."

"I will talk to Ted, Robert. Matthew and I can speak to him." Miriam took his hand, glancing up at the teacher. Miss Rayfield had her eyes down on a book. "I can see a change in you Robert. I will show Ted the note you gave me and Matthew and I can tell him what you did for us in the classroom."

"Yes, of course. Please tell Ted." Robert looked down, feeling ashamed. "Tell Ted I am sorry for the things I said about his wife and you. He will understand."

"She will tell him, Rob." Matthew touched his arm. "And I will do what I can, but you had better take you seat before miss flirt decides to look up and find you still standing."

"Do not worry, Rayfield won't look up until I sit down." Robert looked up at the teacher with hate in his eyes. "We had an understanding of the minds, so to say, so, she will do as I wish or she will have hell to pay." The young man walked back and took his seat, his eyes locking with the demon.

Ted was waiting for Matthew and Miriam when they walked in behind Jenny and the other children. "Alright my darlings, you have snacks waiting in the kitchen." With lots of energy and giggles, the group of children dash off toward the kitchen.

Jenny smiled and walked over to give her husband a hug as Ted kissed her tenderly, then pulled her to his side, his attention falling on Matthew and Miriam.

"You know, don't you?" Matthew stared over at him, always amazed. "You know everything that happened in history class."

"Well, I don't know what happened!" Jenny looked at the three puzzled. "Will someone fill me in, please."

"Matthew is referring to Robert Perkins asking Miriam to give him another chance." Ted placed his finger over Jenny's lips before she could respond. "Robert gave her a note admitting he had been a jerk and he was afraid he had messed up any hope for ever winning her back. Not exactly the same words, but close."

"A much shorter version, but the exact statement, Teddy. I guess you also know how Rob stood up for me and Matthew in front of Miss Rayfield, after she was calling me names and wanting to start something with Matthew."

"Robert sounds like a stand-up guy to me." Jenny was suddenly afraid to say much more, by the way Ted had turned to listen to her speaking. "Well, darling, all I'm saying is, I think it shows Robert does care something for Miriam, after all. Right?"

"Yes, Jenny. I think there could be hope for Robert after all and he did admit he was getting sick and tired of this game, referring to, doing the devil's bidding." Ted winked at his wife, then smiled at Miriam. "You may date Robert Perkins again, Miriam, but only if Matthew and Kathy double date. I do not think the young man would open up if Jenny and I double date with you." Ted put his arm around Jenny.

"Besides, my beautiful wife might forget we are playing

chaperons and tempt me to misbehave."

"Ted!" Jenny blushed and hit his arm playfully.

Ted just pulled her in close to him and smiled over at Miriam. "Miriam, you may tell Robert that I forgive him for speaking ill about my love ones." He kissed her on the cheek. "Now, you and Matthew race off for your snack." Ted slapped Matthew on the back. "Your pretty wife is in there helping mother."

"Great! That makes two snacks for me!" Matthew punched Miriam's arm. "Race you to the kitchen!"

Ted and Jenny watched the young friends race off, side by side, then walked over to the sofa and took a seat.

"Ted, darling, would you please explain just one little detail for me about what you just said before sending those two away for snacks."

"You want to know what Robert said to me that needed forgiving." Ted took her hands in his. "Sweetheart, why? It's over. He asked for forgiveness and I gave it. Just let it drop."

"Ted, please tell me. Was it something about me?" Jenny moved in close to him, her beautiful eyes pleading. "Is that when you almost killed Robert?"

"I'm ashamed to say it was. He made me so angry, I could not control myself. But Jenny, at that moment I thought Robert was a demon." Ted grew serious. "Miriam had been given that rape drug, a stimulant to turn on her sex emotions. She was lying on a black sofa, completely naked and that boy tried to tempt me. He stated the fact that Miriam had always wanted me and now was my time to have her. The words he used was, to lay her and she was waiting for me. Then Perkins said, Jenny would never need to know and that's when I grabbed Robert up by the neck and threw him across the room, slamming him up against the hard wall, where he fell unconscious."

"What an absolute horrible thing for him to say! What kind of sick mind would speak such words to you!" Jenny felt bad for insisting Ted remember that terrible night. "I am really sorry, sweetheart. I realize now why you wanted me to drop it. I should never have asked you to tell me."

"I knew you would not give up until I told you, Jenny. Anyway, that's when I realized Robert was a living, breathing person. The second time when he hit his head, Robert immediately blacked out.

Demons just get dazed for a while, like Robert did on my first throw, and Demons do not shed blood. They have none to shed, but blood was coming from Robert's head."

"When will this date be, Ted? Do I need to share any female advice to Miriam? Words of wisdom she might not be familiar with?" Jenny looked serious, new doubts over this date between Miriam and Robert clouding her thoughts.

Ted gave her his beautiful smile, giving her another invasion of butterflies. "That all depends on what sort of advice my wonderful wife is thinking of sharing. If you are referring to what she should wear as not to look like she wants to draw attention to her female charms, by all means, take her shopping. You've certainly learned how to tone down the low-cut tops." Ted smiled when Jenny narrowed her eyes. "You already have your man, darling, and he can see the real Jenny any time he chooses. I don't wish for other men to enjoy what is mine." He winked when she gave him her biggest smile. "There is one more thing you can help Miriam with. How to hold off a man who is trying to seduce you. You may give her your expert advice on that subject." Ted chuckled at Jenny's shocked expression and started to walk away when she grabbed his arm.

"What's wrong Jenny? That is what you were referring too, right darling?"

"Well, yes! You know it was!" Jenny bit her lip and walked over to the window to avoid his stare. "A little good feminine advice never hurts. And you're right, I've had plenty of experience when it comes to the male sex!"

Ted walked over and pulled Jenny tightly in his embrace. "Jenny darling, you must put all those things behind you. The Holy Father and I know everything you did and we have forgiven you, sweetheart. Please Jenny, forgive yourself and put those things out of your mind. You belong to me now." Ted turned her around to lift up her chin. Jenny could see the deep love reflecting from his loving face. The butterflies returned as he spoke softly, just to her.

"My darling Jenny, I love you as I have never loved before. Only my Holy Family come before you. There is no greater love than how I feel for you and I know your heart reflects the same love for me."

"Oh, Ted!" Jenny buried her head in his chest. "Sometimes I

think I must be dreaming, but then I see you, feel you and your wonderful love." She lifted her head and gave him a smile. "The joy of feeling our girls kicking and dancing inside me, so alive and happy. I thank God that I'm very much alive and the love we have is real!"

Ted kissed Jenny tenderly, then let his hand run gently over her stomach. 'My little family of three beautiful girls, all wrapped up in one beautiful body. Now, about your question. It is Friday night." Ted could see by Jenny's confused face that she had already forgot her question she had previously ask. "The date with Miriam and Robert Perkins. Remember?"

"Oh, yes, I did ask when will the date be." Jenny ran her hand through his shag hair. "All your romantic love words drove all that madness from my mind. You said, Friday night, so I guess you have their night all arranged in your head."

"As a matter of fact, I do. Matthew will drive one of our cars and pick up Robert. He and Kathy will go along as escorts where they will dine at a popular restaurant in the heart of Goldsburg. I chose a place where respectable young couples enjoy going. The four can enjoy their meal while they talk and there's a dance floor if the kids feel like dancing. Nothing sexual, touchy, feely, kind of dance moves, just good old fashion slow dancing with an occasional modern dance, the kids…I think the word is 'dig'.

"Wow! And you came up with all of this?" Jenny titled her head, wondering how this holy man knew so much about this restaurant." "All by yourself? Like you just saw it in your head?"

"Not quite, Jenny." Ted smiled.

"Then, I bet Matthew or Kathy must have told you this would be a great place to take Miriam and Robert, right darling?"

"Not even close." Ted chuckled when Jenny sat down, shaking her head in defeat.

"I give up! How do you know all this when you almost never leave this mountain?"

"The newspaper you insisted on ordering to keep up with the local news, since we do not have a television." Ted continued laughing as he sat down beside her and draped his arm around her. "There was a big advertisement on the fifth page, describing everything the restaurant has to offer and the photo was filled with young people on a dance floor, dancing while others simply seem to enjoy each other's company while eating, what looked like steak, fish, and chicken."

"You observed a lot from one photograph, sweetheart." Jenny smiled. "Now, aren't you glad I insisted that you go to school and learn how to read?"

"I admit, it did come in handy." Ted kissed the top of Jenny's head. "When the night is over, Robert will be taken back to his apartment. Then, we can decide whether or not Robert is sincere or just pretending to care for Miriam. Whatever the outcome, I will know what to do." Ted took her hand and walked toward the kitchen "Now, we wait until Friday night. It's up to Robert."

Chapter Forty-Five

Friday was going to prove to be a busy day, Jeff and Naomi had gotten word that Doctor Luther Raven had suddenly went missing and failed to show up for work. The staff at the doctor's office had to re-schedule Naomi's appointment until Doctor Ward could return. Thanks to Jeff, the old doctor's recovery had gone well and he planned to be back in two weeks. Overjoyed by the news, Naomi hung up the phone and looped her arms gratefully around her husband.

"Jeff, my love, you saved another one from the demons. Doctor Ward is returning in two weeks to resume his practice. Creepy Doctor Raven has mysteriously disappeared!"

"Raven knew we were on to him." Jeff smiled, revealing his sharp teeth. "With the good doctor's quick recovery, he knew he had been caught and that I was just biding my time before striking and exposing the demon."

"Jeff, do you believe Raven if still around, planning something else?" Naomi gently touched her stomach. "Will he try to hurt our baby, darling? He killed hundreds of innocent babies while he lived, just for sick pleasure."

"No one will touch our baby, my love. He would be a fool to try." Jeff pulled Naomi closer to him, his love for her showing in his strong caressing arms. "To answer your question concerning his whereabouts, I am afraid the evil fend is still lurking close by, waiting and watching. But rest assured sweet one, if he is near us, I can sense him and Luther Raven is deathly afraid of my power. You, Teddy, and our new one, are safe."

Aunt Kristine and Grandma Bessie, drove up to the white farmhouse on Goldsburg Mountain. Kris stopped the car and looked around sadly.

"Oh, mother, how could this have happened? That horrible man, going behind the whole town's back to steal this beautiful mountain! It rightly belongs to Ted and his family. Cashton has no right!"

"I know dear. It just isn't fair." Bessie O'Donnell gazed from the car window, tears filling her sad eyes. "It's so quiet and peaceful. I hate to be the barer of bad tidings."

"It won't be easy, but we must tell them, mother. With Ted knowing, there could be a miracle to save the place from that…that devil!" The O'Donnell's climbed out and walked to the front door to find Ted waiting, looking down serious.

"This man, Cashton, wants to take our mountain! How much is he asking?" Both women stood staring at his knowledge in already knowing why they were here. "Kristine, how much money is needed to save our mountain?"

Jenny had been listening and walked up next to her husband. "Money? What on earth is going on, Aunt Kris? Grams? Is someone claiming to own this mountain? I thought the town owned this property and voted to give it to Ted and the orphan children?"

"Yes, Jenny dear, that is all true." Bessie touched her granddaughter's face. "The council voted unanimous for Ted to have it. This new banker, William Cashton and his lawyer friend, a Mr. Tucker, found a loophole in the deed and purchased the mountain without anyone knowing or being informed of their plans."

Kris looked sadly at the loving couple. "I'm afraid the town council forgot to change the deed in Ted's name. We approached both Cashton and Tucker and told them they had no right to go behind the town council's back and purchase this property without a meeting with us. They said, the town still owed back taxes on the property and the bank had all rights to buy it. We had voted to remove any property tax from the mountain because of the charity work in helping unwanted children." Kris pulled out a tissue to wipe her nose. "Then these two…not so nice, men, showed us some statute on some unheard article 666, stating, no property can be excused from paying property taxes. Then Mr. Tucker declared, the loss from back taxes had built up to the maximum amount of close to a half of million, the cap for take over."

"That sounds like a lot of hog-wash!" Jenny's eyes grew angry. "How much to buy it back, Aunt Kris?"

"Yes, how much money do they want, Kristine?" Ted's tone stayed the same, calm and relaxed.

"One billion dollars." Her voice came low at first, then she repeated it, still not believing the ridiculous amount. "ONE

BILLION DOLLARS! Can you believe it? And Ted must come up with it in just one week! They said that was a generous amount of time to waste! That poor man will never come up with our asking price! Their exact words! I just cannot believe it!"

"I can!" Jenny stomped her foot. "That devil will stop at nothing! One billion dollars! He knows perfectly well nobody can come up with that kind of money." Jenny stopped and looked up at Ted, the sudden reality of who might have that kind of money filling her mind. Ted knew the second she looked up at him what she was thinking and he put his arm around her.

"Jenny, I know when it's time to ask for help, so yes, we can give George a call. He is our only hope in this matter."

"George? George Pennington? Can he come up with a billion dollars?" Kris looked baffled. "And if he can, would he just part with it?"

"Gladly, Aunt Kris!" Jenny raced over to the phone and dialed Chicago. "There's not a minute to spare!" Jenny held her breath until she heard a familiar voice on the other end.

"Pennington Industry. May I ask who's calling?"

"Holly? Holly Evans?" Jenny inquired, feeling anxious. "It's Jenny Neenam, on Goldsburg Mountain."

"Jenny! How good to hear your voice!" Holly noticed George perk up at the sound of Jenny's name and get up. "Jenny, George is here and wants to speak to you now. Goodbye."

"Jennifer? What's wrong? Are you and Ted alright?" There was genuine concern in his tone.

"George, we have a really big problem on the mountain and you did tell us to call if we ever needed your help." Jenny grew excited, nervous over the situation.

"Jennifer, slow down, sweetheart. You know I will help you and Ted. I'm just glad you reached out to me." His voice stayed calm. "Tell me what you need, how much and how soon, darling?"

"One billion dollars, George! This new banker, Mr. Cashton has given us one week to come up with one billion dollars!" Jenny held her breath and closed her eyes, before saying "George?"

"I've got it down! One billion dollars, in one week." George was smooth, not shaken by the huge amount of money. "Is that all you need Jennifer? Are you absolutely sure?"

"Yes, George, I'm sure." She could hardly believe her ears. "So, you can come up with that much money? That quick?"

George laughed softly. "Jennifer, one billion dollars is a mere drop in the bucket for what we are making. My God has been good to me. The more I give to charity, the more I make. I'm only grateful you called me for help. Ted's mountain is my favorite charity, pretty woman, so I do not expect to be paid back, get it?"

"George, you're the best!" Jenny turned to the three listening and gave, a thumb's up. "When should I go to the post office and collect your unselfish gift?"

"You need not go at all, Jennifer. I will personally bring it on my private jet, which transports my sports car as well. I'll fly into Charlotte then my lawyer and I will drive out to Goldsburg." He handed his note to Holly to contact the bank for him, plus his personal lawyer. "Now listen, tell Ted I will be there first thing Monday morning. You and Ted can meet us in front of the bank at nine sharp, the time I will make an appointment for. Now, don't you worry about anything, Jennifer. I had some deals with a lot of shady people in the past and I've seen it all." George, spoke with confidence. This Cashton and his lawyer can try any trick in the book the average person would not catch. I, on the other hand, can see right through them, same as Ted, this time." George chuckled. "I wouldn't miss this for the world! It's my chance to really help Ted. Tell the family that they can relax. George is on top of it! Ted's mountain will be safe and in the right man's name before Monday is out. And Jennifer, I do not believe Ted's God up there on top of that peaceful mountain, you know, our God, yours and mine too, would never let those devils up on your mountain anyway! But we will get it done legal, fair and square. Goodbye Jennifer. You did good and be sure to thank Ted for allowing me to help him."

"Goodbye, George. You are the best friend ever." Jenny hung up and gave her husband a bright smile. "Ted. I know you already know everything George had to say."

"To keep it short, Monday morning, nine a.m. sharp, in front of the bank. We meet George, along with his lawyer, who will buy back the deed to Goldsburg Mountain, and have it put in my name legally." Ted said calmly, while Kris and Bessie could only stare in amazement.

"That sums it up nicely, darling." Jenny glanced toward her grandmother and aunt and noticed their confused expression as they stared at Ted. "You two are wondering how my intelligent husband knew everything George was saying standing next to you. Don't try to figure it out, it could make you crazy." Jenny took Ted's hand. "George wants you to have legal ownership of this mountain, darling, although he is sure God would not let those demons anywhere near it."

"George is right, my darling. Without my permission, no evil length to Lucifer can set their foot upon this mountain." Ted gave Jenny a warm hug. "In truth, this mountain belongs to God. No man owns it, but to keep humans happy and content, we shall follow the good laws they made."

"So, I gather Mr. Pennington has the one billion dollars to loan you." Kris finally found her voice. "Being the, fine man he is, I am sure he will give you years to pay it back and probably with no interest."

"It isn't a loan, Aunt Kris. George wants to give this money to Ted, and he is doing it with a glad heart." Jenny felt the incredible act of goodness working all around her and she felt so blessed to have a man as special as Ted love her so deeply and with all of his heart.

"And I do love you deeply, Jenny, with all of my heart." Ted smiled down at his wife. "And you are very special to me too, my wonderful sweetheart. You are one of the kind and I am truly blessed to have you in my life."

Bessie O'Donnell walked over between them as she looped an arm around their shoulders. "You two children are perfect for one another! Ted, I am so happy you came into our Jenny's life." "She has made my life complete, Grandmother Bessie." They exchanged hugs and the elderly woman felt his warm love flow through her tired body. "It makes me glad to see you and Kris have regained the color back in your faces after your trying ordeal"

"Thanks to you! I mean…thanks to God's healing touch, we feel a whole lot better! Fit as a fiddle!" Kris smiled sheepishly and gathered her pocketbook and car keys. "It's time we're running along now, I noticed some children playing outside when we drove up, so I figured school must be out today. I know small children can keep one busy, so we will leave you to it."

"School is out today. That's why I'm here enjoying some extra time with my husband." Jenny clung to Ted's arm. "Pease drive careful down the mountain."

"And thank you both for bringing us this news. It had to be done." Ted led the way back to their car and helped them inside. "You ladies should be safe now, but if you find yourself in any danger, just call my name."

"I won't hesitate!" Kristine's attention went on Jenny, remembering how cripple and helpless her dear niece was and how she prayed to the Lord, asking for help, to be able to walk again. Ted heard and came to her. Yes, Jenny's aunt knew she would whisper his name the moment she or her mother felt threatened. Kris put the key in the ignition and switched on the motor. She called from the open window. "If mother or I can be of help, please call us." Both women smiled and waved, then drove away.

Chapter Forty-Six

Matthew, Kathy, and Miriam stood waiting at the door for Ted's last-minute instructions. He and Jenny walked down the steps holding hands and gazing in each other's eyes. Matthew could not resist to comment on the lovey-dovey pair.

"By the looks of it, I assume someone has been having a little bedtime fun." Matthew cried ouch, when Kathy slapped his arm. "Hey, honey lamb, it's true! Why, look at those bedroom eyes and those connecting hands!"

Ted dropped Jenny's hand and walked straight up to the big cut-up. "Tell me, Matthew, are you sure you can handle this job you're supposed to be doing tonight, without getting lost in Kathy's arms?"

Matthew heard Miriam and Kathy giggle and narrowed his eyes at them. "I know when to resist making it with my wife, Ted!" Matthew pulled himself up straight. "I will not let Robert Perkins do anything to hurt Miriam! You can trust me, despite what these two ladies think!"

Kathy walked over and patted her young husband on the arm. "Ted, if Matthew should get weak and fall for my charms, I promise to remain cool and do the job for you!"

"Don't worry, Teddy, I'm in good hands." Miriam smiled with confidence. "Jenny and I had a girl to girl talk and I learn quite a lot about men. I know I am ready to handle this date better, all by myself."

"Yes, I can see that." Ted hugged his wife, then smiled down at the cute blonde. "If any of you see Robert starting to get fresh, just leave and take him home."

"We've got it, Ted." Matthew opened the door and waved the two girls out. "Alright ladies, we're off to test Perkins' intentions!" he waved over his head at Ted. "And you can stop worrying about my performance Ted!" Matthew closed the door, laughing.

Robert Perkins was waiting outside, in front of the apartments, dressed in black pants and a matching shirt. After spotting the white station wagon, he waved and made his way toward the car. Kathy whispered to Matthew.

"I see he is still wearing all black." She was thoughtful for a second before adding. "But then so does Jeff. Black clothes may be all he has with him."

"Clothes don't make the man, Kath. It's what's in your heart." Matthew winked at his pretty wife. "Take your sexy husband for instant, not the best dresser in the world, but I won your heart, beautiful."

"Matthew Christian, you look very sexy in those jeans and pullover you're wearing tonight! Even out in the field watching those sheep in your old dungarees, you look hot!" Kathy smiled and patted his leg. "No wonder that battle ax teacher can't keep her eyes off my man!"

Matthew chuckled, then rolled down his window and returned the young man's wave. "Hi Rob! Hop in the back seat with Miriam. I hope you're as hungry as we are?"

"I'm starved!" Robert gave Miriam a warm smiled and complimented her blue dress. "You look better than chocolate cake, Miriam."

Matthew's attention went to the rearview mirror as he got eye contact with Robert Perkins. "Miriam is not on the dessert menu, old pal!" Matthew noticed Robert was sitting a good arms-length away from his Christian sister and was keeping his hands to himself. Matthew pulled up at the fancy dining spot as Robert looked out. Matthew cut the motor off and said. "Here we are. Ted made reservations here at the Red Lion."

"The Red Lion? I've heard some really good things about this place. I've heard the food is excellent and they have a really terrific band, along with a fancy lighted dance floor." Robert patted Matthew's shoulder. "Can we have a few dances with our girls before we head home, Matt? I love to dance!"

"If we keep it clean, Rob. No sexy moves on Miriam while you're dancing, I guess we can swirl our dates around the floor a few times. Ted said we might like to dance."

Matthew helped his wife with her chair while whispering in her ear. "Kath, Ted pulled me to one side earlier and gave me enough money to get gas for the car, and cash to pay for all four dinners, plus dessert!"

"I heard that, Matt! Nothing doing!" Robert lend in close to Matthew. "This night is on me! I can never make up for my actions toward Miriam, but I insist on paying for everything tonight."

"Robert, that is very sweet of you to offer, but Matthew and I could not possibly let you buy ours." When Kathy gave the young man a smile, she noticed he returned a genuine smile. "You are a student in high school and I am certain your parents must have you on a tight budget."

"Kathy, I do not enjoy bragging anymore, but I am very wealthy and I have an unlimited budget. My family own a big business in Salem, Mass. And they can afford to give me anything I want." Robert looked down, feeling embarrassed over his family's wealth. "Please, I insist on paying. It might make me feel just a little bit better about my past behavior."

Miriam reached over and took his hand. "Then, thank you, Robert. We except your kind offer." She caught Matthew observing her as she continued. "Kindness and forgiveness have to start somewhere, and I believe it's my place to offer it. Wouldn't you agree, Matthew? Kathy?" she waited for them to nod yes, then looked at the boy she cared so much about. "Robert, what you did to me was very wrong, but I can see how much it is hurting you inside, so I forgive you. I'm not giving you a green light to push yourself back on me, but if you really care, we will see it Robert. We will know the truth."

"Oh Miriam, thank you, sweetheart!" Robert Perkins looked down at her soft hand in his. "I promise I will never hurt you again, not ever." He glanced over at Matthew. "Even if it means double dating with this guy many times."

Robert had insisted that his friends order anything on the menu as he ordered a very special wine for the group. Throughout the meal, they made small conversation, things happening at school, how they were faring with their grades, and then Kathy brought up Miss Rayfield hitting on Matthew.

"I've been watching her from day one. I knew she was up to no good, but it all seems pretty funny to me at first. She had been assigned her mission, to win over one of the Christian boys. She had eyes for Matthew right away and her mission became personal to her." He glanced over at Miriam. "Angela could see what I was up to as well, and she very much approved my actions. I could draw attention away from her evil plans by keeping Miriam and the other two Christian brothers distracted." Robert looked down at his plate, ashamed. "It was all going to plan, when something strange happened to me. I started having special feelings for Miriam."

"Love can do that, buddy. It can change everything." Matthew hugged Kathy. "I was content with my single life, flirting with every pretty face I saw. Who would have ever believed Matthew Christian would become a married man so soon? I just couldn't live without Kath, wanting to make love to her all the time and knowing Ted would only permit us to have sex if we were married." Matthew squeezed his wife's hand under the table. "To be honest, I think Ted and Jenny are the only two that actually waited to have sex."

"I admit, I've had many girls, even married women, but I respect Miriam, and I respect Ted, so I will wait on marriage too."

"That is very brave, Robert, but it isn't easy. Matthew and I loved each other so much we couldn't keep our hands off one another." Kathy laid her head over on Matthew's shoulder. "We know Ted knew about our love making before we spoke the wedding vows, but the dear saint did not waste any time making it right."

"So, you think this thing, these feelings I'm having for Miriam is…love?" Robert gazed into her eyes. I've never experienced love before. I wouldn't know what to look for."

"Rob, you cannot see love, it is a wonderful feeling that captures your whole being." Miriam reached for his hand once more. "Rob, I only know I have the same incredible feelings for you." Miriam returned his warm smile. "I can honestly say, the thing I am feeling, is love."

Robert squeezed her hand, his joy busting inside as he asked "Would you have this dance with me, sweetheart? They are playing a slow number and I promise to behave."

"Yes, you will Rob, because Kath and I will join you lovebirds on the dance floor." Matthew hopped up and pulled Kathy to her feet.

The couples stayed on the dance floor for three dances, two slow and one old fashion b-bop. They returned to their table, ordered another bottle of wine and made casual talk until the wine was finished.

Matthew stretched up his arms after checking his watch. "Well, kids, it's time to go. Ted wants us home no later than ten." He pulled Kathy's chair back and helped her up, then notice Robert did the exact same thing for Miriam. "Thanks, Rob, for buying our meal tonight, That, was real swell of you, buddy."

"Yes, Robert, that was a lovely surprise and I'm sure Ted can use the money we saved." Kathy kissed Matthew when he opened the car door for her. "Such a gentleman." She glanced up at the fancy sign with a red lion painted boldly on it. "The Red Lion had very good steak and that wine was excellent. Only Ted's is better."

"And that dance floor was real cool with those disco lights!" Miriam smiled over at Robert when he climbed in next to her. She noticed how ridged he was sitting, as though he were afraid to even touch her. She reached over and took his hand, bringing a smile to his face. Matthew watched through the rearview mirror and found everything innocent.

Robert seemed to relax as he moved over closer and put his arm gently around her. His attention went to Matthew's reflection, just to see him nod an approval, then he settled back in his seat. When they arrived at the apartment, Matthew stopped the car and turned around to face the couple in the back seat.

"Rob, you may give Miriam a kiss to say goodnight. I think you have earned it." He turned around and moved over to hug Kathy, giving the two love birds behind them their privacy.

Robert gently took Miriam in his arms and kissed her tenderly. They both could feel love sweep through them as he gently rubbed her face and whispered.

"Goodnight, darling."

Ted watched Miriam walk quietly up to her room after telling him goodnight. He turned and pulled Matthew to one side.

"Your honest opinion Matthew, let's have it."

"I honestly think there is some hope for Robert Perkins. He was well behaved tonight, extremely polite and generous enough to pick up the tab." Matthew pulled out the money Ted had given him and handed it over. "It's all there except the money it took to fill the car up with gas."

Ted took the money and placed it back inside his jar on the top shelf, then rested his attention on Matthew.

"So, you think Perkins is on the up and up?"

"I certainly think so, unless Robert Perkins is a very good actor." Matthew snaffled a yawn.

"There is hope for Robert, Matthew and when the time is right, I will talk to him and bring him over. Miriam is in love with the young man and it is obvious, love is growing in his heart." Ted patted Matthew on the back. "I am proud of you, Matthew. You showed me, I can trust you to follow through." Ted gave his warm smile. "Now, go on up to your wife. She is waiting for you in bed, waiting for a little bedtime fun."

Ted chuckled when his young friend swallowed his gum and dashed up the steps. Ted switched off the lights as he thought to himself. "Now, a little more bedtime fun and sporting for me and Jenny."

Chapter Forty-Six

The weekend flew by and Monday morning came with the usual routine of the children getting dressed, fed a hardy breakfast then off to school. Kathy had agreed to stand in for Jenny while she and Ted went to the meeting at Goldsburg Bank, nine sharp.

Arriving early, Jenny and Ted waited in the little sportscar directly in front of the town bank. At ten till nine, a black car pulled up and William Cashton and Mr. Tucker arrived and climbed out laughing as they unlocked the front door and entered.

"Go ahead a laugh while you can, you heartless devils!" Jenny narrowed her eyes. "There goes two demons and they look like ordinary crooks!"

Ted couldn't resist a chuckle. "Jenny, you are a delight, darling." His stare fell on the building, as though he could see the demons through the wall. "That's the same Mr. Tucker that put Kathy in a trance." He paused and looked up. "George is drawing near. He will be pulling up at nine o'clock sharp."

"That's George. Right on time!" Jenny watched him pulled up behind her sportscar, glanced at the clock, nine sharp. "Somethings never change."

As Ted helped Jenny out, George and his lawyer, Roland K. Marshall walked up. George Pennington's eyes lit up as he smiled brightly at Jenny's very pregnant stomach.

"Jennifer, look at you! I can see you and Ted have been busy starting a family!" George reached down to kiss her, then turned to receive Ted's outstretched hand. "My congratulations to you both. This baby is bound to be beautiful with such handsome parents."

"Babies, George! We are having two, twin girls," Jenny smiled brightly and took Ted's hand. "This year has been an unusual year, George. Somethings very bad and our starting our family, extremely good. There are times I feel as though I am dreaming this wonderful life with Ted."

"I can assure you, Jennifer Neenam, you are not dreaming" George winked at Ted and pulled the man, standing silently behind him, up next to him. "Ted, this is my personal lawyer, Roland K.

Marshall and we are prepared to take on this banker and his lawyer."

Thank you, Mr. Marshall, for helping us get our mountain back." Ted shook the lawyer's hand. "These two men you are about to meet will stop at nothing to destroy my rights to that mountain."

"Yes, I am aware at what we are up against, Mr. Neenam. George has filled me in on all the possibilities facing us with this case." Mr. Marshall could not take his eyes off Ted's appearance as he fumbled with his words. "You have nothing to worry about. George is the best at what he does and he will see through anything they will throw at us."

"We trust George, sir. He is a good servant." Ted smiled and gave the lawyer a pat on his back. "Please, do not let my appearance bother you. I wear robes because it what I am, who I am."

The man glanced at George, face flushed with embarrassment. "I am truly sorry for staring at you, Mr. Neenam. George did tell me you were different, but in a very good way. I just never dreamed that you would appear so…religious looking. I promise to do my part in retaining your mountain back in your name."

"Thank you again for getting God's mountain back in my name, Roland." Ted held on to Jenny as he walked toward the bank entrance. "They wait inside for us."

George clutched his briefcase as they followed Ted in the bank and up to the chief banker's secretary. She gave them a hopeful smile as she spoke softly.

"You came!" Flora Lewis looked around nervously. "Listen, I hope you get your mountain back from…" she dropped her volume even softer. "Mr. Cashton. He just showed up one day, a complete stranger, and managed to swindle poor old Mr. McBride out of his bank! As soon as he took over, Cashton began changing everything and now he expects you to come up with a billion dollars to buy back your own mountain! How mean can a person get?"

"As long as people like this serve the devil, Flora, their heart is consumed with hate and sin." Ted checked the clock on the wall and punched George's arm.

"Mrs. McBride, thank you for your support. We appreciate the town standing behind the truth. But if you don't mind my dear, we do have an appointment at nine-thirty with this banker and his lawyer. Are they ready for us?"

"I will check sir." She pressed the button on her phone and

heard him pick up. "Mr. Cashton, the party you are expecting is here, sir."

"Very good, Mrs. McBride, please show them in." Mr. Cashton said with confidence.

George gave the secretary one of his winning smiles as he followed her and motioned the others to follow, whispering "Let me do the talking. I know Jenny has a hard time holding back when it comes to someone hurting her loved one."

"I will try to remain calm, George. That is all I can promise." Jenny squeezed Ted's hand when they entered and the two demons rose and nodded her way, then turned to stare at the well-dressed man with blonde hair and movie star looks.

"I take it you must be Mr. Neenam's lawyer." Mr. Cashton motioned to the chairs before sitting back down. "Well, the papers are all legal, so, if your client hasn't got one billion dollars today to pay off this depth, he will lose the mountain."

"Mr. Cashton, I am George Pennington. I am not a lawyer, but a very good friend to the Neenams. But Mr. Marshall is my personal lawyer, and we have come to collect that deed sir."

"Of course, Mr. Pennington. As long as I see the check for one billion dollars." He faked a smile. "That is the deal sir, take it or leave it."

"Oh, we are going to take it, Mr. Cashton." George unzipped his leather briefcase and pulled out a cashier's check for the full amount. "Before I hand over this check, I will need a copy of the document and have the deed, signed over to Ted Neenam."

"Not so fast, Mr. Pennington! Are you telling us you have that kind of money just lying around?" he sneered.

"You are a big shot banker, Mr. Cashton, and yet, you must not read the business news. If you did, you would be aware of my financial success. I own a very large company in Chicago and our net worth was billions last year and Goldsburg Mountain just happens to be one of my favorite causes." George remained cool and calm. "Like I said before, Ted and Jenny Neenam are my dear friends and I was only glad I could help right a wrong when they ask for my help."

"I guess we are a little rusty about other business' success, Mr. Pennington." Mr. Cashton looked toward the evil lawyer. "Mr. Tucker, perhaps you have heard of the Pennington business in Chicago?"

"The mind doesn't recall any business with the Pennington name attached, I'm afraid." Mr. Tucker stammered. "Although your name seems very familiar. I'm sure I have heard it someplace before."

Ted watched the demons closely. He knew the reason they had never heard of George Pennington or his company, was because they had come straight from hell, where they had been for some eighty years. George had not been born when these men lived and reign in terror. Cashton, a shady businessman, who would cheat his clients out of everything they owned which led them to commit suicide. The crafty lawyer would convince their clients to sign over all their holdings to him, then cleverly murder them, no one being the wiser.

Ted was also aware as to how Tucker was familiar with George's name. Because, before God saved him, George Pennington was bound for hell, just like them. Both demons avoided looking in Ted's direction, because Satan had warned them about Ted's power over them. Ted could feel their great fear of him, but held his tongue until George finished speaking.

Both demons sensed Ted's power growing in their mist and it caused Mr. Cashton's voice to tremble as he focused his attention on the blonde-headed man with the check.

"This check must be checked out to be sure it is legitimate. That amount is far too great to take a man's word for it." The banker kept his eyes on George, who didn't show any signs of worry, but remained completely cool and calm.

"We thought you might question the check, Mr. Cashton, so I took the liberty to have my bank draw up legal papers, stating my great holdings in Chicago Bank and Trust. I am pleased to tell you, I also have signed letters, one from the mayor of Chicago, one from the governor of our find state, Illinois." George never got upset when he was doing business. He was great at what he did best! Make deals! "Mr. Marshall, would you give Mr. Cashton his copies of my outstanding ratings from my state leaders. If these names aren't enough proof of my good citizenship, I also have a written letter from the president."

"President? Do you mean?" Mr. Tucker looked shocked when he took the first two letters from Pennington's private lawyer.

"Yes gentlemen, the president of the United States." George sat back smiling at their gloomy expressions. "If you need more signatures, I can contact every state in the union and have each governor to send me a personal letter. My company does business with every single state and we all have a great relationship. I have built new plants in many of the towns, giving employment to thousands."

"It would appear you have everyone important, backing your good name, Mr. Pennington." Sweating profusely, the banker had stuttered with his words.

"All but the devil himself!" George's eyebrow arched up. "I prefer never to have that evil soul's approval."

Jenny couldn't resist laughing, but quickly looked down nervously when both demons rolled their eyes her way. Ted caressed her hand, then stood up and walked in front of the desk. Rolland Marshall sat up nervously, then looked over at George frightened.

"What's he doing?"

Ted held out his hand for the deed, opening it for them to sign, pointing down to the appropriate line. The demon's hand moved uncontrollable as he signed Ted's name on the line. Staring at the legal paper, the deed moved across the desk as if by an invisible hand, and landed into Ted's. Ted passed the deed to George in exchange for the check, then laid it on the desk.

"You win this time, special one!" Tucker sneered. "Who knew you would have a rich friend!" The evil lawyer turned his attention on Jenny as a wicked smile fell on his lips. "Yes, I can almost feel it!"

"YOU SIR, GET BACK TO HELL WHERE YOU BELONG, ALONG WITH YOUR EVIL FRIEND!" Ted's eyes flashed with anger. "Dare you rape my wife with your evil lustful eyes!" As Ted's anger grew, so did his power and the room began to shake as he shouted "LEAVE ME NOW, BOTH OF YOU!"

Instantly, the demons fell to the floor and started crawling across the room, much like snakes, and fell between a large smoking crack in the wooden floor. They let out an eyrie cry before the floor closed back in on them, bringing complete silence.

Jenny touched Ted's shoulder gently. He turned and gathered her into his arms as he spoke softly "It's over here, darling. Two more have been sent back."

Roland K. Marshall had grown white, shocked by what he had just witnessed. He nervously tapped his client on his back. "George? George? Did this man just say to that lawyer, he was raping his wife with…his eyes? And, where did they go? Why were they slinking across the floor like reptiles?"

"Roland, just relax. I will try to explain everything later." George looped his arm over his lawyer's trembling shoulders. "Just believe it when I say, Ted just did the world a favor by sending those lost souls back where they came from." George walked over to Ted and held out the deed. "Ted, here is your deed to Goldsburg Mountain. In man's eyes, it's legally yours now, lock stock and barrel."

"And here is your check, George. Those evil beings won't have no use for it down there." Ted smiled and laid the check in George's hand.

"Ted, may I give this check to the town of Goldsburg? I feel it might come in good use with all these demons running around." There was sincerity in their rich friend's voice. "It is what I want to do, Ted. Please."

"I am sure the town will put your donation to very good use, George." Ted shook hands with George, then turned to the shaken lawyer. "Roland, thank you for doing your part in making everything legal, in the laws of man." Ted's warm smile and touch made the nervous lawyer feel the warmth of love flow inside his body, causing him to relax and take a breath of relief. "May the peace, and love of God continue to flow in you, Roland as you seek to know the truth."

Rolland Marshall felt like a new man. He did not understand what had just happened inside that office to those bad men, but he knew justice had been served. Not man's justice, but the justice of the Almighty God's, and it felt good, special, that he should be a witness to it.

Out in the lobby, three tellers waited on what few customers they had in line, and the secretary looked up when the small group stopped in front of her. George gave her his handsome smile as he laid the check on her desk.

Mrs. McBride, please have this check deposited in the Town of Goldsburg's account and inform them that it is a donation in honor of my very good friends, Ted and Jennifer Neenam, in the amount of one billion dollars, by George Pennington."

"What about…" the secretary nodded toward the head banker's office "Mr. Cashton?"

"You may relax, dear. It would appear Mr. Cashton and his lawyer have been called away and won't be returning to your fair town. So, please contact the old banker and tell him he may have his bank back." George patted her confused head. "Good day, my dear." Mrs. McBride watched the group walked from the bank before jumping from her chair and shouting the good new to all the unhappy tellers. There would be a celebration in the bank after hours.

Outside in the bright sunlight, Jenny hugged her old enemy. "Thank you, George, you were more than ready to take down those swindlers." She gave him a skeptical glance. "George, did you really have a letter of indorsement from the president?"

"Just a bluff, you, clever girl!" George laughed, returning her hug. "Not that I couldn't have gotten the president to write me a letter of indorsement, or every governor in our great nation. I took a gamble and won, with your husband's help."

"I am sure anyone of importance would be honored to help you, my friend." Ted placed his hands, on George's shoulders. "You've come a long way, George. You have made Heaven happy."

"That's good to here, Ted. I am trying to build my treasures in Heaven now instead of collection for myself a lot of worthless rich items I use to want and nothing I needed." George looked over at Mr. Marshall and found him smiling at him. "I can see my big change has please you too, Roland. Thank you for your assistance. Sometimes, just the presence of a lawyer gets the opponent worried." He patted his lawyer's back. "I guess I should have given you a heads up on what might happen in that meeting."

"Sometimes, you have to see things before you can believe things like that can actually happen." Ted smiled. "We wished you could stay with us a while before heading back to Chicago, George. We still have plenty of demons to fight before we are out of the woods."

"I will stay if I can be of some kind of financial assistance." George smiled down at Jenny's very pregnant stomach. "I'm good at solving business problems Ted, but fighting demons is a little out of my territory. I guess I'll leave that up to you and Jeff Wineworth."

"We would never ask you to help us fight the demons, my friend. We just enjoy your company and friendship." Ted watched as George smiled down at their girls. "Jenny is due in a few months and I would prefer Satan and his demons was gone from our town when our babies arrive."

"Thank you for the invitation to visit, but this is a busy time for you, my friend, fighting these devils and worried about these precious baby girls. I will plan a visit after all this activity is over, but if you need me for anything, please call." George opened his car door. "And thank you both, for letting me help you this time. It felt real, good!" he climbed in, Mr. Marshall getting in the passenger seat. "Holly sends her love and hopes she and Danny can come home to Goldsburg in June so Ted can marry them. Those were her words."

"Tell Holly, I would love to perform the wedding ceremony for her and Danny." Ted put his arm lovingly around his wife. "I am sure Jenny can plan a lovely party for them, to celebrate."

"Jennifer is very good at planning parties. Parties have always been her thing. Nothing too big, nothing too elaborate!" George once again, smiled down at her round belly. "Well, at least, it used to be her thing!"

"Habits change, George. I'm much happier being Ted's wife and the mother of our two little angels." Jenny reached up and kissed her husband. "But I can still plan a wonderful party. It will be good to see Holly and finally meet her Danny."

"Sounds great! I will fly all of us in and the wedding party is on me, Jennifer, so go crazy!" George finally shut his door and put his window down. "We're off to Chicago! Take care." All waved farewell.

Chapter Forty-Eight

Matthew and Miriam carried their bag lunches to a table in the far corner of the school cafeteria. They noticed Robert Perkins waving to them from the short line and he ask if they wanted milk. Matthew nodded as he pulled out their milk money, then smiled down at his blonde headed sister.

"I see you invited Rob to join us for lunch."

"I didn't think you would mind, Matthew." She looked up hopeful. "I knew you would be with me, so I didn't want him to think we were ignoring him already."

"Don't sweat it ducks! I'm cool with it!" Matthew smiled up at Robert when he walked over. "Slide in on the other side of Miriam and here's our milk money. I will not take no, Rob. We are not a charity here."

"Sure thing, Matt." Robert handed him and Miriam the milk before sliding the coins in his pocket. He smiled as he sat down beside the pretty shy blonde. "As always, you look beautiful today, Miriam. I love you in that yellow dress."

"That's sweet, Robert." Miriam pulled out her sandwich and took a bite, then asked between bites. "Hey fellows, have you written your reports yet on our founding fathers? Mrs. Rayfield said it was due Friday."

"Did you have to mention that report, Miriam!" Matthew finished his sandwich and washed down his milk. "I can't seem to find the time to get started on it, much less, finish it on time."

"I've got an ideal, brother. Maybe if you slept with one of your old roommates for a couple of nights, you could find the time to write it, without distractions."

"Miriam might have something there, Matt." Robert smiled over at the frowning young man. "Being alone in that bedroom, with your beautiful Kathy, has to be tempting. My paper is almost finished, but I know if Miriam was staying in the same room, next to me, I couldn't think of a single word to write."

"I get your point! I know I cannot keep my hands of my wife, so I'll just have to get her to help me with this stupid paper."

Matthew faked a smile. "I have got to graduate this year or I will be an old man when I leave school, walking with a cane!"

Miriam and Robert were laughing when the principal, Mr. Morgan, walked up to their table and stopped in front of Robert.

"Robert Perkins! Your father has called and ask me to inform you that he and your grandfather Perkins are on their way to Goldsburg. This is not a family reunion, young man! Your family are very concerned about you! They have had reports that you might require a little parental guidance pertaining to your recent behavior."

"Thank you for letting me know, Mr. Morgan, but I'd rather not see either one of them, sir. I think I know what they want and the meaning behind their visit." Robert stared up at the principal, unblinking. "When are they arriving, sir?"

"Any day now, Robert. We can see you are not acting like yourself." Morgan's attention fell on Miriam, who had been watching and listening carefully to the unusual conversation. "We think 'something' is distracting you from your…lessons." A creepy smile covered his face when he moved in close to the young man. "Remember son, we all have a job to do here and the one at the top is not pleased by your actions. It's not good to make someone, so powerful, angry with you, Robert Perkins!"

"The one at 'the top'? Robert laughed out, obviously not shaken by this man's threats. "A play with words, Morgan?"

"I am sure your father, Professor Perkins can turn you back around, young man!" Morgan looked down a Matthew and Miriam. "Perhaps, a change of friends!"

"You gave me your message, Morgan! You may leave!" Robert's gaze burned on the smart talking Principal. "Goodbye, sir!"

The principal laughed and walked away as Matthew stood up and picked up his folded brown bag, then stared down a Miriam's boyfriend.

"What the heck just happened there, Rob? That man was threating you, man."

"I've got to get lost! I cannot let my father find me!" Robert looked down sadly into Miriam's eyes. "They know about us. They know that I am in love with you, Miriam."

"Oh Robert!" Miriam looked at Matthew for help. "Ted can

hide him, can't he, Matthew? Nothing evil can come on Goldsburg Mountain unless Ted allows it."

"You know what I am?" Robert looked surprised.

"Rob, I think you must realize by now, there is something different about Ted. You had an experience with him, I recall. A small man of statue, but the power of Samson." Matthew got down between Robert and Miriam. "I think it's time Ted had that little talk with you, Robert. By what I heard, it looks like your family is trying to pull you back to the dark side."

"Is that what you want, Robert?" Miriam reached for his hand. "Do you want your family to rescue you from me and resume your mission?"

Robert gathered both of her hands in his as his eyes brimmed with tears. "Miriam, sweetheart, I was dead inside until I met you. I do not want to lose what we have just found." He looked around nervously. "I'll talk to Ted. I cannot let my father get to me."

"You must come home with us today, Rob. It's not safe for you to go back to your apartment." Matthew checked his watch. "One more class to go, then meet us in the parking lot."

"I need my clothes and a few personal things." Robert followed Matthew and Miriam down the hall. "Can we swing by the apartment so I can grab a few things. It won't take long."

"I will have a car filled with kids, Rob, so if there is any sign of your father, I'll keep driving, got it?" Matthew placed a brotherly hand on his shoulder. "If everything looks clear, then get your things fast and get out of there!"

"I understand." Robert smiled with relief. "See you after school." The three went their separate ways.

Matthew met Jenny in the parking lot after school as the home kids ran down the sidewalk toward the white station wagons.

"Jenny, Robert has to come home with us. His evil family are out to pull him back to evil."

"Do you think you should ask Ted first about bringing this boy up to our home?" Jenny waved at the excited children as she placed her books and bag in the trunk, making room for all the backpacks the kids were wearing.

"Jenny, the time doesn't allow my asking permission to bring him. Robert loves Miriam, that's plain to see. The girl finally has her own boyfriend to wrap her thoughts around, so finally she can stop secretly dreaming about a life with 'your' Ted." Matthew whispered in her ear. "His family thinks the devil himself is aware of this new love between Robert and Miriam and they are joining forces to win him back." Matthew nodded his head toward the loving couple walking their way. "Jenny, Ted is Robert's only hope."

"Alright Matthew, I think you are right about getting Robert to safety. He will be safe on the mountain with us." Jenny smiled at Robert and Miriam. "Robert, Matthew has filled me in on your situation and I am sure my husband will understand what we are doing. The fact is, I'm sure Ted already knows everything."

"I am very grateful, Mrs. Neenam. Your family could have well saved my life." Robert spoke softly.

"Jenny, if you will take the smaller children and go directly home, we will be coming just as soon as we collect Robert's things." Matthew read the concern in her eyes. "Jenny, I promise, if there is any sign of danger, I won't stop this car and come directly home. I will never risk the lives of my family over a few clothes and things. I'll loan Robert some of my clothes first."

"Alright Matthew, as long as you don't put those children in any kind of danger." Jenny climbed in and started the motor. "And leave that place as soon as you can!"

"Not to worry ducks!" Matthew smiled. "Tell my beautiful wife, I'll be home soon and she will need to help me with my school paper due Friday."

"Just be careful, Matthew. Ted is counting on us to watch these innocent children." Jenny checked to see that each child was safely in their seat, waved and drove away.

When they drove up to Robert's apartment, all seem quiet, no sign of Robert's family. Matthew looked over at Robert seriously.

"Rob, get in there and grab what you need, then get back out here!"

"Please don't leave me! I'll get back soon, I promise!" Robert kissed Miriam on the cheek, then ran inside the building.

He had been inside for about five minutes when a long black car pulled up with two sour face men inside. Miriam grabbed Matthew's arm.

"Oh Lord! Matthew, it's got to be Robert's father and grandfather! We can't leave him!"

"Miriam, I cannot risk these children for Robert Perkins!" he glanced over and saw her tears and anguish. "Listen, I'll wait for five more minutes. If he can make it out without his family seeing him, then he will be safe."

"Thank you, Matthew." Miriam gave him a hug. "Those men didn't notice us parked over here, so maybe they won't be watching for us to leave with him."

Matthew watched the time closely as the minutes ticked off. After five minutes, he started the motor. He looked over to find Miriam weeping in her hands, then he caught the sight of movement around the back of the building. Robert was slipping around the back of his apartment, carrying his suitcase. Matthew slowed down, giving time for Robert to jump in. He immediately saw Miriam crying and pulled her in his arms, hugging her tenderly. She looked up into his warm eyes as he said.

"Miriam, sweetheart, I'm here! I'm safe!"

She clung to him as she whimpered "Robert! You made it! You made it out! I thought they had caught you! I've never been that scared before!"

"I thought I heard a car pull up and stop, so I stopped to listen. I heard the front door open and knew they were coming in, probably to wait for me to get home from school, since my car was not parked outside. I quickly shut my bag quietly and slipped out the back door, then took off." Robert took a deep breath. "I was afraid you would be gone after seeing them drive up."

"I waited an extra five minutes for you, Rob. Miriam convinced me to wait and since they never caught sight of us, I felt a while longer wouldn't hurt." Matthew turned the station wagon on Mountain Road. "A couple more miles and we will be safe on Goldsburg Mountain."

Chapter Forty-Nine

Ted was waiting for Jenny when she pulled up at the farmhouse. He helped the children out, never taking his eyes off his wife. "Alright kids, wash those hands, snacks are waiting in the kitchen." He patted Leah's head. "Listen to Hannah."

"WE WILL!" Leah looked up at him sheepishly. "I'll use my quiet voice." She frowned at the other children for laughing and they raced off to the house as Ted helped Jenny out.

"You're tired, my darling. The pressures of watching out for demons, being responsible for all these children, the twins growing inside you and now, Robert Perkins, coming here for refuge."

"Oh Ted, the poor boy was so scared of what his father and grandfather would do to him for falling in love with Miriam." Jenny held tight to Ted's hand as he walked her up the steps to the front door. "Poor Miriam is beside herself with worry. She really loves Robert and from what I saw, Robert loves her too."

"It's alright, Jenny, bringing Robert up here on the mountain." His attention went to the door. "Kathy is on her way out. She is worried about Matthew."

No sooner had Ted said those words, Kathy stormed out the door. Jenny gazed up at her husband in amazement and felt her friend grab her.

"Jenny, what's going on? Just the youngest kids came in to have their afterschool snack! Leah informed me Matthew was in danger! Something about taking Robert by to get his things before his mean father shows up!"

"Kathy, you can relax." Ted placed a hand on her shoulder and she grew calm. "As we speak, Matthew is headed up Mountain Road and he should be coming around that curve…now."

Before Kathy could respond, she heard tires coming on the gravel road as Matthew pulled up and stopped. Without a word to each other, Jenny and Kathy shrugged their shoulders, both turning to gaze at Ted in disbelief.

Matthew barely got the car stopped, when he dived out and raced over to Ted. "I guess Jenny filled you in on the reason I'm late and carrying the older children instead of the little elves?"

"Matthew, I did not have to explain anything to my darling husband. He already knew before I arrived. He was out here waiting for me." Jenny laughed softly at Matthew's expression. "You can relax, Ted thinks we did the right thing."

"What am I thinking? Of course, Ted would know. He probably knew before it happened." Matthew bit his lip, regretting his last words when Ted frown at him. "Ted, you know me and my big mouth! I keep sticking my foot in it!" Matthew turned to his wife to avoid Ted's stare. "Well, at least Kathy loves my big mouth, right doll?"

"You bet babe!" Kathy pulled his head down to kiss him. "Just no more risky stunts, got it? The bad people can be dangerous to your health!" she turned to see Miriam and Robert standing there, listening to her ravings. "Sorry kid! No reflection intended on you, Robert."

"Well Kathy, it is, or I should say, it was, I'm afraid to admit." Robert held tight to his bag, not exactly knowing what to expect from the religious man with the incredible powers. "My father and grandfather are the vilest, and they will stop at nothing to get me back into Satan's corner."

"No one will be getting you back in Satan's corner, son, if you choose not to be there." Ted took his suitcase. "Miriam can take you to the kitchen for an afterschool snack, while I put your things away. Then tomorrow, you and I can have that little talk."

As the others went to the kitchen, Ted helped Jenny up to their bedroom, where he insisted she take a well needed nap before supper. As he laid her gently down and removed her clothes, she kept insisting she wasn't tired. After pulling the cool cotton sheet over her, he sat down and took her hand.

"Jenny, stop fighting me darling. You're tire, I can feel it. Now, close your eyes and relax. I'll wake you in time for supper." He bent down and kissed her slowly and lovingly. She let out a sigh and when Ted rose up, Jenny was sound asleep. "Rest, my love. I will return later." Ted slipped quietly from the room and carried Robert's bag to the room he would share with Philip.

Jenny slowly opened her eyes and focused in on Ted, sitting on the side of their bed, gently rubbing her belly. In his other hand he held his old worn Bible and was reading from its pages. Jenny smiled as she observed him, thinking how extremely lucky she was to have such a special man love her. Without looking up, Ted spoke softly.

"I am the lucky one, dearest Jenny."

Jenny rolled her eyes up toward the ceiling then pushed back her sheet. "Ted Neenam, how long did I nap? Ten, fifteen minutes?"

Ted got up laughing and help her out of bed. "You napped for two hours, my love, so now you need to hop in the shower, dress, and be ready to go down for supper."

"Two hours? You have got to be kidding!" Jenny picked up her watch. "Shit! You are right! Have you been sitting there watching the fat lady sleep for two long hours?"

"Jenny, first, you are not fat! You are pregnant! Second, I have not been sitting around watching you sleep. I helped move the sheep to the east pasture, picked vegetables and took my shower, all before waking you up."

"Very well darling, you were right. I guess I was tired!" she jumped up, feeling renewed and danced to the shower. "Give me ten minutes, and I'll be right out. I'd tell you to lay me out something to wear, but I know it's already out and waiting in your arms."

Ted looked down at the blue dress hanging over his arms and shook his head as he whispered, "Everyone around here tries to be funny at my expense." He glanced up when he heard the hair dryer switch off and Jenny came out and slipped into the dress.

"And Ted darling, I am not trying to be funny at your expense!" she patted his surprised face. "What? You don't think I can read minds too?"

"Jenny, I..." Ted was lost for words, then he saw Jeff Wineworth walking from the bathroom laughing.

"That's alright, friend. You can relax, Your, little wife hadn't learned how to read minds. I told Jenny what you were thinking, just as a joke. And I wasn't in your bathroom looking at your sexy wife's very pregnant body. I merely felt the tension between you two love birds and decided to drop in to help. I read it can happen at this time in the pregnancy cycle. The time when sex is limited."

"Nice speech Jeff, but the real reason you're here is because I call you." Ted watched his neighbor closely. "You know my bedroom is private, Jeff, and everyone is forbidden to ender unless I want them here."

"Oh yes, I know!" Jeff smiled and looked around. "All I see is an ordinary bedroom with a bed, just right for lovers." Jeff chuckled at Ted's serious face. "Lighten up, Ted. You can visit our bedroom anytime, except, of course, when Naomi and I are making love. I knew I was safe in coming here this afternoon, with Jenny being so tired and worn out."

"Ted. Sweetheart, this is really quite innocent. Jeff appeared after I had put my bathrobe on. He told me what you were thinking, so I wanted to be special, just once." Jenny smiled through the mirror as she brushed her hair.

"Jenny, my true love, you are very special, all on your on." Ted lend down and kissed her. "Finish getting ready. Jeff and I will be waiting in the hall."

Ted opened the door and waited for his visitor to walked out into the hall, then he followed, closing the door behind them. After speaking to Jeff about his plan to solve Robert's problems, Jeff agreed and disappeared.

Everyone had finished eating before Ted stood up to speak. "Now, children and young people, please listen to my words carefully. Do not get relaxed in school, thinking all the bad people have left our town. They are very much alive and dwelling among us, waiting, hoping we have grown relaxed and think them gone. Then, without warning, they will strike!

When something happens at school, different from your everyday studying and playground playing, search out Jenny, Matthew, or one of your other high school brothers. Stay close to them and you will be safe. Tomorrow is Friday and everyone but Robert will return to school. Robert will stay with me and we will work his problem out, Are there any questions, dearest ones?"

Matthew lend across the table to ask "How will you handle Robert's family? They will stop at nothing to get him back!"

"There is where you are wrong, Matthew!" Ted looked serious as his stare burned on his young friend. "There is one that can easily solve this problem. He has offered his help and I have excepted his plan." Ted's expression changed quickly to his warm smile, feeling the fear that swept through all the children. He laid his hands on the table and looked with love on each face. "My dears, there is nothing to be afraid of. God is always watching over us. Remember what I taught you?"

All the sweet voices, along with the older teens, joined in unison. "One percent of good can always win over one hundred percent of evil!"

"Now, God's peace be with you, little ones, fare youth. Go up now and do your lessons, then cut your lights out at eight, right after your prayers. May you fall into a restful sleep and may your dreams be those of happy things."

Each child got up and hugged Ted, then walked quietly to their room. Ted motioned for the youth to go on up, before he and Jenny ascended the stairs. When Ted closed the door to their bedroom, Jenny ask

"Jeff is the one to help Robert with his family, right?"

Ted smiled and kissed her cheek.

"Yes, my beloved, and I am the one to help Robert find salvation and love."

"Then I know Robert will be in good hands. Jeff, the right man to scare that evil father and grandfather off for good, and you, my darling, to bring the lost sheep home to his Lord."

"You know I could not love you more than I already do, my precious wife." Ted pulled her in his arms and she found their clothes had vanished.

"I'll not ask how you did that, but I will simply enjoy what's to follow!" Jenny looped her arms around his neck. "And I love you too, second only to God!"

Chapter Fifty

The white station wagon drove out of sight as Robert and Ted stood silently watching them. Ted kept his eyes on Jenny until she rounded the curve, out of sight. Robert had been observing him closely and could see the depth of love this man had for his wife and he knew why he was so protective when it came to her.

"It must be wonderful to have such love." Robert spoke softly. "Yours and Jenny's."

"You can know love too, Robert. It has always lived inside your heart and soul." Ted's eyes found Robert's "I think you have already felt it, with Miriam." He placed his arm around the confused young man's shoulder and he instantly felt a peaceful warmth speed through his whole body.

"How can I find this…perfect love, Ted?" Robert asked sincerely. "I will do anything to have just a small part of what you have, then I would have found the perfect love for me."

"It is not hard to find love, son. You only have to believe." Ted started walking toward the mountain trail, Robert following close behind. "First, you must tell me why you really came to Goldsburg? Anyone with a little common sense could see it wasn't because you chose our small school over some bigger high schools closer to your home, far from North Carolina."

"I'm surprised someone hasn't approached me with that question, myself. I can only speculate the demons blocked the ideal from everyone's minds. All except you. They cannot penetrate your mind." Robert's attention went over to the black mountain. "My father wanted me to meet Jeff Wineworth, sir. He had read about him and learned that he was the son of Lucifer. The Satan Times is a monthly newsletter in Salem, put out for witches and warlocks, Those, who follow and worship Lucifer. Jeff has become somewhat of a hero to this evil group, after reading some of the terrible things he has done. Father said, Jeff could make me powerful beyond human hands, much like himself. I guess, in his warp mind, father wanted something better for me, like becoming the great leader, Dakar." The young man trembled at the thought. "Do you know your neighbor, sir? Jeffery Wineworth?"

"Robert, first, please do not call me, sir. Call me, Ted." Ted smiled, knowing they were almost the same age. "And yes, Jeff is my neighbor on Black Mountain. I know him well."

"It did feel strange calling you sir, because you look so young. Almost my age." Robert blushed. "It's that you're so mature and filled with wisdom beyond your years, sir…I mean, Ted, sir." He closed his eyes, feeling embarrassed.

Ted laughed and kept walking. "Robert, Jeff will help you, but not in the way your father has in mind. But first, you must find salvation, so you can find total love."

"Yes, please, I'm ready…Ted." Robert could hear the sound of rocks under his feet as they reached another path, leading up. Just before ascending to the highest point, they stopped.

"This is as far as you can go, son." Ted watched Robert looked upward to the mountain peak, brimming in brilliant light. "That's God's mountain, Robert and I am the only one permitted to go up there, except for three times. My wedding day, when I took a blind child up and little Ruth, when she almost downed."

"Wow! God's mountain!" Robert looked on in wonder as he spoke softly. "Now what?"

"Robert, God has a son, whose name you have heard spoken with lies and hate by Lucifer. His name is Jesus. All men and women sin Robert. Some, more than others, as you have been a witness of, but we all sin and fall short of salvation. Yes, including me, Robert." Ted took Robert's trembling hands. "God, our Father, sent Jesus, His only son, to come to earth, to live among men, to teach them the good news. To show us how we should live and love one another. Because Jesus was of God, He was without sin, the only one, ever, so He died on a Roman cross, a painful death, to save all of God's people by dying for our sins. He loves us that much, Robert."

"You speak as though he is still alive after dying on that cross!" Robert's eyes were filled with tears.

"He is alive Robert! Jesus Christ is very much alive! After His death, they buried him in a cold tomb where he laid until the third day, when he arose from the dead! Jesus Christ is the resurrection and the life! He that believes in Him shall never die!" Ted, spoke from his heart. "Robert, to know salvation, confess your sins to the Lord, asking Him to forgive you, and tell him you truly believe that

He is your Savior, dying on the cross for you and your sins." Ted fell down on his knees, Robert falling down beside him, tears streaming from his cheeks. "Do you want to find that love, Robert? Tell Him what's in your heart."

Robert folded his hands tightly together as he dropped his head in shame. "Jesus, my Lord and Savior, please, please, forgive me! I cannot take back the things I have done, but I believe with all my heart that you can make me clean of all my sins. I truly believe in you, Jesus and I know you died on that cross for my sins just like I believe you arose on the third day and are alive and now live again in Heaven with your Father, our Father. I believe in you as much as I believe in the Father that sent you, because He loves worthless people like me! I believe in you as I believe in Ted and know he is a true child of yours. Perhaps even the son of a great angel! Please show me love, Lord!"

Thundered roared off the mountain as a brisk wind blew around the knelling men, a voice gently whispering.

"You are forgiven, my child, you are saved, my brother, and love is yours forever, as long as you walk in my ways and show your gift of love to those around you." The wind blew gently around Ted. "Listen to the good son, listen to Ted's wisdom. Listen and learn. Return to sin no more." The wind died away and Ted stood to help Robert up on his shaky legs.

Robert threw his arms around Ted and buried his face in his chest as he sobbed, overcome from being saved and hearing the voice of the Almighty. He was finally free, but mostly, Robert Perkins felt true love for the first time in his short life.

Ted remained still, letting the young man release all his new emotions, until he heard the sobbing die down and Robert grew quiet. He pulled him away at arm's length and smiled down into his tear-stained face.

"Welcome home, Robert." Ted's words were soft and gentle. "You need not fear your family anymore. Even if they should kill the body, they can never win back your soul, my son. You have just inherited eternal life."

"I am not afraid, Ted. I feel right for the first time in my life and I actually like myself." Robert followed behind Ted down the rock path. They stopped on the edge of the forest, next to Black Mountain, where the lively green trees stood beside of very dark trees, covered in vines. "Why are we stopping here, Ted? It doesn't look safe." Robert looked around, confused.

"This is where we meet up with him." Ted motioned to a rock and walked over to wait. "Robert, why did you say I was perhaps an angel's son?"

"I've heard the demons discuss the subject." Robert couldn't understand why this very special man did not know who his real father was. "They would joke about how you did not know your father was a very important angel who was in the presence of their creator. These demons I speak of are some of the fallen angels who train the human demons." He noticed Ted questioning eyes. "Maybe they were lying about you for my benefit, trying to impress me with their knowledge of heavenly things. They all knew I was never one of them."

Ted stood quickly, without warning and said "Jeff is approaching. He will help you with your family."

"Jeffery Wineworth? Why on earth would you trust that devil's son to help me?" Robert suddenly grew nervous.

"Because, we can help you, Robert." Ted smiled at Jeff when he suddenly appeared from the woods, followed by Fang and Thorn. "I see you heard my call."

"Yes, and this scared looking rabbit must be Robert Perkins." Jeff's deep voice took the young man by surprise. "So, your father wants you to be more like me?" Jeff's stare gave Robert the creeps. "Has Ted saved you too?"

"You mean…you…but you're the…" Robert was too scared to speak.

"I'm the devil's son? Yes boy, I am the bastard son of Lucifer!" Jeff looked at Ted. "This guy is not much younger than we are. Both of us just turned twenty this year."

"You noticed. Robert happens to be twenty-one years old." Ted smiled at Robert's dropped jaw.

"Both of you are only twenty-years-old? Damn!" Robert blushed and looked down "I mean, darn!"

"No boy, you said, damn and you meant damn!" Jeff finally smiled, revealing his sharp canine teeth. Robert moved over closer to Ted, taking hold of his arm. "Now, listen Robert, I won't bite you! That's a promise. I only nibble on my bride." Jeff laughed. "I will help you with your old man. I will convince him I have taken you under my wing and I will make you one of Lucifer's best disciples, one my father will be proud of."

"But what about…" Robert was cut off by Jeff, who read his mind.

"What about you coming to Ted?" Jeff smiled when he nodded yes, eyes wide with fear. "I came from the neighboring mountain to rescue one of mine and get you away from this Bible thumping do-good-er."

Robert swallowed as he glanced at Ted, confused over Jeff's comments. Was he good or was he still bad?

Ted smiled up at Jeff, who towered over him, then touched his shoulder.

"Robert, at the moment, Jeff is lending toward the good side. I admit, he is proving to be an excellent actor."

"Yes, my friend, my talents are many." Jeff noticed Thorn moving toward Robert, so he snapped his finger. "Back here!" quickly, the wolf fell down at Jeff's feet "Robert, you must not be afraid of anything I say or do in front of your family. I promise, they will be glad to return home to Salem and leave you with me. Just as long as it's not them staying in my presence." Jeff laughed. "They are cowards in the end and believe me, Robert, the end won't be pretty for them."

Chapter Fifty-One

"We will leave now, my one." Jeff kissed Naomi and Teddy. "You are safe here with Ted." Jeff turned to see Robert was holding on to Miriam tightly. "Robert, try and look afraid." Jeff chuckled as his attention went to Ted who was waiting to give the frightened young man a few last words.

"Robert, you will be safe with Jeff so just do as he tells you and your evil family will leave you alone once and for all time." Ted touched his shoulder, sending a warmth of total love inside him. "Remember, God is with you now son, there's nothing to fear."

"Yes sir…I mean, Ted." Robert looked up at the tall dark man and found him smiling. "I'm ready to go now. Let's get this over with."

"Good! That suits me!" Jeff held out his arm. "Alright boy, take a strong hold on my arm, then close your eyes and do not open them until I give you the word." He winked at Naomi, then disappeared with Robert.

Back in Robert's apartment paced old Mr. Perkins and his even more evil son, Doctor Robert K. Perkins, Sr. "How the devil do we get Robert away from that religious fanatic, Ted Neenam! Damn! Protected up there on that mountain!" Doctor Perkins said a few choice words as he swore out loud. "Those demons just informed us they would have a word with the master, but even Lucifer himself could not penetrate that block sat up by that Bible nut! Absolutely nothing evil can set foot on Goldsburg Mountain without that jackass's approval!"

"Now son, calm yourself down! We need to think! There has to be a way!" Robert's grandfather looked from the window and saw the big black mountain looming up next to the green one. "Maybe if we went up to see Jeffery Wineworth, he could surely find a way to get that mixed up boy off that good mountain and back to us."

"Father, let me get this straight! You expect us to just walk right up to that big gloomy castle and knock on his door, then start a small conversation?" the doctor gave a nervous laugh. "I can hear us now.

Look Jeffery, my good man, could we ask you to rescue one of your own from that do-good neighbor of yours?" Robert Perkins, Sr. rolled up his eyes. "Father, do not you remember what kind of animal Jeffery Wineworth is and what he has done to others who got in his way!"

"What other choice do we have, Robert?" Garland Perkins tried to reason with his head-strong son. "I know it's a frightening thought going up to speak to Wineworth, but it's that or goodbye Robert."

"Over my dead body!" Robert Senior's eyes flashed with anger. "I'll not leave here without Robert! Even though the demons said Lucifer could not penetrate that blocked shield, his very alive and remarkable son may know a trick to lure my son across the boundary and onto Black Mountain. We must summon Wineworth to help us!"

"Did someone summon me?" came a strong, deep voice from the shadows in the dark room.

"Who…who's there?" Doctor Perkins moved toward his father and both men coward together, shaking uncontrollable.

"Who the devil, do you think, Perkins?" the tall dark figure moved from the shadows, his eyes blazing with fire. "For starters, never call me, GOOD MAN! I despise the word good in any form, you idiot!" Jeff's black eyes stared at the two frightened men. "Lost your son to the Bible thumper, I see! Very amusing and I thought you had him trained to do my father's biddings, but alas, you failed!"

"Is it our fault the boy met some blonde and fell in love?" the doctor backed away when Jeff let out a loud hiss.

"I HATE THAT WORD! NEVER SAY IT AGAIN, OR DIE!" Jeff rolled his lips back over his canine teeth and gave a low growl. "As for your son, the one you failed, I now possess him, body and soul! He is mine!"

"Robert? You rescued Robert?" Garland Perkins found his voice, although weak.

"No one asked you to speak, old man!" Jeff's eyes blazed with fire as he sized up the grandfather. "It looks like your days are numbered, old man. Your fiery fate is coming to you soon!"

Garland's old shaky fingers grabbed his son's sleeve. "No! I'm not ready to die!" he stuttered.

Perkins Senior yanked his arm away from the frightened man. "Father, shut up and except your fate! Now, stop whining!"

The mad doctor tried to sound brave. "Look Wineworth, we have been good disciples to Satan and won many to our side. Robert was sent here…"

Jeff continued his thought. "So, I could train him to be more like me! I'm no fool, Perkins! Did you think I would not know this!" he sneered. "Robert is mine now! He will do anything I ask of him. Even kill you both if I say the word."

"No! Robert is my son! He could never kill his family, Wineworth." Dr. Perkins jumped when Jeff yelled out.

"QUIET! Find out for yourself, fool!" Jeff turned toward the shadows. "Robert, I summon you to come forward!"

"Yes, master." Robert stepped out, eyes held in a haze as he tried to act the part and show no fear, although on the inside, he was trembling. "What do you wish from me, master."

Both Perkins men looked forlorn at one another, knowing Robert's soul was now in the control of this evil man.

"I want you to kill these two men, Robert!" Jeff willed a sharp ax to appear in Robert's shaking hand. "Now, do as I demand!"

Robert began walking slowly toward his frightened father and grandfather. He could feel his knees trembling as he wondered if Jeff only pretended to be good around Ted but was actually very bad. In his mind he prayed "God, help me."

"Please Robert, we're your father and your grandfather! Surely you know who we are, son." But in fear, they noticed the once bright young man, still came toward them and as he lifted the ax over their head, Jeff yelled out.

"STOP!" Robert closed his eyes as he lowered the deadly ax and drug it back over to Jeff, where it disappeared.

Doctor Perkins and his father fell to their knees, too afraid to move. Robert had never witnessed these strong men so scared in his entire life.

"Now, if you wish to prolong your miserable life, I suggest you get on the next train to Salem and don't look back! My father is not happy with the two of you! Your time on this earth will be limited for your lack of deeds!" Jeff laughed. "But you still may have time to go to the other side, where you won't have to see me for all eternity. But you had better hurry because hell awaits you with fire that will burn your worthless souls forever."

Jeff walked over and yanked them off the floor, holding a man in each hand. "If you don't wish to die before your time, or before you can be…saved, tell no one you spoke with me! No damn demon! No human demon! Absolutely, no one, or I will personally send you to my father! DO YOU HEAR MY COMMAND?" Jeff threw them against the wall. "NEVER try and see Robert, he is mine now!" Jeff snapped his fingers and two of his growling wolves surrounding him. "Fang, Thorn, follow, and if they speak to anyone, KILL!"

The two frightened men looked sadly at Robert, then started backing toward the door, the wolves following near them. "Goodbye, Robert. You belong to him now."

"I am his! See you in hell, father, grandfather!" Robert fought back his tears as they closed the door and disappeared.

"Very good touch, Robert!" Jeff put his arm around the young man's shoulders. "I think there's a pretty blonde waiting for you." Robert saw all the evil swept away from Jeff's handsome face and replaced with kindness. "You're safe now, son. You have nothing to fear from your family again."

"I cannot thank you enough, Jeff. Not just for saving me from them wanting to reclaim me, but feeding them with hope for a better way. I only pray, my family seek out the truth and find salvation. You gave them a path there, now all they have to do is open their heart."

"And with that 1% of Good over the 100% of evil, I just think they might seek that path to salvation. Now that they have felt what hell will be like." Jeff smiled. "You just might see you father and grandfather again, in heaven, if not before." Robert smiled, took Jeff's arm without fear, and they disappeared.

Chapter Fifty-Two

"Monday morning dawned as Jenny slowly opened her eyes and reached over to feel beside her and found the bed empty. She sat up and looked around in the early morning's dim light and found it eerie still. She jumped when she noticed a figure next to the window, only to relax when she recognized Ted's white robe, shining in the first rays of sunlight.

"Jenny, did I startle you, darling?" Ted walked over and climbed in bed beside her, then smothered her with a passionate kiss.

"Mum! Start that, Mr. Neenam and we're both in trouble. Matthew is sure to tease you again if we're late coming down on a school day." Jenny looked into his beautiful blue eyes. "God, I love you!"

"Jenny, my beautiful wife." He pulled her into his warm embrace. "I love you." He pulled her in tightly. "I fear today is the day, my love. I can feel great danger all around. They will strike today!"

Jenny shivered uncontrollable in Ted's warm embrace. "Darling, do you know what they will do? Do you know what I should look out for?"

"They have their plans blocked, dear Jenny. Satan, himself, has blocked it, much like Jeff blocks thoughts from his son, young Teddy." Ted looked deeply into his wife's alluring eyes. "I must be up front with you Jenny. This thing that will happen will be very frightening my darling. It will appear hopeless, but you must not give in to your fears. You must call out for me, in a soft whisper, I will hear you. My dearest love, I will be there for you, to save you and all my love ones."

"Ted, there are so many! So many teachers, so many children and youth!" Jenny swallowed back her fear. "There are far too many demons for you alone to handle!"

"I will not be alone, sweet Jenny. Jeff will help rescue the innocent." Ted's warm embrace assured Jenny and gave her the strength she needed. "We must not tell the children. When the time comes, they will know what they must do. I will inform Matthew and the older youth, so they too will be prepared. Jenny, just be on your guard for anything that will affect everyone in the school."

After being at school for several hours, Jenny was starting to worry when Mr. Morgan came over the school intercom, urging all teachers to get their students to the gym as soon as possible. Ending his frantic announcement with, our school has been ordered to shut-down, beginning immediately!

Like all the other teachers, Jenny began rushing her students to the gym and everyone was waiting inside when the principal swiftly walked in and closed the doors.

"Now, listen everyone! Teachers, please remain in the gym and stay close to the students. Highschool kids, please help the teachers watch the smaller children and try to keep them calm. We had a call from the sheriff headquarters, and he informed us First Peoples Bank had just been robbed at gunpoint. As of now, one teller and two customers have been shot and there could have been more. I'm afraid they couldn't share any more details, except the gunmen, they think three mask men, were last seen headed for the school. I'm going back to my office and call for more information. You are safe here so please, do not leave this gym. We have blocked off this part of the school.

Robert, I need you and Miss Rayfield to come with me so you can help watch for those dangerous men."

"Sir, I'm staying here. My place is with Miriam and the children. They need me more." Robert stared at the principal. "Take Rayfield, she should be enough."

"Robert, I insist that you come with me! Now!" Morgan practically yelled, causing the smaller children to back away.

"We could take Matthew, sir. He could help stand watch." Angela Rayfield took hold of Matthew's arm while Robert pulled on his other arm.

"Matthew, don't go with her! Ted would want you to stay with the children! Jenny needs your help! We all need you, Matthew!"

"Stay out of this, Robert! Matthew, please, it will be safe with me." Miss Rayfield pleaded.

"Leave him alone, Rayfield! Matthew is a married man. You do remember that! You just don't give a shit, do you?" Robert had stepped between the flirty demon teacher and Matthew.

"I know Matthew is married, Robert, he told me, you're right!" she shouted and looked seriously at the handsome young man she wanted to make her own. "I really don't give a shit if you're married, Matthew! I need you to come with me!"

"No, my place is here, with my family." Matthew could see the desperation in Angela's eyes and knew what ever was going to happen, must really be bad.

"Suit yourself, you fool!" she stormed out in front of the principal.

"Women! Always falling for men, they can never have." Morgan sneered, then turned on Robert. "Stay, if that's what you wish, Robert! I will be back with news, when I hear something, so please, wait here. No wondering outside these doors! It could prove dangerous!" Morgan walked out, closing the door behind him.

Everyone stood silently, as if they were afraid to make a sound. Jenny checked her watch and found fifteen minutes had passed since the principal left. She walked over to Matthew and whispered.

"I'll look out and see if I can see any sign of Mr. Morgan." Jenny moved over to the only two doors in the large gym and tried to turn the knob. The double doors were locked. "Matthew?" Jenny's face reflected the worry and fear that was sweeping through her body as Matthew noticed and raced over next to her.

"What is it, Jenny?"

"The doors have been locked from the outside, Matthew! We are trapped in this gym, with no other way out!"

"JENNY! JENNY!" Leah dashed over and grabbed around Jenny, as tears streamed down her cheeks. I SMELL FIRE! THERE'S SMOKE COMING UNDER THE DOOR, JENNY!" the excited girl pointed at the dark smoke seeping under both doors.

"I see it Leah! We will call for Ted Now!" Jenny looked around the room at all the children, who were unaware of the danger they were in.

Matthew was also looking around in a panic, then grabbed Jenny by the arm. "Good Lord, Jenny! You cannot call Ted, there's no telephone in the gym!"

"Matthew?" Jenny patted his back. "I do not need a phone, now step back."

"Oh! You're right! What am I thinking!" Matthew grabbed

Leah's mouth before she could scream out again. "Get quiet, Leah! Jenny will get Ted here in no time!"

Jenny turned to face the closed doors and whispered "Ted, I need you, now!"

Ted and Andrew were out in the garden ever since the school bunch left and were almost finished hoeing the weeds out when Ted dropped his hoe and grabbed his chest. Without hesitation, he started pulling Andrew to the house while speaking in broke-up sentences.

"Jenny and family in danger! All the kids at School! Fire!" Ted closed his eyes and whispered. "Jeff, I need you! Meet me at the school A S A P!" Ted took Andrew by the shoulders. "Look Andrew, go inside with mother, Ruth and Kathy and make sure the doors are locked! Naomi and Teddy are on their way, so let them in!" with that, he vanished.

Jeff stopped hugging Naomi and stared out into space, then looked down at his wife, who had been observing him closely.

"Sweet one, grab Teddy, get in the car and drive straight to Goldsburg Mountain. Wait for me there! They are expecting you!"

"Jeff, what is it?" Naomi quickly picked up their son and strapped him safely in his car seat.

"There's not much time! Ted needs me! Jenny and the family, plus all the kids and teachers at school are in danger! Fire!"

"Go then! Go Jeff!" Naomi got behind the wheel. "I'm on my way to the home! We will be safe!"

Emotions rolled around on Jeff's face as he grabbed his wife before she could shut her door. "Beware of the devil, Naomi! He can turn himself into anyone or anything! Promise! Promise!"

"I will be careful Jeff, I promise!" she kissed him, shut the door and drove away as Jeff stared after her and whispered

"You must be careful, my angel!" within seconds, Jeff vanished.

Chapter Fifty-Three

Ted and Jeff appeared just outside the school, then rushed inside to the gym doors. The fire was burning all around them, yet they were untouched by the fiery furnace. Ted called his wife's name through the thick doors.

"Jenny, get the children and everyone to move back to the far end of the gym! You need to stay clear of the doors when I open them!"

"Alright darling! We are moving back!" Jenny motioned for everyone to move quickly to the far end, away from the exit. "Keep moving back! You will be safe there!" she turned to face the doors, now some distance away, so she spoke loudly. "Everyone has move back, Ted!"

Ted and Jeff bust through the thick doors, fire shooting in past them, but only the heat made it through before both men slammed the doors shut. The children started screaming and crying in fear, so Ted hurried over and knelt down to calm them.

"It will be alright, my little ones. We are going to play a game called, follow the leader, except this time, you must close your eyes and hold the hand in front of you."

"You cannot be serious, young man! We cannot take these children out there! No one will make it through those flames!" The first-grade teacher wrapped her arms around several small children, who started crying again.

"Please, everyone, listen to me! We are going to get you out of here, but you must do as I say!" Ted spoke calmly. "You must believe God is going to help us, you must trust Him!"

A very small girl tugged at Ted's sleeve and he glanced down to find her smiling up at him. "I trust you Jesus! I'm not afraid!"

"Out of the mouths of babes." Ted lifted the child into his arm and look over the group. "Listen, teachers and older students, find the smallest children and carry them. The rest of you brave children, remember to take the hand in front of you and hold it tight. I will lead in front and Jeff will follow, in the back of the line. You must keep your eyes shut at all times and trust us to lead you through safely. Any questions before we start?"

"Mr. Neenam, do you really think we can just walk through that raging fire and live?" Mrs. Collins' hands started to shake as she picked up a small boy. "Look, I have faith, but that's a real fire out there, a blazing furnace!"

"Mrs. Collins, do Jeff or I look like we just walked through those flames?" Ted noticed her tears and reached out to touch her. Suddenly, the teacher felt the love and warmth flow in her veins. "Trust me. Trust God! Believe!"

"I do, I do, Jesus," she whispered.

"We will discuss that later, but for now, Jenny, beside me and take my spare hand." Ted looked back to check for closed eyes and noticed Matthew was looking around. "Matthew, close your eyes." He smiled when the young man jumped and quickly closed his eyes. Then he turned to face the door. "Father, please protect these children of yours, both young and old." Ted opened back the double doors and looked into the chest of a very tall angel. He looked up to find the handsome angel smiling down at him.

"Ted, follow me." As he walked, Ted noticed angels standing on either side of the long hallway leading to the outdoors. Their massive wings spread up to touch the angel on the opposite side, forming a perfect tunnel for the group to walk through.

Jenny tugged at Ted's hand and whispered "Ted, who is talking to you, sweetheart?"

"An angel, my darling. Keep your eyes shut." Ted gazed up at the angel walking in front of him and noticed how much he resembled him. He bent over to whisper to his wife. "I think it's Gabriel."

"You are right, Ted, I am Gabriel." The handsome angel turned and smiled. "I am very proud of you son." He turned and continued down the hallway.

Outside, the television cameras were reporting the terrible fire that would take most of the children and youth in the town of Goldsburg.

"Never in the history of this small town, has anything so remotely happen to destroy this many young lives at the exact same time! To think of the many homes and families that will carry this day with them in painful sorrow. I predict it could take years for mothers and fathers to get over their great loss, perhaps a lifetime! Husbands will morn wives, wives, their husbands! Very small children, not yet school age, will never see their sister or brother, mother or father! It would appear, the only ones to escape this horrible death, are the cafeteria workers and janitors, who worked in the other end of the campus. When the firemen arrived on the scene, the fire was already out of control in the gymnasium where it was reported a school tournament was going on and the entire school, classes first through twelfth grades were competing in different school sports. This was relayed to us by a janitor who was gathering trash from the classrooms and noticed everyone racing off toward the gym. He said the principal, Mr. Morgan, saw him and told him where the students were off to with such excitement.

The old gym has never had the need for a rear exit, until today. I am sure, when the new gym is built, there will be more than one exit, for safety reasons."

The cameras paned over the blazing fire behind the news reporter, who with genuine tears in his eyes, he concluded. "Many faithful Christians who have a loss, might begin to question their faith, But only in our loving God can we find peace for our sorrow and loss. If you believe with all your heart, there is always the hope for a miracle today. All our love ones, might just walk out those exit doors. And, for those two brave men that raced inside that burning building, who knows, they just might be angels."

Inside the safe tunnel, Gabriel called back, "almost at safety, son." Ted's heart was pounding as he recalled the words of Gabriel. He had called him son, twice. Ted saw the sunlight drifting through the burned-out doors just ahead.

"A few more steps Jenny and we will be outside." As Ted stepped out with Jenny and the small girl in his arms, there was a gasp from the large weeping crowd, standing at a safe distanced. The tall handsome angel had disappeared and as the group emerged, safe and sound, the protecting angels vanished and the fire consumed the building.

Ted reached over to kiss his wife, then touched her eyes and the little girl he so lovingly held. "You both may open your eyes, now." He called out to the large group that still had their eyes shut. "You may open your eyes, we are safe."

Jenny blinked at the bright sunshine as everyone wondered around, checking each other out for any fire damage. There was none. Jeff stepped up, a big smile spread across his handsome face.

"That was some tunnel we came through." He winked at Ted, then looked down at the wide-eyed girl in his arms. "Opened your eyes, didn't you, sweetie?"

"An…An…Angels!" she stuttered. "There were so many!"

"It's a long hall, sweetie." Jeff chuckled when he noticed a woman running toward them.

"Emily! My baby, you're alright! You had mommy real scared!" the girl's mother grabbed her daughter from Jeff. "Thank you, sir! Thank you and God bless you and that robed man who led everyone to safety! The fire was out of control! We thought…everyone was gone! We did see a miracle today! Praise the Lord!"

"Looks like, believing is seeing and seeing is believing!" Jeff patted the child on her head. "I guess your little Emily will be talking about angels for a long time." He turned, smiling, and walked back to Ted.

"Some children have to look, Jeff." Ted smiled then sat the little girl down when he saw her parents running up. "When you folks say your prayers tonight, thank God for saving these children and their faithful teachers."

The fire chief ran up between Ted and Jeff, staring with disbelief. "My God! I had just drove up when I saw you two just appear, as if out of the blue, directly in front of the school doors. I blinked my eyes, and you were gone, simply vanished. How in the blue blazes did you save everyone and bring them down that long hall?" Fire Chief Marshall looked from Ted to Jeff. "There was flames everywhere. That fire was completely out of control. Within seconds, as though the devil himself had started it!"

Little Emily Wilson had been listened to the fireman go on and on, so she blurted out "ANGELS! ANGELS SAVED US! I think God sent them because Jesus was with us!"

"Emily's right! Jesus was carrying me, and I heard him talking to an angel named, Gabriel!" Joanie Bradford smiled up at Ted.

"Angels? Jesus?" The fire chief looked confused. "I guess that might explain how you got out, without so much as the smell of smoke on your clothes."

"Excuse me, Mr. Marshall, I am sorry for all the confusion, but everyone mistakes my husband Ted, for Jesus, from his appearance and loving actions. Even I had similar thoughts when I first met this angelic man." Jenny smiled up at the fire chief, who couldn't resist his own smile in return. "I am the English teacher here at Goldsburg School and I would like to report the principal, James Morgan as the one being responsible for starting this fire after locking us in the gym, with no way out."

"I'll not ask how your husband and his strong friend knew you were in danger, my dear, But I'm only glad you found a way to get in touch." The fire chief glanced over at the members of the school board and shook his head. "I have been suggesting a rear exit door and a telephone be placed in the gym for some time, but I was overruled. Not enough money in the budget for something as reasonable as a phone."

"Mr. Marshall, I really do not need a telephone to contact my husband." Jenny smiled up at Ted as she took his arm.

"I'll not ask what you mean by that, but I know it must have something to do with faith in one another." The fire chief cleared his throat. "As for your suspicion of Mr. Morgan being connected to the fire, we will investigate, starting right away." He started to walk away when Jeff gripped his arm.

"Chief Marshall, Jenny Neenam is correct about Mr. Morgan, known to Ohio citizens as James 'arsonist' Morgan, who loved setting fires to buildings filled with lots of people! There is also a History teacher involved with this fire-bug, going under the name of Angela Rayfield, also with a past record!" Jeff smiled over at the school board. "It appears, the school board goofed again, when they hired known felons." He released his tight hold. "They are guilty, but you won't find them anywhere!"

Chapter Fifty-Four

Naomi had just arrived at the home and was safely inside, awaiting news about the school fire. Everyone jumped, when a loud knock came on the front door. Kathy looked out and saw Jeff waiting outside. She smiled over at Naomi.

"It's Jeff, Naomi. You can go find Teddy. He and Ruth are playing hide and seek, and he ran off to hide in the kitchen. I'll let Jeff in."

"Thanks Kathy. Tell him I will be right there." Naomi went quickly to the kitchen, mumbling to herself. "Boy, he got here fast. They just now said the group came out of the school moments before."

At the door, Jeff smiled down at Kathy when she announced Naomi was coming as soon as she collected their son.

"It's good to see you doing better, Kathy. You need to be more careful these days with the devil on the prowl. All the warnings in the world cannot prepare you for my father. He will stop at nothing to get what he wants." Jeff patted her head. "I'm only glad we could save you from his evil."

"You and me both!" Kathy took a deep breath, remembering how close she had been to Lucifer, himself. "Will the family be home soon? I really need to hold my husband after that close call."

They were loading up when I left. Ted decided to ride back with Jenny. He didn't want to let her out of his sight."

"I can understand that feeling, darling." Naomi walked up with Teddy and instantly noticed he had on a different outfit. "Did you swing by the house to make a quick change, Jeff?"

"I didn't want you and Teddy to needlessly have to smell my smoky clothes. That fire was really raging and the smoke was terrible." Jeff put his arm around her. "I'm glad to report, all is well at school. No casualties."

"It did not take you and Ted long to save all those students and teachers, sweetheart." Something seemed different, perhaps, Jeff was just tired.

"With me and Ted on the scene, things moved fast, so grab

Teddy, we're going home. I've had enough screaming kids for one day."

Teddy walked up to Jeff and put out his arms for him to lift him and carry him to the car. "I'm ready, Papa."

"Boy, go let your mama help you in the car!" Jeff walked around to the driver's side as the young boy puckered up and looked down sadly.

"I…I love you, Papa."

Jeff looked around at the back seat, reached back to pat their son's knee. "I know son. Now, get in so we can go home." He switched on the motor and drove away.

After arriving at the castle, Jeff ordered Teddy to go to his room and lie down for a nap. Naomi had been observing her husband closely and she began to worry. After watching to make sure the boy went in his room, Jeff took Naomi's hand and led her to their bedroom, where he insisted she lie down and rest. Pulling a chair up next to the bed, he stared down at her as a wicked, seductive smile fell on his handsome lips. He moved his hand over on her breast and gently rubbed it.

Instead of feeling the warm feeling she got when Jeff touched her, Naomi suddenly felt a cold chill and the nervous feeling would not go away, so hoping he would leave her alone, she admitted to being tired and ask for an hour to rest.

"Then, rest for a short while, my beautiful Naomi, then I shall return and claim what is mine." He smiled to himself and walked out.

Naomi sat straight up, shivering with fear as she recalled Jeff's warning about Satan being able to disguise himself as anyone or anything. Naomi knew in her heart, the person that brought her home, was not Jeff, but an imposter. She scrambled out of bed, but before she could walk out, he was back, demanding she remove her clothes. The smile he delivered gave her goosebumps, as his voice came low and seductive.

"Woman, I MUST have you now!" he reached out for her, but she fought him off and pushed him away.

"Keep your hands off me! I…I know who you are!" Naomi's voice began to tremble as she backed away. "You are not Jeff! You are Jeff's father, Lucifer!"

"Clever girl." Lucifer smiled, revealing sharp teeth like his sons. He reached his long arm out and grabbed her top, ripping it over her breast. Naomi let out a loud scream.

"Jeff! Jeff! Help me!"

Still at school, hearing Naomi scream, Jeff jerked up his head and slung it around to face Ted.

"Naomi is in danger! It is my father! Damn him!" Jeff's eyes blazed, fresh hate raging in his soul.

"Jeff, go! Go to her now!" Ted urged him. "Let not this hate overpower your thinking, my friend! You must stay true to God if you are to help save my angel! Now, go!"

Jeff's heart was falling with complete worry as he simply vanished, right in front of the surrounding children.

"Wow! Did you see that? Where did he go?" Timmy Wilks, a third-grade boy yelled out, eyes wide in disbelief. "He just…disappeared!"

"HE'S MAGIC, STUPID!" Leah spoke loudly, while shaking her red head.

"Leah, do not call people stupid. Name calling is a very bad habit! Just be kind to others. Sweetheart." Ted walked away for privacy and knelt down. "Father, please protect my angel and help Jeff defend his family against Satan!"

Lucifer pulled Naomi to the door and out of the castle. "You, daughter-n-law, are coming with me! Mrs. Mullican is taking care of your boy." Lucifer laughed out. "I am giving the bitch a second chance with my grandson. She is aware what is at stake if she fails me again."

"No! you cannot put that woman near my son! She is mean and cruel and Teddy is petrified of his old nana!" the great dragon only laughed and pulled her in closer as she fought him. "Get your hands off me!" she struggled but knew it was helpless under the devil's grip.

He continued to drag her to the edge of the woods and turned to ripped off her bra, leaving her topless and trying to shield her naked breasts.

"Very well endowed my dear. I know my son must have enjoyed sucking these tits!" Lucifer held her easily and could feel her strength fading. "Next, I will remove those panties and thrust my ready extension deep inside you and kill that baby growing, only to replace it with mine!"

"No! Take your evil hands off me! Jeff!" Naomi screamed and Jeff suddenly appeared and yelled out.

"Get your damn hands off my wife, Lucifer!"

The devil sneered, a wicked grin spreading across his evil face. "Yes, I knew you would come, my son. You are just in time to witness my revenge! I have decided to kill your baby and replace it with mine. If you choose not to go with me, then I will have another son to train and with your woman."

"YOU WILL NEVER HAVE MY WIFE, YOU BASTARD!" With raging anger, Jeff lifted Lucifer over his head and threw him on a big rock. He lay stunned briefly and watched Jeff pick up his wife and carry her to their rose garden,

Jeff ran his fingers through her hair and looked deep into her loving eyes. He took off his shirt and placed it around his wife's trembling shoulders. "Whatever happens my one, remember I love you, my darling." His lips parted over hers in a passionate kiss, then lifted her head as he let down a protective, invisible shield, separating them. Naomi cried out

"No Jeff! Please, darling! You cannot fight the devil and win! Jeff, please!"

Jeff closed his eyes and whispered. "Ted, please come. Naomi and little Teddy need you. I must fight my father and his demons and I do not know how long I can last. My family will need you to protect them when I cannot. Please hurry, my good friend." Jeff looked up into the clear blue sky, his heart pounding with agony. He knew his fate. He would surely die and have to leave his beloved Naomi alone. A loud noise brought him fully alert. Doctor Ravin sneered, as he crept slowly up.

"So, Jeffery, we meet again. Looks like you will be joining us today!" His hands sprang up, revealing long, sharp, fingernails. "Bleed you fool! You could have been the Anti-Christ! You stupid, unfit son!"

Raven lunged forward, hands out ready to strike, but Jeff's quick reactions made the demon stumble and loose his balance. The evil doctor fell hard on his face. Before he could recover, Jeff grabbed him and threw him hard against a large oak tree. The mad doctor shook his head to clear it then stood back up, sneering.

"You cannot get rid of me, you, stupid man, and you know it!" Raven laughed out loud and was suddenly joined by another ugly demon as Naomi watched in horror, afraid to leave and torn with fear for her little boy.

She let out a soft scream when the two demons closed in on her husband, hissing like serpents. "Oh Ted, where are you?"

"I am right by your side, sweet angel." Ted's calm voice fell on her ears and she turned and grabbed him, tears streaming down her beautiful loving face.

"Ted, please…please help Jeff! They will kill him! he doesn't stand a chance up against Satan and his horrible demons!"

"Sweet angel, Jeff must fight his father alone." Ted looked through the clear shield at his newfound friend. "He has asked me to protect you and Teddy for him."

"Teddy!" Naomi's eyes grew wide with more fear. "Ted, that demon nana is with my son! Marna Mullican was Jeff's maid before his mother shot her to protect me! The devil brought her back just to watch Teddy while he tried to rape me!"

"Calm down, sweet girl. Teddy is with me. He is safe now." Ted reached behind him and brought the scared little boy around. "Teddy saw his papa was in danger when we came over and he couldn't watch. Mullican disappeared before I had the chance to send her back, but she will stay clear of me. She fears me more than she does your husband and that's a lot."

Naomi turned at the painful cry from Jeff's throat and saw blood gushing from his forehead and back. She pressed up against the protective shield, crying out.

"God! Jeff! Please…please, leave him alone!"

"Leave him alone my dear daughter-n-law? NEVER!" Lucifer laughed. "I have only begun to punish my son, who has rose up against me!"

After tormenting Jeff a few minutes longer, the two demons backed away as Jeff fell to his knees, breathing heavily. The devil walked over and lifted up his chin.

"My son, my beautiful son. It's not too late to join me. Even now, I would give you the great honor to be my chosen one, by giving you that third six you worked so hard on to achieve. You are my favorite, born of mortal woman. I could destroy you, here and now, and suck your wicked soul back to hell, where I worked on the perfect sperm to put inside my great and powerful body that created you! Once I have you imprisoned forever, I could return and choose your son, my grandson, the perfect image of you and soon the same great qualities that made you special." Lucifer showed genuine concern in his eyes for a brief moment, perhaps, bits and pieces from a time when he too only knew love. "I could mold young Jeffery into another you. Well, perhaps a close second." His long fingers gripped his face. "But damn it, I want you, Jeffery!"

"You will NEVER have me or my son, Lucifer! "NEVER!"

"And who is going to stop me?" he chuckled. "Surely not you! Hell knows it won't be that pitiful weak woman you love! Perhaps this perfect Christ-like neighbor?" Lucifer walked over and smiled at Ted. "He will surely turn the other cheek, like JE-SUS told him to do!" he made his way back to Jeff and knelt down. "No, he hasn't the power to stop the great dragon, my son. I will destroy him too, mark my words, you fool, while you are burning in hell!"

The devil made circles around Jeff's body as he threatened. "Perhaps, more pain may change your mind!" he gave Jeff an evil grin, then moved to one side, revealing Paul Manning and Philip Tucker.

"You will feel the pain of death, Jeffery Wineworth, you, ungrateful son!" the demon lawyer rolled his lips over his row of pointed teeth. "Feel my bite!" he jumped toward Jeff, but the tall powerful man moved quickly to the left and the demon flew right past him into a big rock.

"You cannot escape all of us, Jeffery!" the demon handyman rolled his eyes over to Ted. "Thought you got rid of me, Bible thumper! Lucifer brought me back to help finish the mission we came up to do!" Paul Manning gave a rumble of laughter as he watched Tucker grabbed Jeffery from behind and sink his sharp teeth inside his flesh. Jeff rose to his feet, closing his eyes in pain, then grabbed the lawyer's head and threw him over his shoulders, smashing into Mr. Manning. They slid across the garden and slammed into the rock wall surrounding the rose garden. Both demons lay stunned.

Teddy had buried his head against his mama's legs, as he hugged them with trembling hands. She gently patted his black locks as her own tears raced down her flushed cheeks."

"They're going to kill him! Jeff, my love, my darling, my husband!" Naomi sobbed. "My life!"

Ted could feel his heart breaking, but he knew it was not the time for him to act. He dropped her hand and placed his arm lovingly around her. "Naomi, do not give up hope, my angel. God is present with us, all of us, including Jeff, if he can remember that and call out to Him."

"Oh, Ted, he has to, he just has to." Naomi could hardly speak. Her emotions were running wild with both hope and fear, for the man she gave her heart to. "God in heaven, please have mercy on Jeff, my one true love! Save him!"

She grabbed Ted when she saw all four demons closing in on her husband. He had grown weak from the loss of blood, so his great strength was fading, panting with every breath. The demons jeered as they moved in, smelling their victory close at hand, knowing soon they would get their promised reward for completing the painful killing. Like great hornets, they all swarmed on Jeff's tired body, biting, slashing, stabbing, and sucking their prey, trying to remove all of the life-giving blood that flowed through this handsome man. After what seen like endless minutes, Jeff collapsed on the ground, blood pouring from his once perfect body.

Naomi screamed when the demons stepped away and she finally witness the horrible thing they had done to her wonderful, beautiful, husband and lover. She stared through the invisible shield, trying to make out whether or not Jeff was still breathing. She tried desperately to go to him but found it impossible. Feeling great panic, and anxiety rob her of her strength, she gave way to darkness, as she fainted in Ted's loving arms.

Chapter Fifty-Five

Jenny stared at the note in her hands. It was Ted's handwriting, she knew it well, but it felt odd to receive a note from her husband. But then she thought, with everything that was happening on Black Mountain, the simplest thing could sound strange. Jenny looked down at her very pregnant stomach and gave it a soft pat.

"Well, girls, your daddy has sent for me, or in this case, sent for the three of us." She looked down at the note and re-read it out loud. "My sweet Jenny, I need for you to meet me on the high bluff that joins our mountain to Black Mountain. There is a safe path about halfway up, but I will help you reach the summit by my special powers. I really need for you to come alone. The fewer that knows about our meeting there the better. I promise, there is nothing for you to be afraid of, my dearest darling, for I will be with you in spirit the entire way. That's my brave, smart girl. Your loving husband, Ted." Jenny folded the note and slipped it inside her pocket, thinking it best not to leave evidence of their meeting since Ted made it sound important. "O.K. girls, we must go for a little hike. Your daddy needs us!" Jenny slipped out the door and headed for the forest path.

Jenny finally reached the foot of the high bluff. She suddenly realized why Ted would need his powers to bring her up. The high rock mountain went straight up, almost a third way up the path he told her would be easy. Shielding her eyes from the evening sun, she searched the top for any sign of her husband. She caught a flash of something white near the edge.

"I think I see your daddy, girls. He's waiting at the top." Jenny started her slow climb up the narrow path that led to the foot of the tall cliff, towering over her, casting deep shadows in the valley below. "I cannot see why Ted wanted me to meet him here. This place is almost scary." She thought she heard a noise. "Ted, is that you? I am waiting at the end of the path."

"I'll bring you up." Came the voice, in repeating echo's, across the mountains. "Close your eyes, Jenny. I will tell you when you can open them." Jenny noticed Ted's voice sounded muffled and thought, perhaps it was the distanced from which he had to call down.

"They're close, darling." She said loudly. "Just get me up there with you. It is pretty scary down here."

Jenny could hear a swishing sound in her ears as she felt as though she were floating upward. Then she felt the rocks under her feet and knew she was at the top. With her eyes shut, it was hard to stand up straight from the strong winds that blew across the high bluff. She was glad to finally hear those three needed words.

"Open your eyes."

At first Jenny could only see the flat top of the bluff, empty of all trees. Its menacing rim, which made up its border, was open all the way around, and one wrong step would send you hurling to your death.

"Ted, this place is no better than the end of the path." She knew if he were there, he must still be invisible, because there was no way anything could be hidden to her up here on this God forsaken mountain bluff. "Come on, sweetheart, this is no time to check my bravery! I'm just glad your little girls cannot see this horrible place."

"I agree, Jennifer!" the deep voice came from behind her, causing her to jumped around and see who had lured her up here. "The man was tall and looked a lot like a slightly different version of Jeff Wineworth. Then he smiled, revealing his sharp teeth and she suddenly realized just who had lured her up on this deadly bluff. "Yes, Jennifer has guessed who I am. Now, I wonder if such a beautiful woman can guess why I brought her here."

"Knowing you, Lucifer, it could be many reasons but in the final outcome, it is your evil plan to push me off this mountain and kill me and our daughters. Is that your plan?"

"Clever and beautiful, two good qualities, but to most women, never used together. You did say you was glad your little girls could not see this horrible place, did you not? That is why I stated, I agreed, because it is my plan to let you slip to your death and what a shame to lose such a sexy broad like you."

"Ted will not allow you to hurt his family, Satan! He will, by the grace of God, save us!" Jenny put up a brave front, even though the fear she felt was real.

"Yes, and that is the other reason I lured you here, Mrs. Neenam. Your overly perfect husband is standing in my way at this moment and I needed to distract him so I can complete what I came to do, without his interference." Satan raised his eyebrow in defiance.

"Oh? You are afraid of Ted, aren't you?" Jenny suddenly felt brave.

"Nonsense!" Lucifer forced out a laugh. "That is utterly ridiculous! The great dragon is afraid of NO MAN!"

"But Ted is not just any man, great dragon, and you know it! I know now how you managed to set your foot on our mountain to lure Naomi to go with you. Ted left in such a hurry to save all those children and teachers from the fire, he simply ordered Andrew to go inside the farmhouse and lock the doors! The house had a block on it, but not the mountain!" Jenny gave a real laugh. "Kathy said when you came to pick up Naomi and Teddy, you stayed out on the porch! It was because, you couldn't come inside!" Jenny could see the anger building on his handsome, wicked face, but she was enjoying rubbing some truth in this bad angel. "So, the great dragon is nothing more than a slimy little lizard to my husband, and he will stop you before you complete your devilish plan!"

"Too bad you want live to witness it, Jennifer!" Lucifer snapped his fingers. "Taking a fall off of a big bluff can be extremely frightening, dear girl, but falling backward is twice as horrible!" he smiled when his keen hearing picked up her rapid heartbeat. "Yes, the thought is even terrorizing, poor foolish girl. Perhaps, I shall see you in hell. After all, you had a bad life in your past and that God you serve is not so easy to forget and forgive!"

"With those words, Lucifer, you do not scare me in the least! I know my Lord has forgiven me for all my rotten past. I also know, it can never be the same for you and your followers. You have done the unforgiven act of treason against your Holy Creator, so now you constantly seek revenge, but your 100% of evil will never win over the almighty power of God! You will lose Lucifer, you and all those once beautiful angels who were filled with total love." Jenny's face held sincerity as she said softly. "My heart goes out to all of you, knowing, that even if you wanted it, you can never be forgiven."

For a moment, Lucifer just looked into her eyes, the anger gone, the evil, which moments before, shown on his handsome face, erased. Without another word, the mighty archangel disappeared in silence.

Jenny felt as though she was not alone, for moments before, Satan had snapped his fingers, as if he were calling somethings attention. She suddenly heard what sounded like breathing. She tilted her head, trying to hear how close this predator was to her on this high bluff. Then, her worse fears were realized when she looked into the eyes of four large wolves, twice the size of Jeff's monsters. Jenny knew in that instant, she was facing wolves straight from hell. Their gums were pulled back over their long sharp canine teeth as the growls coming from their throat gave her an uneasy feeling. This was serious and she had nowhere to run, nowhere to hide.

"My God! What kind of danger have I brought to my babies? Lord, help us! Ted, save us!" Jenny took a step backward and the wolves took one step forward, never taking their red-green eyes off of her.

Ted grabbed his heart when he heard Jenny's plea for help. He could instantly feel the danger she was in and he realized now the reason Lucifer had ordered his demons to circle Jeff and start chanting. The old sly devil had blocked his exit from Ted, so he could lure Jenny to the high bluff. Now, Ted found himself in a great situation. He had been waiting for the right moment to step in and help his friend. Ted knew, if he left now to save Jenny, the love of his life, he could not save Jeff and he would leave Naomi and Teddy at the mercy of Lucifer. But his Jenny was in danger! His beautiful girls were in danger and he must help her. He had promised he would always hear her whisper and come to her rescue. Ted fell to his knees, to seek the answer from the one he knew he could trust.

"My Father, please, what am I to do?" Ted pleaded. "I want so much to do your will and help Jeff, but my Jenny, she is the very heartbeat of my life!" Ted felt the wind blow around his head as it whispered

"Ted, my son, I have heard Jenny's prayer for help. Even now I send Michael, my great archangel, to save your family, along with four mighty warrior angels to defeat the menacing foe which stalk her." The wind blew gently, as it brushed his brow with coolness. "Your Jenny is safe in my hands. Carry on, my son."

"From my heart, loving Father, I give you thanks!" Ted stood back up and locked eyes with Satan.

Chapter Fifty-Six

Jenny had never known this much fear in her life. She did not want to die like this, to lose everything, especially her Ted and be the one responsible for their innocent babies dying such a horrible death. Within the stillness around her, she thought she heard a voice call her name. Had she only imagined the soft, yet powerful voice coming from below the cliff. Then she noticed the wolves had stopped their slow advance, ears perked, perhaps wondering their self just who was speaking with a strange unusual accent. Then it came again, this time somewhat louder. "Jenny, God has sent me to help you, child!"

Jenny edge her way closer to the edge and peered down below. She blinked in disbelief at the extremely tall man standing below, pose in a stern stance. She swallowed back her fear and spoke.

"Who…who are you?" she felt her legs wobble standing so near the high drop. "What are you?"

The serious look stayed on his handsome face as he announced calmly "I am Michael! Trust me Jenny! I am God's angel!"

"Michael? The Michael, written of in the Bible?" Jenny ask with wide eyes, knowing ever since she wed Ted, she had heard the angels, but this was the first one to appear to her.

"The Holy word of the Almighty Creator speaks of me in his letter to his chosen, I do recall." He remained the same. "I am honored to be the servant of my loving Aba Father. Do you trust me to save you Jenny? A simple question just requires a simple answer, child."

Jenny heard the wolves growling and she instantly called down "Yes Michael, I trust you! Your help will be greatly appreciated."

"Very well, Jenny, but you must be brave when I ask you to jump." Knowing this would bring a response, he waited.

"Jump? You…want me to jump off this very high, very dangerous, bluff?" Jenny spoke, with new fear.

"Jenny, you 'must' jump. This will save you and your babies from those demon wolves." Michael was clothed in perfect love as he spoke with soft calm. "At this moment, your Ted is praying for you and his daughter's safety."

"Alright, I will jump, Michael!" Jenny held her head up high, knowing her fate if she didn't jump. "Ted needs me! My girls need me to be strong for them, and if He can use me, I am here for my God!"

"A very wise decision, Jenny, because those wolves have regained their bravery and are about to charge you!" Michael held out his strong arms. "Now, Jenny! Jump!"

Jenny took a breath, closed her eyes and jumped off the high cliff. She could feel her body falling swiftly downward. Hearing the wolves howling overhead, brought her eyes open, just in time to see Michael's mighty wings spread out as he flew up to meet her in the air, He caught her gently in his strong arms, then lowered her slowly to the ground below, where the path stopped at the high-walled bluff.

Jenny held on around Michael's strong neck, the gratitude of his saving power pouring into her heart and soul.

"Thank you, Michael! Oh, my merciful God, you saved us! Thank you! Thank God! Thank Ted!" Being overcome with emotion, Jenny fainted in the angel's strong embrace.

Michael had sat down to hold Jenny like one would cradle a child and when she opened her eyes she stared up into his peaceful, loving eyes. Jenny sat up when she heard the wolves still growling and howling above them. Jenny began shaking with fear, just knowing they were still on that cliff.

"The wolves! They're still up there, Michael! Someone else could be in danger, someone we love could get killed!"

Michael stood up to lift Jenny to her feet. She felt like a small child standing next to this great angel. He smiled and pointed up on the bluff. "Look Jenny." Michael's voice came soft and soothing. "Look up at the bluff and see what the hand of the Lord can do!"

Jenny looked up and noticed, this time the four large wolves were the ones backing, in a cowardly manner, their great tails tucked between their legs, the loud growls had turned to whimpers. Then she caught sight at what had them so terrorized. If she had thought Michael was tall, even he looked small next to these mighty giants with flaming swords held out in front of them. Their clothes were that of warriors, ready to battle any foe placed before them. There was no doubt in Jenny's mind, who was going to win this battle. The four mighty warriors walked slowly toward the backing wolves, silently pointed the blazing swords down toward them. Jenny's voice came out weak as she asked.

"God's angels?"

"God's mighty angels, child. They are the great and powerful warrior angels! It would take only one such angel to defeat millions of your human soldiers." Michael draped his arm around Jenny's trembling shoulders. "Relax Jenny, they only fight the evil side. They made a stop here to rid you of these demons before they go to assist Ted. He is outnumbered at the present, but he shall not be for long."

"Ted!" Jenny looked up into the angel's loving eyes. "Is Ted in danger, Michael?"

"No, sweet one, Ted is safe, but he will require our assistance later. Look!" Michael pointed to the wolves dangling on the high ledge. Losing their balance, the pack of wolves tumbled over the bluff to their quick death as the warrior angels disappeared.

"Take my hand Jenny. We are finished here." Jenny gratefully took his outstretched hand. "Now, Jenny, I will take you and your beautiful angelic daughters to your husband."

"You are still here, Ted! Know ye not that your Jenny is about to jump from the bluff bordering these two mountains!" Lucifer could not understand why the religious man looked so at peace. Even in her torment, Naomi had overheard their conversation.

"Ted, you must go to Jenny! I know you are pulled between those you love and want to help all of us!" Naomi grabbed his arm and could not understand his remaining so calm. "Ted, your little girls are in danger as well! Why are you still here?"

"Because, my beautiful, unselfish, angel, my place is here." Ted held up his hand when Naomi started to object, even knowing she could be putting herself and her little boy in danger if he left. "Your heart is always thinking about others, Naomi. Be at peace, Jenny is no longer in danger. Our loving Father has sent help to her and the only ones to jump to their death on that bluff are Satan's demon Wolves."

"What?" Lucifer looked genuinely confused. "You always stand in my way, boy! It was just a lucky break for you this time, but your friend, Jeff, has ran out of luck! Today, he dies!"

"No!" Teddy screamed "Don't kill my papa!" fire shown in his small eyes. "I hate you, grandfather! I hate you!"

"Teddy?" Naomi pulled him back from the invisible shield. "Stay with mama." She watched Lucifer smile broadly at the child, then Ted.

"Yes, the hate is already showing inside my little Jeffery. Now that I see there's a great chance in winning over my grandson, killing my favorite son will come easier!" with one last look at the frowning boy, he returned to finish his job he had started.

Chapter Fifty-Seven

Jeff remained still as the demons continued their chant until the devil held up his hand for silence. Jeff opened his eyes and stood up slowly when he noticed his father standing in front of him. Jeff knew his last battle would be with his evil father, far stronger than all the demons combined. Even in his weak state, Jeff's voice came out strong.

"My wife and son are safe from your clutches! You think you stand a chance with our boy, but that is where you are wrong, father! You cannot harm them anymore! I leave them in Ted's care so I know God will protect them from you forever!"

"For the time being, you may be correct, my poor unfortunate son. Already your son shows signs of hate and he is yet young, not even grown into his sharp teeth." Lucifer mocked him.

"Teddy speaks out of fear for his papa's suffering, Lucifer, nothing more!" Jeff took a deep breath and felt all the sharp pains in his perfect body. "Even the most faithful Christian can show their dislike of the act of mistreating the ones they love."

"You use that word so freely, Jeff. A word you once detested, even killed for if someone said it in your presence." The devil sneered "A lot of good it will do you now, this love that is the cause for your painful death!" he laughed. "Look at you, you are too weak to fight me, just as I planned. Besides, YOU CAN NEVER KILL ME YOU STUPID MAN!" Satan's face grew a bright red as flames shot through his eyes. "You could have had everything you ever desired, but you, poor fool, you fell in LOVE!"

"Yes, yes I did fall in love!" Jeff shouted and fell to his knees, too weak to stand. "And I am glad I did! Naomi saved me! God's love saved me!"

"Listen to you Jeff! Naomi's love! God's love, saved you?" The devil got in his face. "Jeff, you cannot love! You are not just another bastard son of a mortal woman, son, I made sure of that. I made sure you would be my chosen by creating the perfect sperm to deliver to my chosen partner. Your mother was beautiful, a great figure of a woman and easy to turn on. I knew a son with her would be special and very handsome." He laughed. "Call me vain if you choose, because it is true, I am proud of my appearance. I was the most beautiful angel in heaven, even more beautiful than my Creator or His Son! So, why shouldn't I reign! I was handsome, like Him, I was intelligent like Him, I was powerful like Him. Many angels looked up to me, like they did the Almighty! "I was cunning…"

"He is not! You were jealous, He was not! You were envious, He was not!" Jeff took a deep breath. "You are a liar, He is not! And, you thought you could take over His throne and become Him, but you failed and was thrown out! There is and there has always been, only one God!"

"You've become quite the Bible scholar! Too bad it will do you no good!" Lucifer sneered. "You are almost as much of me as I am. I placed inside you 99% of my blood Jeffery and that pitiful mother you had contributed only 1%, by my design. This is why she hated and despised you so much!"

"And it was probably the reason I loathed her so, But if I had it to do over again, I would show her the love she deserved." Jeff closed his eyes in pain.

"And, why, in my name, would you choose to love that woman/" Lucifer raised his eyebrow, uncertain of his son's reasoning.

"Mother gave me the 1% of blood that held love!" Jeff looked up seriously. "And that 1% of love is all I needed to find love! It far outweighs your 99%, father!"

Jeff could hardly move by now, the gashes sliced on his stomach was bleeding badly. The demons had cut his legs and arms, as blood ran down like streams. Unable to hold himself up any longer, Jeff fell forward.

As Naomi watched, she could not control the scream that tore from her throat. "No!" she tried desperately to push her way through the protective shield Jeff had placed in front of her, but her tries were in vain. Ted gently pulled her back to consul her as he waited.

Naomi stood frozen and watched her husband struggling for breath. "Oh, Jeff, my dearest love, don't die, please!"

Jeff managed to turned and look into his wife's tear-stain face. He managed to give her a weak smile as he spoke.

"I love you dear one. You have made me happy for the first time in my worthless life." His eyes fell on the sobbing boy, clinging to his mother. "Teddy, be a good boy and watch after you mama and little brother. I love you, son."

"Oh God, no Jeff, darling. Don't say your goodbyes! Please darling!" Naomi grabbed Ted "Please Ted, do something!"

A devilish smile fell on Lucifer's face and his stared at Ted. "Yes Ted, by all means, do something! You cannot help Jeff and handle me at the same time!" he slung his head around to face his son, poison dripping off his tongue.

"Now, you, ungrateful fool! You were destined to have it all and you threw it back in my face! DAMN YOU, JEFFERY!" Satan gave a loud scream as he dived toward his wounded son to give the final blow. He ripped a great gash through his abdomen with his sharp nails while sinking his sharp teeth deep in the handsome man's neck with one fatal bite. "Now, you die slowly, and soon your soul will be mine anyway where I will reward you with punishment beyond hated!"

Naomi sank to her knees, weeping uncontrollable as Teddy pounded against the invisible shield.

"Papa! Papa! Don't go, Papa!"

Ted had seen enough as he held up his hand and shouted. "THIS STOPS NOW!" he walked through the shield and stood beside Jeff's dying body. Ted's attention was on Satan as his anger grew and he pointed directly at him, shouting. "SATAN, YOU WILL NOT HARM THIS MAN ANY LONGER!" With speed, Ted pointed all ten fingers, and lights, much like lighting shot out of his fingertips as Satan and his demons were trapped inside their own shield, but this one like an inescapable prison. Ted got down next to Jeff and took his hand,

"Jeff, look inside your mind. Let the noise, this hate, fade into silence. Remember the singing, remember the messages written on those pages. It's all there, Jeff, I can see it. Just search your mind, my brother, search your heart."

Jeff relaxed, he could feel the sharp pains throughout his body and he knew he was dying. The screams coming from his beloved Naomi had melted into sobs. He heard her pleading with him not to die because she needed him. Jeff thought, "I want to be with her again. I want to see my one again. I cannot die without finding the truth Ted's speaks of."

Jeff thoughts began to float and he found himself sitting in the small chapel on Ted's mountain. Naomi was by his side holding Teddy in her lap and everyone was singing. Everyone but him. Could he remember the words they sung? There had been two hymns, he thought, and then he heard a voice singing one. Ted's voice sang

"Through your sins be a scarlet, they shall be as white a snow…" Silence fell all around him, as all those watching listened, this time it was Jeff singing, as he repeated the words. Then Ted once again lifted his heavenly voice. "The Savior lives, no more to die. He lives, the Lord, enthroned on high. He lives, triumphant o'er the grave, He lives, eternally to save!"

Jeff once again repeated the song as Naomi stared through her tears, hearing her love one sing for the first time. Little Teddy blinked his eyes as he listened to his father singing.

After the hymns, Jeff began flipping New Testament pages through his mind until he stopped at John 11-(25-26) then he spoke the living word. "Jesus said 'I am the resurrection and the life: he that believeth in me, though he were dead, yet shall he live: And whosoever lives and believeth in me shall never die." Tears ran down Jeff's face and his words were heard clearly.

"Father, forgive me! My sins are many, too many to count. My Savior, you were without sin, yet you died on that horrible cross for sinners like me! I know now the terrible amount of sins I alone, placed upon your shoulders only added that much more to the weight of the pain you bore. I am not worthy to ask you Jesus, but please, Lord, forgive me!"

Jeff gasp for air, the loss of blood had made his once strong voice weak as he lifted up his heart to the Almighty God. "I believe! I believe in you Jesus with all my heart! I have seen your light in Ted and my beautiful Naomi and I want to go to heaven so I can live with my Naomi forever." He sucked in air and knew he couldn't last much longer. "You…you know how much I love her, Lord. She is my life. Her and Ted has spoken of salvation and what I need to find out for myself. I know now what is true, what she and Ted have been trying to tell me. Yes, I love Naomi more than life, But my Father, I love you more."

The wind began to blow, lighting streaked across the dark sky as the thunder shook the ground on which Jeff's wounded body lay.

Naomi stared down at her beloved husband, taken shallow

breathes. She was afraid to take her eyes off of Jeff for fear she would lose him if she blinked her eyes. Was this it, the moment God in heaven would take her dearest Jeff home and leave her a widow to raise two small boys alone?"

No one could hear the voice in the wind, except for Jeff and Ted. It blew gently over Ted and fell over Jeff's slumped body, lying face up where his neighbor and friend had turned him over for this purpose. The voice in the wind spoke softly to Jeff.

"You are forgiven my son. You have passed your greatest test of faith." Then the wind took on a different feel, soft and warm, with the smell of heaven. Jeff opened his eyes and looked into the loving face of Jesus. "Jeff, my brother, how I love you." Not only could Jeffery Wineworth see the perfect look of love on the face of Jesus, he also felt the greatest amount of love known to man descending down and around him.

Jeff could feel his heart stopping and in his dying breath, he whispered "Jesus, my Lord."

Naomi grabbed her mouth to hold in her mournful cry, but she could not control the tears that flooded down her cheeks. She was losing the one, she loved most on earth."

"I am He!" Jesus radiated with great love as he stretched out his nailed pierced hands. "You will be welcomed in My kingdom, my brother, but your time has not come. I need you to remain here on earth until your mission is over. You must live! Teddy, your son, needs his papa, your newborn son needs his papa. Your devoted wife, Naomi, needs her husband and love one, and most of all, Ted needs you. Your task is far from over and it will last until the end, when I return. Heavens time is not like the time of earth. So swift as a hummingbird and slow as a turtle, the time will go. Remember, there is no time in heaven, just now. Until that earthly time, you and Ted must work together to fight evil." The Lord began to fade away as His words said. "I will not leave you to fight this battle alone, my son. Ted will receive my message of warnings and the angels in heaven will be on standby." He continued to fad, as he concluded. "Now, Jeff, close your eyes and when you open them, your wounds will be healed."

Everything grew silent, and all presumed that Jeff had passed away, lying there so still, as though there was no breath left inside him. Lucifer, being an angel, had heard the voice of the Lord, but the human demons could not hear Him, same as Naomi and Teddy. Satan was filled with excessive emotions and he was provoked to rage and wrath, knowing once again the Almighty had won. But this time it was his creation, his favorite son's soul, the Son of God had won and now would use against him in the final battle.

"Jeff, you fool! Desert me to my most hated enemy! You are now a traitor in my eyes! I will work on not desiring your devotion so much and all those beautiful things you did before you found…that damn LOVE! Go, live with your God and be satisfied with holding that girl's hand in God's perfect kingdom! You will never know sex again. I can guarantee you of that!"

"Satan, hold your tongue! I will not let you speak ill of the kingdom of God, my Father!" Ted froze his words, and with a glow about him, he reached down, took Jeff by his hands and lifted him up. Naomi and Teddy looked with disbelief and saw the horrible bloody wounds were completely gone and Jeff's strong tan back glistening with his strong muscles. Her eyes fell on Ted, whose hand was extended for her to come. Without hesitation, Naomi walked through the protective shield and over in front of her husband. Ted gently touched Jeff's eyelids as he spoke softly. "Jeff, my brother, open your eyes."

As Jeff slowly opened his eyes, Naomi let out a small gasp and he dropped them on her. Instead of the cold black eyes he had been born with, Jeff's eyes had turned to a warm heavenly blue, that glistening when he smiled, still showing sharp canine teeth. Lifting her up in his strong arms, Jeff gave her a passionate kiss, then carried her back behind the shield.

"Ted and I have these evil beings to send back, my dearest, before we can celebrate."

Ted motioned Jeff back behind the shield with his family when he felt the presence of some very strong help.

"Do you intend to take on me and my demons all by yourself, Bible thumper?" Satan mocked him. "You are a pitiful warrior to attempt to fight the great archangel Lucifer all alone!"

"LUCIFER!" Michael, the archangel spoke out with authority. "Ted is not alone! Ted, is NEVER alone!" Michael turned to Ted, and nodded, sending him a spirit message that Jenny was safe, then the great heavenly angel turned his attention back on his old enemy and stared sternly at his evil eyes. "Lucifer, I am sending you back to hell! Unless you are invited by some evil force, you must never set foot or soul on these two mountains again!"

"I still see you think you are better than I, Michael! I am not finished! There are other ways to get what I want! My favorite son is gone but there is another he is not aware of, who could be made into my favorite son!" Satan shouted. "And I could always win over my grandson, Jeffery. He will do just fine." Lucifer narrowed his eyes. "Are you afraid to remove the shield which has me a prisoner or do you still think you can fight me and win?"

"Shield be gone!" with that the barrier vanished. "I am not afraid of you, Lucifer and surely not these pitiful lost souls you command! Come and give me your best shot before I send you back, old friend!"

"We shall see who sends who back to where they came from!" the devil snapped his fingers as the fallen angel and his demons walked toward Michael.

Michael gave a great smile as he stood firm. "Indeed, we shall see, Lucifer!" Michael raised his hand and snapped his fingers. The four warrior angels surrounded Satan and the frightened demons, who had never witnessed such magnificent powerful warriors before. Michael stared down at the ground around their evil feet and it began to tremble until it cracked opened and swallowed the group up, closing quickly after them.

Michael stepped to one side, and Jenny smiled at her surprised husband. She ran into his outstretched arms and he held her tight. Ted gazed up into the evening sky and smiled as he whispered.

"Thank you, Father, for saving Jenny and my twins, for saving Naomi and young Teddy, and receiving Jeff as one of us and forgiving him! Thank you for the help of Michael and four of your mighty warriors. I am truly thankful!"

Michael walked up and Ted patted him on his broad shoulder. No words were needed, for the gratitude that reflected from Ted's loving face was enough thanks. The five angels disappeared as Jenny began to cry with happy tears.

"Oh Ted, I love you so much!"

"As I love you, my dearest Jenny." Ted took her hand and waved at a smiling Jeff and Naomi. "It is time to take you home and into a nice warm bed."

"With you lying by my side, husband, I am certain our bed will be very warm this night." Jenny winked at the other couple watching, holding tight to one another as well.

"Do not let us hold you love birds up." Jeff laughed as he gathered his young, sleepy son up in his strong arms. "I can inform you as well, as soon as we feed this growing boy a light supper and put him to bed, we will enjoy a very warm bed of our own too!"

"Jeff!" Naomi blushed, and smiled at her dear friends. "Thank you for everything Ted. Our Father in heaven has blessed us all again! Praise the Lord!" she motioned them away. "Go on and show each other how much. I've got to get my boys home, fed and in bed, since that seems to be their desire. Teddy's yawning, too sleepy to hold his little head up and my wonderful husband, back to his healthy, ready for bed games, self!"

"See you both soon." Ted smiled and taking Jenny by the hand, walked her lovingly home.

Chapter Fifty-Eight

Matthew listened carefully to the person speaking on the other end of the phone line. He looked around the large room and noticed everyone was quiet and waiting to hear what the police report was on the school fire. Matthew was sure Ted would know before he could share the report with the anxious group listening.

"Yes, chief, I will relay the findings to everyone here on the mountain. Thank you, sir. We appreciate your thorough investigation." He hung up and glanced at Ted before speaking, who simply smiled and motioned for him to tell the findings.

"Just as we told the Fire Marshall, the fire was deliberately set in the center hallway, leading to the gym and Miss Angela Rayfield and the principal are nowhere to be found. The authorities have concluded that with all the witness's testimonies, these two appear to be the likely pair that started this dangerous fire, with the intent to kill everyone trapped inside that gym."

"Where did they go?" Kathy glanced up from shelling peas.

"Back to hell, I hope!" Robert took Miriam's hand as he found Ted's eyes. "Do you think they went back, Ted?"

"Rest assured, all of you, they are all back in their rightful place, but they did not choose to go peacefully on their own." Ted knew only those that had witness what had happen yesterday afternoon to Jeff, saw all the demons that had come to their fair town, huddled together when the great angels were sending them back down to hell. Raven, Tucker, and Cashton had wounded Jeff before Lucifer gave the final deadly blow, while Mr. Morgan, Angelia Rayfield, and Marna Mullican, had remain silent as they stood watch by their master's side. Ted stood up and made his way over to the big window overlooking the high peak. "The demons will not be a problem anymore on Goldsburg Mountain or Black Mountain, unless some evil force brings them back. They are afraid of Michael and the great warrior angels, but not Lucifer. He fears no one, not even our God! He must always be watched carefully."

"What sort of evil force is Michael speaking of, darling? Surely, he cannot think Jeff will revert to his evil ways after finding the way and the truth, regarding loving the Lord above all things?" Jenny joined her husband at the window.

"You know the Bible, my love. As long as the earth endures, good and evil will grow side by side. Only at our Lords return, will the weeds be separated from the wheat and it shall then be burned in hell, while the good will receive life eternal." Tears filled his peaceful blue eyes. "We must watch little Teddy carefully, bring him up in faith and hope. The devil will stop at nothing to get what he wants."

Ted jerked his head up, a revelation coming clearly in his mind. He closed his eyes and smiled as he said softly "Mother, father is coming up the mountain road. He plans to surprise us with his unannounced arrival."

"Just like Peter to come without so much as a telegram!" Hannah ran to check herself in the hall mirror. "I must look a mess!"

Ted walked over behind his mother and took around her, smiling at her through the oval mirror. "You look beautiful, mother. I know father will be overjoyed to see his bride." Ted brought out her prettiest laughter as she turned around to kiss him. "Let's meet him at the door. He made the long trip to see you and to greet the twins when they are born."

Mother and son were waiting at the front door when Peter Neenam drove his rental car to a stop in front of the white farmhouse. Seeing the greeting party, Peter climbed quickly from the four door Sedan and made his way to the door to grab his wife and hug her tightly.

"My, how I've missed you, Hannah!" after giving her a tender kiss, he and his special son embraced each other. "I have truly missed you, my boy. I am very proud of you, Ted. You have achieved so much over such a short time. Hannah has written about the fine group of children you are raising and the self-sufficient lifestyle you live here, and in such a modern world. Truly amazing, my son."

"I work not for praise, father, but your approval is always welcome." Ted's smile was warm and genuine as he motioned for Jenny to join them. "And this is the reason for my constant smile. Father, this is my wife, Jenny, the mother of our two adorable twin girls and the other reason for your coming all this distance."

"Yes, yes, my brilliant son." Peter Neenam shook his head in amazement, then smiled down at the beautiful woman in his son's arms. "Jenny, when Hannah received her letter from Ted, informing us about being married, we were, how do the young say it?"

"Blown away?" Jenny laughed when he nodded a positive. "I would know being a high school teacher, Mr. Neenam. The kids in this generation use many different slang words, such as cool, heavy, crazy, meaning good, not insane. I guess you could say, there are times when I see Ted do things or say things no one else can understand, I feel somewhat, blown away myself and wonder how I became so lucky to become his wife. I truly love your son."

"I can see that Jenny and please sweetheart, call me father. You are our daughter now and soon to be the mother of our grandbabies." Peter walked between the couple and placed an arm around each. "I wanted to be here to see my little granddaughters come into the world. I would not miss that for anything."

"Then, you made it just in time, father." Ted picked his suitcase off the floor and casually walked to the staircase. "Jenny will be going into labor today at five o'clock this afternoon. I'll just put your luggage in Hannah's room and show you around until then." He strolled on up the steps, leaving Peter and Hannah staring in disbelief at one another. Jenny walked over to the staircase and stared up.

"I wonder how long he knew that delivery time? This is the first time I am hearing about it!" she turned to smiled at her in-laws. "Well, these little girls have been getting pretty active, so I knew they were ready to come out, any day now."

Naomi walked out of the bathroom and flopped down on the bed. "Jeff, your son is very active today and he is about to wear me out with all his kicking."

Jeff walked over to join her, the Bible in his hand. "It won't be much longer, my one."

She smiled down at the holy book in his hands. "I see you have started at the beginning."

"That I have, sweet one. The old testament must be read as well as the new." His face held a serious expression as he placed a bookmark inside before closing the book. "I also see Lucifer, my father, started his evil work with Eve."

"Yes, I am afraid he has been around a long time." Naomi

glanced out the large bedroom window and feeling anxious at the mention of the evil one's name, ask "Jeff, where is Teddy? Have you seen him leave the house after I ask him to stay in his room and read the new book we bought him about David and the giant?"

"He was playing in his room when I came by." Jeff noticed the worried look on her beautiful face and knowing a mother's sense of danger coming to her child, he said softly. "I will go and check on our son, sweet one, just relax."

Jeff was only gone for a short period before he looked back inside, worry etch across his handsome face. "Teddy is not in his room, Naomi! He is nowhere in the castle!"

"Oh, Jeff!" Naomi jumped up. "We have got to find him! It's not like Teddy to disobey me and run off like this, especially after what he just witnessed happening to you!"

"We will find Teddy, my love. He could not have gone far and I have sent Fang and Thorn to find him and to keep watch until we arrive." They made their way quickly down the steps and noticed the front door standing wide open. Jeff sensed he had gone toward the rose garden and when they arrived, they found it empty. Suddenly, the sound of laughter came from the forest and they made their way quickly toward the sound. The two obedient wolves sat staring in the dark woods, low growls coming from the throat. Jeff knew they felt something menacing and dangerous.

"Teddy, this is your papa! Come out here at once before I come in there after you and spank your butt!" Jeff called out and everything grew silent.

"Teddy Jeffery Wineworth, you heard your papa! Come here son!" Naomi squeezed Jeff's hand "It growing late out here and pretty soon it will be too dark for you to find your way out!"

"Alright mama, papa, I'm coming." Teddy came out smiling, carry a cute little puppy wolf. "Look mama. Papa, I got my very own wolf! Isn't he sweet?"

"Teddy, where did you get that puppy?" Naomi looked at the cute little ball of fur, wiggling in their son's hands.

"A very nice old man gave me this puppy. He said it needed a good home and a special boy like me to raise him, and I seemed like the perfect little fellow, right?" The small child gave a bright happy smile, filled with trust and innocents. "My puppy has a special name too. Want to know what it is?"

"What son, what is his name?" Jeff stared out at the dark forest for the 'old' man who had somehow lured their son outside and gave him a gift.

"My puppy's name is Destiny. Do you know what his name means, papa?" Teddy rubbed the small wolf's ears and laughed as he shook his head. Jeff watched him closely as he asked.

"Yes, I know the meaning Teddy. Do you?"

"Sorta." Teddy scratched the furry belly and giggled at the kicking feet. "The nice man said, everyone has a destiny. Some have a great one while most people have plain ones. He told me I would have a great destiny, like a king, and people would bowl down before me, bringing me great riches! He said I could grow up to be just like my strong papa and rule forever!" the puppy licked Teddy on the face, bringing more childish giggles. He beamed as he looked up at his father with his big black eyes "Can I please keep my puppy, papa?"

"Son, did the nice man tell you who he was?" Jeff knew already but he needed to hear what this evil being told their innocent little boy.

"Oh, yes papa, he did! He told me he was my grandpapa!" Teddy's eyes were wide with excitement. "He said he was my papa's papa. Is this nice old man your papa?"

Naomi grabbed Jeff. "Jeff, he is already after Teddy!"

"Son, listen to papa. You must never have anything to do with that man again, do you hear me?" Jeff knelt down and took around his little boy. "You must never see or speak to him again! He only pretends to be a nice man, my son. He is really very bad."

Teddy pouted up as tears ran down his cheeks. "But…can I keep my puppy, papa? Please?"

"If you promise me and your mama that you will have nothing to do with that man again, and raise your puppy up to be good, then you may keep him." Jeff looked up and received an approval from his wife.

Teddy clapped his hands gleefully. "Thanks papa! Thanks mama!" he gave his parents a big hug. "I'll be real, good and my puppy will be the friendliest wolf around!"

Naomi smiled down at her happy little fellow as she took his hand. "It's almost time for supper, darling. Let's take these fine wolves in and give them something to eat before I make our supper."

Jeff waited until his family had walked away before he turned toward the forest. "I do not know who gave you permission to come back on this mountain, but you can just return to where you came from! You are not welcome here, Satan! You will never win my son's soul, you bastard!"

"I am not the bastard here, son, you are. I was created in this eternal form by the same God you choose to worship instead of me, your own powerful father! If you must know who gave me permission to appear again, it was that innocent child you said I could never control. I merely enticed him by letting him see the puppy outside his bedroom window. He followed it to the forest and called out for him, so I brought him to the boy!" Jeff heard the devil give a devilish laugh. "I will entice him with something far greater when he becomes a young man. The lust of the flesh can make men like you and I do things beyond other simple men. Jeffery must get older, then I shall return!" then there was only silence as Lucifer disappeared.

Jeff made his way slowly in the castle, going over Satan's last words to him, when he noticed Naomi holding her stomach and moaning in pain. He rushed over and grabbed her. "It is time, is it not?"

"Yes! Oh, God!" she squeezed her eyes shut as another labor pain hit, young Teddy staring at her with wide, frightened eyes. "Jeff, the doctor hasn't come back to work yet! This baby is coming…now!"

Jeff picked her up and grabbed Teddy's hand.

"Come son, your baby brother is about to be born! We've got to get your mama to Goldsburg Mountain, right now!"

Chapter Fifty-Nine

Jenny was resting peacefully beside Ted on the long sofa when he casually glanced at the clock on the mantle. It chimed out the hours, one, two, three four and stopped after it chimed five loudly. Jenny sat up and yelled out as she doubled over in a sharp pain.

Hannah and Peter rushed in the big den as Ted carried his wife up the steps and laid her on their bed. His parents looked at each other, knowing Ted had said the labor would start at five sharp and he had been right, again.

After seeing that Jenny was comfortable, he pulled a chair up beside her and had a seat, taking her hand.

"Just squeeze my hand when you feel a pain coming, Jenny. It will be over soon." His eyes followed his mother around their room as she collected the things they would need for delivering a baby. He noticed his father watching her and called him over.

"Father, you may lower the sheets on the other bed we brought in this morning. I knew Naomi would go into labor around the same time as Jenny and her doctor has not return to his practice yet. They all assumed the baby boy would be born in two weeks, not this soon." Ted saw his father's questioning expression. "I should think you would know me by now, father. God, the Father, tells me these things. Now, if you will get Matthew and have Jeff bring his wife in here as soon as they get out of their car."

"Certainly son!" Peter jumped up and walked briskly to the front door and saw the young couple and their small boy walking quickly up the walk to the door. "Ted has you set up inside his bedroom next to their bed." Jeff could not resist smiling, but Naomi looked puzzled.

"Don't ask how Ted knew you would be coming here to have your baby, my dear, but you are in good hands. Hannah has done many delivers and I have done my share." Peter showed Jeff the way and hurried the boy off to the kitchen with Kathy and Miriam and collected Matthew.

Jeff found a chair waiting next to Naomi's bed for him, so sitting down, he gathered her trembling hand in his strong one and told her to squeeze as hard as she needed, remembering his last experience in childbirth.

Jenny let out another scream. "Oh shit! That hurts!" she closed her eyes in pain as she squeezed Ted's hand until the pain subsided.

"I can feel your pain, Jenny, cause, here comes another one! God!" Naomi tried hard not to scream as she squeezed Jeff's strong hand as tight as she could manage, until it eased up.

Hannah gave them a reassuring smile as she gently rubbed their big round bellies. "You are both doing great! If both of you began delivering at the same time, Peter is very gentle with all his patients."

"I'm glad there is something about this nightmare that is gentle." Jenny felt another pain coming, but managed to say, "These two little stinkers are hurting me like…Oh, shit!" Jenny screamed out, while at the exact moment Ted grabbed his stomach and moaned in agony, as he reversed the situation and squeezed Jenny's hand. "Ouch!" Jenny stared over at her husband. "Is that a new way of taking my mind off the labor pains by mashing my hand?"

"No…darling…" he tried to take a breath, scaring his mother.

"Son, are you alright? You're not having chest pains, are you?"

"No mother, I was having a labor pain. I put Jenny's pain inside me…" Ted took a deep breath, still feeling the effects. "just to see what my beautiful wife was feeling! I really admire what women go through to give us men children." Ted closed his eyes in relief when the pains eased up.

"Ted, sweetheart, what a perfectly loving, yet stupid thing, you did, just for me. I know no other men can actually do what you just did, except Jeff, But I grant you, the average Joe out there would never take on the pain of having a baby, no matter how much they love their spouse."

"I can, and I will take on this pain too, for my beloved!" Jeff sat up, preparing for Naomi's next labor pain.

"Jeff, sweetheart, the thought is enough. I cannot ask you to feel this horrible pain just because Ted was brave enough to try it." Naomi smiled, filled with love for this man. "I bet Ted would advise you not to go through with it."

"Jeff, I know you have received some really bad pain lately, but I think you better rethink this ideal, for your own good, my friend. God knew what He was doing when he let women have babies instead of men." Ted looked up serious.

"Ted, I agree, most men should never attempt to feel their wife's pain, but I have unmatched strength, my friend. I will handle this without a cry." Jeff noticed Naomi squeeze her eyes shut and knew a pain was coming. "Soon, I too will know the agony you feel, my dearest one."

Hannah just shook her head when Naomi could not hold in her scream this time, for the pain was extra sharp, indicating the baby was near the birth canal. Within seconds, Jeff doubled over in pain and squeezed his wife's small hand, causing her to let out another cry. But her soft cry was drowned out by Jeff's loud one.

"HOLY SHIT! DAMN! THAT IS BAD!" he stood up rubbing his stomach. "God! That has to be the worst pain in the universe!" he breathed a sigh of relief when the pain ease up, then died away. "Naomi, I am truly sorry I did not listen to your and Ted's sage advice!"

"What's done is done, Jeff, darling, but please do not take my pain anymore! Both of us do not have to suffer." Naomi took a deep breath, knowing the labor would soon be over and with the birth of her new baby boy, all her bad pain would be forgotten when she saw her perfect gift from God. "Besides darling, you just about broke my hand when you squeezed it."

"I can sympathize with you Naomi. These labor pains are bad enough without a sweet caring husband squeezing your fingers off!"

"Jenny, darling, I am truly sorry." Ted grabbed her hand and began rubbing her fingers. "I promise, I will never do that again!"

Hannah could not resist smiling over at her husband, who was trying hard not to laugh at Ted and Jeff. Jeff nodded in agreement with Ted, relieved he did not have to feel that terrible pain again, either.

Jenny almost sat up screaming "Oh! This one is bad! Really bad!"

"The babies are coming out Jenny! Push, daughter, push! I can see the little blonde head coming out!" Hannah took a gentle hold as she continued softly. "Push, honey! You are doing good!"

"Jenny, my love, it's…it's almost out!" Ted's eyes were wide with excitement when the first twin slid out and he heard her cry for the first time. "Welcome, our little Mary." Ted smiled through happy tears as the second head appeared. "Just push Jenny and hold tight to my hand."

"That's it, Jenny, you, brave girl! One more big push and it will be over." Peter beamed when his granddaughter slid into his waiting hands. Within seconds, she too was crying.

"Martha, our precious baby Martha!" Ted kissed Jenny's trembling lips. "I love you so much, Jenny. Our babies are beautiful." He held them down for her to see after his parents placed one in each arm. "Girls, this is your loving mother."

Jenny smiled down at the beautiful, blonde haired twins as tears raced down her cheeks. Her eyes found Ted's "Oh Ted, I love you too, my wonderful husband!"

"Congratulations! I…I think this boy is ready to come out too…right…now!" Naomi cried out as she grabbed Jeff's hand. Peter was standing over her smiling.

"You are correct, sweet angel! I can see its black hair so start pushing hard! Push! Push!" Ted's father gently guided the small infant out and with one last painful cry, Jeff and Naomi's second son came into the world and started crying.

Jeff took his son and gazed down smiling. "Looks like Jacob has black hair, like his old man and brother. I think Jacob is resting his eyes so I'm not sure of their color yet."

"They are as black as the ace of spades, very unusual." Peter looked down at the handsome baby. "Cute little fellow."

"Like his hair, our son gets his black eyes from his father as well. Jeff's were solid black when I met him, but God's saving grace turned them a beautiful blue." Naomi smiled down at her little infant. "He is a handsome boy, just like his papa."

Jeff reached down to touch the tiny cheek. "I hope our next one is a girl, so she will look like her mama."

"A girl would be nice, darling, with a house full of boys, but…" Naomi smiled at Jeff. "I think we will wait for a while before we have her and let me get over having this one first."

"I know what you mean, Naomi." Jenny closed her eyes in relief, knowing, except for raising two little girls, things would be back to normal. "I do want to give Ted a son someday, but I am not ready for Ted to put one inside me just now."

Everyone laughed as Ted blushed. Matthew had been stationed at the bedroom door to keep any child intruder out while the mothers were in labor, but knowing young Teddy had been anxious to meet the babies, he and Kathy escorted the little tot in the room.

"Is it alright to let Teddy in to see his little brother and the girls, he keeps talking about it?" Matthew, in truth, felt the same excitement to witness newborn babies and see what they looked like. Ruth had been the smallest child he had seen up to that point and he thought one day he might be facing this same thing.

"It will be fine for you and Teddy to come in and see our newborns, Matthew." As always, Ted knew Matthew real intention for coming in early. "If it had not made Jenny and Naomi uncomfortable watching the delivery, you could have gotten a few pointers for your son's delivery."

"I'm sure I got plenty of time to worry about that. We are not ready to start a family yet, right Kath?" Matthew looked over at his wife hopeful.

"Not right away, sweetie, but with my age, we cannot wait many more years." Kathy reassured Matthew, although in the back of her mind, her real reason for waiting was after hearing her best friend and Naomi screaming out in great pain.

Everyone's attention was drawn to Teddy as he walked up and looked down at the three infants, staring up at him.

"Wow! They are so little!" his dark eyes fell on the baby resting in his mother's arms. "My brother is real cute, mama. He looks like I did in my baby pictures!" Teddy giggled when Jacob smiled up at him.

"Yes, your brother Jacob looks a great deal like his bigger brother, truly handsome, both like their papa." Naomi lend over and kissed her little boy. "Teddy, you need to be a good big brother to Jacob and you will have a friend for life."

"I'll teach him everything I know and he'll be smart like me, mama." He giggled then turned to see the beautiful blue-eyed blonde in Ted's arms. "Mary is about the prettiest girl I've ever seen, my Ted. Mary will be my wife! Brother Jacob can love Martha."

"Teddy, there's plenty of time before you start thinking about romance, young man!" Jeff reached over and pulled his boy in his lap. He instantly drew his attention on Matthew and Kathy, gave a chuckle as he winked at Ted, who was smiling back. Jenny had been watching the two special men closely and knew they were up to something.

"Hey, you two, what are you up to? Out with it, fellows!"

“Very well! Let me do the honors Ted.” Jeff’s eyes were filled with mischief. “Kathy, may we be the first to congratulate you and Matthew.”

“Con…congratulate us? For what?” Matthew swallowed and stared over at Jeff.

“Looks like you are going to have a baby in eight months!” Jeff could not control his laughter over their shocked expressions.

“I am afraid your waiting is up, my friends. At least, your little boy will have children near his age to play with.” Ted smiled at Matthew, who had turned completely white.

“That is utterly ridiculous, fellows! Don’t you think I would know if I were pregnant or not?” Kathy frowned.

“Kathy, don’t argue with these two. Do not ask me how they always seem to know things, important things, like getting pregnant, but they just have a way of knowing.” Jenny felt for her friend. “But pal, I am sure you are pregnant, so welcome to the mama club.”

“A baby? A boy? Wow!” Kathy smiled and looked over at Matthew, who looked sick. “Honey, are you alright?”

“I…I will be…fine…” Matthew fainted and fell to the floor. Kathy bent down and noticed the pillow under his head.

“Now, how did that pillow get there?”

“We saw it coming and gave him a little soft landing.” Jeff sighed “Poor old cool Matthew, a daddy!”

Chapter Sixty

After a beautiful morning of making passionate love, Ted and Jenny stood smiling down at their sleeping twin girls. Jenny pulled in closer to Ted as she gazed into the angelic faces below them.

"They look like two little cherub angels! Oh, Ted darling, they look so much like you. Can you believe our love made such adorable babies?"

"Yes, my beloved, I can." He pulled Jenny around until his lips met hers. "Our love, our passion, our beautiful gift of happiness and joy. Oh, my beautiful Jenny, I am for certain the happiest man in the universe."

"And I the happiest woman." Jenny smiled up into his handsome face. "My God, my Ted, my daughters and so stands my love."

Ted laughed softly as he hugged her, then watched the girls open their blue eyes and smile up at their parents.

"How sweet they are, and only a month old." Ted beamed. "They are never fussy, except when they're hungry."

"Or have a messy diaper." Jenny picked up Mary. "Isn't it funny how parents can tell twins apart and other people can't? Yes, I can, Mary, my sweet precious girl!" Jenny bent down to kiss Martha's cheeks. "Hi pumpkin, my sweet darling girl. Today is your lucky day, Martha. Daddy is going to feed you your bottle."

"Da da!" the infant giggled. "Da da!"

Ted laughed and reached down to pick her up. "That's right Martha, I am daddy!" the bottles were waiting as they mysteriously were every morning for the couple and they sat down, side by side on the bed, to feed their infants.

Jeff helped Teddy tie up his shoelaces as he sat reading on the side of his bed. "Papa, why did the three little pigs have a big bad wolf after them? Where they mean? Was the bad wolf one from Mrs. Mullican? She made our wolf bad!"

"No, sweet boy, the story about the Three Little Pigs, had nothing to do with that woman! You can stop worrying about your old nana, Teddy. She won't ever be coming back." Jeff took the book from his son and pointed down at the author's name. "This person who wrote this children's book, used only his imagination. I'm really not sure why he made the wolf so bad, same as the bad wolf in Little Red Riding Hood. But the writer of Goldie Locks and the Three Bears, made them friendlier. All three are just stories, not real. Maybe intended to scare little children so they won't run away."

Teddy took the book and threw it down, then announced "Well, it, don't scare me! I'm brave! It will scare my baby brother Jacob, though, so I will hide it in my closet till he's bigger! I will protect my brother, cause I'm big!"

"You are still my little boy, Teddy." Jeff picked him up and gave him a bear hug. "Now, let's go and see if mama and baby brother are ready to pay the family a visit."

"Oh boy! I can see my girlfriend!" Teddy hopped down, giggling.

Naomi had carried the baby down the hall to meet the fellows when she heard her young son's comment. When father and son stepped out into the hall, she frowned down at her little boy.

"You are a bit young to have a girlfriend, Teddy! Mama is not ready for you to start dating just yet!"

"Why not! I love Mary and Mary loves me!" Teddy spoke loudly.

Jeff reached back and spanked his backside lightly. "Son, do not talk so loud! You are hurting my ears! Now, stop being so sassy and listen to your mama before I give you a real spanking!"

"I'm sorry, mama! I'm sorry papa!" Teddy quickly changed the subject by rubbing his brother's small head. "Jacob sure is little."

"He is only one month old, darling." Naomi lend over and kissed the top of Teddy's dark head of hair. "You are thirty months old sweetheart. That is two and a half years."

"Wow! I'm twenty-nine months older than my brother!" Teddy smiled proudly when he heard his papa say, 'smart kid, then pulled Jeff's arm. "Let's go papa, I want to play with Ruth!"

Naomi smiled over at her husband as they made their way to the car. "I have always heard, children at this age was horrible. Now, I know."

When the Wineworths arrived at the farmhouse, Ted and Jenny were waiting outside to welcome them. Filled with excitement, young Teddy jumped from the car and raced passed the greeters, as Jeff and Naomi watched him, shaking their heads.

"That boy could not wait to play with Ruth. That's all he talked about coming over here."

"Ruth? Teddy talked about seeing Ruth?" Ted turned back inside the house quickly, calling over his shoulder. "He is on his way up the stair to see our twins!"

Jenny rushed in behind her husband, followed closely by Teddy's parents. When the last three stepped inside the bedroom, Ted motioned for them to stay quiet and listen. Young Teddy was speaking softly as he looked down at the girls, who both were staring back at him.

"Hi Mary! It's me, your Teddy, your Jeffery." The four adults could hear one of the girls speaking baby talk. Teddy smiled broadly, as if he understood every word she said. "Yes, I know, Mary. I know you love me!"

Jenny turned to see Naomi looking back at her, puzzled, but Jeff and Ted stepped closed together to converse in spirit talk. Unheard by anyone but each other, the men with the special powers spoke to each other.

"My girls have the gift already, like I did at their age, so they can understand Teddy and respond to him." Ted had doubts about telling Jenny too soon, so he had kept this fact to himself.

"I know Teddy has the gift, but he has not tested his brother yet, although Jacob has already spoken to me in spirit." Jeff glanced at their wives to make sure they weren't observing them. "I will speak openly to my son, so our women do not get suspicious." Jeff walked over to his son and knelt down. "Teddy, what else have you talked about with Mary and Martha?"

"I told them about my new puppy." Teddy smiled. They want me to bring him next time."

"Ted, if the girls can understand Teddy, can they respond?" Jenny had walked up to her husband. "Please, darling, I need to know if my daughters are…just like you."

Ted walked over to the babies' crib and looked down, "Girls, can you understand daddy?"

"DaDa, we do!" They thought in unison. "Mama, hear?"

"No, little ones, only daddy." Ted put his hand out for Jenny, who walked up, first, staring at him, then down at her small babies.

"Ted, are you…can they…?"

"There is nothing to be afraid of Jenny, but yes, they have the gift of hearing spirit talk and speaking in it." Ted hugged her. "Everything will be alright, darling."

"You think?" Jenny walked over to the soft chair and slumped down in it. "They have inherited their father's special powers, which means, all three of you will be able to read my mind! Now, I must watch every single thing I think, much less say!" She turned her head to find Naomi watching with sympathetic eyes. "I guess you are the only one that knows how I feel, Naomi."

"Yes, things can get a bit strange at times, Jenny, but our love for our husbands outweighs the unusual powers they have." Naomi took a seat next to her friend and Ted's beautiful wife. Her big eyes gazed down at the baby boy in her lap. "I guess this little guy has the gift too."

"After two weeks, my precious wife. It took Teddy a while before he found his, remember?" Jeff pulled his eldest son over in his arms. "Son, why did you tell Mary you were Jeffery?"

"Cause, I am, Papa! That is my name! Jeffery Teddy Wineworth!" the boy stared up at his father.

"Son, your name is Teddy Jeffery Wineworth, remember?" Jeff took hold of his shoulder, but the boy did not blink.

"I know what you named me, when I was little, just a baby! You are my papa! I want to be like you! Your name is Jeffery!" he jumped from his father's arms and stomped his foot angrily. "So, my name is Jeffery!"

Not wanting Ted to feel hurt from this little boy he loved so dearly, Jeff pulled him in close to his ear and whispered "We will discuss this at home, boy! But for now, get yourself in that kitchen and find Ruth. You had better be nice, Teddy, or I will take you outside and give you a spanking! Do we understand each other?"

"Yes Papa." Teddy ran from the room calling Ruth's name.

Ted had excused himself to go up to the mountain. He had many un-answered questions clouding his mind and Ted hoped today was the day for revelations to free his mind. After reaching the top, everything seemed peaceful and calm as his eyes searched the heavens.

"My Father, I'm aware you know my heart. There for, you know why I have come to you."

The wind blew gently around his feet and up it drifted until it reached his ears and whispered

"My son, there is much troubling you, things you yearn to know."

"Yes, Father, there is." Ted watched a yellow butterfly land softly on a bright wildflower. "I have come to ask you about my real father. The loving being that planted my seed inside my mother twenty years ago."

"I think you already know the answer to this question, my son. Have you not felt it in your heart since you saw his face?" the breeze seemed to kiss Ted's cheek. "Speak his name, Ted."

"Gabriel, the messenger angel, my Father." Ted's eyes were wet with tears, saying his name aloud to the One who had created this mighty angel that helped him through the fire. "I believe he is my true father, Gabriel, your great angel."

"It was time for you to know, my son." The soft voice faded briefly, but returned. "Gabriel is indeed your true father, my devoted child. Peter, your earthly father has knowledge of who your real father is, as does your beautiful mother, Hannah."

"They never spoke of this to me, Father. Nor have I heard them speak this truth to one another." Ted's legs trembled from the knowledge that he was part angel. "He came, Gabriel came that day at school, to help save the children from the raging fire."

"Yes, my son. When you prayed for my help, Gabriel ask to go for you, his son." The voice remained soft and calm.

"I feel him near, Father. He is here now." Ted closed his eyes and he could hear the butterfly's wings lift from the flower and began to grow louder. When Ted opened his eyes, Gabriel was standing right in front of him.

Chapter Sixty-One

Hannah looked up from reading the book in her hand and saw Jenny sitting quietly on the big window seat, gazing lovingly up at the mountain top Ted has just climbed. Hannah could feel in her heart that her son was going to inquire about his real father. Somehow, she had known the moment he returned from the school fire and looked longingly in her eyes. Hannah could since her husband watching her, so she turned and their eyes made contact. At this point, Ted's mother knew it was time to confess the whole story, both to her dear husband and to her loving daughter-in-law. They had a right to know the truth and it wasn't everyday a woman, like Jenny, was married to a man who was half angel.

Peter got up and walked over to his wife. "Hannah, you have something on your mind, my dear. I can see that plainly."

"Yes Peter, my love." She slipped over and patted the space next to her, indicating for him to sit down, then her attention fell on her daughter-in-law. "Jenny, could you come over here, my dear. I have something you and Peter need to hear." Making room on her other side for Ted's wife to sit, Hannah waited for Jenny to climb from her observation seat and walk over to join them. Jenny looked her over, worry showing on her beautiful face.

"Mother, you, are not ill or anything, are you?"

"Heavens no, child, this is something that happened before Ted was born." She smiled, as she recalled that special night. "How to begin? Let me start by telling you how Peter and I tried for years to have a baby. No matter how hard we tried, I just could not get pregnant so we both went for check-ups to determine the cause. The results came back negative and our only recourse was adoption. I had started praying over the hopes that God would grant us a miracle and I would get pregnant and beat the odds, 100 to 1, against. My daily prayers were constant for I truly believed in answered prayer. And then one night of miracles, my prayers were answered. I had a very realistic dream about being visited by the angel Gabriel. Nine months later, after that reverent dream with Gabriel, Ted was born. From the day our son was born I noticed the resemblance between him and the Arch Angel, Gabriel, and the older he became, the more he looked like the angel in my very real dream."

Hannah gazed at her husband with tears in her loving eyes. "Peter, my darling, I never told you about the dream. I could see how overjoyed you were to get the son you wanted. The son we wanted and tried so desperately to have. So, I kept this heavenly miracle to myself, tucked away safely inside my inward heart. I truly believe, somehow, someway, Gabriel came to me and gave me this perfect baby boy, placing it inside me to grow into the wonderful man Ted has become."

"My dearest Hannah, I too had a revelation, nine months before Ted was born. The angel Gabriel came to me as well in a realistic dream. He told me you were going to have a baby and receive that miracle you had been praying for. Gabriel informed me that the Almighty God in heaven had ask him to perform this miracle for Hannah, as well as myself. The doctors had chosen not to refill the fact that it was me who could not produce a sperm healthy enough to form a baby, because of a childhood illness I had while growing up. The blessing that I had survived the plague that had infested our small community was a miracle in itself." Peter looked out as he recalled the night the great angel had paid him the visit and to that day, his words were still crystal clear. "Gabriel told me this child, whose seed he gave to Hannah, would belong to His Holy Creator, and the Almighty would take him under his wing and guide his footsteps, bringing him up to love and serve him by serving those in need. So, our son grew into a loving, faith filled young man, with special powers. Before Gabriel departed, he said we must name our special son, Ted. Then he ended with, I am Ted's true father, and you, Peter, will be his earthly father, to raise and love as your own and Ted's love for you will be powerful and true."

Peter looked down lovingly at his wife, still a very beautiful woman, and reached down to take her hand. "When I awoke that morning, I gazed down at your beautiful face, still asleep, a smile gracing your lips and an amazing glow around your entire body, I knew it was like Gabriel had said. Within a few short weeks, you came to me with the joyful news! We were going to have a baby and I knew in my heart who had made this all possible for us. Not wanting to upset you, I kelp these things in my heart and became the very best father I could be for our angelic son." Hannah stood up and she and Peter melted in a warm embrace. "My sweet Hannah, God smiled down on us and blessed our love with this most special son."

"Oh, my love, you knew all along. We both knew, yet never, until now, let one another know." Hannah laughed softly, then reached up to give him a kiss.

Jenny had been listening in total fascination as she stood to join them. "This is amazing, it's beautiful, its…" Jenny stopped suddenly, the reality hitting her hard. She moved back to the window and stared up on the mountain top. "Oh, my God! I am married to an angel's son! Ted is…half angel!"

Seeing her anguish, Hannah and Peter walked over and stood on either side of her. Hannah draped a loving arm around her.

"All of this must have come as quite a surprise, Jenny, darling. But you must have known Ted was very different and had special powers no one could explain."

"I do, of course I know that!" Jenny swallowed back the nervous lump in her throat. "When I first met Ted, I actually thought he was Jesus, like other people in town."

"That is understandable Jenny dear. Ted has the same appearance and manners. Even Hannah and I were without words when we watched our sixteen-year-old son, climb the hill behind our home in blue jeans and a t-shirt and descend in a robe like he wears today." Peter placed a gentle hand on his daughter-in-law's hand. "My dear, I can assure you, it's something you can never get used to, but I can assure you of Ted's love for you, my dear. The boy only speaks the truth. Never has a lie escaped his lips, Ted only knows love."

"You are right about Ted's love, Father Peter. I know he loves me deeply, second only to our Lord." Jenny finally smiled, knowing she wasn't alone about not really knowing her loving husband. "I love Ted more than anyone or anything, except of course my Lord. Ted finally drilled that through my thick head. I guess you could say, he saved my soul."

"Ted has always loved his God first, as should we all, and I know how deeply he loves and adores you, Jenny. Those beautiful granddaughters are the results of the incredible love you share." Hannah beamed. "Just because you know Ted is the son of an angel does not change the way you both feel for one another. You see sweetheart, Ted is also half human, so he has the same feelings we do when it comes to the loved one in his life. That, my dear, includes making love."

"Making love? That brings me to another question, which might not be any of my business and if so, just tell me you wish to keep that secret to yourself." Jenny looked down and spoke softly. "Just how did Gabriel make love to you, Hannah?"

Hannah smiled down shyly, then glanced up at Peter for his permission to reveal what had happened. Always the trusting husband, Peter reached over and rubbed his wife's blushing cheeks.

"Do tell us dear. I have often wondered how it happened myself. I promise not to get upset Hannah, I realize some sex had to happen to get you pregnant."

"Of course, angels do it different, although I remember him pulling his robe over his blonde hair. The wings seem to vanish as he knelt his tall frame down. I can still see his amazing blue eyes gazing down at me as he climbed on top, and even though I never seen his…well, you know, I felt it go inside me. For a moment he seemed unsure of what to do, I assumed it was his first time with a woman, but suddenly he began to move, first in a slow motion, then quite rapidly, until he closed his eyes and smiled. I knew at that moment Gabriel had put Ted inside me for I could feel myself moving with heavenly passion and tremendous love. The handsome angel was lit up by a bright light and as soon as I became pregnant, I too lit up in that same bright light. I suppose the light was coming from Ted, already growing inside me." This time it was Hannah gazing up at the mountain top. "When I woke up, at first, I thought it had been just a dream, but I realized I could still feel where Gabriel had made love to me. Let me just say, that male angel was very well endowed."

Hannah noticed how quiet it had become and turn to find husband and daughter-in-law listening to her every word. She tried to read Peter's emotions after confessing to what she would call, an innocent, unexpected onetime affair with a mighty angel.

"I hope this hasn't upset you Peter, dearest. I can assure you, every time we have made love, it has been a wonderful, passionate experience. You are a spectacular lover Peter Neenam and you've always considered pleasing me before finding pleasure for yourself. I deeply love you, Peter and I have ever since the first day I saw you step outside your door."

Jenny smiled as she watched the loving couple embrace. They pulled apart as they suddenly remember they were not alone by the window.

"Jenny dear, perhaps I have said too much in front of you about Peter and my personal life." Hannah blushed, thinking she might have been too outspoken about her and Peter's sex life. "I hope I have not embarrassed you, darling."

Embarrassed me? Speaking about sex?" Jenny could not resist her chuckle. "Trust me, mother, that is one topic I can write a book about, I am just happy that you both enjoy sporting in bed. That keeps a marriage exciting."

"That makes me feel better, Jenny." Hannah smiled up at her husband. "You never told me how you feel about how I became pregnant with an angel's son, Peter."

"My darling Hannah, I could never be upset with you, you who are practically an angel yourself. I will always put your needs first, my love. I remember that fresh out of college face smiling shyly at me and I knew right away, I was in love with you, from the very first sight."

Jenny came between them and wrapped an arm around each in law. "I can see Ted gets some of his perfect love from his earthly parents. Dear Hannah, I may sleep with an angel's son, but you were blessed to sleep with God's messenger angel. The same angel that told Mary she was the chosen one of God, and would have the Savior of the world. Then, he spoke to Joseph, in a real-life dream, much like your own. What a gift! Such a beautiful gift!" Once again, the reality of Ted's true identity hit her. "Gabriel is Ted's father! The messenger angel, Gabriel, is my…father-in-law!"

Chapter Sixty-Two

Ted and Gabriel stood looking at one another, until the great, powerful angel held open his arms, a magnificent smile spread across his handsome face. Ted and father embraced for the first time, love flowing between them like a magic stream. With his soft yet powerful voice, Gabriel spoke.

"Ted, my son! I am so proud of you!" Gabriel's eyes lit up with joy. "Our Creator has done well in guiding your life, son. I knew He would, of course! There was never any doubt to the outcome. The almighty God is greater than better in all He does and you are no exception. The perfect example for all men to follow. I have been with the Holy Father a very long time, so I can truly say, much the same way the Creator Father guided, His own Son, while He dwelt on earth, did He guide you, Ted. The big difference though, you must never forget, is that Jesus was always a part of the Trinity, the Son of God, who came down to save His people, including you, from their sins."

"Yes, I know this father." Ted smiled, understanding clearly what his father was trying to tell him. "I know the Father of all creation, is forming me in the image of Jesus, His Son, Not into the Lord's number two son. I know my human weaknesses and that all men and women fall short of salvation and receive Christ, the crucified, as our Savior. I am aware that Jesus is the Son of God, and that I, Ted Neenam is the son of Gabriel, God's messenger angel, who brought the news to Mary that she would bare the Son of the Most-High God! Somehow, I knew I was the son of an angel, I just never guessed it would be such an important, high-ranking angel who takes council with the Almighty Father in heaven! God's messenger angel!"

"One of many, yes I am." Gabriel returned Ted's brilliant smile. "I was just the lucky one chosen to bring the good news to that small faithful girl, who happened to see my light inside the stable she had just left, and came back to see what caused it." Gabriel beamed as he recalled telling Mary the good news. "What a delight it was to tell such a bright eyed, intelligent young girl that she was going to have the Son of God!"

"Our Holy Book says that Mary was frightened when she saw you and heard your declaration." Ted loved the fact his father was remembering the best event known to man.

"Mary was innocent and very much in love with Joseph. It's true she was frightened, while at the same time, the faith-filled girl felt humble, yet overjoyed, that God would choose her out of so many other girls." Gabriel held out his palm and two white doves flew down to rest. "Over the many years, I've had lots of happy messages, some, not so happy, but the day I was ask to bring you into this world, was met with mixed emotions, my son."

"This time, God was giving you a message, father. I am sure it seemed like an unusual request from our Heavenly Father." Ted tried to imagine Gabriel's reaction to the news.

"I must admit I was confused over such a request. I began to understand the reason for wishing to bless this religious woman with a child after hearing all her moving prayers. They came constant and each one filled with hope in the promise of our Lord," Gabriel began to pace, back and forth, "I had never been with a woman and needless to say, the thought of making love was very terrorizing to me. Strangely enough I knew what to do, perhaps from watching humans make love for more years than even you could imagine. There was something special about your mother, making it easier to be intimate with her." Gabriel looked deeply into his son's blue eyes. "I even think I fell in love with her, myself, and when I see you, the beautiful son we made together, I still feel a special bond with Hannah."

"Father, I am sure you know all about my Jenny." Ted placed his hand on his father's strong arm. "And our beautiful daughters, Mary and Martha."

"I certainly do, my son. Your Jenny is the perfect woman for you. She loves you as woman is meant to love her man." Gabriel reached for Ted's hands. "And my granddaughters, what joy they bring me. My fellow angels are still patting my shoulder and calling me Grandpa Gabriel. It never fails to bring a big happy smile on my face."

"It's good to finally know who I am father and why I am like I am." The wind began to blow around Ted's robe and tears filled his blue eyes. "You are leaving now. Will I see you again on earth, Gabriel?"

"Ted, my loving son, now that I have had a chance to see you and know you better, I need you as much as you need me." The mighty angel sparkled with pure light. "I shall see you soon. Tell Hannah…" Gabriel hesitated.

"That you love her?" Ted flashed him a beautiful, knowing smile. "Peter will understand, father. He knows everyone loves my mother, she is very easy to love, as you well know. Peter is a devoted husband and has always been a wonderful, caring father to me and I love and respect him deeply." His eyes grew serious as they filled with fresh tears. "I love you too, my father, Gabriel."

"Ted, my beautiful son, I love you too!" Gabriel faded away as his soft voice began to drift. "And tell Hannah I love her." Gabriel was gone, but not the Holy Father.

"Now you know the whole truth about your mysterious birth. Beware of future troubles! Not right away, there will be a short time of peace, while our old foe waits. This peaceful time will give your small ones, time to grow stronger. Watch Teddy carefully, my son, when he, insist everyone call him Jeffery. Lucifer has his sights on the boy because he's so much like his favorite son, Teddy's father. Yet, there is another to be aware of. He comes pretending to be a friend of the family, when in fact, he is consumed with the ideal of power, the kind of power only granted by Lucifer. Be on your guard for him, and keep watch over the young boy."

"Yes Father, I know little Teddy has to make choices on his own as he gets older and finding his own powers can turn his head to want more power." Ted looked around sadly, knowing the family's great cost if Teddy chooses evil over good and the thought of his father fading away. "Young Teddy breaks my heart when I see him already showing anger and wanting to be called Jeffery. I promise, we will do all we can to bring him up in a strong faith, Father."

"That is all that is expected of you, my son." The soft breeze blew gently through Ted's long hair. "It is time for you to go down now, my boy. Your Jenny anxiously awaits your return. She knows about Gabriel, being your real father. Hannah and Peter finally shared their stories with one another as well as Jenny. Now, she is consumed with uncertainty and fear, because Gabriel is your real father, which makes you half angel, same as Jeff. But son, Jenny loves you deeply, only you can make her feel safe." God's voice grew softer. "Now go and love go with you." The voice was gone and Ted turned quickly toward the path that would lead him back to his wife.

Jenny had returned to her window seat, her attention glued to the mountain top as her fingers nervously thumped on the wide seal. Hannah and Peter had joined her at the window, bringing her a hot cup of tea, to help relax her nerves. Taking the cup with shaky fingers, she thanked them and took a small sip.

"Ted will be back soon, Jenny dear. I know you will feel a whole lot better when you see him." Hannah reassured her daughter-in-law as she too gazed out the big window. Instantly Hannah spotted a flash of white coming down the mountain path. Happy at last to spot Ted, Hannah stood up straight and pointed in his direction. "Halfway down, It's Ted coming down!"

Seeing her husband getting close. Jenny sat the teacup aside and jumped up, racing out the front door, Ted's parents close behind her. Ted seemed to have a glow all around him as he gave them his special smile. The three watching felt his great love reaching out to caress each one of them, but when his gaze fell on Jenny, the love in his incredible eyes, doubled. Ted walked straight into his wife's arms and hugged her tenderly, yet protectively. Jenny could feel her entire body relax and she knew she was safe in the arms of the man she loved so dearly. Ted's words came soft to her ear.

"Jenny, my dearest love, you know my father is Gabriel, God's angel!"

"Yes darling, I know everything." Jenny hardly recognize her own voice as it trembled and she felt herself shaking again. She began to cry as she buried her face in his chest. "Ted…Ted…you are…part angel!"

"Jenny, my love, I have not changed. I'm still the man who loves you more than anything, save the Holy Trinity." Ted's lips found hers and she relaxed as he whispered, "I am still the husband who delights in making love to you, until the wee hours of the morning." He lifted up her chin to face him. "I am just your Ted, Jenny."

"Oh Ted!" Jenny laughed through her tears. "And I am just your Jenny, forever and ever!" Ted grabbed her in a hug as they joined in laughter, then Ted looked over at his mother, a hint of mischief on his handsome face.

"Mother, Gabriel sent you a message." Ted smiled at her blushing cheeks. "He told me to tell you that he loved you."

"He did?" Hannah felt for the porch bench before sinking down on it, and looked sheepishly up at her smiling husband, "Peter, I...don't know what to say!"

Peter chuckled as he joined her on the bench. "Hannah! Hannah! Be happy! An angel just declared his love to you! Who wouldn't love you, Hannah, dearest." Peter wrapped his arm over her shoulder. "Gabriel might love you, Miss Hannah, but Peter Neenam is the man who stole your heart and married you!"

Everyone joined in laughter, then Ted knelt down in front of his parents. "Peter, you will always be my father. You brought me up with such love, the kind of love only a father could bestow. I love you very much and I always will." Ted reached over and patted his mama's head. "I love you too, mother! You and Peter taught me everything I needed to know to begin my life here on the mountain." Ted smiled up, knowing Jeff and Naomi had arrived and stood looking down at him helplessly. "It's Teddy, isn't it?"

"My little boy is changing, Ted. He wants to be called Jeffery and so far, we have been able to forbid his change. Now, Teddy is always wanting things he cannot have and gets mad and stomps his foot when we deny him his wants!" Naomi had genuine concern written on her sweet, beautiful face.

"The devil has already approached Teddy!" Jeff knew Ted was reading his mind when his good neighbor said softly.

"He lured him with a cute puppy named Destiny. Satan's gift to a grandson from Teddy's grandfather!"

Jenny had been listening and joined the group, taking Ted's hand. "We can all work with Teddy. He is really a smart and sweet little fellow."

"We will instill love and faith inside his heart, so should he slip and fall, the deep-rooted love will consume the hate and lift him up!" Ted hugged the young girl he had took in and loved, while speaking to Jeff in spirit talk, revealing the warning from God. Jeff nodded his understanding.

"Ted is right, my sweet one. All of us will guide our son down the right path. If I made it through, there is even more hope for this boy." Jeff put his arm around his wife and pulled her up close, as he watched Teddy come running up, carrying his new best friend.

"Look my Ted, my Jenny! This is Destiny, my very own puppy! Isn't he cute?" Teddy smiled up at them and revealed his new sharp canine teeth!"

Author's Notes

Good is always fighting evil! Now the odds are even better since Jeff has joined forces with Ted, to fight Lucifer and his demons! With the knowledge of Gabriel being Ted's father, the odds have grown greater!

The years of peace are quickly fading and the trouble begins when a stranger, with a very familiar face, shows up at Wineworth castle! To make matters worse, a small group of runaway children find themselves in all sorts of trouble and by God's design, meet Ted.

Book# 3 in "The Good Seed-The Bad Seed" series entitled: *The Lost Sheep*

www.ingramcontent.com/pod-product-compliance
Lightning Source LLC
Chambersburg PA
CBHW072122250626
47159CB00007B/2539
* 9 7 8 1 6 3 0 6 6 5 1 5 9 *